FIVE ELEMENTS. ONE REALM. ONE CHOICE.

FROM
FLAME
AND
AsH

NEW YORK TIMES BESTSELLING AUTHOR

CARRIE ANN
RYAN

From Flame and Ash: An Elements of Five Novel
© 2019 Carrie Ann Ryan

ISBN: 978-1-947007-76-5
Cover design by Charity Hendry
Book design by Inkstain Design Studio

FROM
FLAME
AND
ASH

"Carrie Ann Ryan writes sexy shifters in a world full of passionate happily-ever-afters."

—VIVIAN AREND
New York Times **bestselling author**

Carrie Ann Ryan's books are wickedly funny and deliciously hot, with plenty of twists to keep you guessing. They'll keep you up all night!"

—CARI QUINN
USA Today **Bestselling Author**

"Once again, Carrie Ann Ryan knocks the Dante's Circle series out of the park. The queen of hot, sexy, enthralling paranormal romance, Carrie Ann is an author not to miss!"

—MARIE HARTE
New York Times **bestselling Author**

To Liz & Jillian.

Thank you for always being there, for loving these worlds,
and for showing me who else I could be.

FROM
FLAME
AND
ASH

CHAPTER 1

I hadn't had this dream in a while. The fact that I knew it was a dream right off the bat told me I wasn't going to like where it led. Of course, knowing what I did now, none of the dreams from my past had been very good for me either. Though they might have told me some important things, stuff that *meant* something, it didn't mean I had to like them.

Or their underlying message.

This time, I stood at the center of a star with five points. Before I knew that everything I dreamed was true, I'd always thought of where I stood as the four corners of the seasons, each of the elements, or the four cardinal directions.

But I had been wrong…even as I'd been right.

I hadn't known there was a fifth.

But then again, I hadn't known much at the time.

I still felt like I didn't. Not at all.

I stood at the crossroads, my hair blowing in the wind and the screams of a thousand voices echoing in my mind. I knew they were my own. My screams mixed with those of my friends, those I loved, and others I didn't know.

These were memories. My dreams weren't really dreams.

But each time the visions came, I didn't know if they would be my memories or a future that would never come. I didn't know if they were the memories of those who kept sending me these nightmares, or if it was just something to try and scare me into coming back.

I didn't want to go back.

Or maybe I did.

The fact that I was still deciding on *when* told me I wasn't ready. But I pushed those thoughts out of my head and tried to focus on what the dream was trying to tell me—if it was trying to tell me anything at all.

The element that I was most afraid of was in front of me. Spirit. And I did not know a single person who possessed it. I didn't know anyone who could Wield it like the others. Every time I looked into the face of this element, I could feel the fear crawling up my back, into my shoulders, moving down to my belly to latch on. Because I didn't know what Spirit Wielders could do, other than walk in my dreams. Yet I knew it could be so much more.

It had to be.

Because if it weren't, then the others wouldn't have tried to kill the Spirit Wielders for their powers.

In the far right upper corner of the star, there was Fire. Below that, Earth. To the left, Air, and above, Water.

All elements. All coming at me...and yet not.

The Air blew my blond hair back from my face, and I lifted my chin, letting the heat of Fire warm my pale skin. I'd gotten slightly tanner outside of my dreams this past year by being outside, but within my visions, it was as if the sun had been leached from my skin altogether. As if I were just a pale shadow of who I once was.

As with the elements, and like with anything, there were different types of people, various Wielders who used their powers and magic in ways that were either helpful or hurtful depending on the individual. There were those who Wielded their elements and used them to protect others or to harm even more. They used them to their advantage and had had *hundreds* of years to perfect those skills.

I had been born human. And I still was…maybe. Even in my dreams. Here, I didn't possess the elements that had been thrust upon me, unlocking inside of me with bone-breaking agony and pain. The torment of which was so haunting, I knew I would never forget.

In these dreams, I was the girl I had been before. And I was powerless.

I hadn't been without power in the end, and yet in these dreams, I was reminded of what I'd been, and what I might become if I went back without knowing what was to come.

I had left the Maison realm because I was afraid. Because I had been beaten. I'd lost my best friend and so much more. I'd died with a sword in my belly and blood on my hands.

And the Spirit Wielders, those who'd remained hidden for centuries from the other Wielders, saved me.

The boy I loved—who I thought I *could* love, at least—the one I thought was my soulmate, hadn't been able to save me. There hadn't been that true connection. Legend said that a soulmate could heal a mortal wound. And he couldn't heal mine.

Now, Rhodes was gone, off to his own kingdom. And I was in the human realm, hiding. He had his people to protect…and I had to find a way to heal.

But what I was living right now was a dream, I reminded myself. Just a dream.

Water from its corner of the star lapped at my feet, cold and icy. It wasn't like that time on the beach as a child, playing in the sand and letting the waves crash into me. I had been a strong swimmer, but my mother had always warned me about the rip tides, the strong currents. They could take you out into the abyss and drown you, take you away from everything you'd ever known, and no one would be able to hear you scream.

As I thought that, the waves grew stronger, knocking into my knees until I went weak, shaking just slightly. Sand scraped my skin, but I did not fall. Not now.

This was just a dream.

And I wasn't that girl anymore.

The ground rumbled beneath my feet, and I knew that Earth was angry. I reminded myself that there was more to come from that land. More to take. Because while the king of the Fire and Earth territories was one man—one who had saved me—the Lord of Earth was not as welcoming, not as forgiving.

I owed their lord a favor, one I was afraid I might not ever be able to repay.

The man who ruled the territory had not killed me, and therefore, I owed him. It was funny how being able to breathe could be something owed, a *favor*. The mere idea that I could walk away with my life in my hands, *that* was what I owed someone.

The earth cracked ever so slightly beneath me, jagged lines appearing that sent dust spiraling into the air, but I did not falter. I did pull myself back from thoughts of what I owed, however.

Because unlike with Water, I could Wield this element. I could feel Earth, and it tugged on something within me, a part so deep that it caused warmth to spread through my fingers. And though I didn't actually possess that element in this dream, I knew that once I woke up, I would be able to.

And then the Fire came at me, and I held back a wince. Fire, such heat.

I didn't possess this element, even though its twin, Earth, called to me. Earth and Fire were friends, tangling with each other not only in magic and genetics but also within a kingdom that was falling apart under its new king. The new ruler who had come into his title as the kingdom fell apart around him.

I didn't know if I would be enough to save it.

I disregarded the Fire and what it represented, ignored its temptation. It had called to me since I was a child, and it still called.

It was not the Water with its siren song that lured me, but the Fire that burned.

And then I remembered that Water could douse the flames, even though Fire could dance above the waves.

All of that might soon unlock within me. And I wasn't sure I was strong enough.

I turned myself fully within the star to face the first element that had ever unlocked within me. Air. I had unlocked it to save the boy that I thought I could love—and myself. I could still feel the wind dancing between my fingers and tangling in my hair. It was the warmest of elements, even more so than Fire in my opinion. Because Fire raged and burned, while Air hugged and caressed.

But it could kill.

I knew that firsthand.

And I possessed this element.

That was something I was still coming to understand.

Even a year later.

"You're wondering why you're here," a voice said from behind me. I turned in the direction I had faced at first, towards the Spirit element.

That element meant nothing to me. All I knew was that it was a void. That was the only way I knew it was Spirit at all. I had no idea what it could do. Hadn't truly met anyone who could Wield it.

While the rest of the elements were physical, Spirit seemed to dwell within.

I knew the Spirit Wielders could walk within my dreams and *give* me dreams. I knew that they could heal. But I didn't know if that was because it was me, or if it was their element.

Though it wasn't as if I could ask them.

When the Spirit Wielders came into my dream, they tended to talk to me, not *with* me.

I should have found that annoying, but that was how all of my training had gone for the past year once I returned to the human realm and moved away from the Maisons.

I had quickly found out that the world was not as it seemed. Another world was pressed tightly up against ours, connected by portals that led from the human world to the Maison realm.

And a thousand years ago when the Maison realm was five territories, five kingdoms with kings and queens who worked together, there had been peace. And then, over time, Earth and Fire had become the Obscurité Kingdom, and Water and Air had become the Lumiére.

Light and dark. Opposites.

And they had warred.

I didn't know the reason for the war, although it is said that the King of Obscurité started it all.

But after meeting the latest king and his mother, the late queen, I wasn't sure if anything I had been told about the Fall was true. When the war had paused and became what it was now, at least in its abstract form, the Fall had begun. The Spirit Wielders had left the Maison realm to hide with the humans.

I didn't know if my ancestors had been among those to hide, but none of that mattered now. Because everything had changed. The Maison realm was fracturing. It was failing.

People were losing their ability to Wield. Some had been stripped of their Wielding powers by magical forces, others nearly losing it because the crystals that powered the Maison realm were dying, as well.

And I knew all about this because, apparently, I was the fabled Spirit Priestess.

The one who could save them all.

Or so they told me.

"Why am I here?" I asked the Spirit Wielder in front of me. I couldn't see his face, his cloak covered him completely. Although I wasn't sure I would *ever* be able to see the Spirit Wielders' faces. For all I knew, this was all just my imagination trying to help me come up with answers for what I needed to know to remain sane.

"You are here to learn. You are here to remember. You can't stay here forever, Lyric."

I shook my head, not wanting to hear the words.

It had been a year since I ran from my responsibilities and what could be. I'd needed to figure out who I was, and I still wasn't sure.

But I didn't have time for myths and dreams.

But they apparently had time for me.

A movement in the dream, a shift in the wind, caused me to pause. Then the elements around me burned, flooded, ached. This wasn't my dream. And it wasn't the man in front of me.

"You must go, Lyric."

"Where?"

There were so many places I could go within the kingdoms once I left the human realm. But it wasn't like I could just figure out my journey without help. I didn't know what I needed to do, and nobody was actually guiding me.

Not anymore.

"All is not what it seems."

I resisted the urge to roll my eyes because that was the understatement of my year. Of my life.

But then, before I could speak again, Earth rumbled harder, and Fire lashed out at me. Water seemed to wrap itself around my ankles, and Air slammed into me, so hard that it felt like ice sticking to my skin.

This was different. This wasn't the same type of dream I'd had before. And then the Spirit Wielder lifted his hood, vacant, dark pools of shadow where eyes should have been.

"You must go. Before he finds you. Before they *all* find you. The Gray is coming. And you are still too weak."

And then the elements slammed into me with such ferocity that I screamed.

I startled awake and winced as the others in the classroom around me clapped. I wasn't in the Maison realm, and I wasn't alone. I was in a classroom with a bunch of students, most of them glaring at me. I had fallen asleep, and the others had seen.

I had left the Maison realm to find myself, to heal. But I had been left wanting. I waited to learn the next step, but the nothingness around me only pulled me farther away from where I knew, deep down, I needed to be. A place I was afraid I'd never reach again.

I had left those who needed me.

And I knew I needed to go back.

No matter the cost.

CHAPTER 2

I had already packed my go-bag weeks earlier, knowing this time would come. I repacked it every night, ensuring that I had what I would need, unpacking and changing things out when I thought better of it. Items made in the human world didn't last long in the other realm. So, I had most of the things I'd taken with me when I left the Maisons, as well as some stuff Alura, a friend of Rhodes and Rosamond who also lived on my block and happened to go to school with me, had given me over the past year.

I was ready to go back. And my new friend—my *only* friend these days—wasn't of this realm either, so it seemed I wasn't really alone.

I paused at that thought, wondering why that seemed to be the first thing that popped into my mind.

Maybe it was because the idea swept over me with each passing day and every passing dream, all the memories of what I had left behind.

I'd abandoned it all because I was scared. Because I'd needed time to regroup. But so much time had passed at this point, I wasn't sure what would happen next.

I wanted to go back. I didn't know if it was about facing my destiny because, honestly, I didn't know if there *was* a true destiny there for me. But I had to go back because people were counting on me, even if I wasn't sure I could rely on myself.

I couldn't just walk away again and pretend that nothing had happened.

The very evidence of what had happened currently sat in my bag, purring and licking her toes.

My little polydactyl cat, the one with bat wings.

Yes, a cat with extra toes was extraordinary on its own. A cat with extra toes on each foot *and* wings? That wasn't of this world, or of this realm.

But Braelynn, my best friend in the entire world, *had* once been from this realm.

"Please stop getting your cat hair all over my clothes," I said, reaching out to pick her up out of the bag. "I swear, you're mostly black, but your little white hairs on the tuxedo part of your front stick to my clothing, showing themselves to the world."

She just snorted.

Damn cat.

I tended to wear black these days. I didn't know if it was because the color happened to look good on me, or if it was because I was in mourning.

Grieving the fact that my best friend had died, only to come back as a cat that was now in my arms. Or maybe it was me mourning what I once had.

I had once thought my life was normal. Normal heading into boring. I hadn't been able to pick my major, I was almost about to watch my friend and my ex-girlfriend—the only two people I truly talked to often—walk away from me as they went off to undergo their own college careers.

Braelynn was never going to college now. She had lost that opportunity when she came with me into the Maison realm to see what my dreams were about.

I had known she was following her own path, figuring out why she felt as if she didn't belong either. But in the end...in the end, it was my fault that she was dead. Or at least changed. And my ex?

She was never coming back either.

She couldn't.

Brae bumped my chin with the top of her head, and I looked down to see her glaring at me as if she knew where my thoughts had gone.

"You can't really read my thoughts, can you?" I asked.

She just gave me a look that said she could do whatever she wanted and to bow before her regalness. Okay, maybe that was just the look of a cat in general. I liked felines, though the idea that this cat happened to be my best friend was still a little weird.

I mean, once you clean your bestie's litter box, there's no going back. And let's not get started on the hairballs and the self-cleaning, and everything else that comes with being a cat.

I didn't think Braelynn as a cat could actually read my thoughts, but sometimes it sure seemed like it. I forgot, when I wasn't thinking too closely about it, that she wasn't actually a cat. Nor was she human anymore. It was this weird dichotomy where I felt like I was still speaking to my friend even though she couldn't talk back.

I slipped my go-bag into the closet, wondering when I would finally come back for it. It wasn't like I could just venture into the Maison realm and know that I would be safe. When Easton had dropped me off here, he hadn't told me how I could get in contact with him again, only that he would be here for me when I was ready.

That was so not helpful, but I had been a little shaken about the fact that not only was my best friend dead, at least as I had known her, *I* had died. Though the Spirit Wielders had somehow helped me out of that.

Oh, and the boy that I had thought was my soulmate, Rhodes? As it turned out, he wasn't my soulmate at all, and that meant he couldn't actually be with me. Or maybe he *could* be with me, but we weren't actually talking to each other beyond the letters that he wrote to me that Alura brought. I wrote him too, and Alura passed the messages on, as well as the ones I wrote to Rosamond, though I had no idea how she did it.

It was all so confusing, and I hadn't asked Easton more about the rules. I only knew that I could go back. I just didn't know how or when.

When Alura had come to the house a week after I came home, devastated, broken, and having to act like everything was normal, I had taken it as par for the course. *Of course*, a Wielder would be watching over me, making sure I didn't end up in harm's way like I tended to do these days.

She had been the one I'd seen the day before everything changed. She'd been talking to Rhodes and Rosamond about something—me, most likely—and hadn't gone hiking with us when the Neg had tried to kill me, thus starting everything. She'd stayed behind, saying that it wasn't her time yet. She was the most mystical girl I'd ever met, with long hair that seemed to flow in the wind just like Rosamond's did. I didn't know what kind of Wielder Alura was, only that she was one, and have been living in the human realm for some time. I didn't know why she was here. And, honestly, I didn't know if I should or would ask.

With the way the Maison realm was breaking, each territory slowly fighting each other before they fought against the kingdom itself, I knew there had to be people fleeing. It wasn't safe for everybody back there anymore. So, retreating to a realm where there wasn't any magic or Wielding might be the safest place for them.

But when Alura had shown up on my doorstep with a note from Rosamond in her hands, saying that, yes, she was a Wielder and that she was here to answer my questions, I figured I should listen. Not that Alura had answered any of my inquiries. Not really. She was good at mumbling and going on and on about history and random things, but she didn't really answer any specific queries I made.

It was like one of those mystical orbs that told you things in riddles and fortunes and then left you to try and figure them out on your own.

I'd never been good with riddles, but I had a feeling if I were going to continue down this path, I should figure out exactly how to learn that talent.

I hadn't been sitting on my hands the entire year, though.

Easton had spelled my parents to make them think that I hadn't been gone for as long as I had. I didn't know how he'd done it, but he'd explained that he had extra gifts that came with his bloodline. The same with Rosamond and the others since they were of the Lumiére Kingdom. Easton had made it seem to my mom and dad like I had been gone for a weekend with the girls, and that everything was just fine. He'd also spelled Emory's and Braelynn's parents so they wouldn't miss their daughters because Braelynn wasn't the same as she had been before, and I knew there was no going back to the girl with the soft smiles. The one that had started to fall in love with a Lumiére warrior named Luken.

And Emory…I tried not to think about Emory.

She had been my ex-girlfriend, and then my friend, but had slowly turned into my enemy. That process had begun long before we learned that there were such things as Wielders and realms and the fact that I was the prophesied Spirit Priestess.

She had begun to hate me and tried to control me way before we stepped into the Maison realm.

When she tried to go off on her own, attempted to come back home because she hadn't liked what I was becoming—or so she'd said—she had been kidnapped. Taken.

I sucked in a breath and tried not to think about that. Except it was all I thought about sometimes. I hadn't known what had happened to her, and I didn't know where she was now. I only knew that once we entered the Fire territory and met with the lord and lady of that estate, Emory had shown up, chained and screaming profanities and evil things. At me.

She'd seemed to truly hate me, and clearly wanted me dead. I just didn't know why.

Someone had thrust Wielding magic into her, and it had twisted her. She might've started warping on her own, but the magic had secured that final lock, turned that last key. Now, she was some sort of being that could suck out Wielding and hurt others.

The last time I saw her, I had thought she died. Instead, she'd just been *poofed* into the dungeon of the Fire Estate.

I had been fighting my own war at the time, my own battles, and I hadn't been able to go back for her—not that I thought she would have accepted my help.

Though getting a sword thrust through your gut so you could feel every single slice of the blade, every bit of heat and tiny fraction of change and movement sort of made it so that you didn't think about much of anything except for the pain.

After, I had run away because I didn't know how to save her. And, honestly, I hadn't known how to save myself either.

But in the year that I'd been back, I had studied the large tome that Rhodes' older sister—by at least a couple of centuries—had given me.

Rosamond had told me to learn my history, and so I had.

I shook my head. "Sometimes, it kind of blows my mind that everybody is so much older than us," I said quietly. "Don't you think, Braelynn?"

Braelynn gave me sort of a nod. I had to think it was a nod and not just like a cat sneeze or something. Yes, I was talking to my cat, like people with normal cats did every day. And those cats answered back with meows and gestures. My cat just happened to be a former human.

Rosamond had been the whole reason that we had gone into the Maison realm a year ago in the first place. And once we found her, I woke after healing to find her sitting on my bed petting Braelynn.

I still remembered my shock at seeing a cat with wings, one that I would learn was actually my best friend. Rosamond had given me a book and basically told me that knowledge was power. Or something like that. My mind had been a little full and bleary at that point after coming back from the dead. And so, I had read up on the history of the Maisons.

At least, the one the Lumiére wrote. I didn't know where Rosamond had gotten such a book since we had been in the Obscurité Kingdom when I saw her last.

The Lumiére and the Obscurité were two halves of a whole. Once, they had been one realm of five territories, five elements. As time passed, those territories had turned into two large kingdoms with the Spirit territory slicing between them. Those kingdoms had warred, and during the Great Fall, a war to end all wars, the kings of each kingdom had died, leaving their power to their children.

I had met one of those children, Cameo, the former queen of the Obscurité.

She had died to protect me. I could still remember the look in her eyes at the sacrifice I knew she had made. Because she hadn't been a bad person. She had just been trying to save her people in the only way she knew how, even if she hadn't seen the betrayal right in front of her that undermined every move she made. And when she died, she did so because her knight had thrust power into her, a blow meant to kill me. She had sacrificed herself for me, and I would never forget that.

Sometimes, I woke up screaming, thinking that the power was inside me. Watching as Cameo stood over my corpse. I lay blinking, wondering why I was there at all.

But I remembered that queen, and I would always do so. And I would never forget her son, the current king of the Obscurité.

Easton.

The boy who had saved my life. The one I knew would probably never forgive me for what had happened to his mother. But he was the one who had made me a promise to come back as soon as I needed him.

I just didn't know what any of that meant.

The Maison realm was fracturing. The crystals that made up each realm and helped to bring in the Wielding powers of the elements and then push them out into the realm's people had either been ill-used or broken during the Fall. The history had written it one way, but I had seen them another when I watched the knight manifest his magic in an evil and putrid way.

Again, I didn't know if what Rosamond's history book said was the actual truth or just one side of the war.

Wasn't there a saying that the truth of history is only with those who wrote it? Because there's always another side to the story.

It was said that the King of Obscurité—the old one, Cameo's father and Easton's grandfather—had broken many rules. That he had tried to take over the entire realm and forced the King of Lumiére into fighting when he didn't want to. The resulting war had killed thousands—maybe even millions in the end.

And since the Maisons were long-lived, a lot of the warriors who had been alive during the Fall over five hundred years ago were still around. That history was always within them.

It was a lot for me to take in and deal with, yet I was smack in the center of it.

Because that was another tale, another myth. A story of someone called the Spirit Priestess. One who was supposed to unite the kingdoms and the territories under one banner. The history just didn't actually lay out how that should happen.

As the supposedly foretold Spirit Priestess, I would've liked some instruction. Maybe even a note. A to-do list of what I was supposed to accomplish in order to save my friends and so many people that I did not know.

Because with every single day that passed as I sat in my university classes, working towards my history major—one that I didn't even know I really wanted—I knew I didn't belong. I had only picked the major because I hadn't been able to choose anything else. I wasn't going to be a scientist, I wasn't going to be a doctor. I wasn't going to be a lawyer. The only thing I could do was look back. Pore over the histories and wonder how people got through such tragedies, overcame the wars that devastated civilizations. Because maybe there was an answer for me with regards to the Maison realm in what the people of my world had done. Maybe there was something in what was already written that could tell me what was to come.

Or maybe I was just losing my mind and needed to go back to the place I thought would be the end of me.

Braelynn tapped my chin again, and I looked down at her.

"What?"

In answer, the doorbell rang, and I shook my head.

"You're scaring me now." I swore Braelynn shrugged, not that a cat could actually shrug, but her little tail twitch thing told me something. I ignored her and went to the door, knowing who it would be.

Because, after all, I only had one friend these days.

"Alura."

"It's time."

I blinked.

"It's time?"

"Do you remember what Rosamond said? She told you to trust me."

I nodded, letting Alura in.

Rhodes had written to me, telling me what he was doing in his realm. After the fight with the knight in the Obscurité Kingdom, he had gone back to his court, called by his father and uncle. His uncle was the king of the Lumiére, his father the Lord of Water. And, apparently, his grandfather, his mother's father, was the Lord of Air. Rhodes, the boy I had fallen for, the one who was apparently not my soulmate despite what I had thought, despite what he'd thought, had some major connections.

He was royal blood, through and through.

And I was just human. A human who had unlocked two of the five elements within herself.

My hands twitched, and I looked down at my fingertips. I could still Wield in this realm and had been practicing with Alura for the past year.

It wasn't the training that I truly needed, though, since she wasn't an Air or an Earth Wielder. Those were the two elements I had, and that meant that Alura had one of the other three Wielding elements. Not that she told me what they were. She didn't show me anything, just helped me focus so I didn't blow anything up while we were in the forest of the foothills on the Rocky Mountains. It was the only place I could safely practice my Wielding without anyone seeing.

It just wasn't the same as in the Maison realm.

Alura tapped my bracelet, the one she had given me. It was a silver chain with tiny little charms on it. Each one represented an element. Alura had told me it was for protection, but I didn't know exactly what that meant.

Rosamond had written to me, just like Rhodes had, and told me to trust Alura. So, I did. And I wore the bracelet. And packed and repacked, knowing that I would be going back to the Maison realm any day now.

When Alura looked me in the eyes, I knew that day was today.

I had to go back to the Maison realm. Maybe I would be going back to Rhodes. Perhaps I would be going back to Easton's kingdom.

Two kingdoms needed me, and I had friends—or at least people I knew—in each.

The time had come.

There was no holding back any longer.

CHAPTER 3

I didn't know exactly where we were going or who we were about to meet, only that this was the start of a new beginning. Or perhaps it was the continuation of the start I had run from when I needed to learn to breathe again.

It might seem odd for me to so blindly trust Alura after everything that had happened. But then again, when I truly thought about it, it didn't. I knew Alura was a Wielder and someone that Rosamond trusted. I had almost sacrificed everything to find Rosamond after the Obscurité knight and his Negs had taken her, and I would *still* do whatever I could to help her.

I trusted her because her mere presence demanded it. She'd saved me, even if I hadn't known it at the time. It had been a year since I saw any of the others. Nearly a full three hundred and sixty-five days, yet I could still feel the connection that I had to Rhodes and even Rosamond.

I rubbed my hand on my chest, annoyed with myself for even thinking about that connection to Rhodes. Because it wasn't really true, was it?

Maybe it was because the others thought I was the prophesied Spirit Priestess. Something I was beginning to believe myself. That could have been why I'd felt such a strong pull towards Rhodes at the beginning. And maybe that was why I felt like I could truly trust and be friends with Rosamond.

Before I found out about any of the world beyond mine, I had been inexplicably pulled to Rosamond. Emory and Braelynn had been ready to move on with the rest of their lives. They had made choices about colleges and majors that had nothing to do with me. And I had understood that. Because growing up meant making the hard choices and figuring out who you were as an adult.

But I hadn't figured out what path I needed to be on. Until I discovered that there was a darkness beneath my skin—and perhaps a lightness, as well. I hadn't truly found my path until I found out that I wasn't who I thought I was. And, yes, I had run from that also, but it was because I had been forced into it. No, that wasn't right. I ran because I was scared. Because I needed time. And I wasn't going to get that time sitting in a realm that I wasn't sure even wanted me.

Oh, they may *say* that they wanted the Spirit Priestess to save the day, but what did that really even mean?

Did they really want change to happen?

Because the knight of the Obscurité Kingdom hadn't wanted me to help anyone. He'd wanted the power for himself. Lore had threatened the entire realm because of his greed and his anger towards everyone that he thought had slighted him. He had stolen the Wielding power from those he thought weaker. He'd either killed them or forced them to become weaker shells of themselves until they couldn't fight back.

Thinking about him, thinking about what he'd stood for, I wasn't sure that anybody really wanted me to come back and save the world.

I huffed out a laugh, shaking my head.

Save the world? Sometimes, I wasn't even sure I could save myself. I couldn't do it when that sword had slid into my belly, and I had seen the horror in Easton's and Rhodes' gazes. They had tried to keep me from sliding down onto that blade, kept it from cutting even deeper. But I had been impaled against the stone wall behind me because of Lore's Wielding.

It had been Rhodes who kept me still, and Easton who had slid the sword back out with a fire so hot that it scorched both of us as he pulled the blade from my skin.

Both Rhodes and Easton had tried to save me, but it hadn't been enough.

I wasn't Rhodes' soulmate, that much I now knew. Because if I had been, he would have been able to heal my mortal wound. That was what soulmates did, after all. At least one of the many things they did according to myths and legends.

But he hadn't been able to do it.

Nobody had.

I had been alone until the Spirit Wielders had connected to me from wherever they were on whatever realm and found a way to heal me. They had brought me back, and even though I was weak, we had found a way to save the realm. If even for a day.

Lore was no more. The knight had faded into the darkness.

Now, Easton was the King of Obscurité, and Rhodes was gone.

When I woke up with Braelynn biting at my hair, I had known that things would be different.

But I trusted Rosamond. I put my faith in her because she was a Seer and had never led me astray. And maybe that was stupid. Perhaps I was just naïve. But I needed to trust in something. Because if I didn't, I wasn't sure I could take any of the next steps that I needed to.

So, I let out a breath and packed my bags again, ensuring that I had everything I might need.

"Are you ready?" Alura asked, stepping into my bedroom. I was on the top floor, my bedroom still looking like it had throughout high school. With white drapes and a huge duvet, delicate furniture, and books that I had read before but hadn't picked up since I came back. I'd focused on what I could learn about the other part of myself and the classes I knew I wouldn't be going back to.

I held back a shiver as I looked at the bed. I'd had so many nightmares here, I couldn't even count them all. The dreams had to be because of who I was, but no one had ever been able to explain them to me. And believe me, I had asked.

I had written to Rosamond, asking her why I had the dreams, why they seemed to torture me, but she hadn't given me any details I could use. She hadn't said much of anything, so I didn't know if she actually knew. She'd told me before that sometimes being a Seer meant knowing things and determining *when* to tell others about them.

Lore had even been able to slice into one of my dreams at one point, and he had burned Rhodes in the process because Rhodes had been sleeping next to me in a tent at the time.

The dreams had to mean something, but nobody would tell me what.

Either they didn't know, or they didn't think I should know.

Because Rosamond was a Seer, I had a feeling it was the latter. And since Alura seemed to like being mysterious and didn't like telling me things, that made them not wanting me to know ring true even more. The dreams had to mean something, that much I knew. They had rattled my entire being while I slept in this room and when I'd been fully human—or at least *thought* I was—but I hadn't known that there was anything more to them.

"Where am I going?" I had asked this before, and I wanted the answer. Just saying, "the Maison realm," fractured as it was, wasn't really helpful. I knew that there was an entryway near my house up in the foothills of the Rocky Mountains. That would get me into the southern Spirit territory. I had only ever been there, and to the Fire and Earth territories. I hadn't ventured into the Lumiére Kingdom at all, nor had I ever been to the northern Spirit territory.

I had spent most of my time in the Earth territory. Because between the actual *pirates* that had kidnapped us, and the Lord and Lady of Earth's sentries and guards, I had been on multiple journeys across the whole territory. I had seen so much of it and had even fallen in love with parts because of the sheer beauty of the place. It hadn't mattered that my feet were sore, or that I had blisters on my blisters, it had still felt like I was part of something. I had only been in the border territories for a little bit, and in the Fire territory for an even shorter period of time. We hadn't had to walk long distances, not like we did in the Earth territory. Others' Wieldings had brought us from one place to the other.

I didn't think I would be able to use Wielding like that anytime soon, not until I trained more. And maybe not ever since I knew that not everyone could do that.

So, wherever I was going, I knew I would have to walk. A lot.

Thankfully, I had been training. I was far stronger than I had been the first time I walked into the Maison realm, but that didn't really mean much since I hadn't known what I was facing then. And for some reason, I felt like I had no idea what I would be facing now.

"We're going where you need to go." Alura held Braelynn in her arms, scratching beneath my cat's chin.

"So, are we going to the same place that I went last time?" I slid the bag over my shoulders, making sure the weight was evenly distributed so I could keep up with any pace that I needed to with it on. I had learned how to do that better when I was in the other realm. So, hopefully, I wouldn't tire out too quickly wherever I was going.

"You'll be going into the southern Spirit territory. Same place that you went before."

Surprised, I blinked and took a step back. It was very unlike Alura to actually straight out tell me details. That probably meant she was keeping other secrets. Because as much as Rosamond had told me to trust her—and I did—it was kind of hard sometimes to truly understand what Alura wanted me to do.

I had no idea what kind of Wielder she was, and I really didn't know her on a personal level despite the fact that I considered her a friend. But I knew there had to be a reason she was here. Maybe it was because I was all alone and didn't have anyone else. Anyone except for Braelynn.

My cat looked at me as if she knew I hadn't immediately thought of her, and I closed my eyes for a moment.

It was just so like a cat to make me feel guilty, and, for some reason, Braelynn was acting more cat-like than human these days. Or maybe I was just losing my mind because it had been a year since I'd had any contact with anyone beyond the letters we exchanged. Maybe that was why I clung to Alura, this woman that I didn't really know.

"Did you work the spell that you needed to with my parents?" I asked, my throat a little dry. She had explained to me that there was a way we could make it so my parents would forget that I even existed. She had assured me it could be temporary, though. It was similar to the memory spell that Easton had used to ensure that they didn't notice that I was gone for as long as I had been in the other realm. The last time, my parents had sent out police cruisers and even made a stack of flyers with my face on it to let everyone know that I was missing and that they were looking for me. Braelynn's and Emory's families had done the same, although from what Alura had told me, Emory's parents really hadn't put much effort into it.

That saddened me, but I pushed those thoughts away, trying not to think about Emory at all. It hurt no matter what I thought of.

But, somehow, the memory spell had erased all evidence of what had occurred when I was gone. No one had known to miss me or put in a police report. Anyone who had seen it on a flyer or screen or anywhere else had simply forgotten about it.

I knew that was strong Wielding, forceful magic. So much that I wasn't sure that anyone else could have done it. But the King of Obscurité had the power.

I didn't know if it was his Fire or Earth Wielding that could do it. Maybe it was just something inherent in all Maisons. Some things weren't elemental. Some things just seemed to be Maison.

Perhaps keeping the Maisons a secret from the human realm was the strongest magic of all.

I had read something about that in the book that Rosamond had given me. About how the Maisons were forced to stay secret because the humans wouldn't understand. The fact that I had understood that at all when everything had first happened told me that there was a purpose. Or maybe I had just been reaching for something because I didn't feel like I belonged. Braelynn had been the same way, but Emory had been the one to back away. Emory hadn't wanted to believe.

In the end, she had been forced to believe. Had been compelled to feel the magic running through her veins. I didn't know where she was or how she felt, but I knew it had to be different for her now. As if she were a completely different person.

Once again, I put those thoughts from my mind, knowing that I didn't have time.

"So, are you coming with me?" I asked, unsure what I wanted the answer to be.

Alura shook her head, and I immediately felt disappointment, though not as much as I should have. Maybe it was because I really didn't know her well, or perhaps it was just that she sometimes freaked me out, even with the trust we'd built.

"You'll be bringing Braelynn with you, though," Alura said. "She needs to be back in the realm because she can't...no, I'd better not say anything."

I moved forward, pulling Braelynn into my arms. She purred against my neck and then looked over at Alura with what I could only guess was an accusatory stare. Braelynn seemed to give those often. Then again, she was a cat. I really did like cats, but it was strange to talk to my best friend as one.

"I thought I was going to have to leave her behind." I didn't have the same disappointment I had before. Instead, I felt a little elated. I would be bringing Brae with me. She wouldn't be alone here in a place that didn't know who she really was, and I wouldn't be alone in the Maison realm. Even though I knew I likely wouldn't be alone there because someone had to be meeting me. Because if Alura were telling me it was time to go, there had to be someone waiting for me on the other side. It was probably Rosamond. Maybe even Rhodes.

I ignored the clutch in my belly at the thought of him. It had to be them. Nobody else would be there for me.

"She's going with you, and I'm going to attach this little carrier to your bag so she doesn't have to walk the whole way. It'll be like she's a parrot on your shoulder with her little head out and her little paws." I just shook my head, laughing a bit as Alura righted the pack with Braelynn's little section.

"On the other side, we'll attach the things she needs, but I'm sure when you're there, there'll be enough supplies for the both of you. Now, we must be going."

"But my parents? You finished with that part, too?" I knew I was jumping all over the place, but I was really worried. I had been waiting for this day for a year, sitting in place as if everything were just in stasis, on pause as my life tumbled out of control.

I'd said goodbye as if I were going on a walk earlier, but Mom and Dad hadn't seen me. Not really. They hadn't seen the pain in my eyes. The knowledge that I was leaving them—this time possibly for good. I loved my parents with every ounce of my being, even if I couldn't tell them everything that had happened. They didn't even see Brae as a cat with wings, just a feline that I called Braelynn. They thought it was funny that I'd named my pet after my best friend. They had no idea she *was* my best friend.

I couldn't tell them anything without either putting them in danger, or having them think I needed to be put in a mental institution for believing in the unbelievable.

"Your parents won't remember you, and they won't be staying here, either. I'm going to have them and Braelynn's family go on vacation together, maybe even a long one where they resettle somewhere else. Just in case those who don't want a Spirit Priestess in their world for reasons of their own come to find them."

I swallowed hard, holding Braelynn close. "You think they would hurt my parents?" I knew that there were people out there who didn't want me to save the Maison realm. They didn't want me and my powers to take what they thought was theirs. Not that I was going to, but they had reasons of their own that only they understood. Or maybe, like the knight, they wanted my power for themselves. For those reasons, I was glad that others were thinking of my parents and trying to protect them. But it didn't make any of it any easier to swallow.

"They will be fine. No one will even know where they are. I'll do my best to make sure neither of you even know where they are."

"As long as they're safe." I might not truly connect to my parents the way I should, but I loved them. And they loved me. And Braelynn's family loved her, even if they couldn't remember her because of the memory spell. My parents wouldn't remember me soon either. And it was all for a reason. For a purpose. But it didn't make it any easier. And so, with that, I brought Braelynn close, and we started on our way to the mountains. Alura drove, competent and acting as if this were an everyday occurrence. As if I weren't walking into a realm that wasn't the one I had been born into, one that called to me with its siren song in my dreams *and* during my waking hours.

This was rote for her. But for me, it wasn't.

It couldn't be.

Because I was the only Spirit Priestess. The one they had all been searching for. The one Rhodes and Rosamond had been looking for. And they had found me.

Others were looking for me, but it had been Rhodes and Rosamond who eventually fulfilled that part of the prophecy. Apparently, even Easton had started the search long ago, though he'd quit while trying to save his kingdom. I didn't know how I felt about that. Then again, I didn't know much about Easton or how I felt about him saving me or him helping me in the end when Rhodes had walked away.

I let out a shuddering breath as we got out of the car, Braelynn in a pouch on my back with her little paws perched on my shoulder. We walked towards the mountain.

I must have looked weird with a cat sitting perfectly still on my back and shoulder, but there was no one to really look at us. We made it through the place where I had fallen that first time. The area where a Neg had wrapped its spindly fingers around my ankle and tugged me down the mountainside. I had almost died, but Rosamond had saved me. And Rhodes had been the one to try and pull me back.

We passed that place without saying a word. I wasn't out of breath. My body didn't hurt. I had trained for this. Alura looked as if she were gliding over the trail. As if she hadn't a care in the world. Maybe she didn't. Perhaps this was just part of her journey.

One day, I would find out. One day, I would ask more. But this was not that day. When we made it to the crevice in the side of the mountain where I could feel the pull of the Maison realm, I knew it was time. I understood that this was why I was here. This was what I had been waiting for. I was stronger than I was before. I was smarter. I knew more.

Now it was time for me to find my other elements. I still needed Water, Fire, and Spirit.

I needed all five to fully complete who I was.

Once that was done, I could figure out what it all meant.

Because there wasn't a direct path that I could follow, not yet. But there was at least something.

"Trust yourself, Lyric. You know more than you think you do." Alura hugged me then, kissed the top of Braelynn's head, and then bussed my forehead.

"But you're not coming," I reiterated, my voice deceptively calm.

"It's not my time. It will be soon. But it's not time yet." I vaguely remembered her saying something similar when I first saw her talking to Rhodes and Rosamond on the street. Before everything had changed. Before *I* had changed. I still didn't know what she meant, but when she gave me a little wave, I gave her a nod in return and turned towards the crevice.

The magic pulled at me, licked at my skin. This was where I needed to be. Soon, I would see my friends. Soon, I would know what path I needed to take and would stop hiding. Because the others needed me, and frankly, I needed them. So I took a step, and then another. The magic tugged at me, pulling, fraying. Braelynn purred against my neck as if she enjoyed the feeling. If I were honest with myself, maybe I was enjoying it, too. It was as if I were coming home after a long journey to something familiar and sweet.

It didn't make any sense because I had only been here once before, yet I knew this was where I needed to be.

And as I stepped into the bright light that was the southern Spirit territory, I shielded my eyes with my hand. Braelynn leaned into me, still purring as she faced forward. I focused on the three shadows coming towards me. Three figures that didn't feel like the dark energy of the Negs or as if they were trying to hurt me.

But they didn't feel familiar.

When they walked into the light in my line of sight, they didn't *look* like anyone I knew either.

I held up my hands, the earth beneath me rattling just a bit, and the air sliding between my fingers. I was ready to fight back if needed.

But then a man held up his hands, his deep voice rumbling. I froze. I did not know these people, but it seemed they knew me.

"Lyric? Good, Alura said you would be here."

I didn't know this man, but he clearly knew me. Or *of* me.

"Who are you?" I asked, not backing down on my Wielding. I had learned to protect myself, at least somewhat, and that was better than when I'd first stepped foot into this realm a year ago.

The woman standing beside the man who'd spoken rolled her eyes.

"Really, Teagan? You're just going to call out her name and act like we aren't strangers?" She came forward then, her dark hair lustrous. She was absolutely stunning, but I had no idea who she was.

"Sorry for that. I'm Aerwyna, but call me Wyn. This is Teagan." She pointed over to the bigger man who had first talked. "And this is Arwin," she said, pointing to the smaller male who looked more like a boy than a man. But I couldn't really tell what age anybody was. Considering that Rhodes and Easton were in their two hundreds and looked my age, I probably wouldn't be able to.

"That doesn't really help me," I said, my voice terse. "Just because you know my name doesn't mean I should know you."

"I knew this was going to happen." Wyn shook her head, tossing her hair back from her face. "We're Easton's friends. From the Obscurité Kingdom. And we're here to take you back to the court so you can begin your training."

Training?

"Easton?" I asked, my voice breathy, my palms going clammy.

This wasn't how it was supposed to go. I was supposed to contact *him* if I needed him. And I hadn't. I didn't need him. And if I kept telling myself that, maybe I would believe it. Because contacting Easton meant that I was making a choice, and I didn't want to do that at all. I didn't want to decide between the two kingdoms. I wanted to save them both. I needed to help them. However I could.

But that meant that Rhodes and Rosamond hadn't sent for me. Hadn't wanted to help.

I swallowed hard and studied the three people in front of me. Wyn had her hair down, the strands blowing around her shoulders. Her skin was paler than mine, making the red of her lips stand out. She had huge, light blue eyes that were almost gray and seemed to be filled with knowledge and humor at the same time.

Teagan was just as large as Luken, Rhodes' second in command and friend. He was broad, and while Luken was light and blond, Teagan had darker hair that wasn't quite as long, though it looked like he raked it back with his fingers often. Teagan's skin appeared tan, maybe from being outdoors often, while the other man was a bit paler with shorter hair that had designs cut into it.

Now that I looked at them, felt their Wielding, I knew they weren't Lumiére. I could feel the Wielding of Fire and Earth on them, though I couldn't tell which person held which magic. But these three were not of the Lumiére Kingdom.

These were Obscurité.

The other kingdom.

And not my friends.

CHAPTER 4

"I have a note from Easton," Wyn said, coming forward slowly, her hands out as if to say that she came in peace. She shook her head and sighed. "I knew he should have come with us, or at least had us bring someone you might have met in the court. But everything's a little… uneasy at the moment, so we're the ones who came to take you home."

I didn't take a step back like I wanted as she moved towards me. For some reason, I felt as if they were telling the truth. It wasn't like I could truly trust them since I had no idea who they were, nor did I know if I could actually trust Easton, but he *had* helped me when I needed it. He had tried to help his people, as well. Now, he was trying to rule them.

I had no idea about his character or who he truly was, other than the fact that he had fought by Rhodes' side as if they had done it for decades. Maybe they had fought like that for decades. *Centuries.* It wasn't as if I truly knew anything about their history. The time I had been with Rhodes had told me that I could fall for him, that I thought maybe he would be mine. That perhaps the connection between us was important.

But I had been wrong about that.

I pushed those thoughts from my head, wondering why they had come at all. Because it didn't really matter right then. The only thing that mattered was these three people in front of me as I stood in front of the crevice that led to the human realm. We were out in the open, the glaring sun from the Spirit territory shining down on us.

I had always thought that this area had a sepia tone over it as if the sun got a little too bright yet not bright enough at the same time. It was a large desert with craggy rocks all around, the ground so dry that it had broken pieces in it as if it had once been a great area of water but was now just barren desert.

I knew there were trees to the east of us towards the Earth territory, but I didn't know if there were any north or to the west.

In fact, now that I really thought about the terrain, I figured the two courts were directly north of us. The way the Spirit territories were divided, each was a triangle of sorts, with the peaks coming together to contain the Obscurité and Lumiére courts. The courts themselves didn't touch, their borders dark with magic until it was so opaque that I knew no one could get through. Maybe they could have in the past, but not after the Fall.

From what I'd read, the Spirit territories did not have courts. There hadn't been a king or queen for those territories, especially not after the Fall. I didn't know who ruled them, or if anyone had. Because once the Fall happened, all of the Spirit Wielders left the realm. They had either hidden amongst the others, died, or had gone to the human realm, never to be heard from again.

I knew there were at least twelve.

Twelve who had stood on a clock in my dreams, facing me in order to tell me that something was coming, that I was needed. Those twelve had all helped me, had tried to save me.

In fact, they *had* saved me in the end. Although, for some reason, I knew that might be the one and only time they could ever do it.

It had taken great energy to even connect to me. I knew that much somehow, but I didn't really know much else.

"Lyric? Can we take you with us? Can we take you home?"

I blinked at Wyn's voice, pulling my thoughts from Spirit Wielders and histories that didn't need to be gone through just then. Some said you needed to look past the history and what had come so you could look towards the future. I didn't believe that. Yes, I needed to look forward, but I also needed to know what had come before, what had made all of us so I could figure out where my place was, what my purpose was.

"You keep saying *home*. You mean the Obscurité Court. *Your* home?"

Wyn winced. "Yes, sorry about that. I know your home is in the human realm where you just came from. Right? That's at least what Easton said. He said he actually took you back there before. And that you could have contacted him at any point to come and bring you back, but you didn't."

"You seem to know a lot about what Easton told me." I didn't know who this woman was, or her relationship to Easton, but she did have almost all of the information that Easton would have had about me. Almost.

"I'm just telling you what he told me."

"And yet, you're here. So that means you contacted Alura? How do you know her?" I didn't just want to go off with these people, even though I really didn't have a choice at this point. I couldn't go back to the human realm, I knew that. I needed to find my place here. But I couldn't find my way to the Lumiére Kingdom on my own. Rhodes and Rosamond hadn't asked for me, but I also hadn't asked to go to them. The fault lay with both of us, and only one kingdom had actually brought people out to come for me.

Maybe I had to trust in that.

The Air between my fingers sizzled, and I let out a breath. My Wielding loved being back in this realm, and I could feel it deep down in my bones that I was supposed to be here.

I had known that I was meant to be in this realm the first time I stepped onto its ground, though I hadn't known what it really signified at the time.

Now, I was here for a purpose.

"I don't really know what else to tell you other than we should probably get going. The Negs could be here. They've been patrolling more often."

"Why is that? Is everyone okay?" I needed to stop thinking about just myself and instead think about the people here that needed help. They were dying because of not only what the knight had done, but also because the crystals that fed the Maisons their Wielding and life forces were failing. The more the crystals dimmed, the more people we would lose.

"We're getting better. Lore screwed us up a bit, but we're not going to let that stop us from rebuilding." Teagan was the one who spoke that time. I turned to him. He was strong, and he looked it. His voice was low, and there was such promise in his tone that I really did believe that he wanted to help his people. I just didn't know where I fit into that.

"I know you don't know us, and you didn't really have a lot of time in the Obscurité Kingdom to actually meet everybody, but we're here to help you back to the court." It was Arwin that spoke this time, and I looked at the younger man. For all I knew, he could be hundreds of years older than I was, but he seemed younger in the way he spoke and the manner with which he held himself. I didn't really know. It was just a feeling.

"Alura told me to trust who was on the other side." As soon as I said her name, the bracelet on my wrist warmed, and I looked down at it. The Fire and Earth elemental charms brightened on my wrist, and my eyes widened. It seemed the magic that she had put into whatever I was wearing wanted me to go to the Obscurité Court.

I might have been seeing things, but I knew I had to go. After all, there was nowhere else to go.

"Alura gave you that?" Wyn asked, her voice careful.

I lowered my hand and stared at her. "Yes. She said it was for protection and other things she didn't elaborate on. She doesn't seem to tell me much."

Wyn's shoulders dropped as if she were releasing tension. "That's good. Protection is good."

"What did you think it was?" I asked.

"Oh, it could have been anything when it comes to Alura. But if she says it's for protection, then it's for protection. She would never lie about that."

I swallowed hard. "So you're saying she would lie about something else?"

Teagan let out a gruff laugh. "Great job, Wyn, you're making sure that you stress her out and make her not want to trust us at all."

"Oh, shut up. I'm sorry, Lyric. It's been a long journey, and we still have a longer one to go. Easton would have opened a portal through the crystal to get us back quickly, but none of us wanted to waste the energy. I hope you understand. We're going to have to make our way back to the court on foot."

I nodded, having expected that—only with Rhodes to the Lumiére, and not Easton or his people to the Obscurité. "I figured. And I don't want to use any more energy than we need to. I know that the land needs the crystal. That the people need it. And I'm going to do whatever I can to help fix that. Not that I actually know what I'm doing," I added when all of their eyes warmed just a bit as if they were waiting for me to come out with all the answers. I had none. And from what I could see, they didn't have any answers either.

"Well, let's be off. We're going straight north instead of through one of the other territories. We should be fine, but we're going to move quickly. It'll take a couple days, mostly because we're going on foot. But then we'll make it to the Obscurité Kingdom, and we'll be able to see Easton. And then he'll tell us exactly what we're doing."

I nodded at Wyn's words and then followed them as they turned back to where they had stashed their packs.

It seemed the four of us were going on a journey, something that reminded me of my first trip here.

Braelynn nuzzled my neck, and I blinked, having forgotten about my best friend on my shoulder.

The fact that the others hadn't commented on the cat with wings stashed in my pack told me that either she had hidden the whole time during the conversation or Easton had warned them.

"Is your friend going to be okay during the journey?" Wyn asked, seeming genuinely interested. She reached out a hand, and Braelynn sniffed it before nuzzling her. Such a typical cat gesture. I was actually surprised that she didn't lash out. Braelynn wasn't violent, but if somebody came at her a little too quickly, she got startled and used her claws rather than her purrs.

"Alura said she would be fine and hooked up this whole harness thing."

"If she gets too heavy for you, one of us can carry her. I don't think those wings of hers are ready for flight just yet." Teagan winked as he said it, and Braelynn let out a little mewling sound.

Yet? Would Braelynn ever be able to fly?

I pondered that as Braelynn let Teagan pet her before doing the same with Arwin. Then the five of us were off for our long walk up the Spirit territory towards the Obscurité Court.

I had been here before, though I hadn't been in this part of the territory. The closer we got to the Obscurité Kingdom, the more rock faces there were.

There weren't ruins or evidence of large civilizations. It was as if all of that had been erased from the face of the territory altogether.

It probably should have worried me, wondering where all the Spirit Wielders once lived. But after five hundred years, half a millennium of harsh winds and even harsher sunlight, maybe none of that survived. Perhaps the evidence of who those people were had gotten just as lost as the people themselves.

"So, do you all work for Easton?"

Teagan laughed again but nodded.

"Sort of. Easton and I have been best friends since we were kids. He's an asshole, but he's my king." Teagan did a sort of bow thing as we kept going, and I snorted.

"Well, Easton was kind of a butthead to me, but he did save my life." I paused at that, remembering the pain, the Fire. But he had tried to protect me, and he had watched as his mother died as she sacrificed herself to save me. I didn't think I would ever be able to find a way to repay that selflessness. And I didn't imagine the boy I had seen would ever be able to forgive me for what his mother had done.

But that was something I would have to face soon. We were only a couple of days' journey from where Easton was, where the King of Obscurité was. I would have to face him sooner rather than later and confront exactly what it meant to see the boy who might blame me for his mother's death.

Maybe I shouldn't have come with these people after all.

"He doesn't blame you," Wyn said softly as the others moved forward. Braelynn was now on Teagan's shoulder, her little harness attached to his bag. Braelynn hadn't been too heavy for me, but Teagan had said that he didn't want me to tire out. In fact, he'd been kind of gruff about it, mumbling about how weak I would be if I kept moving at this pace while holding a cat. I couldn't make any sense of it, but I let him take her away because she seemed to trust him. Brae was my barometer of trust these days. As were most cats.

If a cat didn't like you, there was likely a good reason.

Or maybe that was dogs.

Either way, Brae was my test, and I was sticking to it.

"What?" I asked as Wyn nudged me.

"I said, Easton doesn't blame you."

I swallowed hard. "How did you know what I was thinking about?"

Wyn just sighed. "I can't read minds, and I'm not a Seer. But I know when people are feeling guilt or something painful. It almost hits me. Maybe I'm an emotional Seer. Who knows? But I know that you're in pain. And it's not just from what happened to you when Lore betrayed us. I know it has to do with what you saw, and what Queen Cameo did. Easton doesn't blame you. How could he? You're the Spirit Priestess."

I didn't flinch at Wyn's use of the title. That had to count for progress, right? "You say that, yet I can blame myself for it. She didn't have to do that. Yes, I will always blame Lore for what happened, but I had some role in it, too. If I had been fast enough, if I had found a way, maybe it wouldn't have happened at all. Maybe Cameo would still be here."

"And maybe if the three of us—me, Teagan, and Arwin—hadn't been on patrol on the other side of the Spirit territory dealing with a roundup of Negs, we would have been able to save the queen. Maybe if we hadn't been so positive that something was wrong, so sure that we needed to leave because we were trying to save our people, we would have been in that throne room to help Easton. But we weren't. We weren't there, and now the queen is dead. Long live the king."

We didn't speak much after Wyn's whispered words, my thoughts rolling around from one topic to another. I knew I was here to train, to figure out my role in all of this, but maybe everybody else was, as well. Perhaps nobody knew where they truly fit into this war that didn't seem so much like a war but an ongoing battle that never seemed to end.

I knew we would figure it out. We had to. Because there wasn't going to be another choice.

Wyn might not think that Easton blamed me for his mother's death, but I could blame myself. I did. And I had a feeling that Easton held me responsible, too. How could he not?

But I didn't know him. I didn't know this court. I didn't know anybody except myself and the cat currently peeking over Teagan's shoulder.

I used to ask myself how everything could come to be like this, but not anymore. I knew that this was how it would always be from now on, no matter what.

We walked for two days straight, only resting for a few hours at a time to sleep, eat, and drink water. It was weird, but the journey felt so much like the time I had moved from the Earth territory to the Fire one. We just kept walking. Nobody in the group spoke much, but Arwin was the quietest of them all. He seemed so sweet, though, always making sure I had enough water and food. And he really seemed to like Braelynn. He held her close, even carrying her in his arms so she could have a better look around. They were all warriors, I knew that, but Arwin seemed almost...innocent.

It seemed weird that there could be innocence in a world where people died all the time because of other people's greed. But there was goodness in the human world, as well. Sometimes I forgot that.

My legs burned, and I was exhausted and really just wanted a bath, but I knew we were getting close.

When the magic through my body shimmered, I looked down at the Air Wielding humming in my fingers, the earth rumbling beneath my feet.

We were getting close.

Or perhaps we had arrived.

"Oh, it's about time," Teagan said with a grumble as we slid our way towards the wards. The magic looked like a soap bubble on a clear surface so I could see past it to the court ahead, but I couldn't really tell what was blocking us.

"You and Braelynn are invited, so you should be able to walk through the wards easily. You'll also be able to leave because you're not prisoners here," Wyn explained as we moved our way through the magic. "It won't hurt you, but if you hadn't been invited or if you were Lumiére? Then it may hurt."

"I'm an Air Wielder, as well," I put in.

"Oh, we know. But you're a guest here. The wards aren't to hurt people, they're to keep us safe. That's the difference."

I didn't know what she meant by *difference*. Maybe the other court's wards were intended to hurt? Or perhaps I was reading too much into Wyn's words.

The court looked much the same as it had before, only shinier and brighter.

This was the dark court, the Obscurité. In my head, before I had ever met Easton or the rest of them, I had thought them perhaps the enemy. The evil court. After all, I had only met those of the Lumiére before.

Lumiére was light, good. But there was good and evil on both sides, something I would do well to remember. After all, I held elements within me from both kingdoms. One day, I hoped I would hold the other three elements, as well. Meaning I would be of both kingdoms *and* the Spirit territory.

The dark castle before me was made of black stone and a nearly purple crystal. It was gorgeous with its turrets and even a moat. It looked very medieval but almost serene. It probably shouldn't seem that way, but that was the word that came to me.

As if there were peace or at least a semblance of it. And maybe that was the case since Lore was no more. His evil was no longer lurking and sucking the magic and life force from the Obscurité people. That darkness was gone.

Yes, the crystal was still failing, but there wasn't death surrounding them anymore, no shroud pulling the kingdom deeper.

I really just wanted to brush my hair and teeth before we had to deal with anything, but I could tell that wasn't going to be the case. Because before we'd even walked onto the bridge that led to the castle itself, a very familiar Wielder strutted out, his hair falling across his forehead.

His light brown skin glistened under the sunlight, his black eyes narrowing even as his lips quirked into a familiar smirk.

"It's about time you got here. I was about to send out the cavalry, and then I realized you *were* my cavalry."

Easton.

The king.

But not *my* king.

"Long time, no see," I said, giving him my best haughty tone. I didn't know why, but he just bugged me.

"Ah, the fabled one. Welcome to your new training. And welcome to my home." He gave me an exaggerated deep bow that almost made me smile. Almost.

Teagan and Wyn both held back grins while Braelynn gave me a look over Teagan's shoulder. Arwin, on the other hand, looked about ready to faint. Because the king was bowing to me? Or perhaps because I wasn't curtseying back.

Either way, I didn't know, and it didn't really matter.

I was here. And there was no going back.

But then again, there never had been.

CHAPTER 5

The last time I was here, I had died. Now that was a weird thought to think at this exact moment. I looked down at Braelynn, who was currently cleaning her paws while giving me a strange look. Seriously, only cats could do that.

Well, the last time we had been here, we had *both* died. Only I had found my way through it and came out somewhat whole. Braelynn had come back a cat. With wings.

My life had really taken a strange turn at some point. I don't really remember the exact moment of that change.

When Easton finally let us into the castle—yes, a real castle—the maids had sent me up alone to my room. It was a different suite than I had before, or at least I thought. I looked around again, frowning. No, this was the same room I had woken up in after the battle, it'd just been cleaned up a bit since then.

This was the space where I had finally seen Rosamond again, sitting at the end of my bed with Braelynn in her lap. Right before she had handed me the large book that I had left behind back at my house in the human realm. It had been too heavy for me to carry for the long journey, and I had most of it memorized anyway. It was really the only book, other than the history books from my own world that I had read in the past year.

I had hidden it under my bed and hoped that my parents wouldn't find it. If they did for some reason, maybe I could explain to them that it was just a dictionary and history of fantasy and wasn't real.

It wasn't as if I could tell them that any of this was real.

Regardless, this was the room that I had been in when I tried to wake up and realize exactly what I needed to do next. I had felt so lost, trying to figure out who I was and what the next step should be. It wasn't as if I had known what I was supposed to do back then. I didn't know what I was supposed to do right now.

Almost dying had scared me to the point that I needed to take some time for myself. And I had taken it.

Now, it was time to *train*—as Easton had put it.

Wyn, Teagan, and Arwin had left me to my own devices, but all had promised that I would see them again.

So, I took a bath and washed away the grunge from the past day's walk. The maids and other staff had left hot water for me in the cast iron tub, and I was grateful. The one thing I truly missed about my world was full indoor plumbing. The castle seemed to have some of it, at least from what I remembered, but not in this room. No, this suite was a little medieval.

And maybe Easton had put me in it *because* of that fact.

Or perhaps he had just put me in here because it had been my room before and thought I might need something familiar.

I still didn't know why he had been the one to call on me and not Rhodes.

It worried me, but it wasn't like I knew what I was doing. I needed to learn how to better control my Earth Wielding abilities. And at some point, I needed to unlock my Fire Wielding. Easton would be the one to teach me that—or at least one of his people would be. I hoped.

And one day soon, I hoped I would go to the Lumiére Kingdom and learn how to better Wield my Air and unlock my Water Wielding. It didn't make any of this easier, but I would find my way through. I had already done a lot, and I would just keep going.

I dressed in soft leather pants, boots, and a long tunic that had flowers embroidered on the edges of the hem and cuffs, and paired it with a belt to cinch it at the waist. I sort of looked like a mix between what I had been before and what I was now. They weren't the same battle leathers that I had worn when I was here last, nor was it the same type of leathers that Wyn had worn when I first met her in the Spirit territory.

This seemed more like just casualwear without having to wear a dress. And for that, I was grateful. I wasn't the most graceful person when it came to dresses, so maybe I could move around better in this.

There was a knock on the door. Before I could answer, it opened, and Wyn stuck her head through the gap, her hair falling into her face before she tucked it behind her ear. "Oh, good, you're dressed. Easton wants you to meet a few people and to show you around."

"Oh? Am I going to start training today then?" I bent down and scratched Braelynn behind the ears, needing the way she purred against my leg to keep me steady.

"I don't really know if training's going to start today, but for sure tomorrow. I think today you're just going to get settled. I know we're technically at war with the Lumiére, but if you want, I can find a way for you to contact your friends." She whispered the last part, and my eyes widened.

"You would do that?"

"You're the Spirit Priestess. You're the one who's supposed to make us all come together and save the world. How can I help you do that if I don't let you contact those of the Lumiére? Just think about it. I have my ways." She winked and then walked fully into the room to kneel down on the ground. Braelynn looked at me and then swished her tail before going right over to Wyn and jumping into her arms.

I held back a smile. "I see that Braelynn trusts you."

"Of course, she does. I'm very trustworthy. I'll hang out with her for now if you want. That way, she's not alone while I show her around the court a bit. I don't want others to think that she's just some ordinary cat." Wyn looked down at Braelynn and trailed her finger along one of Brae's wings. "Not that anyone's really going to believe that. I don't know if I've ever seen anyone like her before. And I've seen a lot of different things considering where I grew up."

I perked up, wanting to know more about these people I would be staying with. "Where did you grow up?"

Wyn's brow rose, and she gave me a wry smile. "My parents are the Lord and Lady of Earth. Technically, I'm a princess of Obscurité, a lady in her own right."

I blinked, remembering my last, not-so-nice encounter with the Earth Estate. "I...I didn't know that."

Wyn just snorted. "Yeah, I see you know them. And, yes, I'm their daughter. I grew up in the court though because my parents had this idea that I should marry Easton. So, they stuck us together."

That made me blink again. "Oh?"

This time, Wyn laughed. "We're a court system. As long as the bloodlines aren't mixed too much, our families like to marry within and keep the power with them. Easton and I found it funny and trained so I would be in his inner circle as a warrior instead of just his wife."

I felt like I was four steps behind again. "I have no idea what to say to that."

Wyn just shrugged. "There isn't much *to* say. But it's not important. Really. I'm here to protect this kingdom. And Easton is my king. It's what we do. You'll learn more about it all on your own today when you go off with Easton."

"So you're not coming with me today?" I asked, feeling a little lost. Of course, that was something I was quite used to these days.

"No, I don't think you need me. After all, you've known Easton longer than you've known me. Just don't let him push you around. He gets all grumpy when he's stressed out, and he's really stressed out right now."

"So I guess you know Easton really well." I wasn't really asking too deep of a question, but it sounded far more curious than I had planned.

Wyn just laughed. "Probably not the way you're thinking. Easton and I have never been that close, at least not in that kind of relationship. But he is my best friend. At least, one of them. Teagan is the other." She rolled her eyes. "Teagan, on the other hand...*he* I *did* date. But he's a jerk—even though I love him."

I swallowed hard. "Oh."

Not really sure what else to say, I just sat there patting my hands against my thighs. I didn't know how old Wyn or Teagan were. I still didn't even know what kind of Wielding they had. I was so far out of my depth, it was crazy, but I'd find my way. I had to.

"Sorry, I kind of blurt things out when I'm nervous."

"You're nervous? Why would you be nervous? I thought I should be the nervous one."

"Oh, you have total rights to be nervous right now. And I wouldn't blame you if you wanted to run out that door and never talk to us again. It would be kind of strange to be in a realm that isn't yours and get asked to do things that no one can explain or tell you what they actually entail. But I'm nervous because I can't believe that Rhodes and his sister actually found you. I mean, I know you're still Lyric, but you're also the Spirit Priestess. And I guess that's a lot to put on your shoulders. And I don't like that. I'd love to be able to help, but I'll just have to figure out how to do that while you figure out how to help yourself." She paused. "And that made no sense. So just ignore me and let me take you to where Easton and the uncles are."

She turned on her heel, Braelynn still in her arms, and I followed, feeling more confused now than I had when I started.

"So, uncles?" I walked next to Wyn, trying to look around as I did so. Part of the court had been destroyed when we fought against the knight and his men. So much magic running through the halls had broken some of the stone and the crystals. But a lot of it had been rebuilt in the year I'd been gone.

There was still the dark stonework and even darker floors, but it had more of a shine to it than it had in the past. It wasn't as dull, didn't seem quite as...evil. Not that I thought that dark was evil and light was good, I had learned through reading Rosamond's book and just from what I had seen that there was good and bad on both sides. I just needed to figure out which was which when I was facing it.

"Justise is Easton's uncle, Cameo's brother. Not that everybody really knew that Justise was related to her. But that's not my story to tell. Anyway, Justise is married to Ridley, who's our healer. Justise is the blacksmith and helps with our weapons. They're hanging out with Easton today and are dying to meet you."

"Oh, that's...I didn't realize people really knew about me. Or wanted to meet me." I didn't know what to say to that. I hadn't realized I'd be meeting some of Easton's family. Frankly, I just wanted to begin my training so I could go to the Lumiére Kingdom when it was time and try to figure out what the next step was. For some reason, this felt like a way station, and I really shouldn't think about it that way. I had things to do, elements to learn, and I needed to focus and not yearn to be somewhere else when I was here.

"You'll like them, I promise. Justise is a grumpy butthead, but with what he's been through, he's earned it. Ridley is our not-so-grumpy healer. At least that's what I call him. But I love the both of them, and Easton hasn't had a father figure in his life for quite a long time, so I've always enjoyed the fact that he has his uncles with him."

Before I could say anything to that, wondering exactly what Easton thought of Wyn airing some of his possible secrets to me, we ended up in the middle of the courtyard with the sun shining down, and people milling about. This was far different from the last time I had been in the court with so many people hiding, so many scared.

Maybe that was just the parts I remembered because I had been fighting for my life. I could still recall the sound of the children laughing and playing in the streets of the border to the Fire lands. There hadn't been children hiding in pain or in terror. They had all been smiling. They had been happy. Yes, terrors were happening all around them, but there had still been hope.

And now I could see some of that on the faces of the people that looked up to Easton as their king.

There were so many of them around us. Some were Fire Wielders, some Earth, some I could sense were a mixture of the two. And some, yes, some were Danes, Maisons without any Wielding powers. I had learned from reading Rosamond's book and from what the others had told me, that Danes were becoming far more prevalent as time passed. When the Maison realm had fractured in two, it had changed the way magic and Wielding moved within its own people.

Before he died, the old knight had used the crystal that tried to protect its people against them. He had siphoned the magic and Wielding from them to create Danes. Some had been born that way, others were forced into it.

When we were last here, Braelynn had been called a Dane, while Emory had just been considered human. I was neither because I was the foretold Spirit Priestess—or so they told me.

Oh, I believed it now, but sometimes it was quite hard to keep on believing it when I didn't have a clue what I was going to do about it, or even what I *could* do about it.

Nobody knew why Braelynn had been considered a Dane, but maybe that was why she'd come back as she did after she died. Nobody explained to me exactly how it had happened, though I didn't think anybody really knew. It was just one of those things, something that happened that I was supposed to just go along with.

So, I would listen, and I would learn. I wouldn't just go along with it this time.

"Ah, you're here," Easton said, raising that dark brow of his.

I really did not want to like him, even as he smirked at me. Oh, he might be one of the most attractive people I had ever met in my life, but he was also one of the most annoying. He always had that smirk. As if he knew something I didn't. And because I knew that he actually did know way more than I did, it just annoyed me. It wasn't my fault that I was a couple of hundred years younger than he was. Anybody with that much time to learn things would have a leg up. It wasn't nice to gloat about it.

"Oh? There she is," one of the others in the courtyard said, grinning. Two men stood beside Easton, both with dark brown skin and darker hair. One wore a smile and leathers and a tunic similar to my own, just without the embroidery. The other had on something similar but with a leather smock over it. That male was not smiling.

I could guess who was the grumpy weapons maker and blacksmith, and who was the not-so-grumpy healer.

"Ah, yes, Ridley, meet Lyric, the Spirit Priestess." Easton gestured towards him, his voice oddly formal as if he didn't really know what to do right now either. That made me feel a little more comfortable.

"Hi, I just go by Lyric though, if that's okay," I said, giving a little wave.

Ridley came up to me and wrapped me in a hug so tight, I swore my back cracked a few times. However, it felt good in the end, so maybe he had done it on purpose. He was a healer after all, not that I actually knew if what he did was done by magic or if he was like a doctor. Rosamond's book hadn't been very specific about that.

"It's so good to finally meet you. We've heard all about you, of course. And from the look on your face, you haven't heard about us. But why should you? You've had to focus on exactly what this whole magical world means. But, any questions you have, we're here for you. And if my nephew tries to hurt you while you're in training, I can hurt him back, and I can heal you. It's sort of my job." He winked, and his husband at his side rolled his eyes before holding out his hand.

"I'm Justise. It's good to meet you." I took his hand, his firm grip squeezing my fingers ever so slightly. And though his words were gruff, I could tell that he actually meant them. So, maybe he wasn't all that grumpy.

"Thanks for inviting me." I really needed to work on what I was going to say before I actually said it. I hated sounding inept.

"We weren't just going to let you stay there in the human realm and rot, were we?" Easton asked, buffing his nails. He really was a jerk. A very big one. With really pretty eyes.

Of course, then I thought of Rhodes' silver eyes, and I got a little sad.

I swore Easton could tell where my thoughts had gone because his eyes narrowed and he came closer, holding out his hand.

I looked down at it before taking it, not sure why I did, but also not wanting to offend anyone by *not* doing so.

"Let me show you around a bit, and you can tell me what you've been doing for the past year. My uncles need to go back to work, but I wanted them to meet you. If you have any questions during training while you're here, they're here to help you. As are Teagan, Wyn, and even Arwin. Arwin is still in training himself, but he's still one of the higher-ups here, and I trust him with my life—therefore, yours. I want you to learn how to deal with your elements. And that's why you're here. Nothing more."

That last bit was a very odd thing to say, but I just nodded, saying my goodbyes as the uncles walked back to where they presumably worked, Ridley leaning in to Justise's side ever so slightly as they did. They were seriously a cute couple, and I was glad that there was at least some happiness in a world that seemed to be failing around the Maisons.

"So, that's why I'm here? To figure out what I'm doing?"

"Of course. But, tell me, what *have* you been doing for the past year?" Easton let go of my hand when he turned the corner to move down the hall, and I wondered why I felt the loss. It wasn't as if he were *mine*, after all. No one was. Not even Rhodes. Or Emory. No one.

"I would've thought you'd have spies watching me or something," I said in jest, pulling myself out of my thoughts. And now I was afraid that maybe he *had* put people on me. Perhaps the others had, too. It did seem highly unlikely that everyone would just leave me to my own devices while I was in the human realm.

"I wasn't watching you while you slept or anything," he said as he rolled his eyes. "But, really? What were you doing?"

"Alura was helping me train. And I read, trying to catch up and just heal while I figured out the next step."

"And did you figure it out? The next step?"

"Not at all. But I guess that's the point. I'm probably not going to figure it out until I'm already stepping."

"Truer words have never been said."

We moved over the cobblestone bridge, and I looked around, taking in the vast beauty of the Obscurité Court. It had seemed so much more somber the last time I was here, but then again, I had died. Everything had appeared a little darker.

I was so focused on not paying attention to Easton that I tripped over my own foot and ended up slamming right into his chest. He looked down at me, raising a brow as he caught me. I growled then reached out and punched him in the chest as he laughed. I moved back to standing.

"Oh, stop it," I said, snapping.

"I knew you just wanted to touch me. All you had to do was ask."

"You're a jerk."

"Yes, I am. But I'm also the king. So, you better watch what you're saying."

"You're not my king, Easton."

"Ah, so Rhodes' family is your court, then?"

"No, I'm not from either court. Period. And you would do well to remember that."

"Maybe."

Easton studied me a minute before waving off the conversation. Then he snapped his fingers, a slight flame appearing. It looked as if he'd done it out of habit. Like he was thinking. But I knew my eyes lit up. I smiled, watching the fire. I had always liked fire.

"You like Fire?" he asked as he doused the blaze.

"Of course." I breathed, unsure why I'd said the words so quickly, so I backtracked. "But then again, aren't I supposed to have that element too at some point?"

"Then you need to learn it." The words sent a shiver down my spine, but I nodded. It took so much out of me to unlock an element. It wasn't going to be easy. It never was. The other two elements I'd unlocked already had hurt, so I had a feeling this was going to hurt just as much. It likely had to.

Rhodes had told me before that Fire was the hardest element to control. Therefore, it would probably be the hardest one to gain, as well.

"So, Alura has been teaching you more about Earth and Air? How can she when she has neither?"

"Do you know what element she does have?" I asked, curious.

Easton shook his head. "Not my place to say. I probably already said too much, but then again, I always do."

No, he usually said just enough to annoy me. Well, fine then.

I spread out my fingers, feeling the earth beneath me, and I rumbled it just slightly. Easton's eyes lit up, and he did the same with his Earth Wielding. It was weird, mixing our elements together and using just one Wielding. I had never done that before, but I liked it.

"You're better than you used to be. Alura's teaching you well."

"Well, that one does seem easier to me, though I still can't like do waves of dirt and all that." I had seen the Earth pirates and sentries move rocks, boulders, and hills of dirt with just their Wielding. I might be better than I was, but I was nowhere near that level of proficiency.

Easton nodded. "We can help you with that. Once you figure out the basics, it's just putting it all together over time. And you're good with Air, too?" I nodded, pushing at him just slightly with my Wielding. He didn't take a step back, but he did smile. "Oh, I can see you're tough with it."

I narrowed my eyes. "I've always wanted to try something." And then I focused on him, letting the Wielding slide from my shoulders and move down my arms and through my fingertips. The Air slid under him, lifting him up ever so slightly.

Easton's eyes widened, and he threw back his head and laughed. "Now that's a good one, little one. Can you make me do spins?"

I shook my head, laughing with him as I lowered him to his feet.

"If I did that, I'd probably end up bashing your head in, and that's not something I really want to do." I paused. "At least not at the moment. Treason and all."

"Well, I'm grateful for that. Training begins tomorrow. The uncles will probably begin with you. I have things to do."

"So, you're not going to be in charge of my training?" I asked, still a little confused as to why I was here. With him. Alone.

A strange look covered his face, and he shook his head. "I'm king now. I have other things to do. My people will help you. And maybe then you can help us."

There wasn't much to say after that. After all, it had been my fault that his mother died, my fault that he was now king. And I still didn't know how I was supposed to save everyone. I could barely save myself.

So, without words, he walked me back to the castle as the sun set around us, then led me to my room. He still didn't speak as I closed the door behind me without even saying goodbye to him.

Braelynn was already in the suite, obviously having come back from her trip with Wyn, though I didn't know when. And though I was hungry, I knew I couldn't eat. Not when I was so confused. Not when I missed all the things I'd once had, everything I knew I couldn't have again.

And so, I lay in bed, willing myself to at least go to sleep or wait for the next part to come. Braelynn jumped into my lap, purring as I tried to hold myself together. I didn't know what was coming next, but I knew what I missed. I missed silver eyes. Missed when things had just been about a crush on a boy and me finding myself. I'd already found a part of myself, but I didn't know what it all meant.

And there was more to come. There always was. And now it seemed Easton would be part of it, at least in the periphery.

And I still had no idea how I felt about that.

CHAPTER 6

When they told me I would be training, I had thought about using the sword that had impaled me, going into some kind of medieval or Viking sparring where I would sweat and cry and maybe even bleed. I had pictured going through every motion, trying to fight for my life and learning how to use weapons that were not just my elements.

I remembered Luken, Rhodes' best friend and fellow warrior. He had used his sword and his Air Wielding together as if they were one. He'd sent his Wielding along the sword as a way to direct where he needed to send his magic and where he needed to fight.

I knew he also used the sword against the Danes who were just as strong as he was, using weapons that they could hold because they didn't have the Wielding within their bodies.

So, when Easton and the others had said it was time to train, that is what

Me wearing battle leathers and trying to fight for my life as I learned how to build muscle and use weapons that I had never held before.

I suppressed a shiver.

Oh, I'd held a sword before. Now that I thought about it, I had picked it up from the ground, bloody and still warm, after it had slid from my body and from Easton's hands when he used it against the knight. I'd used it to block the magic that the knight had sent to me directly from the crystal. The power that had ripped Braelynn open, killing her, and had done the same to the queen.

Braelynn hadn't had enough magic within her body, even though she had been a Dane, and had burned to a crisp, turning to ash and blowing away before she came back later as a cat.

Rosamond still hadn't told me exactly how that had occurred.

Queen Cameo had had enough magic within her system to not fade away completely into dust. So, she had died, but she hadn't turned to ash. Her body had lain there, lifeless.

So, I had held the sword and pulled it towards my body to protect myself from the blast of energy and magic. And then I had pointed it towards the knight, directing all of that Wielding from the crystal back at him.

And it had killed him.

So, yes, I had held a sword before. But it didn't appear I would be holding one today.

"So, we're not going to do any actual Wielding?" I asked, my voice a little soft as I sat with Ridley in the middle of the garden area.

I had slept horribly the night before. Dreams of what had happened the last time I was here mixing with the last time I had seen Emory writhing on the floor with such anger in her eyes. I had dreamt of Rhodes reaching out to me but never able to catch me. And I dreamt of Easton, smirking at me but then giving me weird looks that I didn't understand.

I felt like I didn't understand a lot these days, and that stood in the way of me becoming who I needed to be, what I needed to focus on. Because every time I took two steps forward to find my destiny, something pushed me three steps back, making me even more confused.

Wyn had woken me early that morning, taking me down to the mess hall where many of the warriors were eating their breakfast before they went out to their various training sessions or sentry duties. I didn't really know what everybody did, but I would hopefully learn soon. It wasn't like I was trying to learn the ins and outs of the court security system, but I wanted to know how things worked. Apparently, these were my people. At least, some of them. And that meant I wanted to know who they were and how they worked. How they lived.

I could barely function in the human world, though it seemed there had been a reason for that. I didn't have a true purpose. I hadn't had one until I came here.

I wanted to know exactly what it meant to be part of the Maison realm, even as broken as it was.

But I had no idea where to start.

I'd sat between Arwin and Teagan across the table from Wyn as I dug into my breakfast, trying to enjoy the food even though it all just felt and tasted like sawdust in my mouth. I'd been a little worried about what my training would be and what I would have to face. Nothing I had faced before had been easy. After breakfast, the three warriors had gone on their way, and Ridley had come to get me, taking me to the center of the courtyard but in a different part of the castle where there wasn't anyone around.

It was almost like a garden.

It was calming, soothing. I sat on the ground, my legs crossed. Ridley did the same directly in front of me, and I wondered what I was doing.

"I'm not going to be the one to teach you to fight. There are others to do that. But you also have to train your mind. Because Wielding is within you. You have to understand exactly what parts of you breathe in that element in order for you to use it."

I swallowed hard and nodded. "I guess that makes sense."

"It'll make more sense once you learn more. I know that you were thrust into this whole situation far faster than you could have dreamed. Or rather, I guess faster than *we* dreamed. I don't suppose you dreamt of anything like this."

I didn't say anything for a moment, then, without even meaning to, I told him more than I had anyone before.

"Actually, the dreams were the only thing I had before at all. I dreamt of standing between five elements, in the middle of the five directions. I dreamt of standing at the center of a clock where all the numbers seemed to shadow me, wanting me to go in different directions. I dreamt of the Negs and so many other demonic things." I paused. "At least, I thought they were demonic. But I guess maybe they were the absence of everything?"

Ridley's eyes widened before he nodded. "Have you told anyone else about these dreams?"

"I don't think so." My words were soft, and I realized that they were true. I hadn't really told anybody about the details of my dreams before. And I honestly didn't know why I had told Ridley just then. But maybe it was because I needed a connection between when I thought I was just human and lost to where I was now, still just as lost but in a completely new landscape where I felt as if I were falling behind again.

"I don't know what they mean, but they have to mean something I guess."

"Dreams can mean anything that we need them to mean, or they can just be something to set us on the right path. Sometimes, I dream that I'm lost and trying to find my way out of something or somewhere, and it's only because I had a bad day, or I had a fight with the one I love. Or maybe because I couldn't heal the way I needed to and someone was hurting because I wasn't strong enough. Dreams can be manifestations, or they can just be dreams."

"Mine never really felt like just dreams." I swallowed hard, remembering waking up in a ball, covered in sweat and having to wash my sheets over and over again because I dreamt so vividly that I felt like I was actually there.

"Later, when you know me a bit more, I'd like you to tell me more about this dream. If you want. I'm not a healer of the mind or the soul. I'm a healer of the body. But I can try to help. If you'll let me."

I just sat there silently, not knowing if there was really anything I could say to that. Because I didn't know Ridley. Not yet. I didn't even know Easton or the others. I was here because something had drawn me to this court, and the warriors had been the ones there for me on the other side when I needed a place to go.

But I didn't know these people, not really, and I didn't know if I was ready to share everything that was in my heart. I wasn't sure I could share everything that made up my deepest fear.

Maybe one day. Someday I might find some people that I could actually trust with everything that I was.

"Okay, for now, that's enough of that. I want you to close your eyes and focus. I want you to think about what it means to be a Wielder."

"What if I don't know what that is?" I asked, not realizing I was going to voice the words until they were out of my mouth.

"There is no one answer. It's just what it means to you. And if that meaning is confusion and being last, then that's a true feeling that you need to work through. You don't have to tell me anything you're thinking. You don't even have to speak another word for the rest of the time we're together. All

I want you to do is focus on what's inside of you. Focus on the mental strain it takes to use your Air and Earth Wielding. And, one day soon, we can talk about the other three Wieldings that you will have. One day soon."

So, I closed my eyes and tried to think about what Ridley was telling me. I wasn't one to meditate or sit down and be silent for long.

It wasn't that I thought it wasn't helpful, it just wasn't something I'd done yet.

But I knew that when I actually focused within myself, that was when I could use my Wielding the best.

If I followed Ridley's advice and tried to center my mind, maybe I could get stronger. Perhaps I could actually do something with what I had.

So, I closed my eyes and tried to think about my Wielding as an onion, something I could peel slowly, layer by layer. I held back a smile, remembering a movie I had seen when I was a kid about something very similar to that. Because an onion wasn't the most pretty. Wasn't the most decadent thing you could have and think about.

I focused again, thinking about the Air sliding through my body. That was always the easiest to pull forth. Maybe it was because it was the one that I had first unlocked, or perhaps it was because it was the element I had first seen Rhodes use. It was the first element I had seen Wielded at all.

Maybe that was why I was so close to it.

It reminded me of Rhodes.

I ignored the pain in my heart at that thought. I hadn't seen him in so long, and I missed him and his family. I missed them all, though I knew I would see them soon. It was only a matter of when.

"You're doing great, there," Ridley said softly.

I just nodded, focused again on what was inside me. The Wielding seemed to swirl around me, large clouds of Air and Earth mixing together.

It didn't make any sense, but somehow, it was like I could visualize the Air Wielding moving inside my body, pulsing beneath my skin, trying to get out. It could be rough, it could be like a full-force tornado. But it was also gentle. A soft caress, a sweet breeze.

It was nothing like the Earth Wielding that also surged within my system. That was like a rough earthquake, jagged and fierce.

I knew I could make it soft, delicate with how I used it. But it was also brutal. Jagged-edged.

Then again, so was Air. So were all of the elements. They could all be used to help, but they could also be used to take away.

I didn't know how long I had sat there, thinking about what was inside of me, but then I heard Ridley's voice seemingly from far away. I moved towards it, slowly coming out of whatever trance I had accidentally put myself in. When I opened my eyes, the healer was looking at me with a smile on his face, and pure admiration in his gaze.

"You're doing wonderfully, Lyric."

I blinked, slowly rolling my shoulders back as I tried to figure out exactly how long I had been out.

"Did I fall asleep?"

"No, but you were in a deep meditative state."

That was weird. "Really? Did you help me with that?"

I didn't really know what a healer did, but that sounded like something they'd do. Maybe.

"No, I could've helped if you needed it, but I think you have been on your journey for so long, that sometimes you just need to focus on what's inside before you can move forward. Maybe next time I'll have to ease you into it, but this time, you fell right in. Now, you're probably wondering what this all means, and that's something you're going to have to figure out for yourself.

But once you know what's inside you, you'll be able to use it. The others will help you with combat training. But I want to make sure that you're mentally settled and emotionally secure before you take any next steps."

I nodded, even though I knew I would probably never be mentally and emotionally secure and stable. There was no way I could be when everything was faltering and changing around me. Sometimes, I felt like I was running as fast as I could yet standing in place. It was hard enough being a teenager on the cusp of adulthood in the human realm, let alone in this realm.

Ridley helped me to my feet, and I stretched and grinned at him. And then Easton came up to us, a placid smile on his face, and I resisted the urge to punch him. I had no idea why I wanted to hit him. It just felt like it'd be so easy. Like he had a very punchable face—at least when he smirked.

But as soon as Easton looked at Ridley, he stopped smiling. In fact, he started to look much like his other uncle, his grumpy expression mirroring Justise's.

"Are you almost done? I need your help, Ridley. One of the sentries tripped and hurt himself, and they could use you. I'm sure Lyric is just fine on her own, and one of the other babysitters will be around to help."

I hated him. "Seriously? I don't need a babysitter."

"You need what I tell you you need."

And with that, Easton stomped off. I just glared at him, wondering how the hell he could be so sweet sometimes yet so disastrously annoying at others.

"Don't worry about him, Lyric. They grow out of it. Eventually. So I hear."

I looked up at Ridley, my eyes wide. "Why would I care?" I knew that was a little rude, but honestly, Easton just sent me over the edge, and now it seemed I was lashing out at everybody. "I'm sorry. Forget I said that. He just gets under my skin."

Ridley gave me a weird look much like Easton had. And then he shook his head. "Never mind, Lyric." A pause. "I guess we'll figure that out, too."

I still had no idea what either of them was talking about, but as I walked away from Ridley, headed back to my room as people started to stare and whisper, I wondered once again why I was here.

Why couldn't I be with people I knew? People I had fought beside.

Because I didn't know these people, I didn't know this court. But now I needed to learn it. I'd never felt more alone, even surrounded by so many others.

Sure, I had been alone before. And I knew I would be alone again.

But right then, all I wanted was a place to call home.

I just didn't know where that was.

CHAPTER 7

Sharp pain radiated from my backside as I tried to roll to my knees from where I was currently splayed on the ground. I sneezed as the dust around me settled, and I had a feeling I looked just as embarrassed as I felt.

"Yeah, you probably shouldn't have landed on your butt like that. Maybe we need to teach you how to fall."

I glowered up at Teagan, who just grinned at me, holding out a hand.

Reluctantly, I put my palm in his and staggered to my feet, wiping off my leather pants since I was caked in dirt. I had a few scrapes, too, and some blood. But that's what happened when you were training to be a warrior…or whatever the hell I was doing.

I didn't actually know what I was training for. I only knew that I was still very much a novice when it came to elemental Wielding and how to protect myself.

I had always been a runner. That had been my thing. I ran.

In retrospect, I could see that I ran from decisions and having to figure out where I fit into the world, too. But I didn't really want to think about that right then. So I wasn't going to.

But I always jogged when I needed to set my mind straight or tried to work through aspects of decisions I needed to make. I also ran when I needed to think about nothing and just focus on breathing.

I had been good at running when the Negs came after me. And I had run well when Rhodes screamed at me to keep going and try to save myself.

Not that I had actually done much of that, at least not until the end. Because Rhodes had done his best to save me, and then I had been forced to save myself when everything seemed bleak.

But I wasn't going to think about that. I wasn't going to think about the fact that my stomach churned, and I had that little ache in my belly when I thought about Rhodes and the fact that he wasn't mine.

Because I had seen the way he looked at me, like everything he'd thought possible and true had been completely ripped away from him, his steadying force no longer secure.

I had seen that, and I hadn't known how to react to it. So, I hadn't.

I ran.

"Hey? Are you okay? Did I really hurt you?" Teagan asked. He reached forward as if he were going to touch me but thought better of it at the last moment. No one really touched me here. It was as if they were afraid they'd hurt me.

Or someone would hurt *them* if they touched me.

I didn't understand it, but I had other things to worry about.

Teagan cleared his throat and then looked over my shoulder to where Arwin and Wyn were standing.

"Lyric?" Wyn asked as she walked up to me.

I shook myself out of whatever thoughts I was having and looked over at the other woman. She had pulled her hair back into a loose braid and stared at me as if worried that Teagan had somehow accidentally broken me.

"I'm fine. Just got the wind knocked out of me." Not a lie, but not the complete truth either. I really didn't want them to know that I was just annoyed with myself. That I felt I wasn't really good at anything.

"If you're sure. We can take a break if you'd like," Arwin said.

I looked over at him, and he smiled. Even though I knew he was probably older than I was, he *felt* much younger. As if he hadn't had the experiences that age brought even though he was so much older than I.

But that was just how the Maisons worked. They aged far slower than humans did. That's why, while Rhodes and even Easton were in their two hundreds, they felt around the same age as me. Rosamond was in her four hundreds, yet sometimes she felt the same age as me. Other times, she felt so much older.

But that was probably because she was a Seer and held so much of the weight of the world on her shoulders.

I might have similar burdens, but it felt far different. Maybe because it didn't feel real. It hadn't felt real when I was hiding in the human realm, trying to read up on as much as I could and training with Alura on the side.

But now that I was back in the Maison realm, albeit in the Obscurité Kingdom rather than the Lumiére one like I thought I would be, I was still just trying to catch up. Responsibilities on my shoulders or no.

"I'm fine. Really. I just wasn't expecting the floor to come at me like that."

Teagan grinned. "That was Wyn. Not me. I'm the Fire Wielder, remember?" He held out his hands, and a little ball of flame danced along his fingertips.

I stared at it, transfixed.

I had always loved fire, probably to my detriment. I used to like playing with matches when I was a kid, even though I knew I wasn't supposed to. I loved sitting next to a campfire. I adored the smell of it, the way you couldn't control it even if you thought you could. It wasn't that I wanted to destroy things. No, far from it. I'd always loved the fact that it felt like it was alive unlike anything else.

It was the one element that I knew I would probably either fear or love once I could Wield it. Others had told me that it was the hardest one to Wield, and that's why so many Fire Wielders had terrible attitudes or lost control the easiest.

I was afraid of it, I knew that, but I would learn.

Just like I was learning Earth and Air.

"I didn't make the earth rumble that much," Wyn said quickly. I looked over at her, and she blushed. She was so strong, so confident, yet sometimes it felt like she was just one of the girls, as if she were my age instead of in her two hundreds like the rest of them.

Wyn was an Earth Wielder—and a very strong one at that. She was not an Earth shaker like the man I had met in the Earth territory when he tried to kill us. That man had been one of the pirates under Slavik's command and not a very good man at all.

Wyn, though, she could create waves of soil and dirt and earth to drown and destroy her enemies. Not that she'd told me about it, but it had been in the material that I had read from Rosamond's book. Wyn was still training to learn how to create full earthquakes and even build mountains out of the land around her. That was something I wanted, as well. Because using what was around you was the best way to fight those who wanted to take something from you.

It was so odd to think about my life in these contexts, but I wasn't a human girl anymore. I wasn't thinking about what college to go to or what I would be when I grew up.

I was a Spirit Priestess, at least two of the five elements told me so. I might not know how to save the Maison realm or how I would protect those I cared about, but I knew that I needed to train. Hiding from myself and everything around me wasn't going to help anyone.

"Okay, want to go again?" Wyn asked, wiping her hand on her pants. "We can start with just focusing on what's below you. If you can stay steady when the earth shakes, that means you'll be able to Wield the Earth right under your feet while everything else is being Wielded by the other person. It's one of the first things they teach us when we're younger and first learning how to use our Wielding. It helps us maintain at least some semblance of control of what we can physically touch, rather than just what our Wielding can touch from far away."

I nodded, remembering reading this in the history book. It had been more about the Lumiére powers than the Obscurité, but I was learning quickly. At least, I hoped I was.

I closed my eyes and tried to focus on the Wielding inside of me. It was weird to hone in on just Earth and not Air. Today was only about Earth, though, and that was something I was just fine with. There weren't any other Air Wielders around me, so it wasn't like I could ask them for help.

In fact, the three helping me had said they hadn't really seen Air Wielders at work, other than when they were fighting against them in the small skirmishes that had broken out over the past one hundred years or so.

The Obscurité and Lumiére weren't at full-scale war with large and dramatic battles. That had happened when the Fall had occurred.

Now, it was more like border territory wars while everybody tried to figure out what the next step was. I knew that Teagan and Wyn had fought often on the lines of battle between the Lumiére and Obscurité. Arwin was still learning and had only fought a few times.

In fact, apparently, I had been in just as many battles as he had, and mine had only been by accident when I was trying to find Rosamond back when I first heard about everything that wasn't human.

I had been in this realm for about two weeks, so between training physically with these three, and working mentally with Ridley, I was exhausted. But thriving.

At least, I thought I was. I *hoped* I was.

I could call on my Earth Wielding without thinking too hard. Though even now, I still wasn't great at the offensive. Defensive was good though, and that meant I could at least protect myself and anyone close to me. At least for short periods of time.

Wyn pushed again, using her Earth Wielding to come at me. I threw up my hands, pushing outward so I could create a wall.

I remembered that Lore, Cameo's knight, had created a wall of Earth so thin that I could see him through it. He had used almost minuscule particles of sand rather than the dirt itself to protect him. I didn't know how that power could come about, other than through pure evil. He had literally sucked the energy from the crystal itself, using those connected to it and their powers against us. I never wanted to be that powerful. Not if it meant sacrificing others.

I wasn't even sure I wanted that power if it came to me naturally. They'd said I was going to be the most powerful Wielder of all, or at least the one who could use my powers the best to save others. Though no one knew what that meant.

It was starting to get under my skin because it was like they all expected me to just…know.

How was I supposed to know when, only a year ago, I hadn't known that any of this existed?

Wyn pushed again, and I kept steady this time, keeping my hands up so the barrier could stay between us.

Sweat dripped from my brow and down my spine, and I clenched my jaw, my teeth practically rattling.

The Air moving within me pushed, wanting to help, but I tamped it down. In my training the day before, I had used both elements and had been able to push Wyn out of the way and win our round. But Teagan had come with Fire, and only because of his strength and knowing where to aim it, did I escape and avoid being burned.

I still remembered the way Easton had come out of nowhere. How he'd screamed at the top of his lungs at Teagan because he'd dared to almost burn me.

It was kind of funny considering that Easton had only come down to observe a rare few times. I hadn't even known he was there. Suddenly, he was standing near me, watching. And apparently angry that training had gone too far.

The thing was, it hadn't gotten too far. Teagan had never been out of control, and I had known that he was coming at me. I just didn't know how to fight against it yet. But we were learning. They were training me.

Apparently, Easton didn't understand.

But I didn't understand *him*.

Though it wasn't like I really needed to.

We worked on my Earth walls more and more until I was finally exhausted and had to call it quits.

"Okay, I think I'm done for the day."

"You're not going to be able to just call it quits for the day when you're in a real battle," Easton said, growling.

I looked over at him, once again surprised that he was there. He had an excellent knack for just coming out of nowhere and surprising all of us. He tossed his black hair back from his face, his dark eyes narrowed. His jaw looked so tight and clenched that I was afraid he would break a molar.

"It's just training, Easton. Lighten up." Teagan started packing up our supplies and refreshments that we'd used throughout the day. Wyn just shook her head and went to help him. Arwin stared between us before going to help the others.

That left Easton and me on the training field, sweat making my skin damp and my hair stick to my face. I'd had my hair back in a loose braid, much like Wyn, but now, parts of it were out, and I was sure there was dirt on my face. I likely didn't look at all interesting. I actually probably looked more like a dirt-covered rat.

And yet, Easton just stared at me. It made me really uncomfortable.

"What?" I asked finally. "What's wrong with you?"

He shook his head as if coming out of a trance. Or as if he'd ignored everything I'd just said. Same difference.

"If you walk away when you're tired, you're going to end up hurt later when it really matters. You have to keep fighting. Keep pushing through."

"I am."

"No, you're not. And no one's truly testing you."

"Hey," Wyn put in, but Teagan pulled her back. I noticed that she looked down at where he touched her and frowned. I wondered what that was about. Then again, it wasn't any of my business.

"If you're so picky about how I'm being trained, why aren't you helping? Your friends are. Your uncle is. But you haven't helped at all."

"I have more important things to do in this kingdom than try to help you."

I didn't know why that hurt, but it did. The other three mumbled under their breath at each other, or rather Teagan and Wyn grumbled, and Arwin just looked at them, his eyes wide.

"I understand. You're the king. I don't expect you to help me. But I do expect you to not treat me like trash just because you think I'm not training the way *you* want me to. If you want me trained a certain way, then do it yourself. If not? Then butt out."

"She has you there," Teagan said with a laugh.

"Oh, shut up," Easton snapped, though thankfully, not at me. If he had, I probably would've used my inner Wielding to toss him off his feet. King or no.

"Forces are coming, Lyric. Things that are stronger than all of us."

I froze, the hairs on the back of my neck standing on end. "What do you mean?"

"Can't you feel it? Don't you know that there's something greater than all of us pulling the strings?"

His words. They meant something...but, what?

I didn't know.

I didn't understand.

I nodded, unaware that I was doing so until it was already done. "I've always felt like that, but I thought it was just because I was new to this."

"No, there's something. We need to keep fighting. You need to push. And I'm going to be mean. I'm going to be a bastard. But all that is just me wanting to make sure that my people can live through this. If we have to rely on you, then you have to be the strongest you can be. My friends there? They're the people I trust with my life. I'm entrusting your life to them. I can't help because I have to make sure everyone else is breathing. That whatever Lore did to my people isn't lasting.

"But we already know it is. We already know that I may lose more of my people because of what that sick psycho did. That's what I'm forcing others to do. I'm training them. I'm teaching myself. I'm trying to keep this kingdom intact. And to do that, I need to know you're protected. I need to know that you're ready for what's to come. That means I can't be there to hold your hand.

"So, get your act together and be the best Earth Wielder you can possibly be. And find a way to unlock that Fire Wielding. Because once you're the full Spirit Priestess, you need to be stronger than you ever thought possible. I don't know if I'm the person to help you with that, but I trust in my people. And they're the ones who will do it."

Then Easton turned on his heel and walked away, leaving me completely lost.

I had never seen him so impassioned, yet I shouldn't have been surprised. I knew he loved his people. He hadn't been out searching for the Spirit Priestess like Rhodes had because Easton had been forced to step back and deal with what was in front of him. Help with what was tangible: the fact that his people were dying.

Apparently, Rhodes had had the luxury—at least according to Easton—of searching for me.

Rhodes had found me. He had saved me.

Now, Easton apparently needed me.

Then again, they all did.

The walk back to the castle was quiet with Arwin right at my side and Teagan and Wyn behind me.

We didn't say anything. Really, there wasn't much left to say. Easton had said it all.

We were training, and not just for fun. Because something was coming.

Only we didn't know what that was.

I was caught in the middle, lost just like last time.

But I wasn't going to run. Not like before. I was going to fight. I just had to be strong enough. Easton had seen. Easton had seen I wasn't enough.

I would show him. I was going to show all of them. I would be strong enough.

No matter what.

CHAPTER 8

I ate most of my meals in the dining hall with the other Wielders, sitting by Wyn, Teagan, and sometimes Arwin. I usually ate my other meals alone in my room, poring over textbooks that Ridley and the quiet and grumpy Justise had given me. Everybody seemed to want me to learn how to Wield Earth and Air with the best of my abilities. They all had this idea that I had some higher purpose. And while the prophecy said I did, it was still hard to get really deep down into it.

But I knew the details would come.

First, I had to finish training.

So, while I generally ate my meals with people I knew, I was also surrounded by those I didn't. Some came to introduce themselves to me but were pretty quiet about it. No one really sat long enough for me to get to know them, or for them to get to know me. I didn't know if it was because I

Maybe it was because I was sitting with what I figured must be the most powerful Wielders in the room, and everybody just sat with their friends.

Or Easton had told everyone to leave me alone. That sounded more like it. Easton always had reasons for what he did, not that I actually understood any of them. Tonight, however, the fact that we were eating as a group in Easton's personal quarters confused me.

I had never been to this section of the castle before. I hadn't even known it existed. I wished Braelynn were with me, but she'd wanted to spend time in my room curled up at the end of my bed. She trained with me most days, but she didn't like coming to dinner or other places with other Wielders. Maybe it reminded her that while she might still be my best friend, she wasn't really *here* anymore. It made *me* remember.

And I didn't know how to process any of that.

"So, are you ready to see where the illusive Easton eats and sleeps and does all his breathing?" Wyn asked, elbowing me in the side.

I looked at her, rolling my eyes. "Really? Really?"

"What? I can't help it. I'm never really allowed in his rooms." She stopped where she was, and I almost tripped over myself to look back at her. "That sounded really bad. Not that I want to get into his rooms. I just like to bother him, and in order to do that, I have to be near him."

"You bother me just by existing," Teagan said, deadpan.

"You know, I can curse you. I can use my Wielding and curse you." She narrowed her eyes on him, and Teagan grinned before wrapping his hand around the back of her head and placing a really hard, loud, very wet kiss on her lips. I just stood there, blinking as I looked between the two of them.

"You know, I hate you," she said as she wiped her mouth with the back of her hand. She slung the moisture off exaggeratedly before she grinned.

"Hey, you used to like my kisses."

"I used to like a lot of things. And those kisses…eh. I guess they were okay."

"Okay? I thought I was the god of all kissing."

"Son, you really don't want her to keep wondering why you guys aren't together anymore," Justise said as he and Ridley strolled into the hallway. "The first rule of being broken up is to never ask *why* when it might have to do with kissing and other deeds."

"Dear God, husband, was that a joke? Wow. Gasp," Ridley said, clutching his hand over his heart and taking a couple of staggering steps back. "Quick, Lyric, protect us all. Surely the apocalypse has come."

"Ha ha, dear husband. I can be funny. *I* am hilarious."

Only Arwin laughed, but it was more like a nervous chuckle while the rest of us just stared at the men.

"What?" Arwin said quickly. "I was afraid he was going to like, throw his hammer at me or something."

"I could still do it, boy," Justise said, deepening his voice and lowering his brow.

Ridley patted Justise's cheek and grinned. "Ignore him, Arwin. He's just a big teddy bear. A big, grumpy, growly teddy bear."

"You're going to pay for that later, dear."

Ridley rolled his eyes and took Arwin by the arm before walking down the hallway. "Promises, husband. Promises, promises, promises."

And that was how I found myself laughing while leaning against Wyn as the rest of us headed into the small dining room that was part of Easton's quarters.

According to Wyn while we had been dressing, these had always been Easton's rooms. He hadn't moved in to the king and queen's section of the estate, and I wasn't sure he would. While I didn't know him as well as the others did, I had a feeling that he had made his home here. Having to assume the mantle of king was already a major piece. A big change. Having to move everything into the place where his mother had once lived? Yeah, I didn't know if I could ever do that. And knowing what I did of Easton, I wasn't sure he would be able to do it either.

Easton was near the window at the edge of the room when we entered, his hands clasped behind his back as he stared out at part of the kingdom.

He looked so alone there, dark and maybe brooding like Wyn had said.

It occurred to me that though he did have friends who tried to get to know him and joked with him, he was alone.

He was a king without a queen, without a real court. I didn't know how he was dealing with the Earth or the Fire Estates or how they were reacting to their new king. I hadn't asked because I was honestly a little scared.

Rhodes and I owed the Lord of Earth a favor. Not because he had saved our lives, but because he hadn't killed us outright.

I had a feeling that the Lord of Dirt, as Rhodes called him, would one day call upon us to cash in that favor.

And that scared me. A favor to someone so high up for someone like me, one who might someday find connections that the lord might want to use for his own gain… I didn't want to think about.

The Lord of Fire and his lady had been nicer, if a little scarier.

As far as I knew, they still had Emory trapped in their dungeons. I would've tried to get her out by now or found a way to help her, but I didn't know how. And, apparently, she was a siphon, one that could take away Wielding from others.

I still didn't know how that had happened or what it might mean for her in the future, but one day I would have to talk with the Lord and Lady of Fire and figure out what to do for my former friend.

Before all of that, though, I had to think about what to do with the king by the window, the one who still hadn't spoken to us as everyone got their drinks off the sideboard and started to move around the table, taking their places.

Apparently, this was not unusual for Easton, standing there letting others talk while he brooded or had deep thoughts.

But I didn't like him standing there alone, so I walked up to him, knowing it was probably a mistake.

"Thanks for having us over for dinner tonight," I said, my voice a little soft. The others were still talking, but I was fully aware that they were trying to listen in on our conversation and wondering what I was doing.

"I figured it was about time." Easton ran his hand through his hair and then frowned.

"It's beautiful here, did I tell you that?" I asked, wondering what I was supposed to say. I was never really good at any of this. I had never been. Dinner parties weren't my thing and hadn't been even when I was still in the human realm. My parents had them occasionally when they had to deal with work associates, and I had always been quiet. The one that people asked simple questions to and then ignored. Sometimes, I had my friends over for dinner, but it was just a normal meal before we were on our way.

I really wasn't good at small talk.

Easton looked at me for a moment before looking out at his kingdom again. *His* kingdom. "The place is beautiful. It used to be more. Not so barren."

"I've seen some of the territory. It's not barren. There's so much growth and life in it."

"I suppose." He shook his head and then turned to face me.

His eyes were dark, reaching.

They searched my face as if he were trying to see something that he wasn't sure was there. Or maybe I was the one reaching.

He had saved my life, even though he hadn't been able to fully protect me. And now he had brought me here so I could train. I was grateful for that. Ridley was helping me stay calm, and the others were teaching me what they knew about Wielding. And while Alura had helped some, it was like I was back with Rhodes and Luken while they taught me Air Wielding.

They had helped me so much, and now this new group of people was helping me, as well.

But sometimes I couldn't help but feel as though I were caught in the middle of one war and then another. Or as if I were caught in the middle of two separate people that I didn't really understand.

"So, I hear you're better at your Earth Wielding."

"Really? They said that?" I was pleasantly surprised, and it knocked me out of whatever mood I was in.

"Well, Teagan, Wyn, and Arwin say you're pretty good. Or at least, you could be if you weren't so far in your head."

"We did not say that," Wyn corrected. "Lyric, we did not say that."

I snorted, looking at Easton. "Oh, I assumed Easton was the one who thought it. Even though I'm pretty sure you're the one who's always in your head. Correct, oh, wise one?"

That made Justise laugh.

"Why are you laughing at her calling me wise?" Easton asked his uncle, shaking his head.

"Oh, pretty much the obvious reason. *My king.*"

Easton flipped him off, and I smiled. Apparently, no matter what realm you were in, that action seemed to be the same. Or, it was the fact that we were near the Americas and therefore it was something they'd learned from crisscrossing the realms. I still didn't know if there were more access points to other realms in other parts of the world. While the book had alluded to them, I hadn't outright asked yet. I was a little too worried about what would happen if I did. Because the world seemed too large as it was, finding out that there was even more out there than just what I was standing in?

Nope, not going to think about that.

"Okay, let's eat," Easton said, taking my hand and pulling me towards the table.

I stumbled slightly, looking down at his hand over mine.

Easton generally did his best to avoid touching me, something I was just now noticing. Was it because I was the reason his mother was dead? I wouldn't blame him for that if it were.

I wouldn't blame him for a lot of things.

He gave my hand a squeeze, flashed me a smile that didn't quite reach his eyes, and then went to sit at the head of the table. Wyn had left me a seat on the other end, and that put me the farthest distance away from Easton as possible.

Since that was basically what he had been doing the entire time I had been there so far, keeping as much distance as possible between us, it didn't bother me in the slightest.

The food was amazing: rich and tasty, with the sweets at the end perfection. Even though I was staying in a castle at the moment, we didn't usually eat like this. Most of the time, it was good food but rations.

Teagan and Wyn had explained to me that a lot of the food that might usually come to the castle was now being sent back to the land and its people rather than being kept for the court itself. Lore had hurt the people more than by just making the Maisons Danes and stripping them of their powers. He'd also begun to take their land and food, as well as supplies and other things. Lore had done so much damage under his title of knight. I wasn't sorry he was dead.

Even if it was by my hands.

I didn't understand how the queen hadn't seen everything her knight had been doing. But for all I knew, the knight had used magic to ensure that didn't happen. Cameo hadn't been my favorite person. She'd scared me. I'd thought she tried to take Rosamond and her Seer powers. I'd thought I had almost died multiple times for her. And though quietly, she had still been at war with the King of Lumiére because they couldn't find common ground. But she had given her life for mine, so I was never going to talk bad about her. However, I had to wonder how the kingdom had come to this.

But, not right then. Now, I was going to eat some amazing food, laugh with my new friends, and hope that tomorrow I'd be able to train a little bit harder and learn more.

Because something was coming. Easton had said that before, and he was right. I could feel it. Something was orchestrating all of this. And there was a reason I was here. Therefore, I was going to fight. I was going to make sure I was the best I could possibly be for that reason.

Just as I set my water glass down, I gasped, the bracelet that Alura had given me burning my wrist. The glass I held fell to the table, spilling the rest of its contents on the tablecloth. Everyone froze before looking at me.

I looked down at my wrist. The water element charm glowed hot against my skin.

"Ow," I whispered, shaking my hand as if trying to let the heat out. But it stung. Easton was on his feet and by my side before anyone else could even move. He held my wrist gently, bringing it to his face as he looked down at the charm.

"This is the bracelet from Alura?"

I nodded, grateful that the burning had stopped and the water element symbol was no longer heating against my skin.

"That's Seer magic there," Ridley said, his voice soft. "Powerful Seer magic."

"Very much so," Justise said as he stood up and looked over Easton's shoulder. "And whatever blacksmith made this knew what he was doing. I'd say someone in the Water territory needs you."

I looked up at Justise for a moment before glancing at Easton.

"What?"

He ran his thumb along the inner skin of my wrist, and we both sucked in a breath before he let go of me.

He cleared his throat. "If that is what Alura gave you, and if my uncle's right—and since he's the best blacksmith in the entire Maison realm, I would assume he's right—that means that you need to head to the Lumiére Kingdom." He met my gaze again. "Soon."

I let out a breath, trying to collect my thoughts. "Okay. That's…I guess there's no, like, phone calls here to tell me that they need me?"

"No, you're not in the human realm anymore," Easton said sharply.

"I know that. I've known that for a long time. I just don't understand how you guys communicate." I was shouting now and had pushed back in my seat so I could go at Easton face-to-face. The others stood as well as if waiting for the fight, not knowing exactly what they were going to do.

"We communicate through magic, and through other means. All I know is that's Seer magic. So, it might not be someone communicating directly with you." He paused. "Or, it could be Rosamond saying she needs you. Who knows? But if Alura gave that to you, then you need to head to the Lumiére Kingdom."

"Why do you keep saying *if* Alura gave it to me? What makes Alura giving it to me so special?" I paused, something clicking. "Is she a Seer?"

Easton shook his head. "No. But her secret's not mine to tell." I hated when they said things like that. Over and over again I heard the riddles. "All that matters now is that you need to go to the Lumiére Kingdom, and you can't go alone." Teagan cleared his throat.

"I'll go. I'll make sure she's safe."

Warmth filled me at the thought of Teagan—or *anyone*—wanting to help me. But I didn't want him to get hurt.

"I'm going, too," Wyn added before she looked over at Teagan and they nodded at each other.

"I'll go, as well," Arwin said, shrugging. "I want to go. I want to help you, Lyric. I just hope you want me to go with you."

I cleared my throat, a little nervous. "You'll all be going into an enemy kingdom. Are you sure I shouldn't just go by myself? Rhodes and Rosamond know me. I should be safe. I don't know if I should bring Braelynn, but still…"

"Braelynn can stay here," Easton growled. "As for you? Who knows if you'll be safe? You know, some people don't want the Spirit Priestess to win. You saw that yourself with Lore." Easton spat out the man's name, and I refused to take a step back even though parts of me wanted to. "The three of them will go with you, and they'll protect you. And they'll keep up with your training."

Ridley sighed before looking at his nephew. "You can't go." He paused, and I froze. Easton? Going? There was no way Easton could go. He had responsibilities here. And while it might make me feel safer—something I was *not* going to think about just then—he couldn't come with us. It wouldn't be safe…*for him.*

"Yeah, I know," Easton said softly.

Ridley spoke again. "But you know you need to."

Easton nodded. And I blinked. "I know that, too," he said softly.

"I…I'll be fine. I'm not their enemy. If this is all Seer magic, and I'm supposed to be in the Lumiére Kingdom, I will be okay. There's a reason I need to be there."

"That's fine. But you're not going alone. Not now. I'm going with you.

That's final."

Then he turned on his heel and stormed past me. I wondered what was going on.

The others looked just as confused as I felt, but then we were moving, everyone going to pack and do whatever they needed to prepare for the long journey. I just stood there, looking at the uncles and wondering how all of this had happened.

The water charm on my bracelet burned again, and I looked down at it, knowing it was calling me to the Water territory. I'd never been there before, but now I was going to see it.

I was going to see the Lumiére.

I was going to see Rhodes.

CHAPTER 9

I felt like I had been at the Obscurité Kingdom forever, even though it had only been a few weeks. And now, I was packing up again, wondering how long I would be gone. Or if I would ever come back.

I wasn't actually thinking about my own death, the idea of mortality and what would come from a battle in which I was ill prepared for.

However, that was always in the back of my mind. I couldn't really help it because I had watched one friend die, only to come back as my so-called Familiar. I had watched another friend come back as if she had been changed into something totally different. I watched the queen die for me. I watched the knight die at my hands. And I had died myself. Only to come back, as well.

So, the idea of death and what came after was constantly on my mind. Even if it wasn't the primary focus of my day.

"Okay, stop thinking about death, just get to work. I need to pack. I need to make sure Braelynn is fine, and then I need to be on my merry way."

Braelynn looked up at me, and I swore she was smirking. How could a cat smirk? Well, other than their normal cat face, because sometimes they looked like they were always smirking.

"What? I'm getting ready for you." And talking to myself, but here we were. "I just need to get packed, and then I'm leaving. But I'm not leaving you for long. I promise."

Braelynn looked at me again before she turned her back on me, raising her tail in the air and showing me her butt. Seriously? We had definitely crossed a boundary in our friendship. I'd thought the major one had been when I cleaned up her poop in the litter box, but apparently, that wasn't it. It was now, when she showed her displeasure by sauntering away, her butt facing me.

It was a little ridiculous.

"Knock knock, are you ready?" Wyn asked as she walked into my room. She looked around, surveying what I held, and I wondered why she always did that. It wasn't like I really had anything to my name these days. Everything I really owned, even the mesh jacket I had loved with all of my heart, was back in the human realm. The only things I had left were what Alura had given me from Rosamond and Rhodes' house, and the small things that I had picked up in the weeks I had been here. I had no money, no real clothes or personal effects. Really, the only thing that I had that was mine was a bracelet, and that had been a gift.

I was here to train, and apparently, to save the world, and I had to rely on everyone else's charity in order to do that and survive.

I didn't know why I felt so grumpy about that just then. Maybe it was the fact that it was finally hitting me that I was once again completely out of my depth.

"I'm almost ready. I think. I'm not really good about packing for long trips where I've no idea where I'm going or what the weather's going to be like, especially when I don't really have anything to pack."

Wyn just smiled, shaking her head, her long hair framing her face. She was beautiful, seriously gorgeous, but she didn't give me that clutch in my belly that Rhodes did. Or even Easton.

No, I wasn't going to let my thoughts go down *those* strange paths.

"Well, considering you have mostly battle leathers and training clothes, you should bring all of that. And you should be able to fit it all in your pack. You are your own weapon, so you're good there. And the uncles are already packing up food and water for us that we'll split between the group. Just make sure you have that bracelet of yours, and make sure Braelynn is all set up for the uncles to take care of her."

Braelynn let out a little mewling purr, and I didn't know if she was happy or sad that she wasn't going.

And then I remembered exactly why Braelynn might be acting like this. Luken.

Luken was an Air Wielder and Rhodes' best friend and fellow warrior. He lived in the Lumière Kingdom, and I knew he was probably near Rhodes himself. He'd also been very close to Braelynn and had grieved over her so openly and vividly that I had broken down. They had only known each other for a short while, but I felt as if they loved each other. But he had walked away because he had to go with Rhodes, and Braelynn had been forced to go with me.

I had no idea what he felt for my friend now, nor could I figure out what Braelynn felt for him.

But, like me and Rhodes, their ill-fated love connection hadn't actually worked out.

"I kind of want her to come with us, but it's not safe. I know there are…

people she needs to see in the Lumière Kingdom, but I know she can't come."

Braelynn jumped on the edge of the bed, and I petted her, scratching beneath her chin.

"The uncles will take care of her. She'll be safe here, and it's a reason for you to come back." Wyn gave me a smile as she said it, and then I frowned.

"What do you mean?"

"Well, we're headed to where your first friends are. Where your real friends are." She shrugged, and I wanted to reach out and hug her, to let her know that those words weren't truly the case anymore since she was my friend, but she continued before I had the chance to do so. "Even if we ignore all the reasons you're here in the first place, and the destiny that surrounds us all, the people you connected to first live there. After all, your man is there." She winked then, and I winced.

"Rhodes isn't mine." I was too quick to say that, and her brows rose.

"Okay, I won't touch on that again. Unless you want me to. But, either way, Braelynn will be here for you. So, that means you have to come back. With us. Even for a short time."

"I've never been to the Lumière Kingdom, Wyn. Of course, I want to come back here. It's the only place that almost feels like home." I shook my head. "But I really can't think that far ahead. Because if I do, I'll start to stress out about the fact that I have no idea what I'm doing."

"Your Wielding is getting far better. You're strong, Lyric."

I finished packing as we spoke, needing to keep my hands busy. "You say that, and maybe I'm training well, but I don't know what comes next. And because of that, it's a little stressful. And because I don't know how I'm supposed to unite the kingdoms and make everything okay, I'm just going to work on the here and now and take the next steps that I need to when I need to. So, yes, I'm coming back to the Obscurité Kingdom." At least, I hoped I would be. Because I had to. Braelynn was here. And I didn't want to die. "But that doesn't mean I'm actually going to stay here. I don't know if I'm going to stay in the Lumiére Kingdom either. I don't know if I should just stay in the Spirit territory and hide there. Or maybe I should go home and forget all of this ever happened. Not that home in the human realm really feels like home anymore since my parents are gone and don't even remember me. There's really nothing there for me anymore."

"You sound even more stressed than usual," Wyn said, her words careful.

"Yes, stress is just the tip of the iceberg. But, like I said, I don't want to think about all of that so, let's just make sure I'm all packed, and then we can head out and meet the guys."

"Speaking of *guys*, I'm really glad you're coming." Wyn leaned over and helped me finish packing the last of my list.

"Well, I kind of have to. It's my calling." I gave her a weird look.

She shook her head. "Yes, I get that. But it's kind of nice to hang out with another girl. There are a lot of female warriors, don't get me wrong. There are many talented female Wielders who are even stronger than I am. But I'm in Easton's inner circle, and because he keeps it such a tight-knit group, you and Arwin are pretty much the only newer people. So, yes, it's kind of nice having another girl."

"Well, I'm glad you want me to be here. It makes me feel needed." Beyond the whole being needed to save the world thing. Again, I wasn't going to think about that.

I picked up my bag and nodded at Braelynn. Soon, the three of us were walking out into the throne room. I didn't come here often, mostly because Easton hardly ever sat on his throne. Therefore, this place didn't have a lot of people in it. But this was where we had all decided to meet before we started our journey.

94

Braelynn left me quickly and walked over to Justise before hopping into his lap. There were other chairs in the room other than the throne itself, so Justise was sitting there, going over paperwork of some sort as we all milled around. Arwin and Teagen were already there, their packs on their backs. Ridley was pacing, going through something in his head. I figured it was either just nerves or he was working out a problem with his healing. Ridley did that often, and I found it quite endearing. He was never *not* thinking, much like his husband and his nephew.

"Hey there, little girl," Justise said, and I looked up, a little worried that he had called me that since he never had before. Then I realized that he was talking to Braelynn in his lap and not me. "I bet you're going to miss your friend and the rest of them," he whispered, even though we could all hear. It was very unlike Justise to be cooing over a cat, even though Brae really wasn't just a feline. Apparently, there were different layers to all of us.

"I'm very sorry that we have to leave you," I said again to Braelynn, hoping that she would listen to me. She just gave me a glance and then burped. An actual burp. Only it wasn't really a burp because a little trail of smoke came out of her mouth.

I blinked, wondering if I had imagined it. Then she stretched out on Justise's lap and curled into a ball. I had no idea what had just happened. No one looked as if anything weird had happened, so maybe I'd imagined the whole thing. But I was sure there had literally been a little ring, a puff of smoke coming out of my best friend's mouth.

How did a cat with bat wings breathe fire?

No, she hadn't, I was just all in my head and thinking too hard about it.

There was nothing weird about Braelynn.

Other than the fact that she was my reincarnated best friend and now a cat with bat wings.

Everything else was normal. There had been no smoke.

Easton stomped into the room soon after I went through my mental tirade and glowered at all of us.

"Are we ready to go?" he asked, tightening his pack over his shoulders. I looked at my bag on the floor next to Wyn's and nodded.

There was something I needed to do first, though, and it wasn't going to be pleasant. "I am. But you can't go."

Easton's brow rose very haughtily. "Oh? Are you telling me what I can and cannot do?"

"I'm not actually telling you that, other than the fact that you are the king of the Obscurité Kingdom. You're not supposed to be going through the Lumiére Kingdom at all. The others can help me. You don't need to be there."

Everyone was oddly quiet as I faced off with Easton, and I had no idea what that was about.

"I'm going. And that's the end of it."

"You're not my king," I reminded him. "And while I'm grateful that you want to be there to help me, I don't want you to get hurt, and I don't want this kingdom to lose another one of their leaders because of me." I shut my mouth as soon as I said it, my pulse racing, and my eyes wide.

I swore you could hear a pin drop in the room with how quiet it got. I hadn't meant to say that. I'd been very careful about not mentioning his mother or that I had been there when she died. Or the fact that I was the reason she was dead. I didn't want to remind them all that I was at the middle of it. That it was my fault Cameo was gone.

No one spoke as Easton stepped up to me, placing one foot in front of the other with intent. The glare on his face looked like it hurt, and his jaw was so tight that I was afraid he might break his back molars.

"Lyric," he began, his voice low, deep. I was a little scared, but I still raised my chin, not afraid. Or at least pretending I wasn't. "I'm going. I'm going to protect you. And maybe I have other reasons of my own for going. You can't stop me. My kingdom will be just fine under Justise's and Ridley's attention. They will care for the people. I trust them with everything that I have. Even your little friend, that cat over there, will help protect the kingdom. I can leave because you are important. And because I have reasons. So, don't think that I'm not aware of the danger. That I'm not aware of what my role is. I live it, Lyric. I'm keenly aware of who isn't here anymore. And why that is."

I swallowed hard, the Air Wielding between my fingers going soft. I hadn't meant to start using my magic, but I was scared, his voice so calm, so controlled. I knew there had to be something far deeper beneath those words.

"Do you understand, Lyric?" He paused, those dark eyes boring into me. "I need to hear the words, Lyric."

Why did he keep saying my name like that? So determined. So... unusual. "I understand. But I don't want you to get hurt."

Then he laughed, though I didn't think it actually reached his soul—it definitely didn't reach his eyes. "You don't need to worry about me. You're the one we're all worried about."

He stepped away, and it was as if a bubble had burst, suddenly letting the sound and the warmth of the room fill us again. At first, during those moments, it had felt as if it were just the two of us. But everyone else had been watching, and I had wondered what they'd seen.

"Wait," I said, reaching out and then jerking my hand back. I did not touch him, ever. That was somehow an unsaid rule, and I was being very good about it. "Your words just hit me. What do you mean, Braelynn can protect the kingdom?"

Braelynn let out a little hiss and then turned her back to me. I wondered what the hell was going on.

"I said that? Interesting."

And then Easton walked over to talk to his uncles, and I was left standing there wondering what dimension I was actually in. Yes, I was in a different realm than I had been born in, but apparently, I was missing a whole bunch of things. Like what Braelynn *really* was, and why she was here. And why everyone seemed to know things that I didn't, that they didn't seem inclined to share. However, I was used to not knowing things until they happened.

"So, what happens when we get there, and they realize that you're Easton?" I said quickly. "Because you're kind of memorable."

He looked over at me and smiled. This time, it reached his eyes. I sucked in a breath, wondering why it looked so different. "Memorable? You say the sweetest things, Lyric."

"That's not what I meant. Shut up."

"I can't answer your question and shut up at the same time."

"You're insufferable."

"Well, I can't help that. You just bring out the worst in me."

I was aware that everyone was staring at us as if they were at a tennis match, watching a ball volley from side to side. "Easton. What are your plans?"

"It's like you don't trust me."

"You make it very hard to trust you when you don't actually tell me anything. And then you glower. And growl. And act all broody."

That forced a snicker from Wyn, and Teagan started laughing outright.

"Shut up, you two," Easton snapped.

"Well, she's got you there," Teagan said. "Like, really well. I can just picture it in my mind."

Easton just shook his head, a small smile playing on his lips.

"Well, Lyric, since you're new to this whole Wielding thing, I'm going to teach you a trick. There's a special spell we can use from one of the old books so I can go as an unobtrusive Wielder using glamour. No one's going to know who I am, other than the people in this room. In fact, if you look really closely, you can see the edges around me blur slightly. That means the glamour's already on. Nobody other than us knows I'm Easton. Everyone just sees a guy with brown hair and brown eyes, who can use some Wielding. Totally anonymous, totally inconspicuous."

"Really?" I asked, incredulous.

He held out his arms. "Inspect me, dear Lyric.

That made Teagan let out another snicker, who then grunted as Wyn elbowed him in the gut. Arwin was watching everything unfold, very quiet as if he were trying to take in everything and not knowing exactly what was going on at the same time. He wasn't alone, as I had no idea what was going on either.

But I took a step forward and focused on Easton, his face, his shoulders, and then his broad chest. He grinned as I stared, and I ignored it, knowing there was something I needed to see. Then I saw it.

His edges were indeed blurred as if there were a different kind of lighting on him, one that made him slightly out of focus. I didn't know what the others saw, but to me, he was Easton.

The insufferable king who confused me like no other.

"Seen enough, Lyric?"

My gaze traveled back to his face, and I narrowed my eyes. "Well, it's your head if someone figures it out." I looked over at the others. "Are we ready to go?"

"We're ready," Wyn said softly. "I guess it's time."

I looked around at those who were going to help me make my way to a place they'd never been to before. They were going to protect me as I learned to defend myself. We'd be going through the northern Spirit territory, a place I had never been. There was so much I didn't understand, so many things

I still had to learn, but as I looked down at my bracelet which once again warmed at the Water symbol charm, I knew we were going to the right place. I knew this was what I needed to do.

I hadn't believed in magic for so long, but now, it was what I strived for, what I leaned on.

As I looked around at the others, I hoped that no one else would get hurt for a prophecy that I didn't understand, for something that I knew would take more out of me than I could bargain for.

I went to the uncles and kissed their cheeks to say goodbye, knowing that this might be the last time I saw them. Ridley was sweet, making sure to add extra bandages and other first-aid things to my pack. Justise glowered, much like his nephew, and then kissed my cheek back, wishing me a safe journey. I held Braelynn in my arms, kissing the top of her head. She purred and then hugged me a bit like a human would.

It was times like these that I remembered that this was my best friend, the one that I could share things with even if I was afraid of them myself. She had journeyed with me into this realm because something had drawn her here, and she'd wanted to be by my side.

Now, I was leaving her behind because I had to keep her safe. The safest she could be in this new life of hers. And I was so worried, so scared that this could be the end.

But the Lumiére Kingdom was calling me. It was time.

The journey would be hard, but I was stronger than I had been before. I knew so much more.

I would finally be able to see Rhodes again and make sure that we had made the right choice by walking away from each other. Yet, at the same time, I wondered what our connection had really been at the beginning. Why we'd thought we had a chance at something when fate had decided something else was for us.

Easton looked at me as I thought about Rhodes, and I had to wonder once again if he could read my thoughts.

His jaw tightened, and then he set off down the corridor and away from the throne room. I picked up my bag, and we all followed. And then the journey began.

I was once again a traveler, lost in a realm I didn't understand, but one I was becoming to know as home. I didn't want to die today, I didn't want to think about mortality, but once again, it was at the forefront of my mind.

This was the life we led, one that was mine.

I wasn't Lyric the lost, human girl anymore.

I was Lyric, the perhaps-one-day-soon Spirit Priestess, the one who could Wield two elements, the one who had loved and lost. The one who needed to journey again.

I was Lyric, and I would find my way.

Somehow.

CHAPTER 10

My feet hurt. Honestly, that was the first thing that came to mind when it came to traveling long distances between the Obscurité Kingdom and the Lumiére.

I know I should have been used to this type of traveling, considering how much I had done over the past year—or even longer if I thought about it—but it still wasn't my favorite thing.

Technology from the human realm didn't work correctly in the Maison realm. And because of that, it wasn't like we could just hop on a train or a plane or even in a car.

I figured there had to be boats or ships of some sort because there were creeks and streams around, and if what I had read about the Water territory was correct, most of the area was actually seas, oceans, and various rivers. With floating cities and different land masses where the people lived. So

Once we left the Obscurité Court, we walked into the northern Spirit territory after taking a little detour across the farthest corner of the Fire territory since we had to find entrances through the wards.

It was very much like the southern Spirit territory, all desert-like with a sepia tone to it.

And while the southern Spirit territory had the Negs, the absence of all magic, beings full of darkness that had come to try and attack us the last time I was here, the northern territory felt almost emptier.

I wasn't even sure how that was possible.

There were cracks in the ground as if it had once been part of a larger mass, maybe even a salt bed where a large body of water had once sat centuries ago.

I wasn't a hundred percent sure as I didn't know what the Spirit territories looked like before the Fall. I'd asked Rhodes once, and he had said that he wasn't exactly sure. After all, he hadn't been born then, and others didn't talk about it often, as if they were afraid to talk about what was lost, or as if it hurt to think about what wasn't there anymore.

I didn't ask my current companions about it either. I was afraid of the same answer, and I didn't know if they'd have an answer at all.

Teagan and Arwin were up front, talking animatedly about training and different techniques when in battle. Well, Teagan was talking animatedly. Arwin was listening as if he were ready to take notes. If he had a piece of paper to write down everything Teagan was trying to teach him, I was sure he'd be doing just that. I wanted to learn too, and had heard so much history about fighting from the others, but this seemed different.

I hadn't actually been in a full-on battle like Teagan was talking about.

Yes, I'd fought against the Negs and even some Earth-Wielding pirates. I'd fought against Fire guards who had come at us and tried to pull us against our will towards the Fire territory. The same with the Earth guards in their territory, now that I thought about it.

I had fought against magic no one had even heard of when it came to the knight and the queen of the Obscurité Kingdom. I had done all of that, but I hadn't been in a full battle like they showed in the movies with CGI. No, Teagan, Wyn, and even Easton had fought side by side, their Wielding full and up front as they battled for their lives and that of their people.

The Fall had happened so long ago that the actual battles that were fought then were a long-distant memory.

But there were still skirmishes along the borders here and there at times.

And those were the battles that Teagan was revealing to Arwin now.

How Water and Air Wielders fought against the Fire and Earth Wielders.

How people died, and how people were injured.

Or when people lost their Wielding or weren't strong enough even though they were the strongest of their line.

I could barely imagine it and was honestly only half-listening at the moment because of who walked beside me.

Wyn was behind us, guarding the rear as she walked in silence. She had been walking alongside me for a while but had traded places with Easton in his glamour a full day into our travels.

I hadn't known why, but she liked being the rear guard, as if protecting her king and the rest of us was her sole responsibility.

Her strength was amazing, and part of me wished I was attracted to someone like her rather than Rhodes—or even the boy by my side. Because if I were honest with myself, I knew that I was somewhat attracted to Easton, despite the fact that he annoyed me like no other. Even if I knew he thought I was beneath him. It didn't matter that I was his so-called Spirit Priestess.

To him, I would always be the girl who got his mother killed, the one who didn't know what she was doing and didn't have enough magic to protect the realm. Easton was the one who had to fight, who had to use all of his power to protect everyone.

To him, I was just learning, and I wasn't enough. I wasn't what he had been expecting, and I could see it clear as day with every look he gave me.

So, yes, walking side by side with him as we made our way through the northern Spirit territory wasn't the easiest or the most comfortable.

In fact, it was quite painful.

"How much longer until we get to the other kingdom?" I asked. It was the first time I had spoken up. I had done my best not to keep asking if we were there yet.

I didn't have a scope of the distance, though. Because it wasn't like there were street signs or landmarks for me to gauge where we were. I had never been here before, and nobody was really telling me which direction we were going, other than west. We just kept moving west towards the Lumiére Kingdom.

And although we could have gone straight through the Obscurité Court to the Lumiére Court because they practically touched with the way the area was laid out, it wasn't done.

The magic surrounding the courts was so strong that you couldn't just walk into the other kingdom from the other side. You had to go through certain pockets where the warding was weaker. I didn't know how they knew where those spots were, but considering they'd had hundreds of years to test the warding along the borders, I assumed they just learned over time.

And because the Spirit territory split the two kingdoms apart, they didn't have the same type of borders that the territories within the kingdoms did.

So, the Fire and the Earth territories, because they were in the same kingdom, had their own combination of borders. It was an actual strip of land that was a mix between the two types of Wieldings.

I figured that the Air and Water probably had something similar in their kingdom.

But because the Spirit territory was so different, there wasn't an actual mix of the two Wieldings at each of the borders.

And that meant that once we left the wards of the Obscurité Kingdom and made our way into the northern Spirit territory, we were on our own. There was nothing of Earth or Fire about it, just something unique and obscure.

And while it was beautiful, it was also haunting.

There were no structures—ruins or otherwise. No way of knowing if anyone had lived here before.

I didn't know how many Spirit Wielders there had been before the Fall, but there must have been more than just a few to be able to take care of this entire territory.

But now it was barren and empty. Desolate. There was nothing here to show the history of a people that were no longer there. It was as if their mark had been erased, slowly eroded away over time as their memory faded from the minds of those who had been alive when the Spirit Wielders had lived in the Maison realm.

Because when the Fall occurred, the Spirit Wielders had left. They'd fled the Maison realm and went into the human realm—and perhaps even into the other territories if the legends were true.

And considering that I was a walking legend, or so they said, I tended to believe that idea.

The history of this territory was even worse. It turned out that the old kings of each kingdom had used the Spirit Wielders and their magic to increase their power.

I wasn't sure exactly how that had happened, but considering that I had witnessed some version of that with the knight, Lore, using those within his kingdom and stripping their Wielding through the crystal, I figured that was probably how it had been done.

But I didn't want to think too hard about that since it wasn't something I could stomach well.

"We should be there eventually."

Easton's voice brought me out of my thoughts, and I shook my head. He had taken so long to answer, I had forgotten I had asked him a question. And his answer really wasn't an answer at all.

"Really? Eventually? I'm so glad you cleared that up."

He huffed out a breath. I wasn't sure if he was laughing or just grunting at me. Most likely grunting because…this was Easton.

"Eventually because sometimes the Spirit territory makes you feel like you're closer than you really are. We are walking through a desert, after all. We should be there within two days, but, knowing this territory, it could take longer. Or we could be there tomorrow. It just really depends on the magic in the air."

I almost tripped over my feet as I narrowed my eyes at him. "Like there's a time vortex or something? Or magic making us think we're going farther than we are?"

"No. More like things aren't really how they seem here. I don't know how else to explain it. I'm not exactly a Spirit Wielder, am I?"

"I'm not either," I said quickly.

"But you will be soon. One day."

I nodded, my mouth going a little dry.

That was the one Wielding aspect that truly worried me. Over time, I had met each of the other types of Wielders. I knew that eventually, I'd be able to be trained by someone. And even though the Fire Wielding was the one that tempted me the most, it scared me, too. However, it wasn't the one that worried me the most.

No, that was the Spirit Wielding and the fact that I did not know any other Spirit Wielders who could help me when I gained that element.

My dreams came back to me, and I let myself mull them over. I guess I *had* met a few Spirit Wielders, the ones that haunted my dreams. They had been the ones to call out to me, the ones who gave me the strength to save myself from the sword that had been in my gut. There were twelve of them, each standing on a different hour of the clock at the cardinal directions, watching and speaking to me.

They had been so otherworldly, so *different* from any other type of Wielder I had met.

And I had no idea where they were in the waking world. Or how they could help me. *If* they could help me.

Easton reached out and brushed my hair from my face as we walked, and I tripped over myself. His hands were instantly on my elbows as he held me steady.

"Are you okay?" He looked down at me, his voice low as he spoke.

I blinked, looking up at him. "Yeah. You just startled me."

He cleared his throat. "Sorry. You just looked so pensive, I wanted to see if you were okay."

Then why did you touch me?

I didn't ask that question, but it was the first thing that came to mind.

I didn't know what I was about to say, but when I opened my mouth to speak, Teagan shouted, changing everything.

"Brace yourselves!"

I looked over at him, wondering what he could possibly mean. Because there was nothing here, the area was completely empty.

But then I knew I was wrong.

It looked as if there was something flying through the air, bobbing up and down as it came towards us, its mouth open, its jagged teeth as long as I was tall.

But I couldn't be seeing what I thought I was seeing.

It was as if it were partly there, and somewhat gone. Like a ghost. It looked like a dragon, that much I knew, but then again, I didn't know if dragons were real.

It had a long beard on its face that blew in the wind as the creature came towards us. Its body was skeletal, you could actually see the fact that there was nothing inside this dragon that was coming at us.

But it was as if it was out of phase. Sometimes it was a little more solid. Sometimes, a lot more translucent.

It was a ghost dragon, and it was coming at us.

And then it blew fire, and Easton grabbed me and slammed me to the ground. My head hit hard, and I rolled under him as he covered my body with his, screaming at the others to take cover, as well.

The heat above us didn't burn. Instead, it tried to lick at us, almost wrapping around us.

"Don't let it touch you," Easton said, his voice right near my ear.

I stiffened, attempting to see around him yet trying to pull him closer and away from the fire at the same time. "I won't. It's fire."

"It's not just fire. It's ghost fire. You don't know that it's hot until you can't breathe and then, suddenly, you burn from the inside out. It's worse than any normal flame, worse than any Fire Wielding I could ever do. Just hold on."

I'd tucked myself in as much as I could, trying not to let anything touch me. However, with Easton on top of me, with his body covering mine, there was no way that the ghost fire could actually burn me.

No, it would have to get through Easton first.

But I refused to let him die for me, refused to let him get hurt for me. But, if I pushed him away, he could get hurt anyway.

That meant I would let him do this for now, and then…we would just have to have a talk about this whole the-king-not-sacrificing-himself-for-me thing.

Easton rolled off me suddenly and then pulled me to my feet, looking around as if he were on alert.

His hands were out, the earth shaking under our feet. I didn't know if it was him or me that was creating that Wielding.

I let my Air slide from my fingers, not knowing if I could actually use my Wielding against a ghost dragon.

Easton had flames on his fingertips, and I hoped that if he could use that to protect us, maybe I could use Air, as well.

I remembered the first time I'd met Easton before I even knew his name. He had used his Fire Wielding to protect us from the Negs, and I had somehow used my Air Wielding to lift his Fire higher to direct it the right way. We had never talked about it, had never done it again. Now, I wondered if that had been a coincidence or if we could do it again.

Because I had no idea how to fight this thing.

"It's a Domovoi," Easton said quickly. The others surrounded us, ready to use their Wielding even though none of us knew how to fight this thing.

"A Domovoi?" I asked, not sure I could say the word properly.

"It's a dragon like you see, but this one's pretty big. It usually has six to ten legs, and this one doesn't have wings even though it's flying. It'll bring fire, the ghost fire that I told you about. Don't let it bite you. Its bite is venomous. And if it gets too close, its skin will create this fume that can kill you."

I blinked up at Easton, still on alert. "It doesn't *have* skin, though."

"Not right now. That's because its rider is on it. But once the rider drops down from the Domovoi's back, its skin will likely come around to create its shield."

"Rider?"

Easton jerked his chin towards the Domovoi.

"Look." I turned towards the dragon as it circled us, fire spewing from its mouth. And then I glanced on top of the creature and saw what I had missed the first time.

There indeed was a rider, and it was just like its Domovoi counterpart.

The male, at least I thought it was male, was translucent at times and sometimes solid. A ghost.

He wore robes that floated in a breeze that wasn't there, with a hood that covered his head. I knew he was dead. Or at least was something *like* dead.

The rider had arrows coming out of its back, and its chest and arms looked as if it had been murdered in a battle that had come with weapons that were before my time.

I couldn't see its face, I didn't even know if it had one. It scared me.

It was as if death were coming for us, and it wore only a hood, not a face.

"Be ready!" Easton called out. "The rider can't leave the dragon's back unless it's called, but we don't know who's calling it. Aim all of your Wielding towards the dragon's side rather than its head. Its side is weaker. And then we can get it to go back where it came from. There's no killing a Domovoi," Easton added, and I figured that tidbit was mostly for my benefit since no one had looked shocked at seeing this thing, rather only that it was there at all.

And so, I let my Air Wielding slide through my fingers and hoped it would be enough.

"Now!" Easton called out. We worked as a unit, and while the others were far more trained than I was and had worked as a group before, I felt like I could help. That I *needed* to help.

Easton used both his Fire and Earth in tandem, slamming a wave of flaming Earth into the side of the Domovoi.

Teagan used his Fire Wielding to create a tornado of fumes and plumes of flame that went under the dragon, trying to crisp it from below rather than directly where Easton had hit it. Wyn had her Earth Wielding, sending rocks into the Domovoi's side with the same type of dirt and soil wave that Easton had used.

And then Arwin added his Earth Wielding as well, bolstering Teagan's Fire and slamming soil and other debris up into the dragon. Everyone worked as one to bring the thing down.

I wasn't going to help with my Earth Wielding, the others were much better at it than I was.

But I had one thing they didn't. Air.

So, I held it in my hands and pushed it from my body, the Air Wielding ripping from me but without pain. It was as if it were always meant to be there, just a slight prickling sensation and then a wave of triumph.

The Air Wielding wrapped itself around the other four's Wielding and moved it faster, harder into the dragon.

The Domovoi screamed, as did its rider, and it was like no other sound I had ever heard in my life.

I wanted to slap my hands over my ears so I couldn't hear anymore, but I couldn't, not when I needed to use my Air Wielding.

Easton shouted, and the others moved closer, their Wielding feeling even stronger around me. So I did the same, trying to use what I had to protect my friends, to protect Easton. To defend myself.

And then the cloaked rider figure looked at me, and I could feel whatever eyes it had directly on me. I knew this was death. If he touched me, I would die.

But then Easton put his body between the cloaked figure and me, blocking my view and making my Air Wielding falter for just a moment.

"Fade, go away! Run back to the hole you crawled out of," Easton shouted. The masked figure looked at Easton and then practically through him to me. Then, suddenly, they were gone.

The Domovoi and his rider were gone, and all of us let our Wielding fall. My body shook as I tried to figure out if I had burnt myself out or not.

I was so angry. So livid with Easton.

He had to stop trying to sacrifice himself for me. He had to stop doing the things that he kept doing that confused me.

But before I could say anything, before I could figure out exactly what I was feeling, there were footsteps on the ground beside us. We all turned, ready to use our Wielding again.

But this time, it wasn't the rider. It wasn't the Domovoi.

No, this was someone I had seen before in a dream. Someone I knew yet didn't know.

An old man in robes, his face worn, and his eyes looking as if he were both seeing for the first time and ageless.

He grinned at us, and Easton growled. "About time you got here. Okay, then. I guess you want some fish? Okay. Glad you took down the Domovoi. It's been very annoying recently. Well, come on now. Dinner's ready."

And then the man I knew as a Spirit Wielder, one I thought had been on the face of the clock in my dream, turned around and walked towards a set of caves I hadn't seen before.

I wondered what the hell had just happened.

CHAPTER 11

The others once again had their Wielding queued, ready to fight this man, but Easton gave them a look, and they all stood down. As if the boy by my side knew that the Spirit Wielder might be dangerous but not in a way we all knew outright.

How I knew that, I didn't understand, but this was a step. I could tell. A beginning. I just needed to figure it out. The others gave me a weird look, and I just shrugged before we all followed the old man.

Why? Because, apparently, this was my life now, and I had no idea what we were doing. No, that wasn't right. We were following him because I *knew* we needed to, and while the others trusted me, they also knew we were there for a reason. We were going on Seer magic, and from clues from the bracelet on my wrist at this point, and the others knew more than I did. At least, I

Easton moved closer to me, his body warm. I figured it must be from the excess adrenaline rushing through his system. We were all a little out of breath, a bit sweaty from our fight so that just made sense.

"He's a Spirit Wielder. Can't you feel it?"

I held back a shiver and nodded. "I still have trouble figuring out which element is which within someone, other than knowing whether someone's a Wielder or not." I paused, that sense of *knowing* creeping in yet again. "But, yes, I knew he was a Spirit Wielder."

Easton gave me an odd look. "You'll be able to figure out the differences the more you get used to us. That much I know. Plus, you'll eventually have all five elements running through your system. It's no wonder you get some of them confused because like reaches out to like and all that. But I have a feeling you knew this man was a Spirit Wielder for other reasons. Care to share?"

We were talking softly, the others walking in front of us as if keeping us safe from the Spirit Wielder. I wondered why Easton seemed to know so much. Of course, that always seemed to be the case with him. He saw too much, knew too much, yet never revealed anything about himself.

A typical king, I would think.

"I saw him in my dreams," I said, not knowing where that answer had come from. I hadn't meant to say anything, but there it was, the words out of my mouth and me unable to do anything about it.

"Your dreams," Easton repeated, his voice low as if his mouth were getting used to the words and sounds.

I didn't want to tell him all of it, and I didn't think I was going to just then. But I could tell him at least the part about the dreams. After all, keeping everything to myself likely wouldn't help me or anyone else.

"I've had dreams and nightmares for as long as I can remember. Sometimes, it seems like I've always been meant for this point in my life, as if something's been reaching out to me, wanting me to know I should be here, that I should have been here long ago. I can't explain it. But, yes, he's been in my dreams, although I've never seen his face before today. He and eleven others. Like the hours on a clock."

Easton gave me a shocked look and then nodded. "We've always known the Spirit Wielders were out there. I guess it makes sense that they would reach out to you." He frowned again. "There's more to that story, though. And I know you're not going to tell me right now. But if you need to share, I'm here. But be careful, Lyric. Anything that reaches out to you in dreams or in visions has the power to connect to you in ways that you may not be ready for. Something you may never want." At his warning, I shivered.

"I know. I know."

Because I didn't know why the Spirit Wielders had helped me before, why they had helped me in my dreams and tried to speak to me.

All I knew was that it wasn't easy trying to figure out where I was positioned and how to interact in a world that wasn't my own, even though maybe it should have been.

I couldn't believe that I'd actually talked to Easton about it at all. I shouldn't have.

He never shared anything with me, and I really didn't even know him.

But now I wasn't sure what to do. Because I shouldn't have spoken to him.

I shouldn't have bared that part of myself. Yet it seemed like the only thing I could do at the time.

Maybe using my Wielding as I had was a little too much for me and the lack of oxygen to my brain was impacting more than I thought. Because I wasn't really making any sense, it seemed my thoughts were a step or two behind everything else.

"Why are we following him?"

"Because he's a Spirit Wielder living out here alone. I want to see what he's up to. We're still going in the right direction towards the Lumiére Kingdom. But I have a feeling there's a reason he is here, and I want to figure it out."

I nodded, agreeing. "I want to know, too. Plus, I've never met a Spirit Wielder before." My tongue tripped over the words. "I...I was kind of worried I would never find one."

Easton gave me a knowing look, and then we ended our conversation, walking side by side in silence as the others surrounded the old man. I wondered exactly what would happen next.

We didn't walk far, only to the caves that had been near us when we fought the Domovoi. The old man seemed to have created a home for himself inside the caves. It didn't make much sense to me, but he was here, and there had to be a reason for it.

Though maybe there was no reason, and this was just a way for the Negs to come at us. Or for something else to come at us.

I had to remember that the Lumiére and the Obscurité were at war. They still had battles and skirmishes, and there were still rules against going into each other's kingdom. There were no full-scale wars right now, no true battles that seemed to take ages, but I had a feeling that was coming.

As if with the queen gone and Easton now in his new position, we were just waiting for whatever would happen next. Because Lore, the knight, had taken so much out of the Obscurité Kingdom that I had a feeling there had to be a mirror version of it in the Lumiére.

Everything just seemed...off. Easton had been right before when he warned me with that deep voice of his.

It felt like a puppet master was pulling strings, and we were only in one part of what would happen. There was more to come.

Because the realm was dying, and I was supposed to save it.

From the look of the barren landscape in front of me, I was afraid I was too late.

The old man stopped, surrounded by some of his things but mostly just dirt and dying plants.

He was talking to himself as if there were people all around him. Some part of me kind of hoped that maybe he was talking to spirits or even the other Spirit Wielders, just in another part of the world.

I had no idea what Spirit Wielders did, and no one else really seemed to know either. There was nothing written about them, and I didn't know what their Wielding entailed. But this man looked insane. So, either being alone had done this to him, or it was the Spirit Wielding itself. I honestly hoped that this wasn't my future.

"So, Lyric. About time you got here. Now, I haven't really seen people in a while. Couple hundred years or so. Not really sure. I usually hide from them, but I can't really help it because sometimes they just find me. And then there's that dragon thing, and it just comes at you out of nowhere." The old man started rambling, and my eyes widened. Easton had put himself in between us just slightly so it didn't look too obtrusive, but I still half-glared at him.

He really needed to stop this whole trying-to-save-me thing.

I could save myself.

Or at least I could try.

Teagan, Wyn, and Arwin were stationed around the area, looking over their shoulders yet still watching the man.

None of this felt right, but I knew we had to be here. There was a reason we were here. And then I looked down at my bracelet and intuited that, yes, we were here for a reason.

The star on my charm bracelet, the one that I knew was part of the Spirit Wielding, flared just once, warm against my skin. And then I realized that, yes, we were here because we were supposed to be.

My whole life was now filled with magic, built on prophecy and the unknown. The fact that I was taking my cues from a bracelet that came from a Seer of some sort—or whatever Alura was—probably cemented that, but it didn't matter.

Because I needed to know more.

And tonight, maybe I would find out more.

Easton must have seen me glance down because he gave me a tight nod and then pressed in even closer as if wanting to let me know that he was by my side.

I wasn't sure exactly how I felt about that, but it was nice to have someone to rely on even if it was a little confusing.

"How did you know my name?" I asked, my voice soft.

The old man just shook his head and rolled his eyes. "We're not really going to start at that point in time, are we? Because you already know who I am. We've spoken. A little. You know all about the blood and the sword and the like. It wasn't really fun, but I'm very glad you're okay. Because if you had died, it kind of would have messed up the whole prophecy thing, and then everyone would've died, and it would've been a whole thing. We really don't want it to be a thing."

I blinked, trying to follow his line of conversation.

The others gave me a confused look, but I didn't fill them in.

The only one who didn't seem confused was Easton, and that was probably because I had just told him about the fact that I had seen this man in my dreams.

If Easton could put two and two together, he would probably figure out that, yes, the Spirit Wielders had been there when I died and came back.

I had no idea what I was doing.

"Okay, I remember you. What are you doing out here all alone?"

The others seemed to know to let me lead this conversation, even though I really didn't think I would be the best at it. They were all so much older than I was, with so much more experience. For all I knew, I was going to say the wrong thing and ruin it all. But then again, this felt right. Even if I could be wrong.

"I'm glad you're here, Lyric."

That didn't answer my question.

"I've been here for a while. As long as I can remember. And I can remember pretty far, if you know what I mean. I remember when the ruins weren't ruins, and the buildings touched the sky, and the people laughed and milled about on the streets. I remember the sound of children and the smiles of their mothers."

I let out a shiver, and Easton pressed even closer to me as if reassuring me. Or maybe that was just what I needed, and so I took that as the meaning of his action.

"There was a city here?"

"Yes, of course, there was, little one. There were cities here as well as in the lower territory. There were so many people. But it wasn't all happiness. Though you know that. There wouldn't be ruins if there hadn't been heartache. Because we were lost, forgotten, and then remembered when we shouldn't have been. And because of that memory, they took us. They killed us. They stripped us of our souls and our magic. They used their Wieldings in the worst possible ways. And then we were gone. Not here, nor there. But I remained. Because without a memory, does something even exist? Without someone to tell others of the cities that were born and the children that smiled and laughed, did it exist in any realm?"

Tears pricked my eyes, and I blinked them away, not knowing why I was crying for people who had been born long before I was even a speck of memory.

Civilizations in the human realm had been built and had fallen in the time the Spirit territories had been vacated. Yet it felt like it was yesterday. As if I could hear the children dancing in the street and smell the warm bread from the bakery and see people walking around as if they had no cares in the world.

And it hurt. It hurt so much, but I couldn't do anything about it. After all, there was nothing to do.

"But, Lyric, you're here to save the day, aren't you?"

I blinked, looking up at the old man. "What?"

"Well, you need to save the day. You're not here just for giggles and to lean into that boy over there." He winked, and Easton and I separated. I hadn't even realized that we were leaning into each other until the man pointed it out.

Heat spread across my cheeks, and Wyn raised a brow at me. Both Teagan and Arwin were looking in the other direction, but I had a feeling their attention was also on me.

Well, that was weird.

"What's your name?" I asked, wondering why he wouldn't tell me.

He waved me off. "It doesn't matter. Names come and go, time comes and goes. That's what time is, after all, something that passes in the distance as we try to keep up."

Okay, so the man was a little insane. And loved to talk in riddles. Apparently, being alone for over five hundred years did that to someone.

"So, Lyric? The dreams weren't enough? What more do you need? How many clues do we need to give you so you can fix what happened?"

I sucked in a breath, but I didn't lean towards Easton, and he didn't move towards me. "So, you *were* in my dreams. I didn't make that up?"

The others looked at me, but Easton didn't. After all, he already knew the answer.

"Of course, I was. I'm a Dream Walker."

This time, Easton sucked in a breath, and I looked over at him. He gave me a sharp look, then leaned close to my ear, his breath warm against my skin. I held back a shiver as I always did when it came to him.

"Dream Walkers are rare. As the name implies, they can walk in dreams. And legend says they can steal your soul through your dreams."

He leaned away, and I blinked, frozen in place. My soul? They could steal my soul?

My...spirit?

I didn't have time to think about this. The Dream Walker studied us curiously before opening his mouth to speak again.

"The others need me," the man continued. "They all need me. Oh, fish. I forgot your fish." He went off to look for fish, even though I didn't know how there could be fish in a place with no rivers or lakes. I wasn't sure I wanted to ask.

I blinked, looking at the others as if hoping they would know what to do because I had no idea.

"What? What do you mean? What am I supposed to do? Do you know something about the prophecy? Why are we here?"

I had so many questions, and this man was not giving me any answers. I didn't even know if he had any. All he was doing was confusing me and, honestly, annoying me just a little.

"The Spirit Priestess will come of five, yet of none at all.
She will be strength of light, of darkness, and choice.
You will lose what you had.

You will lose what you want.

You will lose what you will.

You will lose what you sow.

Then you will find the will.

Find the fortune.

And then you will make a choice.

A choice above all.

A sacrifice above will.

A fate left denied.

And a loss meant to soothe."

I froze once again. Those words...they were what I'd wanted to hear, what I needed to know. Yet I had no idea what any of it meant. I needed to deconstruct it...yet it wasn't enough. I needed more, and I had no time. There was never any time.

"Lyric, it will all make sense. Though that's not all of the prophecy." The man met my gaze, and I saw such clarity there. I blinked. "I was the sixth, the one behind you to the south. The one in your dreams. The one who was there when it all ended. I know what was, and so I understand what needs to be. If you ever find your way to where I am again, I will show you our history. At least what I can remember of it. The Spirit territories used to be lush and filled with life. And they need to be once more. The Maison realm needs to be abundant once more. The Spirit territories look as they do because there is no one here to give them life. And I'm afraid the rest of the realm will look like this soon if you don't give life back to the crystals. If you don't seal the fracture."

And then he blinked, and his eyes suddenly went less clear. I wondered what had just happened.

I looked over at Easton, our gazes connecting, and I saw darkness there

123

mixed with a warmth that told me that I would be okay. That I wouldn't be alone. That I would have someone by my side no matter what. Then he blinked, and the look was gone in an instant.

I didn't know what to say to anyone. I was more confused than ever.

"Go. You must go. You can't be late."

"Will you be safe here?" I asked, feeling more unnerved than ever. He'd spoken of the prophecy. It was the first I'd heard of it, in any detail at any rate. And yet...yet I was so confused. What did it all mean?

The Spirit Wielder cupped my face, and I sucked in a breath, the power beneath his hands scaring me with its strength.

"Go, Lyric. You will find what you need, though it might not be what you want. The world is changing, as are you. Find your path. And once you do, you will find your power. Go. You know what you must do. Or you will soon."

"Thank you," I whispered, not knowing what else to say.

Easton tugged on my hand, and his touch pulled me from whatever trance I felt like I had fallen into.

"Thank you for your kindness," Easton said solemnly to the old man.

"Thank you for protecting the Priestess, Your Highness."

I froze, wondering how the old man knew. Easton was under glamour, and from the way he leaned into me just a bit, I knew he had been startled by the address, as well.

"You know more than you're saying." Easton's voice was so low that I could feel the danger in my veins.

"Of course, I do. I'm an old man. I know more than most. Now, go. The sun will set soon, and you don't want to be out after dark. Protect her with everything you have, Your Highness. With *everything*."

Easton pulled me away then, not saying a word, and I couldn't help but wonder what that meant. I wondered what everything meant now. There was a reason we had seen this man, if only for a moment. Maybe the reason was just to reassure me that we were on the right path.

I didn't know what that look had meant earlier, or if it'd meant anything at all.

But I knew we needed to get to the Lumiére Kingdom. I needed to know why I was being pulled there. And I needed to see Rhodes. I needed him to understand who I was and learn what could happen in the future. I needed to know why we weren't soulmates and discover what our connection had been. I needed to make sure that Rhodes knew that we had a chance even without that bond.

But, above all else, I needed to know my history, and I needed to determine what would happen next.

Any connection I felt with Rhodes, or even Easton for that matter, would have to be put aside. Because first, I had to figure out who I was.

And decipher what that old man had meant.

Because this was only the beginning. Or perhaps it was the middle. The end was coming, and I was worried.

CHAPTER 12

"We need to get going," Teagan said, looking off into the distance. "That was weird, man, but we need to get going." He repeated the words, and I looked over at Easton, wondering what we were going to do next. This was all just so surreal. But then again, my *life* was a bit surreal these days.

"I don't know what a Dream Walker is," Arwin said, his voice soft. "And I didn't want to ask him since I felt like if any of us talked other than Lyric, he wasn't going to answer, or maybe just stop talking altogether and push us out."

I looked over at the youngest member of our guard and studied his face. I knew he had to be at least a hundred years old because I had overheard them talking about his last century, but he looked younger than me, even though I was only eighteen. The way the Maisons aged and lived was so different than how I had been raised, but sometimes I forgot that they could have a century

"I don't really know what that is either," I said. "I mean, he was in my dreams, I know that much." I winced, not really wanting to mention that. "He, um, was in my nightmares, but not like he was evil or anything. I just remember having a vision of him. I figured that was maybe what Dream Walkers do? I don't really know."

I hated sounding weak and uninformed .

"Dream Walkers are a subset of the Spirit Wielders," Easton answered for all of us. "Much like how each set of Wielding has its own versions. How Earth Wielders can trigger earthquakes or create large domes of earth to come at you. Or some are Earth shakers. How Water Wielders can sometimes move oceans or just creeks. And how some can actually boil the water within your body or pull it from you completely, desiccating you."

My eyes widened at that. I hadn't known Water Wielders could do that, but from the looks on the others' faces, they had. Having Wielding was dangerous, yet it protected you at the same time. It was just so odd to be able to talk about magic and death as if it were an everyday occurrence. As if these powers weren't something that was new and shiny. But they were for me.

"Dream Walkers are the rarest of the Spirit Wielders, at least that's what I remember reading when I was in school. Not much is known about the Spirit Wielders, but the Dream Walkers can walk in your dreams and can bring others with them. I don't know why they would do that, but that's what I know, all I know other than…other than they can…they say they can steal your soul within your dreams. I wish people had written down more about the Spirit Wielders, or that whatever *had* been written down about them had been kept. But after the Fall, everything changed. And I only got the scraps that my mom could find."

Wyn cleared her throat. "I remember learning right alongside you, Easton. There isn't much at all." She looked at me, a sad expression coming over her face. "There's a reason we can only help you with some of your Wielding, and why I hope the Lumiére will be able to help you with your others. But as for the Spirit Wielders? We don't know their magic. We weren't allowed to learn when we were younger, and any myths and stories that might have been passed down have long since been forgotten. But we will find a way, Lyric."

She said it as a promise, and I wanted to believe her, but it was hard when she was voicing some of my own fears. That I wouldn't be able to learn everything that I needed to in time, and that whatever I was supposed to do wouldn't be enough.

The idea that I had the weight of a realm on my shoulders even though I didn't quite believe in it was something hard to comprehend.

But the others were looking at me as if they trusted me to save their realm, though none of us knew exactly how that was going to happen. "We're going to find a way," Easton said, his voice sure. "I haven't been going through all of this training and getting you into the Obscurité Kingdom and now the Lumière Kingdom only for you to fail because we don't know how to Wield the fifth. So, we'll figure it out. I'm not wasting my time."

I glared at him. "Really? So, we're going to make this all about you."

"Of course. I am the king." He laughed as he said it, but it didn't feel real. As if he were just trying to lighten the mood because the tension surrounding all of us was a little too much to bear. We had gone from training to traveling to fighting to confusion. And now we'd be traveling again.

"And Teagan is right, we need to go. Because I don't want to spend another night in this area. Something feels...off."

"Something always feels off," I said, agreeing with him. "But that could be the fact that I'm like a fish out of water."

"Considering we're headed to the Water territory, that's probably an apt description," he said, and I knew there was a joke there. But I just shook my head, falling into step at his side as the five of us continued our journey.

Everything felt the same as we walked, making our way to the Water territory. There were no real discernible landmarks, so I had no idea where we were going, but the others seemed to know, and I trusted them. After all, I had been with them for long enough that I could. They had helped me, tried to make sure that I was ready for whatever might come at us.

And Easton had saved me once before. Even though he annoyed me sometimes, and was arrogant as hell, he was still on this mission with us, still going where he shouldn't to make sure I was safe. I couldn't forget that.

We had walked for another day, well out of the way of where the Dream Walker had been, when the hairs on the back of my neck stood on end, and I tripped over my feet.

"Negs," Easton said softly, holding out his hands. His Fire Wielding was ready to go, so I mirrored his actions, using my Air Wielding. Everyone got into position, and then the monsters came at us.

The Negs were creatures that looked like demons straight from hell. They had long fangs covered in drool, red eyes, and dark bodies. They growled menacingly, their teeth sharp enough that I knew I wouldn't make it if they bit into me.

"You stay by my side," Easton barked at me. "You've fought these before, and you're even more trained now, but do not leave my side. Do you get me?"

I looked up at him for a bare instant before I looked back at the Negs. "Okay, but you don't get to die for me. Do you get *me*?"

"No one's going to be dying today other than the Negs."

And then the monsters were upon us.

Two of them came at Teagan, who used his Fire Wielding to burn them. They screamed, a menacing sound that practically burst my eardrums, but then they rolled to the ground, still not dead, just slightly charred.

Wyn and Arwin worked as one, building their Earth Wielding and combining it as they pushed the closest Neg violently into another, rolling them under mounds and mounds of dirt.

I had my Earth Wielding as well, lifting one Neg up with as much power as I could and then tossing it towards another.

Easton looked over his shoulder, winking at me with a menacing grin on his face.

It was as if he were having fun with this, even though I knew that his eyes didn't hold laughter. No, he understood the danger, but the fact that I was working with him? Using my Wielding just as he was? Maybe that was worth a grin. Because I could feel the power within my body. I could feel myself working alongside him—Easton using his Fire and Earth, me using my Air and Earth. We took out two Negs, and then another. He burned one as I buried the other. And then I used my Air Wielding to lift his Fire Wielding even higher, directly into the face of another Neg.

We hadn't trained for this, and I hadn't known that I could even do it, but it was as if it were natural, something inherent in my abilities.

Easton's arm brushed mine, and I could feel the heat of him while I sucked in a breath. The intensity of his Fire Wielding was high, but it didn't burn. Instead, it was almost as if I knew that no matter what happened, we could work together and destroy the monsters.

I didn't know why they were here, but we must be close to a border. That was the only reason the Negs would be here. Right?

Unless they had been sent by someone else. I remembered Rhodes saying that the Negs liked to stay in the border territories. Because with so much magic intermingling, so much Wielding intensified, the absence of magic itself tended to congregate. That they were coming out more and more said something about the lack of stability when it came to the realm.

These Negs were the absence of light, yet still the absence of the darkness of the Obscurité.

They were the monsters that filled the night, but they weren't the only monsters out here. Just look at Lore, the knight who had tried to kill us all.

And I knew there were more monsters, ones without sharp teeth and claws.

Ones that would kill anyone in their path to try and take their power and their Wielding.

But Lore was dead, and though we all knew that there had to be something greater out there, something or someone that was orchestrating all of this, it didn't matter just then.

It was just me and the others against the Negs.

And so, we fought. I pulled in my arms and then pushed them out. My palms widespread and my fingers splayed as I used my Air Wielding to blow another Neg out of the way and into the Fire tunnel that Easton had created.

The smell of burnt flesh and crisped hair filled my nose, but I ignored it, trying not to think about exactly what we were doing.

I was helping to kill things, but I knew we had to. If we didn't, they would kill us. There were at least fifteen Negs, maybe more. I had lost count, but they kept coming at us, kept trying to fight and kill.

Sweat poured down my back and covered my palms, but it did not interfere with my Wielding.

I knew the others were stronger than I was because they had been training longer, but I had this well inside of me as if I'd been collecting energy and power over time and just had to use it and let it out.

But no amount of Wielding was infinite. The finite resolutions that we had meant one of us would tire out soon if we didn't take out all of the Negs.

And so, I pulled back the power inside me and pushed harder, using my Earth and Air in conjunction with Easton's Fire and Earth. And I screamed.

I couldn't let the others get hurt. No matter the cost.

Wyn fell, having been pushed down by a Neg, but then Teagan was there, pulling the Neg off her with his bare hands before he burned the creature to a crisp.

Arwin was in the center of it all, using his Earth Wielding to push the Neg that had tried to take Wyn out.

I couldn't help them because more Negs were coming at us. Soon, I knew we would be okay.

We were all working as a unit, a team.

And then the last Neg fell, and Easton looked at me, his chest heaving as we all fought for breath.

"Are you okay?" He asked me the question first, and as I nodded, he gave me a tight nod himself and then looked at the others. "All of you?" he asked, his voice rough and growly.

"We're fine. That last one came at me out of nowhere. It was like they were targeting us. What the hell, Easton?" Wyn asked the question, and I frowned.

"Don't all Negs just come at us like that?" I asked, wondering why Wyn looked so confused and stricken.

"No," Easton answered. "We're not as close to the border as we should be for a Neg attack like this. There's something else at work. Can't you sense it? The fight isn't over."

I looked into the distance, trying to see what he could. I shook my head. "So, someone sent these? Like the ones that came to Rhodes' house and took Rosamond?"

At the sound of Rhodes' name, Easton glared, and I wondered what that was about. Maybe because they were on opposite sides of a coin in the battle of a war that nobody really wanted to fight—other than those who wanted more power? I didn't know, but I didn't have time to think about the grand scheme of things right now, not when Easton was so sure that something else was coming.

"Those Negs came right at us. And, like I said, we're not close enough to a border. That means whatever's directing them has to be close. It was far too much of a coincidence to actually *be* a coincidence."

"Who's directing them? Who could be around?" I asked, my voice soft. Because we were so far away from any other civilizations here and were in the Spirit territory, that meant that whoever was coming for us wasn't in the territory that they were allowed to use for battle.

Maybe I was wrong. As I looked off into the distance and saw the shadows coming, I knew I was dead wrong.

"It's the League!" Teagan shouted, and I looked over at Easton.

"Who?"

"The League. They're Water Wielders. They're known as the spies of the territory. I don't really see them out in the open like this often, but they must not want us here. It's not uncommon for them to patrol for the King of Lumière. They can't know that I'm the king, do we all understand that?" Easton asked. We all nodded. Of course, we wouldn't let them know that Easton was the King of Obscurité. If they found out that he was coming towards the Water territory, it could mean a full-out war rather than just memories of one and intermittent skirmishes. Of course, I didn't know where I stood in any of it, so I didn't say anything. I just hoped nobody would recognize what or who I was.

"The League works for the king and only the king. Or, at least they *should*. But they could also be working for one of the lords, so be on the lookout. We don't know why they're here. Or what they want."

"Isn't Rhodes' father the Lord of Water? Why would he send them out?"

Easton shook his head as he looked around. There was nowhere for us to take cover. So, unless the League just wanted to talk, we would have to fight hand-to-hand. I really hoped they just wanted to talk.

"Yes, Rhodes' father is the Lord of Water. And his grandfather is the Lord of Air. And his uncle is the king. He's very connected, but that doesn't really matter. Because while you may be safe from Rhodes and the others, we are Obscurité. You said yourself that I'm not your king, and that means Rhodes' family isn't either. So, you should be safe, unless, like Lore, someone doesn't want you around. Do you know what I mean?"

I sort of did, but I was still a little confused, wondering exactly what Easton meant by all of that. Because he was right, the knight hadn't wanted me around, hadn't wanted anyone to stop his power grab.

Was it the same in the Lumiére Kingdom? I didn't know, and because I didn't know, I was going to be vigilant.

I trusted Easton, even though it was a fragile trust at best.

With both kingdoms so fervently trying to attack one another, I wasn't sure that anybody really wanted the realm to come together. Maybe they didn't believe that it was actually shattering.

Maybe they didn't want a Spirit Priestess.

Or maybe a few did, and those in power wanted me gone. After all, that's what had happened in the Obscurité Kingdom at first. That's what I had thought Queen Cameo wanted. I had been wrong but hadn't known that until it was too late.

I had to remember that while I trusted Rhodes and Rosamond, I didn't know any of their family, I didn't know what they wanted from me. Or what I could do.

The League walked to us, their heads held high. They wore long, blue robes that billowed in the wind. All were perfect copies of one another, despite the fact that while they each had shaved heads, they all had different skin tones and eyes of different colors. They looked like a unit though, through and through.

I wondered if they had sent the Negs. Or maybe it was someone else. Or perhaps it was all just a big coincidence. The fact that there were no answers, and everything was just coming at us all at once made things harder to believe. "I'll be the one who talks," Teagan said. "You stand behind Lyric, Easton. Look like you're just a pageboy or something. If you can, my king," he said sarcastically and gave us a wink.

I knew we were all on edge, and I was a little worried.

"How can we help you?" one of the men said as he walked up to us. "You're coming nearer to the Water territory than you should, Obscurité."

"We're just on a mission, one to meet with the Lord of Water." Teagan smiled, holding out his arms. "As you can see. We mean no harm. We just took out some Negs. You wouldn't know anything about that, would you?"

"I don't know what you mean."

"We are just on our way for a training session. You should be careful, you don't know what could be out there."

I frowned, wondering what the hell all of the undercurrents meant. It was all so confusing, and it was clear that no one was actually saying what they meant.

I must have looked nervous because Easton reached out and tangled his fingers with mine just for an instant before giving them a squeeze.

I was so shocked that I looked up at him. He shook his head slightly but still leaned into me as if knowing I needed some reassurance. After all, I had no idea what was going on. But knowing Easton was beside me made me feel safe. It was as if I knew that I might need to fight my way out but felt better because I wouldn't be alone. No matter what.

"We were just passing through," one of the League members said, his gaze directly on me.

"As are we," Teagan said.

"Thank you for taking out the Negs, it saves us some time. Travel safely, all of you."

And then the League turned on their heels as one and walked the other way as if they weren't going to fight us and had nothing to do with what had just happened.

"What's going on?" I whispered, leaning into Easton even more as I asked.

"I have no idea, I think the League just wanted to test us or check out our Wielding before they come at us. And them being on a training exercise? Don't believe that for a minute. So, we need to keep our guards up and just get you to Rhodes and the others. Because while they're going the other way, I have a feeling we're going to see them again. Soon."

I watched as the League walked away, going so far into the distance that soon they just looked like little dots until they were no more.

They were all Water Wielders, ones with a lot of strength, that much I could tell.

I just wondered exactly who they were and why and if they had sent the Negs after us. And exactly what had just happened. Because they weren't just going away, wouldn't just leave us in the middle of a territory that wasn't ours or theirs. They were watching us.

And I knew this wouldn't be the last time we saw them.

No, this wouldn't be the last time at all.

CHAPTER 13

We decided to set up our campsite instead of trekking all the way through the wards. Doing so could possibly create another incident far too quickly—or worse.

The border between the Spirit territories and any of the other four elemental territories wasn't like the other borders. Between the Water and Air, and the Earth and Fire territories, there were actual amalgamations of the two elements that were reflected in the environment and the people who lived within the borders. It wasn't the same within the Spirit territories.

I had never been to the Lumière inner border, and while I might one day, from what I had seen of the Obscurité inner border, it was like its own section of the world. I didn't know if the Spirit territory borders had been like the other borders at some point, but I didn't think so.

Now, the border was stark, a clear line of non-amalgamation where one began and the other ended. There was no true evidence of what the Spirit

Wielders had once been, and even if there had once been a clear sign of their power and a trace of elements here, there were no signs of the blending of the two now, not like with the other inner borders.

To me, at least, the Spirit Wielders, however they had lived, seemed a little distant. A little disconnected from the other elements.

Maybe it was because the only Spirit Wielder I'd ever met in person was the crazy man who had said a bunch of things that didn't make any sense. Or maybe it was because they had been eradicated and forced to flee after the Fall.

Those who had wanted to use the Spirit Wielders for their gain, to appropriate their powers to increase their own, told me more about who the Spirit Wielders were more than anything else written about them.

Either way, after seeing the Water Wielders come at us as they had, even if the League hadn't really questioned us or attacked us, we wanted to collect our forces and make sure that we were ready for what was to come.

Because we didn't know what we were walking into.

The League, perhaps the entire Water territory, knew that we were on our way into the Lumière Kingdom. We couldn't hide that. And considering that I was supposed to be allowed into both kingdoms, at least according to what others had said, it shouldn't have been an issue. I should've been allowed to have my guard and just walk in and ask for help with my training. But we all knew that nothing was ever that easy.

Everything seemed to be shrouded in shadow, and I would just have to hope that we all made it through somehow.

"What's wrong?" I looked up at the sound of Easton's voice and frowned. I hadn't realized that he was so near, but I should have known. There was always someone near me, as if they were afraid I'd run off and hurt myself. Or maybe, more likely, fearful that one of the League members would come back, and we'd end up in a fight that I wasn't ready to have. Because while I was better than I had been even a few weeks ago, I still wasn't up to the same level of skill as the others. But that's what happened when you had a century to learn. I'd had a year.

A year where I hadn't really even been in the company of others that could actually train me well. Alura had helped, but I still didn't know her motivations, and everyone kept saying that she had secrets that weren't theirs to tell.

To say that annoyed me would be an understatement.

"Lyric?" I blinked, not realizing that Easton had crouched in front of me. He was so close, I could feel the heat of him, and I wasn't sure that I liked it.

"I'm fine." I said the words quickly if a little harshly. But then again, I tended to be like that when I was around Easton. I didn't know what it was about him, but he just set me on edge, even though I knew he wouldn't hurt me. He had done everything in his power to make sure that I was okay, even if he wasn't the nicest about it.

"You looked lost, at least in your thoughts. What's going on in that head of yours?"

I shrugged and leaned back from him. It was hard to think when he was so close. And, I tried not to think about that. Tried not to think about the fact that I felt a little clutch in my belly when he was near. Attempted not to recognize that I knew there was some kind of connection between us.

Maybe it was just because we got on each other's nerves. Or maybe it was because there was something more.

But I wasn't going to think about that. Because I had thought about something like that before. I had thought that I could be someone special. And I had been wrong.

I wasn't going to be wrong again.

I wasn't going to let myself feel like that.

Because, no matter what, I didn't have time for things like that. I didn't have time for crushes or thinking about boys or girls that gave me flutters in my stomach.

Because, apparently, I was supposed to save the world, only I didn't know how to do that.

Somehow, putting it into terms like that, when it all sounded so big and farfetched, let me breathe easier. Because when I thought about each minuscule task that I had to complete, each step on the list that didn't actually exist yet, I couldn't catch my breath.

"I'm just thinking." I looked away for a moment before turning back to him. "Are you on guard for the camp or are you going to sleep, as well?"

Easton studied my face again before shaking his head. And then he sat down on the log next to me and looked around.

"Wyn, Teagan, and Arwin are on patrol. We're not a huge camp, so we're all really within each other's views. And it's not like we're in tents."

I nodded, looking up at the bright sky above us.

There wasn't a single cloud. But then again, I wasn't sure if there had been clouds in the sunlight. Everything was so sepia-toned, as if the sky itself couldn't hold clouds nor have the blue color of the human realm or other parts of the Maison realm.

Because even in the Fire territory, there had been blue sky. Not everything had been painted in reds and blacks, not really. It'd been just as vibrant as the Earth territory, if a bit warmer.

Nothing was as it seemed, at least not in the Maison realm.

And not when it came to me. Not anymore.

"So, why aren't you sleeping yet?" I asked, not looking at Easton.

"Well, number one, I'm not tired. I don't think I'll be sleeping tonight.

Hard to do when I'm already on edge and trying to make sure my people don't get hurt. The League is around. I can't feel them, but they won't just leave us alone to walk near their territory. There's something up with them, and I want to figure out what it is."

"You're not going to go out and follow them, are you?" I asked and put my hand right on his shoulder. I hadn't meant to touch him, and we both froze. He looked down at where my hand was, and I pulled it back as if I'd burned him or myself.

I swallowed hard and met his gaze, wondering what the hell I was doing.

"I'm not going to follow them. Because that would leave you unprotected."

I swallowed hard. Not understanding. "The others will be here. I'd still be protected. You would be the one without help."

"I'm the king, and stronger than you think I am."

"Are you?" I asked, my voice low. I didn't know why I said it. Why I even thought it.

I watched as he licked his lips, and I wondered why I was noticing that at all. I didn't even like him. Or maybe I liked him too much. Perhaps I was just falling into this trap because I was scared and I'd rather think about Easton's jawline and his lips and not the fact that we were going into a territory that I'd never been to before. Either way, I was being thrust into a world of magic and mayhem that didn't make any sense.

I'd rather think about that little clutch in my belly rather than the possible danger, even though I shouldn't. I'd much rather do that than think about the fact that I was this prophesied destiny that didn't make any sense.

I didn't even know what the prophecy meant. Nor did I know all of it, only what others had told me. If it weren't for the fact that I could feel the Wielding in my veins, that I'd actually used Earth and Air Wielding in the past, I still would've thought it was all fake. That it was all just a story to tell others.

I would think that I had been born with nothing, no Wielding at all. But now it was unlocked in me.

So I knew what I was. I knew what the others told me I was.

I just didn't know what to think or do about it.

So, yes, maybe I would think about Easton and the way he was looking at me, a way I didn't understand, rather than anything else.

It just made more sense.

"You should get some sleep, though," Easton said softly. "We don't know what's coming tomorrow."

"We never know. Right?" I hadn't known anything since the Negs first attacked me when I was on that mountain.

His jaw tightened, and I resisted the urge to reach out and press my fingers to it. Why was I acting like this? It made no sense.

I didn't even know him, yet I wanted to touch him.

Maybe I really did need sleep. Because I didn't like this pull I felt towards him, this connection.

I didn't trust connections, not anymore.

Not when I had felt pulled towards Emory, and that had ended in horror. Not when I had felt that pull towards Rhodes, and that had ended with him leaving after not being able to save me from a mortal wound because we weren't soulmates.

And, apparently, that was the be all and end all when it came to Maisons.

I didn't want to feel this connection. I thought maybe it was stress. Maybe my mind needed to latch on to those possible bonds rather than fixate on the danger we were facing.

Yes, that had to be it. There was no actual connection. It was just me stressing out and being stupid.

"Get some sleep," he said softly again. "I'm trying not to think about the

Negs. Or what happened to you. Unless you want to talk about it. If so, I can bring Wyn over."

I snorted, knowing it wasn't very ladylike, but it didn't really matter. "Really? You're going to send over the only other girl if I need to talk about my feelings? Oh, but Easton, what if I really want to talk to you? Bare my soul and tell you everything that's worrying me."

I'd said it in jest, but now I knew it had been a mistake. I could see in his eyes that he shut down. And I pulled away because I didn't want to talk about anything. I just wanted to be left alone with my thoughts as I tried to work out my Wielding. I needed to unlock the other elements, and worrying about everything else was just making things harder for me.

"I don't know what's with you, Lyric. You act one way, and then you act another. You're really confusing."

"Hi, pot. Meet kettle."

He frowned. "What?"

"It's a human saying."

He gave me a weird look. "I know most of the human sayings. It's not like I've been stuck in the Maison realm for my entire existence. But really, you need to sleep."

"I really wish you would stop telling me to go to sleep. It's not going to make tomorrow any easier. Because I know the League is coming. I know that something's going to happen, I can feel it just like you can. And I know we're just camping to regroup and make sure that if the League is watching us, they don't know what we're doing. I'm still going to be on alert. And I don't think any amount of naps will help with that."

"You may be right. But at least try."

"You have to first."

He narrowed his eyes at me and gave me a tight nod.

"We'll both lay down next to this log of yours and at least try to relax. Because I'm not letting you out of my sight. Not when the League is lurking. Not when I feel like something's coming."

He settled in next to me, and I swallowed hard. I didn't like when he was so close. It made my thoughts blur, and made everything a little too confusing.

"I don't want to fight the Lumière," I said softly. "I don't want to fight the Obscurité either. I just want to figure out what I'm supposed to do. But the more I learn about the Maisons, the more I learn about my own elements, the more I feel like there's more questions than answers."

"I had been searching for the Spirit Priestess for years before you were even born," Easton began, looking off into the distance. "You were always more of a question than an answer. A figment of what could maybe help our realm. But I had to stop searching for you because my kingdom was dying. I didn't know that it was Lore. I didn't know that he was killing my people, stripping them of their powers and their dignity. If I had known, maybe I would've been able to stop it sooner. But I had thought we were just breaking down because the crystal was breaking. I didn't know it was being helped along."

His shoulders fell a bit, and I almost reached out to touch him, barely holding myself back.

"There's no coming back from that. Unless we figure out exactly what your prophecy means and how to fix us, how to glue back together the fragmented pieces that are our realm, I don't know how we're going to come back from it all. I left my kingdom in the hands of my uncles because I trust them. As soon as I can, I'm going back. I will protect my people. Just like I'm going to protect you. Because you're important. But so are my people. I failed them once, even as I failed you by not finding you when I should have. I can't take that back."

He wasn't looking at me. I wasn't even sure he was actually speaking to me at all, even though he was directing his conversation towards me.

It hurt to hear his words. Not that he blamed me for anything, but because he was in pain.

He was so strong, so defiant, and yet he felt like he had failed everyone.

I was right there with him, unable to figure out what I needed to do.

And so, I reached out and gripped his hand for a moment before letting it go.

"We'll figure it out. We have to."

He didn't say anything. There wasn't anything to say. We just looked out into the distance, no longer pretending to try and sleep. Because it wasn't going to be easy. It was never going to be easy. Tomorrow, we would walk into the Water territory and we would take that next step. Easton would be one more step away from his kingdom, from the people he was sworn to protect.

All because he was here to protect me.

CHAPTER 14

I knew that the Water territory would be vastly different than any other I'd seen before, but even in my wildest dreams, I didn't think I could have imagined something quite like this.

It was the morning after Easton and I had spoken next to the log without really looking at each other. We had all eaten a quick breakfast and then made our way towards the border. There hadn't been much of the camp to pack up since we all wanted to be able to move at a moment's notice. So, it was easy for us to just walk our way towards the border.

Although we were all on edge, on alert just in case the League came back, the path towards the entrance to the Water territory had been quite anticlimactic. Considering all the fighting that I had been dealing with since I first found out about the Maison realm, I was just fine with that.

But now we were standing at the border between the Spirit and Water

Beauty didn't even begin to describe what I saw. Stunning. Exquisite. Breathtaking. None of those words were quite right either. Nothing combined or separate could ever explain exactly what I saw before me. And I knew this was only the beginning. We were still at the border, no longer in the barren landscape of a territory that had once been full of people and magic. But now, we were entering an area that was unlike anything I'd ever seen or imagined.

"All I can say is…wow," I whispered and looked up as Easton tensed next to me. "Just, wow."

Easton shrugged and then looked over at the vast expanse in front of us. "It's the Lumière Kingdom. All Water and Air. That's their substance."

I elbowed him in the side. "Hey, I thought we were supposed to have peace between our kingdoms. We can't really do that if you're saying things like that."

"It's not my kingdom. But the Lumière Kingdom does know how to create a border."

He wasn't joking.

Right past the wards at the entrance to the Lumière Kingdom were cliff faces complete with waterfalls as far as you could see. The sound was overwhelming, and I actually had to shout over it in order to be able to speak to Easton. But it was worth it.

As the water crashed to the seas and lakes below, the mist rose up, and the sun hit it just right so there were rainbows everywhere you looked.

I had been to Niagara Falls on both the United States and the Canadian sides when I was younger, yet that had been nothing compared to what I saw now.

From what I could see, the entire border was one large set of waterfalls.

It was as if the land from the Spirit territory were ending and just poured into what would be the Water territory.

"Where does the water come from to make these waterfalls?" I asked since it seemed that they just came out of nowhere.

"It's part of the magic of the Water territory. Just like the other territories. Over time, their geographies changed to supplement the people and their Wielding. Or maybe it was the other way around. No one really knows, and it's just how it's always been for me. But the water begins here, though it's fed from the seas that you see in front of you as well as the crystal salt."

"The Lumière crystal."

"Of course. But despite the many spies I send, I still don't know the strength of that crystal compared to the one in the Obscurité Kingdom."

I narrowed my eyes at him. "Spies? Are you going to be a spy yourself this time?"

He just gave me a grin and then looked over to the vast expanse in front of us. "I could. But you'll never know for sure, will you?"

I just shook my head and looked in front of me. "It's just…wow." I kept repeating that word, but honestly, there wasn't much more I could say.

"If you say so," he said a little grumpily.

I had read that the Water territory was actually mostly made of seas, oceans, rivers and floating cities. There were a few actual land masses, including a large one far out west where the Water Estate was located. Plus, there was a long island that bisected the territory itself with small tributaries and rivers sliding through it to connect the two largest bodies of water.

It was insane how beautiful the area was. Everything was lush blues and purples with waves cresting as the wind picked up.

The waterfalls were reasonably tall, and I had no idea how we were going to get down to sea level, nor did I know how we were actually going to get to the Water Estate.

I looked at my bracelet and shook my wrist. "So, is this supposed to tell me where to go? Because it's not like I know if we can just swim over anywhere."

Easton snorted. "We'll find a boat. We always do."

"Yeah, remember that time we found that Viking-like vessel," Teagan said laughing. "I'm pretty sure my shoulders are still sore from all the rowing."

"Well, it didn't help that you were sitting the entire time and we all tried to ignore you." Wyn just smiled at him, even though we were all still on alert.

After all, we were now standing at the edge of a new territory.

I could feel the wards in front of me and knew we were technically still on the Spirit territory side. One step forward, and we'd be in a new kingdom.

"What we're going to do is get you to the Water Estate. That's the best place for you, even though it's on pretty much the exact opposite side of where we're standing right now." I once again turned to Easton as he spoke.

"And how are we going to do that?"

"Once we get through the wards, though it's not going to be easy considering none of us are Lumière, we're going to find a boat like I said. There are always small fishing vessels available. Though the smaller the boat we have, the harder it will be to actually cross this sea. But we'll get there."

"How are we going to get through the wards?"

Easton looked at me and shrugged. "The same way you got through *my* wards. There's a hole. We'll slide through, and then we'll just pray that no one's on the other side ready to catch us."

I held back a wince as my belly clenched at the memory of how we had gotten into the Earth territory. Or at least how I had gotten in with my other friends. It was as if I were running along parallels, yet everything was much different this time. I wasn't denying who I was anymore, even if I was still unsure of how to proceed. I also knew that there was far more riding on this than just searching for someone. I was looking for something more now.

Somehow, I also had to unlock my elements along the way, and I still didn't know how to do that. Hopefully, Rosamond would be able to help once I reached her. Because she was a Seer, and I always felt like she had this sense of knowing, of realizing exactly what I needed to do next...even if she told me she couldn't See it all.

"I guess we just need to get there."

"You'll be safe, Lyric. We'll get you to your friends. And then you can train."

I looked at him. Worry filled me as I tried to formulate words. "What about you? What about the rest of you? I knew you were going to get me to the Lumière Kingdom, but for some reason, I hoped someone would be here to meet us."

I had hoped that Rhodes would be here.

But he wasn't.

He wasn't ever going to be here for me in the way I hoped.

And I was oddly okay with that. At least in the sense that I wasn't pining for Rhodes like some lovesick schoolgirl. But that wasn't important now. What was important was the safety of my friends, and the path I needed to take.

"It would've been nice if loverboy would've been here for you, but he's not," Easton said, and I glared at him.

"Stop it. Just stop for a second."

"I really don't want to. We'll make it through these wards and get you to the estate. Then the others can figure out what that symbol lighting up on your bracelet means. And why you're here."

"And then you'll leave? You'll go back to the other kingdom and just leave me behind?" I knew the others were watching, and I wondered why I was pushing.

"I'll leave because I have a kingdom to run. But I'll make sure you're safe first."

I swallowed hard, trying to see exactly what was wrong with Easton. I could never read him, and it was worrying. We had come here because the Seer magic in my bracelet had told me I needed to go to the Spirit and Water territories, but that didn't mean we would be safe.

"We need to go before we lose the light."

Then Easton turned on his heel, and I followed him, wondering if I was once again making a mistake.

This time, the hole in the wards was far more visible to me than it had been when I first looked into the Earth territory. Maybe it was because I actually had two of my five elements now, or perhaps it was because I knew what to look for this time.

It was like a little seam, a tear in the wards themselves. You couldn't sense them, though, unlike the ones at the Earth territory. And these were opaque. I couldn't see through them at all into the Water territory itself.

But as we slid through the hole in the wards—Easton first and then Arwin, and then me—as if we were sliding through a hole in a chain-link fence, the hairs on the back of my neck stood on end, and I bumped right into Arwin.

Easton was in front of me in a flash, gripping my wrist.

As Wyn slid in behind me with Teagan following her, I knew we weren't alone.

The League stood there waiting for us, their faces shadowed in blue hoods, the water behind them churning as if they were using their Water Wielding.

None of us held that element.

I was the only one with a Lumière element at all. And I didn't know if it was going to help.

"You shouldn't have come here, Spirit Priestess," the man who I assumed was their leader sneered.

I stiffened and tried to pull myself from Easton's hold, but he didn't let go.

"You shouldn't be here. You should have stayed in your precious little human realm away from all of this. This doesn't concern you. It's far bigger than you could ever know, little girl."

I remembered when Easton had called me *little girl* once upon a time, and I had hated it. This time, it felt like bile was rising up my throat until my skin crawled.

Because these people weren't just teasing, and they weren't going to help me.

No, they clearly wanted me dead. And I didn't know why.

"Who do you work for?" Easton asked, his voice low. From the way the others were looking at him, the League didn't know that they were actually talking to the King of Obscurité. And for that, I was grateful. The glamour seemed to be holding.

While these warriors obviously didn't want me here as the Spirit Priestess, even though they had walked right past us before without hurting me, they would likely be up in arms if they found out that the King of Obscurité was in their midst.

This was a dangerous game. Easton shouldn't have come.

If he got hurt because of me, I would never forgive myself.

But as I looked at the thirty or so men and possibly women in cloaks in front of me, I worried that I wouldn't make it through this to be sorry at all.

"The King of Lumière sends his regards," the first man said and then lifted his arms. A wall of seawater lifted behind him.

I knew these were all Water Wielders, but I hadn't really seen Water Wielding in action as much as the others. Rhodes might have used it before, but he used Air more than Water, at least in front of me. The magic was smooth, a dance of beauty. Each of the Wielders lifted their hands, and more parts of the sea behind them rose, swirling into a vortex before dancing in the air.

They were waiting for us, and I didn't know what to say.

What to do.

The King of Lumière wanted me dead?

Or maybe this was all just a ruse.

After all, the knight of the Obscurité had framed the queen, Easton's mother, so the world had thought she wanted me dead. He had made it appear that she had been the one to kidnap Rosamond and orchestrate everything.

But Queen Cameo had wanted me alive. She'd wanted me to help save her kingdom and then the realm.

And she had died for that wish.

So, maybe it wasn't the king at all. Perhaps it wasn't Rhodes' uncle. Maybe it was just these men or another puppet master at work.

I didn't know, but I didn't have any time to think about it either.

Because the first man moved.

And I screamed.

CHAPTER 15

They came at us in waves. Literal. Waves.

I had never seen such brutality in something that was meant to be so beautiful.

When I was younger, I had been fascinated with the waves on a beach much like I had been fascinated with the undulations of flame. Although fire had always called to me more, water had still pulled me. But then again, so did a gentle breeze and the feeling of the earth between my fingers as I planted seeds.

All those moments, all of those elements when I had thought I was only human came at me so fast, it was as if I saw my life flash before my eyes. I had been drawn to the elements without even knowing that was what called to me.

But right then, it wasn't about Fire or Air or Earth.

It was about Water and how it came at us, in one swift blade of death.

demise, and destruction.

It wasn't a trickle.

It wasn't a *drip, drip, drip.*

It was a *wave.*

And though we all threw up our hands, using our Wielding to try and protect ourselves and each other, it wasn't enough.

Arwin and Wyn both raised their hands up high, a wave of Earth blocking some of the initial impact of the Water.

The ground beneath me shuddered, and I pushed my hands forward, palms out, to lend my own strength and Earth Wielding.

I was stronger than Arwin, but not as skilled as Wyn yet.

But I thought maybe I could help.

Sweat dripped down my brow as the wave, a massive tsunami, started to crawl over the wall of Earth that we had made.

Easton cursed under his breath and added his own Wielding to ours. This time, flames danced up the wall. When Teagan joined Easton, the flames leapt and evaporated some of the water coming at us, but it wasn't going to be enough.

Although fire could heat water, water doused flame.

And while I added my own Air Wielding to the mix of Earth and Air to try and lift up some of Easton's Fire, it wasn't enough.

The earth trembled and caved in.

And then the water was on us.

Easton grabbed me by the waist and tossed me to the side as the initial wave slammed into the others. I landed on my hands and knees, both grateful and annoyed that he'd been so quick to move me out of the way. By the time I got to my feet, I was shaking, and my hands were dirty and bloody from the impact.

With so many powerful Water Wielders pitted against us, I wasn't sure how we were going to survive this. I wasn't sure who this League was.

Nor did I know what they truly wanted.

What I did know was what I *didn't* know. Whether our efforts would be enough.

I only had a second to glimpse Wyn, her dark hair blowing around her face from the sudden gust of air made by the wave crashing to the ground in front of us.

And then she was swept away, her eyes wide as she looked over at me, her mouth parted. She couldn't even let out a scream as she was knocked off her feet. And I couldn't see where she had gone.

I reached out to her, but then Easton was suddenly in front of me, his hands up, creating another wave of Earth Wielding.

"Stop panicking and *do* something. We just need to get through the first assault, and then we can get to the League. But *do something*, Lyric."

The sharp rasp of Easton's words was like a slap, and I was thankful for them.

I had never seen anything like this before, and it had rattled me to the point that I was making mistakes. I wasn't focusing on how to protect us. Instead, I was focusing on how we were all going to die because we weren't strong enough.

But that was a mistake. And I knew it.

So, I nodded at Easton and let out a breath. "Okay. What can I do?"

He glanced at me, an odd look in his eyes. I didn't know if he was proud of me or honestly just tired of me. Because I knew I hadn't been helping.

"Arwin is searching for Wyn. Teagan is going to work with Fire. I'll work with Earth. You work with Air, we'll do what we can. Just breathe, Lyric. Keep fighting. No matter what."

I glanced over my shoulder just for a moment to see where Arwin was running down the side of the newly-made river through the Spirit territory.

Somehow, the Water Wielders had changed the landscape of the territory itself as they kept sending wave after wave at us.

Easton threw up one arm and pushed out his palm, and then whipped up the other. Each time a new wall of Earth Wielding slammed into the wave of Water Wielding, the resulting mess was mud, a slosh that made a sickening sound as it slammed back to the ground. It made an almost sucking sound as if it were going into a vacuum as the water receded into the earth.

And then they were at it again, the elements slamming into one another.

I added my Air Wielding to both Easton's on one side, and Teagan's on my other.

My Air slid under the Earth wall that Easton made, lifting it a little higher so it could slam over the Water wave like a cap, bringing it down to the ground with a nearly deafening splat.

And then I used my other arm, splitting my resources to lift the Fire that Teagan Wielded towards the water itself.

Yes, the water doused the flame, but not before it was forced to stop due to the sheer heat of the fire.

Even as I worked, I noticed that my Wielding worked better with Easton's than it did Teagan's. Was it because Easton was the king and therefore stronger? Or was it just because I had worked with Easton like this before? I didn't know. All I could do was keep moving, one palm out and the other raised to the sky.

My left palm faced the Earth mound that Easton Wielded, my right palm turned up as I moved both arms so I could help both men with their Wielding. I had learned this from the others. Even from reading the book that Rosamond had given me. Yet it wasn't enough.

My arms shook, and the power within me felt like it wouldn't be enough.

And still, the Water Wielders kept moving closer.

One step. A wave.

Another step. A wave.

And then another.

And another.

The water receded before coming at us once more.

And I screamed again.

The waves slammed into us, breaking through our defenses.

Wyn was back, somehow making it to the front of the battle with Arwin at her side. But she was screaming since we were now in a sea of our own, no longer standing on the Spirit territory side, but within the wave itself.

We were drowning, suffocating, and I didn't know how to save us.

Teagan swam through the white caps, shouting as he tried to get to Wyn.

She had one arm up in the waves, trying to keep afloat as she used her other to hold Arwin up. The young Earth Wielder had somehow been knocked out. Blood ran down his face from a large gash on his head.

There were rocks and stones in the water, not from our Earth Wielding but from the sheer velocity and force of the wave the water had created when it slammed into the Spirit territory's land.

I was treading water, trying to stop swallowing buckets full as each wave slammed into us.

I didn't feel strong enough, I felt like we were losing.

Another wave came at us, and I wondered if the Water Wielders were actually going to use the entire sea of the Water territory itself to drown us.

Another small swell came at me from behind, surprising me, and I went under.

Easton's screams reverberated in my ears, and I looked underwater, my eyes wide even as they burned.

I couldn't see much, only wave after wave, the dark blues mixing with the turquoises and light blues of the sea itself.

There wasn't rain, wasn't any actual wind other than what the waves themselves made.

So the sunlight coming directly from both territories stabbed into the water, creating a kaleidoscope of colors under the surface.

I could see Teagan thrashing as he swam towards Wyn and Arwin.

And I saw Easton reaching for me, trying to come to me, but the League seemed to know that we needed each other.

Because they sent more Water at us, more Wielding to separate us.

I couldn't breathe.

My lungs burned, and my whole body shook as I tried to swim to the surface, only to be pulled down deeper.

The pressure made my ears pop and my eyes hurt, but I kept kicking, kept reaching for the surface. I was afraid I was going to die here.

That I was going to drown.

Terrified that I wouldn't survive to do what others thought I could.

I would never find out what the true prophecy meant. I would never find out what the other three elements felt like.

I would become nothing, and all because these Wielders were more powerful than I was. I wasn't enough.

I reached up, trying to find a way to the surface, trying to suck in air even though there was nothing for me to breathe.

I didn't have gills, I couldn't magically become a fish or a mermaid like Braelynn had become a cat. I could do none of that.

I wasn't a Water Wielder, and I didn't know how to create an Air bubble to breathe underwater like I had read some Air Wielders could do.

I could do none of that.

I was dying. Drowning.

Another wave hit, and I was suddenly thrust up into the air, just enough that I could gasp a breath, choking as I spit up water, the action sending hot pokers down my throat. And then I was slammed back under again, only this time, I wasn't alone.

All of my friends were underwater, as well. Each of them trying to use their Wielding to protect themselves.

But we couldn't do it, not on this border, and not with so many fighting against us.

They wanted us to die.

They wanted *me* to die.

And then something inside me snapped. Not like the other times, not when it was like a lock clicking into place.

No, this was as if the lock itself had shattered, not into a million pieces but just enough that I could feel water trickling out of the crevices, filling my body as if I had been empty before.

My fingers tingled, and my eyes opened. Suddenly, I wasn't drowning anymore.

I was the Spirit Priestess.

I would protect those who couldn't defend themselves.

But first, I needed to save myself. I needed to rescue my friends.

While I was still underwater, and even though my lungs were on fire since I needed oxygen to breathe, I held out my hands and screamed.

It was as if a volcano had erupted beneath the waves and I was at the center.

Bubbles rose from my skin in rapid succession as if I were boiling, but I wasn't hot, wasn't even warm. In fact, I knew my lips probably had to be blue at this point, my body was so cold I was shivering, but it didn't matter.

I had unlocked my third element.

I was Air. Earth. And now I was Water.

I could fight back.

And the League would lose.

I knew I was probably going to use too much power, I was already using too much just by staying under the waves. But I would survive, and it would be enough.

It had to be enough.

I pushed out my hands, my palms facing forward, my fingers spread, and the water moved.

I had no idea what I was doing, but I was operating on instinct, and I just *knew* that this was right.

The Air and the Earth and the Water mixed within me, fighting each other for dominance, smashing into one another.

I didn't know how to fix that right now, but I knew that control would come.

First, though, I had to make sure my friends stayed alive, and then I had to destroy those who had come to kill us.

There was no sense of what was right or wrong just then. There were only the elements, the Water itself. I could hear it screaming in my ears, a siren's song shouting at me that I had to obliterate those who had come to murder us. Who'd come to drown us.

I knew that there were other ways to Wield Water. Ones that could tear the moisture from your skin and your actual cells. But these Wielders hadn't done that.

They had used sheer force and brutality. Therefore, I would do the same.

And they would fear me.

I didn't know where those thoughts had come from or even if they were mine, but it didn't matter right now.

I pushed the water away, back at the Water Wielders.

They were screaming, shouting.

The heat around me burned.

It wasn't from Fire Wielding, though. It wasn't even from within myself.

It was from the sheer power and beauty of the Wielding.

My eyes were open, but I didn't blink.

The League members looked at each other and then me, their arms outstretched as they tried to move the water back, but they were never going to be strong enough. Not at this first show of Wielding, not with my first temptation of the darkness. The abyss.

I pushed out, slamming the water that they had used against us at them.

They screamed. They writhed. They reached out, trying to control what they had once been able to touch and Wield, but they couldn't do it anymore because the water was mine.

All of this was mine. The world around me would be mine, and they would call out to me in infamy. They would beg for forgiveness and mercy. But it would never be enough.

Arwin was still on the ground, bleeding and unconscious. Wyn had him cradled in her arms, trying to resuscitate him. I didn't know if he was alive or dead.

The League would pay for that.

Teagan was standing above her, his arms outstretched and Fire dancing along his skin as he readied to use his Wielding. But he wouldn't have to. Because I would be the one to destroy those who came at us.

Easton stood apart from me, staring at me as if he had never seen me before.

He hadn't, not like this.

Because I was the Spirit Priestess, and this was my power.

I lashed out at the Water Wielders, and they screamed. They drowned. They couldn't fight back.

And then…they were gone.

Dead, by my hands. As they should be.

As quickly as the power had come, it slid away from me, shocking me back to reality, into the cold.

I blinked, my teeth chattering as I looked up at Easton.

"What? What just happened?" I asked as I fell to my knees, my whole body shaking, my bones rattling, my soul…empty. Yet not.

Water surged out of my pores as if it were seeping from my body itself.

Air seemed to puff out of my fingertips violently and sporadically. I couldn't control it.

The earth shuddered beneath my feet, cracking in some places. I looked up at Easton, trying to control my power.

Those thoughts earlier hadn't been mine. I knew that now. None of that had been mine. Sure, the Wielding had been, but none of the rest. It'd been too much, and somehow, I had broken.

I didn't *want* to kill. I'd only wanted to protect those who needed it.

But I had done it.

I had used power. So much. And I couldn't control it.

Somehow, something had changed within me. And even in those few moments, I didn't like it.

"Lyric. Shut it down. Control it."

Easton shouted at me, but tears just poured down my face, a mixture of air and dirt and water, all my Wielding. I was scared.

"I can't. I…can't."

"Lyric. Do it." And then he was in front of me, gripping my shoulders.

I pulled away.

I was terrified. I was going to kill them all. I couldn't control it. Those thoughts I'd had before, hadn't been mine. The feelings weren't mine. Or maybe they were, somewhere deep down. It was all too much. I couldn't do this.

I couldn't do any of it. I felt like I was going to blow. Crack. I wasn't going to make it.

None of this had been mine before, but now this was mine to take.

This was my consequence.

And I couldn't handle it.

I couldn't control it.

I could do nothing.

CHAPTER 16

My body felt as if it were breaking, shattering from the inside out. Every inch of me ached, burned, then cooled and heated again.

I couldn't control the power within me. I felt as if it were trying to control me instead. I had no idea where that voice inside me had come from. Had no idea what I was going to do about it.

But I was afraid that if I didn't find a way to release all of this excess energy and figure out how to control what was inside me, currently breaking me apart piece by piece, cell by cell, it wouldn't matter that I didn't know.

Because nothing would matter, and I wouldn't be here anymore.

I looked over to where Wyn and Arwin sat on the ground, both of them bleeding. Teagan stood over them, trying to help them up.

Arwin was at least blinking now, so he was alive.

But whatever sense of relief I got from that was gone quickly.

Because all I could do was focus on the fact that I couldn't breathe. That my hands were shaking, and I couldn't stop the elements within me from trying to break free.

Easton came towards me, leaning in even farther, whispering to me—though he could be shouting for all I knew. "Breathe, Lyric. Just push through it. Focus."

"I can't," I called out. "I can't. I can't do anything. Why won't it stop? The two were working just fine. Why is three so much?"

"Because it's different. It will always be different. They're layered on top of one another. It amplifies the effect of all. But we're going to get you out of this. Just breathe."

Panic slammed into me, choking me, gripping my throat and heart until I couldn't handle anything but Easton's voice. "I can't. It's too much. The water…it's falling from me. Why can't I stop it?"

I was still on my knees, shaking. I looked down at my skin and sucked in a breath.

Water poured from my pores as if I were drowning from the inside out.

I could feel it dripping from my hair, but not because I'd been doused in water, because it was coming from my actual scalp.

My Air Wielding continued to puff out of my fingertips, even out of my elbows and my shoulders. My knees and toes.

I was a teapot, set on steam, and I couldn't stop it.

The earth around me still shook, large crevices spreading out from my fingertips as I dug them into the soil.

Mud sloshed every time I hiccupped a sob. I tried to control it and spit out more water, more dirt, more air.

I didn't know where it was all coming from. I didn't know how to control any of it. I was choking on my own elements, on my own Wielding.

And I feared I would hurt everyone around me because I couldn't stop it.

Easton reached for me again, and I scrambled back and shakily got to my feet. I held up my hands and shook my head.

"No. Don't touch me. If you do, I could break. I could hurt you. Do something. I need to…I need to go. I can't be here. I'm going to kill you all." And then I ran.

I ran towards the edge of the Spirit territory where we had been before.

Everything looked different now, at least from this side. There was mud everywhere, broken pieces of ground where the water had latched onto it.

But we were still on a cliff. I could sense the waterfalls all around us.

Far ahead, the sea was calm as if there hadn't been over a dozen Wielders trying to kill us moments ago. Trying to drown us.

But it didn't matter now.

They were dead.

And I was going to die. From my own Wielding, not theirs.

They hadn't killed me. I was going to kill myself.

The ground rattled beneath my feet, each stone starting to fall, pebble by pebble.

The water right below where I stood started to thrash, and I swallowed hard, my hair blowing in a wind of my own creation.

I couldn't control it. Why was everything so amplified?

I had been fine with Earth and Air, even though those two weren't connected and were of separate kingdoms.

Why was Water so much harder?

I cried out, my body convulsing.

This was it. Maybe I wasn't the true Spirit Priestess. Perhaps the elements had been wrong. The prophecy flawed. I was going to die.

Suddenly, strong arms were around me.

Easton pulled me to his chest and ran his hands over my hair as he whispered in my ear.

"You're fine. Just breathe. Lean into me. *Trust me*. I've got you. I've got you, Lyric. No matter what happens. *I've got you.*"

Easton held me as the trembling racked my body. Air slammed into him through me, and I cried out. But he didn't move, didn't scream. He just took the elements I gave him. Took the pounding of pain and fury.

I shook, tears falling down my face. I hated feeling so weak. But I wasn't strong enough to control this. I clearly wasn't the right person for the job. This was too much.

Water started to pool around us, coming from the sea as my Wielding spun out of control once more.

It slammed into Easton's back and then into our sides, but still, he didn't move.

"I've got you, Lyric. Just breathe. Focus. I've got you."

He repeated those words over and over again, and I tried to hold on. I believed him. But it was hard.

I couldn't breathe. Couldn't focus.

Then Easton ran his hands through my hair, despite the gusts of wind slamming into us. He pulled me closer, so close I could feel every inch of him, and I took a deep breath. All of a sudden, I didn't sense the elements.

I just sensed the Fire within him, the Earth as well, but mostly the Fire.

And the king he was.

Just Easton.

I could breathe.

As the water slowly began to recede, and the earth quit its shaking, I let out a breath.

The air around us stilled, calming.

I let out more breath.

Easton didn't stop speaking to me. Didn't stop whispering.

Because he had me.

I could breathe.

As I sank to my knees, leaning deeper into his hold, he didn't let me fall. Instead, he caught me and lowered down with me. And I cried in his arms.

It was too much.

I had killed those men. And I hadn't even thought twice about it.

Whatever voice had surged up inside of me, whatever power had taken over, I hadn't been strong enough to withstand or control it.

I had let the elements rule me, and I had almost failed. I had nearly hurt and killed those who were there to protect me. If it hadn't been for Easton, if it weren't for his calming force, I likely would have lost control of it all.

And so, I wept. I grieved for so much.

For the fact that this was my life now. That I still had no idea what was going to happen next. I wept for Brae. I cried for Rhodes, a boy I would never have. Someone I wasn't sure I even wanted anymore. I wept for the life I once had. I mourned my parents who no longer remembered me.

I wept for it all.

And then when there were no more tears to cry, I sucked in a ragged breath and pushed away from Easton.

I shoved away because I was scared. Because I didn't know what to say.

I rose to my feet, shaky but not as much as I had been before.

Easton stood too, in one graceful move. It was as if he had practiced it for hundreds of years. Perhaps he had.

"Lyric?" he asked, his voice softer than I had ever heard it. He didn't look like the boy who had smirked at me. Didn't look like the boy who had yelled at me to try and teach me.

He just looked like Easton. The one who had held me when I broke. The one who comforted me when I cried.

"I'm not the right person. How can I be the Spirit Priestess if I can't handle three elements? How am I supposed to handle five? I'm not the right person."

"You are, Lyric."

"No. I can't be. If I was, I wouldn't have broken like that. I'm weak. I'm not strong enough."

Easton stormed towards me, closing the two steps between us. He loomed over me, anger on his face. "Yes, you are. Now, shut up."

And then he kissed me, so hard and fast I could barely understand what was happening.

His hands were suddenly on my face as he brought his mouth to mine. I sucked in a breath at the feeling of soft lips against my own.

He was kissing me.

Easton was kissing me.

And it felt...right. It felt like everything had been coming to a thousand times of needs, a thousand times of wants.

It was something I'd never had before, a kiss that didn't make any sense. No, I couldn't kiss Easton.

What was wrong with me?

I pushed him away, shaking my head. "I can't." I sucked in a breath. "What was that?"

I looked at him as he glowered at me. "You know what that was. What it's always been." Each word was uttered with a growl, and my eyes widened.

"Are you saying you're my...?"

I couldn't finish the sentence, couldn't say anything more. I just looked at Easton. And I knew. I knew what he could be to me. I knew what that feeling inside of me was and had always been. Why I had been drawn to the boy with Fire. Why I didn't understand exactly what I felt for Rhodes and why it was so different with Easton.

I looked at him. I could still taste him on my lips. Feel how swollen mine were.

And I knew.

That connection between us.

There was something.

But I had no idea what to do about it.

Before I could do or say anything more, Easton lifted his head and pulled me behind him.

Suddenly, Teagan, Wyn, and Arwin were at our sides, pointedly looking at me.

They had seen everything, had seen me break, had seen me fall, and had seen Easton kiss me.

They had seen it all.

But no one was paying attention to me now.

Because I wasn't the important one here.

No, that was the Water Wielders coming at us, this time on a ship, surfing on a wave made from Wielding as they came towards us nearest the lowest waterfall.

I could see them in their blue robes, their strong features that spoke of ages past. I could sense the power within them.

And I had just killed others like them. I didn't want to do it again.

"Remember," Easton growled, "I'm just a Wielder. Don't call me by name." He was still under his glamour. The others couldn't know he was the king.

I looked at him and swallowed hard.

I couldn't think. And I needed to focus. Not on him but on the task at hand.

"Are you Lyric?" one of the men asked as he stepped off the boat and onto a rock nearest the edge of the waterfall. "Rosamond sent us. We are the guards of the Lord of Water. It's time to take you to your friends."

Easton stiffened ever so slightly, but I didn't lean into him. I didn't do anything. I just looked at those in front of us. Those with a connection to my friends.

And I knew this was why we had come. Why the Water charm on my bracelet still warmed.

This was why we were here. To get to the Lord of Water.

Rosamond, the Seer, had Seen me. She had sent for me. Rhodes had sent for me.

Now, we were ready for the next task.

I just had to push away everything that had just happened recently so I could focus.

No matter how hard it was. No matter how much my mind wanted to rebel.

Because I was the Spirit Priestess, even if I couldn't control the power within me. Even if I might die because of it.

But others were relying on me. I couldn't focus on feelings or connections right now. I had to concentrate on strength.

Even if sometimes I felt like I had none.

CHAPTER 17

To get to the Water Estate with the Lord of Water's guards, we had to travel over the sea. Unlike the Earth territory when the Lord of Fire had sent us in a caravan, and we took turns hiking and sometimes using the wagons, this time, we were on a ship.

A huge wooden vessel not powered by mere sails or oars or even the mechanics of an engine one could find in the human realm. Instead, the Water Wielders used their powers to guide the ship through the water towards their destination. The ship still had sails, so unless they were just for show, I figured they were used at times with Air, though no one mentioned it.

As Air and Water were allies, it kind of made the lack of mention odd.

Of course, I didn't really know the situation within the Lumière Kingdom. I only knew bits and pieces from what Rhodes, Luken, and Rosamond had told me, and from what I had read in the history book that Rosamond had given me.

But that had been more about the Fall and the mechanics of Wielding rather than the current climate within the kingdoms.

I knew more about the Obscurité Kingdom than I did the Lumière now. Maybe that should have worried me, but it didn't. Because there was still so much to learn when it came to both kingdoms as well as the Spirit territory that lay between them.

Once the lord's guards had taken us to the ship, things had moved quickly. The Water charm on my bracelet kept heating up, so I knew we were going the right way, even if it felt like I was doing something that could irrevocably change my life. It seemed everything was changing my life these days.

The guards hadn't even introduced themselves by name. Instead, they had put one fist over their hearts, crossing their bodies with their arms as they bowed their heads regally. And they had done this to me and no one else. I didn't really know how I felt about that.

They called me the Spirit Priestess, and they rarely used my name when addressing me. I was just a title, their prophecy.

Maybe I needed to stop thinking things like that. It was just going to stress me out more than I already was, and we were on our way somewhere I had never been before.

It was odd to think that we were amongst people we didn't know, going to a place we didn't know, and yet I knew it was the right thing to do. Just like Wyn knew it was right because of her emotional Seeing.

Not that there was an actual title or term for that. But I trusted when Wyn had feelings about things.

Of course, just because someone believed they were telling the truth didn't mean they actually were. It depended on what they thought true at the time they were speaking. That was what Wyn could read, those moments. At least if we put our faith in the talent that Wyn might have.

We weren't a hundred percent sure that it was actually a gift, but we still followed it. That and the indications of the bracelet on my wrist.

"Do you ever have a feeling that you're here not as a guest but as something or someone who isn't really allowed to go anywhere else?" Wyn asked, her voice just a whisper in my ear.

We stood on the deck of the ship, all five of us surrounded by the lord's guard.

"Well, now that you mention it," I whispered back, my shoulders tightening. "I mean, we aren't prisoners, right?" I asked, my voice so low I was afraid Wyn wouldn't be able to hear me. It wasn't like we had any privacy on the deck, not really. None of us had been invited below deck, nor had we been given any accommodations or sustenance other than some water and bread. We had declined it all, stating that we had our own rations. I didn't know if that had been the wrong thing to do or maybe the perfect response.

It didn't matter that I was a Spirit Priestess and was supposed to be part of each kingdom. It mattered that the people I was traveling with were not from this kingdom. They were not supposed to be here at all, and yet the guard had told them to come with me.

I didn't know what was going to happen next, or if my new friends were in any danger. I just had to hope that once we got to wherever we were going, Rhodes, Luken, and Rosamond would make sure that my new friends were safe. After all, we were all fighting for the same purpose now. Right?

"I don't know, Lyric, but keep your guard up. I've never actually been to where we're going, so it's all just as new for me as it is to you."

I looked over at Wyn, my eyes slightly wide. "Really? I would have thought all of you would have found your way into the other kingdom at some point."

"Oh, I've been to the Air territory a couple of times, as well as to the border between the two within the Lumière Kingdom, but I've only ever been to the waterfalls that we passed that create the border between the Spirit and Water territories. It wasn't like I didn't want to go, but my orders usually took me to the other side. Teagan has been here, though. As has Easton." She winced and looked over her shoulder. Thankfully, no one was listening to us or even making any sudden moves as if they had heard. "I mean, Frederic."

I rolled my eyes and smiled. Easton was going by *Frederic* at the moment, and it was hilarious. Easton did not look like a Frederic at all, and he was the only one who was actually good at remembering that was his new name. All of us kept slipping up even though there wasn't anything funny about what would happen if those of the Lumière Kingdom found out that it was actually Easton and not just an Obscurité Wielder named Frederic with us.

"Anyway," Wyn began, speaking quickly. "Arwin hasn't been here either. So, we'll take in the sights. We'll figure out what you're supposed to do—prophecy and all."

"I hate the unknown. I hate that I feel like I'm right on the verge of something that's important, but it's not really making any sense. It's a little too much. You know?"

"I know exactly what you mean. Well, maybe not *exactly* since I'm not actually unlocking Wielding like you are, but…three out of five? That's a lot. And you're getting there."

I swallowed hard and looked down at my hands, at the power beneath my skin. We were surrounded by water on all sides, a vast sea of nothingness. And it called to me. A siren song as if it begged me to start using my Wielding. Tempting me to train.

But I couldn't. Not right then.

I was afraid of what could happen if I did. Would I be able to control it? Would I be able to use my Air and Earth at the same time without breaking down or being overwhelmed?

I never wanted to feel like I had felt when my body was breaking down. Or worse, how I was when it felt as if something had taken over my mind and I wasn't strong enough to fight back.

And I had been able to get out of it because of Easton.

And that scared me. Maybe even more than the power itself.

Because I couldn't let myself rely on him. I didn't know what his motivations were, and I didn't know what he felt about me.

But I could remember the feeling when we had spoken when he kissed me. I remembered the fact that I had felt a connection to him, even if I shouldn't.

I was afraid that he was the one person that could mean the most to me. Even if I didn't know what to do about it.

"What are we talking about over here, ladies?" Easton said as he came over.

"Just the sights," Wyn said. "What do you think, Frederic? Enjoying all the water?"

Easton gave us a look and just rolled his eyes. A smile played on his lips, and for that I was grateful. Because if he could at least retain some humor in the situation, maybe it wasn't all that bad. Perhaps we weren't prisoners on our way to another dungeon like I had been during my previous trip to the Maison realm.

It was starting to really get on my nerves that every time someone found out that we were entering a new territory, we were taken directly to the lord's estate against our will.

Yes, I wanted to eventually visit them all and try to unlock my elements as I unearthed the prophecy, but that didn't mean I wanted to be forced into any of it.

Although it seemed I didn't have much choice.

"Just wait until you see what's below the water."

I looked up at Easton and frowned. "What do you mean? I mean, there has to be like fish and things, but what are you actually talking about?"

He just shook his head and then put his hand on the small of my back, gently pushing me towards the edge of the ship. Wyn took a discreet step back and then another before she was slowly walking away towards Teagan and Arwin.

I noticed her giving me a strange look, leaving me alone with Easton, and I wondered what that was about. Because I still hadn't had a chance to talk to her about the fact that I had kissed Easton. They had all seen it, and nobody was talking about it. Everyone was doing an excellent job of not talking about it.

And maybe that should worry me.

"Look over there," Easton said, his voice low, barely a whisper against my ear. I shivered at the sensation of his breath on my neck and wondered why he was doing this to me. Because I had more important things to worry about than whether or not Easton was my soulmate.

Apparently, I had to save the world.

I didn't have time for boys. Or girls.

"What am I supposed to be looking for?"

"Look directly at the horizon, and then just watch."

I looked where Easton pointed and did as he told me to, and then my mouth dropped open.

A large bird, far bigger than a pelican or anything I had ever seen, dove down into the water and came up with a fish.

Only this fish seemed to have two tails. It slid down the gullet of the bird.

"Is that an albatross?" I asked, trying to remember the name of the large bird from the human realm.

"No, but it's similar. Here, our birds are slightly bigger."

"What's it called?"

"A cascade, or at least, that's what *we* call it. The Water Wielders may have another name for them. But it's quite big, and it has been known to try and eat small children—and even Wielders who don't really know how to fight back."

I froze and looked up at him. "You're just kidding with me, right?"

He shrugged, pushing a piece of hair behind my ear. I had it in a long braid down my back, but tendrils kept coming loose.

"I wish I was. They don't usually come near ships though because large groups of people are too much for them. But if you were alone and playing out in the water and one happened to come near you? I'd use my Wielding. Or I'd run. Really fast."

I tore my gaze away from him and looked where the cascade dove again into the water and picked up another fish with two tails. "That thing's huge."

"Yep. But don't worry, you're safe here. Well, safe enough. And not all fish here have two tails, that's just one of the special ones. They come up to the top to get some sunlight since they don't really like being in the dark, but in doing so, they're ripe for the cascades' pickings. So, they have to be careful and usually form large schools even though most fish that big don't form schools. But, that's just the Water territory. Weird yet beautiful at the same time."

I looked up at him and frowned. "I never would have thought you'd say anything in the Lumière Kingdom is beautiful."

He shook his head, his gaze focused off in the distance. "You can think something's beautiful and yet know it's not for you. Know that it's dangerous for you and that it doesn't want you. That it will do anything it can to keep you away. So, yes, the Lumière Kingdom is beautiful, but it's not for me."

I had the strangest feeling that he wasn't exactly talking about the Lumière Kingdom anymore, but I didn't broach the subject. I didn't say anything at all. Instead, I stood in front of Easton with his hands on either side of me on the railing and did my best not to lean back into him.

The guards sometimes gave us curious looks but didn't say anything. And for that, I was grateful.

All I could do was watch the realm that was not mine pass me by and try to take in all I could.

It was so different from anything I'd ever seen before. And wonderful.

"Look at that," Easton said, his voice soft. "But don't make too sudden a movement."

I tilted my head to him and studied where he pointed, and then sucked in a sharp breath. "Was that a tentacle?" I asked, my voice a little shaky.

"That was either a giant squid or a Kraken. The Wielders are on top of it, though. That's why we're shifting just slightly west. We should be safe, but I would keep that new Water Wielding power of yours handy."

I swallowed hard. "A Kraken? Like...like a real Kraken?" I shook, trying to figure out what to say.

A Kraken. Mythological creatures that could take down ships and break them in half with just their tentacles. The creature men in armor yelled to release when they were at war in the movies. The same creature that would ultimately eat them just like a large octopus would. I tried to keep my breathing steady, but I was having a hard time of it. Easton snorted and rubbed my shoulder. That just sent my breath into another fit, and I wondered again what I was doing.

"We're safe. It's not as close as it looks. If it was going to get us, we wouldn't be able to see it first. They come up from below and wrap their tentacles around the sides of the boat, breaking it in half before pulling it under along with the crew. So, the fact that we can see it at all means it's just letting us know it's there and it's not going to attack."

"You know, I don't really feel that much more reassured."

"Well, I'm doing my best here. We may have things in our kingdom that can kill you, but I swear it's the things that are beneath the surface that seem a little more dangerous. You know?"

Oh, I knew. I was still a little too stressed out to focus on anything else.

Easton continued to show me different animals and sea life as we traveled through the Water territory. The others came up to us at some point to listen, and then we all just stood there, taking in the territory that wasn't ours.

There were whales, more birds, and even dolphins. Everything just looked slightly off from the human realm, as if magic and evolution had altered things ever so slightly. And from all the stories that Easton was telling me, I knew I really didn't want to get in the water and swim.

Because, no matter what, I would always wonder if the Kraken would come at me from below. Or a cascade would come at me from above.

Either way, the Water territory seemed far more dangerous now, and we weren't even in the part where there was land, and we could discuss politics.

Because I had a feeling that was going to be the hardest—and scariest— part.

Because while animals were dangerous, you could see their true natures. People? Not so much.

We had already been attacked more than once on our journey here, and I had killed to protect my friends and myself.

And though we were visiting the Lord of Water, he still answered to another. His brother, the King of Lumière.

The same regent who might have sent others to kill me.

So, I didn't know what we were going to face, but I was glad I wasn't alone.

Even if it was dangerous for them, I was glad they had come.

Because our journey was only just beginning. I was sure that what was to come would be just as deadly.

CHAPTER 18

Unlike in the Earth territory, or even any of the other territories we had been in, it only took a day to traverse the sea.

I didn't think it was because the Water territory was any smaller than the others. In fact, from what I had read, each territory had the same square mileage as any of the others. It was just that the Water Wielders pushed us across the sea at such an incredible speed that we moved faster. I didn't think any of the other territories had the means to do that. With the exception of moving via Wielding and the crystal, of course. Like Easton had done to transport us to the court to meet his mother.

Maybe the Air territory had similar means, but I didn't know how they traveled their lands.

It wasn't like the Fire territory could send you along a wave of flame. The same with the Earth territory. There wasn't just a mound of dirt that could

I thought back to what I had read in Rosamond's book and tried to remember exactly how each of the territories had been formed.

Not much was known about the history spanning the centuries before the Fall. Just the fact that as each set of Wielders started to intermate and have children with either dual powers or just one strong power, the land began to look like the magic that was centered in that area. Some scholars thought the land had always looked like that, and the Wielders sprang from that.

I wasn't sure, but given the fact that every territory was almost the exact same size, I had a feeling that either the magic had wanted everything to be even, or someone had made that happen, and then everything else had come from that. I didn't know for sure, and it wasn't like I would ever be able to find out. Not really. But it was still interesting to me to imagine how things had been formed.

Even when I was in the human realm, I had liked to know how cities rose up where they were and why things had evolved as they had.

A thousand different decisions could make a city. Millions of choices and steps.

It seemed to be the same within the Maison realm.

Now was one of those choices. A decision.

As soon as we hit the land mass where the estate had been built, the Water charm on my bracelet tingled again. I stood straighter.

I could feel the hairs on the back of my neck rise, and I knew we were about to enter the land of some powerful Wielders.

The land where I hoped Rhodes was.

He might be in the royal court for all I knew, and that was at the center of the entire realm, across the way from the Obscurité Court. Rhodes had told me once that he had rooms there and sometimes stayed with his uncle and cousin.

I didn't know if he would be there now, or what I would say to him when I saw him.

Because the thing of it was, I wasn't the same person I had been when I first met him. Nor was I the same person who took that journey with him.

I wasn't even the same person I had been when I woke up from death and realized that he wasn't mine.

Because there was something different inside me now, some power that I was still trying to find and understand.

Plus a connection that I wasn't ready to talk about.

A bond with the boy at my side. A king.

The king who was in hiding because he couldn't let the others know who he was.

And it wasn't a choice I wanted to make, or a choice I *had* to make at that moment—maybe not at all. There were more important things to worry about than the fact that I might be seeing Rhodes soon or the idea that the boy at my side might be anything more than my friend.

If he was even my friend at all.

I couldn't think about any of that.

Because I was about to meet the Lord and Lady of Water. I was about to go to a new estate and learn a new territory.

I had to discover how to use my Water Wielding without draining myself and perhaps fracturing the world.

I had to be better. About that and so many other things.

So I couldn't think about Rhodes.

I couldn't think about Easton.

I couldn't even think about myself right now.

"Are you ready? Because I do believe we are here," Easton said, his voice low. He had that same sarcastic tone that I knew would give him away if

Rhodes or anyone else heard.

No matter what glamour he wore, you couldn't take the Easton out of Easton.

"I'm as ready as I'll ever be," I said quickly, my voice soft. I was nervous. Why was I so nervous?

Okay, it could be the fact that I had a new element to Wield, I had just killed a bunch of Water Wielders and didn't know who they owed their allegiance to. I had fought a ghost dragon, learned part of the prophecy, was having feelings for someone that I still didn't fully know, and my best friend was a cat and not by my side.

Oh, and my ex-girlfriend was stuck in a dungeon somewhere, and I couldn't help her. But, apparently, I still had to save the world—or at least this realm.

No wonder I felt weird.

I couldn't think about any of that right now, though. So, I pushed all of my thoughts aside and raised my chin.

"It's time to meet them."

"You're strong, Lyric. You'll make it through this. It's just one more step. And you won't be alone." Easton cleared his throat. "Because Wyn and the others will be here. So will your man."

I gave him a look. "Don't start. Please? Because you know you can't act like you usually do. You get that, right?"

"You don't have to tell me how to protect myself. And I'm the one who needs to protect you, remember, little girl?"

"Shut up," I muttered under my breath.

Before either of us could say anything more, the ship let down its gangplank at the dock.

I looked around at the land, my eyes wide.

Although the sea had been vast, a mix of blues and greens and purples and even black, the land was lush and green and covered by water. Not as if there'd been a rainstorm, but with small streams and tributaries everywhere. In the distance, I could hear the sound of waterfalls, and even the air seemed to have a mist to it as if everything were wet.

But I couldn't feel the moisture on my face, not really. It wasn't like it was miserable, and my hair wasn't curling in the steam or humidity. It was just that everything was lush, and water truly was everywhere.

It didn't seem to bother any of the non-Water Wielders, and for that, I was grateful. There was nothing worse than being wet and uncomfortable. Okay, many things could be worse, but that was up there on the list.

We walked the ramp, Teagan and Arwin in front, me in the middle, and Easton right behind me. Wyn took up the rear as usual, always on guard. All of us were.

We still didn't know if we were prisoners, nor did we know what was going to happen next.

For all I knew, the Water Wielders were going to take me into custody and kill the rest of my group.

All of us had our Wieldings ready, though I tried to hold back my Water Wielding. I had no idea how to summon it yet, and there was no way I could control it without training. But I could still feel it pulsing within me, one beat to the next.

I worried that if I used my Air or Earth Wielding, my Water Wielding would spill out, and I'd end up drowning myself.

As soon as we hit the end of the dock, I immediately saw two individuals that I knew.

There were people everywhere, guards and others in long white and soft blue robes. Everyone looked regal as if they were waiting for someone of great import. I let the others pay attention to those around us. I just smiled and focused on the girl running towards me.

Rosamond grinned, her eyes bright, her arms outstretched.

A smile filled her face, her light brown skin shining beneath the sunlight and mist. Her dark brown curls flew behind her as if dancing in the wind as she bounded up the dock and threw her arms around me. I caught her, taking a staggering step back, so I landed against Easton. He put his hands on my shoulders to steady me and then backed away.

"You're here. I Saw you coming, but I was so afraid that I was wrong. Not that I'm usually wrong, but it was more that I was afraid I wouldn't get to see you. But you're here. I'm so glad you're here." Rosamond held my face, kissed me on the mouth hard, and then hugged me again.

I laughed, my eyes stinging with tears.

I had missed her. I didn't know her as well as the others I'd been on the journey with. After all, Rosamond had been kidnapped by the knight of the Obscurité Kingdom, and that was why we had come to the Maison realm in the first place. But now Rose was here, and I felt such a strong connection to her. Not a soulmate connection, but as a friend. Someone I could trust.

Her letters to me while I had been hiding and licking my wounds in the human realm had been a steadying force for me.

I was so glad she was here.

"It's good to see you, Rosamond. You look wonderful."

"You look gorgeous. I love these leathers on you. You look like a warrior. Like a true Spirit Priestess." She kissed my cheeks and then danced around a bit, doing a little bop-wiggle. "I know I'm supposed to be a little bit better about controlling myself and acting more regal right now, but I can't help it. You're my friend. My family."

I blinked, wondering what she meant by that. But then she moved out of the way. Suddenly, Rhodes was there. He took two quick strides to me, hugged me hard, and then kissed me hard on the mouth.

I froze, wondering what he was doing. The last time I had seen him, he had walked away from me, saying I wasn't his. It had been one of the hardest things I'd ever overcome in my life. Standing there, watching him walk away once we both realized that the dream of what we could have had, had slipped through our fingers.

He wasn't my soulmate. Wasn't my other half. He hadn't been connected to me in a way that meant he would stay. That he could save me as I could save him. He had walked away from me and towards his responsibilities. He'd left me, the one person I'd thought he needed.

I couldn't close my eyes, couldn't even lean into the kiss.

Because it felt wrong.

Because Easton was right beside me.

Rhodes wasn't my soulmate, he wasn't the person that I felt that mystical connection to. He was something to me, but I didn't know what that something was.

But right here, now, out in the open when I was so confused? I felt like this wasn't the time. Wasn't the place. I honestly didn't know what was happening.

So, I put my hands on Rhodes' chest and gently pushed him away. I didn't want to make a scene. I didn't want to hurt him. But I was confused, and this wasn't helping.

Rhodes didn't look offended, didn't look hurt that I had pushed him away. Instead, he tucked a piece of hair behind my ear and smiled at me. "It's good that you're here. We've missed you, Lyric. And I can sense the Water Wielding beneath your skin. You unlocked another element. I hope you'll tell me the story, and I hope you'll let me help you learn the craft. You are so strong, Lyric. I'm proud of you."

He said all the right words, and I knew they were true. I really and truly appreciated them, but I was still so far out of my depth, it wasn't even funny. I didn't know what to say to his praise, so I just smiled and nodded before taking a step back and gesturing towards the others.

"Thanks for letting me come. Letting *us* come. Or, I guess, showing me to come." I held out my wrist and jangled my bracelet.

Rosamond stood by Rhodes and smiled widely. She clapped her hands in front of her and nodded. "Oh, good. Alura gave you that. No, I didn't make it, but I did give it to her to give to you. It's special."

"I figured that out on my own," I said dryly. Wyn and Teagan snorted behind me, and I shook my head.

"So, I think I need to introduce you guys to everyone. This is Wyn, Teagan, Arwin, and Frederic." I didn't trip over the last name, and I was proud of myself. "Guys, these are my...friends, Rosamond and Rhodes."

Everyone said hello, making sure that they were all polite to each other. After all, they were in a territory that wasn't theirs, and this was all complicated and probably a little confusing.

But when I watched Rhodes nod tightly at Easton as Rosamond just gave a little finger wave, I had a feeling the Seer could See through Easton's glamour.

And that meant Rhodes could, as well. Or at least he knew something.

Wow, this was going to be interesting.

It didn't seem that anyone else knew that Easton was here, that the King of Obscurité was in the so-called enemy realm.

I just really hoped that ignorance would remain.

We still stood on two different sides of the battle. Rhodes and Rosamond on one, I and the Obscurité members on the other. Easton put his hand on my shoulder and gave me a quick squeeze. While I really wanted it to be reassurance, I knew he did it just for Rhodes' sake.

Because Rhodes' jaw tightened, and he narrowed his eyes. Just for a moment, but I saw it.

I didn't shake Easton's touch away in that moment, but I really didn't want to be in the middle of this. This was not about me. Not even a little. It was about the two of them and their issues. I just happened to be stuck in the middle of it, and if it weren't for the fact that the world seemed to be watching, I likely wouldn't be standing there at all. Not by choice anyway.

Before I could figure out what to do about that, the Lord and Lady of Water came forward.

The lord looked just like Rhodes: regal. He was a little softer but still a warrior. He had silver eyes, too, just a little dimmer than Rhodes', as if they didn't have quite the same luster and magic that Rhodes' did.

The lady beside him looked much like Rosamond but frailer. She looked almost a little sick, and I was worried about her. She leaned heavily on the lord—Durin as he was introduced—but smiled softly.

"Welcome and well met, Spirit Priestess. Let us drink and be merry. For the foretold Priestess is here to save us." Durin grinned as he said it, his voice booming and bellowing. He had one arm around his wife as the other moved about as if showcasing his strength.

"And my boy. My precious, baby boy. He is the one who found her. He is the one who knows her."

He put an emphasis on the word *know* and winked at me. A sensation crawled up my spine, and I did my best not to lean into Easton or anyone else for comfort. Rhodes' face went carefully blank, and I couldn't tell what he thought about his father's words or how he'd spoken about Rhodes at all. I didn't like it. Not even a little.

Baby boy? How could he call his son that in front of so many people?

And to mention our connection? I didn't understand.

The lord was a little odd, a bit too much for me. Almost a farce. Because I knew this wasn't his normal face or demeanor. Wasn't the way he usually spoke to others.

I could tell that the others knew that, too.

Something was happening. Something was coming.

I just didn't know what it was yet.

"Well, let us go inside and show the Spirit Priestess some of the territory, a bit of the estate that she will grow to love and call home. Yes, yes this is a very good day indeed."

Durin bowed just slightly, not enough to actually show reverence—not that I needed it—and then turned, leading his frail wife away as if he expected all of us to follow.

The other Water Wielders began moving, but Rhodes and Rosamond stayed on the dock with us. Neither looked directly at their parents, and both seemed to be doing their best not to show any emotion on their faces.

I had no idea what might happen next, but I knew it would be important whatever it was.

I had a feeling that whatever personality, whatever emotion ran beneath the surface of the façade the Lord of Water affected, *those* were the ones that would be important.

That would help me set the course for my destiny.

No matter the past and my future.

CHAPTER 19

By the time we made it into the estate itself, I was exhausted and felt like I needed a bath. What I really wanted was a hot shower, but I didn't think they were actually going to have that. After all, none of the other estates or courts I had been to had put showers in every room or even had them at all.

"So, do you think they'll put us in the dungeon?" Wyn asked. I held back a laugh. Not because it was funny, more because I was actually worried about that, too, and not sure what to say.

The Lord of Water and the others had seemed understanding of the fact that I had brought some of the Obscurité Court with me, but that didn't mean they would be understanding when I was out of earshot.

"How about we just stay together no matter what?" I asked and leaned into her so I could lower my voice even more. "Hopefully, whatever chambers they put us in will either be in the same room or close. And the guys will be near. Because while I trust Rhodes and Rosamond, I just..." I trailed off, not wanting to voice my opinions when we were walking in the hall where anyone could hear us.

But Wyn gave me a nod. I looked over my shoulder at the three guys.

They followed us but didn't seem to have heard our conversation since we had talked low enough. I was getting pretty good at this, but that didn't mean I would be good at it forever.

Rhodes and Rosamond walked in front of us, leading us towards our rooms. And since we were going upstairs, I figured that we wouldn't actually go into a dungeon.

That was always good.

"I've put you all in separate rooms," Rosamond said. "I figured you could use your privacy." She looked directly at me and smiled. "Your friends are safe here. I know that it seems unheard of for the two kingdoms to come together like this, but you are the Spirit Priestess, and we are trying to save our realm. So, that means, at least for the time being, that my father has lifted the ban on members of Obscurité within the estate."

I let out a relieved breath, but then Easton came forward, narrowing his eyes at us.

"And what about the king? Because while the lord runs the estate, the king runs you all. What about his ban?"

"Why don't we go into Lyric's room for a moment and talk about that," Rhodes said, growling.

I really did *not* want to get into the middle of this, but it seemed like we weren't going to get away from it.

So, we all went into my room. I barely noticed the high, arching bed with its canopy above and the huge window that looked out over a landing.

Everything was ornate with silver and gold filigree everywhere.

It was a truly gorgeous room. Much softer than any other suite I had ever been in, except for maybe the one at the Obscurité Court's castle.

We all clamored into the room, and Rhodes closed the door behind us.

"Okay, *King*, why are you here?"

I looked between Rhodes and Easton and shook my head. I really did not want them to fight, considering that they always fought with each other unless they were working side by side as warriors. The only time I had ever seen them not glower or start bickering had been when they were fighting Lore together.

I wished they could just figure out how to make things work.

Then again, I wished I could do the same.

"He's here because I needed help getting through the Spirit territory, and then into this one. The bracelet told me to come here, and since everyone but me knew this was Seer magic, I came. But they didn't want me to come alone."

"He was supposed to come, Rhodes. You know this. I told you." Rosamond just shook her head and then smiled at me. "The others won't be able to see through your glamour. I only can because of my gift. Rhodes can because he has that gift, as well. The gift of truth. Much like our grandmother does. But no one else here will be able to tell. We will go along calling you Frederic. It's safer if we do. But you need to be here. Because while we want the Spirit Priestess to help piece together the fractured realm, not everyone does."

"Yes, some want the Lumière to rule, much like I know some in the Obscurité want to rule," Rhodes bit out. "There have been rumblings against you, Lyric," Rhodes said directly to me, and I blinked.

"What kind of rumblings?" I asked.

"That we never should have found you. That if you were gone, it would make taking over the Obscurité Kingdom easier. Those people don't know how the crystals work, though. They can't. They think they can overcome it with just sheer power and sacrifice." Rhodes shook his head, his hands fisting at his sides.

Easton stood beside me, glowering.

"There are some in the Obscurité Kingdom who think the same. I am not one of them," Easton added when Rhodes glared. "I know the two of us don't see eye to eye, but I want what's best for this realm. And that means not having our two kingdoms fighting each other constantly until we die because we've used up too much of the crystals' magic."

"So, what are we going to do about it?" I asked, thankful that we were actually speaking about plans rather than just fighting.

"I don't know," Rosamond said, frowning. "I can't See what I need to. All I know is that the people you are with need to be here. They're here to protect you, and so are we. You have three of the elements unlocked. When you have the fifth, everything will fall into place. But until then, you need to train, and we need to keep you safe. We'll figure out what to do. We'll figure out how to make our uncle see what is needed. Right now, he's angry. And I just don't know how to fix that."

"My mother was angry, as well," Easton said softly. "But she tried. It's just that no one realized that Lore was the one orchestrating it all. He fractured the crystal to the point where I don't know what we're going to do."

"Our uncle thinks that he's high and mighty and that he can control the crystal, or at least what's left of it. But he doesn't have to hide behind a knight." Rhodes shook his head. "I didn't mean it like that. I meant that he doesn't need to use a knight. He's enough of an egomaniac on his own."

It was odd hearing them talk so openly treasonous about the King of Lumière, a man I had never met, and one I wasn't sure I wanted to.

"For now, though, you must clean up and dress for dinner. Our father and mother want you to come and have a formal meal with us. You and your companions. Just be safe and know that some of us want peace. So many have been born to and lived through war. They want nothing to do with the Obscurité Kingdom. They don't see that the world is falling apart around us, and that we need to change. They only see what they've been told, that the enemy needs to die. So, just be safe." And on that scary pronouncement, Rosamond left, taking Teagan, Arwin, and Wyn with her.

I didn't know if they had shared a look or something, but somehow, I was left with just Rhodes and Easton.

"Lyric, can I talk to you for a moment?"

Easton looked between Rhodes and me and glared. "She needs to get ready, didn't you just hear your sister?"

Rhodes took a step towards Easton, but I moved between them.

"We really don't have time for this." I turned to Easton. "Rhodes is my friend. You go get ready. I will meet you out in the hall. Okay?"

He searched my face for a moment, and then slowly slid his knuckle down my cheek. I didn't have to ask why he'd done that, because Rhodes practically growled at my side.

I really did not want to deal with this. And, frankly, I wasn't going to. I was going to see what Rhodes had to say, and then I would just bury all my emotions. Because I couldn't handle them right now. I needed to figure out the politics of this territory and unravel the rest of the prophecy. I didn't have time to deal with these boys and their egos.

"Please, Easton," I pleaded. "I'll meet you in the hallway."

Easton looked between Rhodes and me and then walked away, closing the door behind him.

Honestly, I was a little surprised he had closed the door at all, but then again, most things about Easton surprised me these days.

"It's good to see you, Lyric," Rhodes said, his voice low. He stood facing the door, not looking directly at me, and I wondered what he saw. I wondered what he had seen when I first walked off the ship, and why he had kissed me.

He turned to me then, and his eyes were bright, the silver a deep pool of everything that I had once wanted, and everything that had kept me safe on my first journey.

"You changed." He looked at me and then reached out to touch my cheek, just like Easton had done. "I can sense the power in you, the results of your training. And while you might not be trained in everything, I can sense the intensity of it. You're amazing, Lyric. You were before when I was just getting to know you and watching you in that neighborhood in the human realm. You were amazing when you fought back against the Negs and when you had nothing but your fists and the ability to run. And you were amazing when you stepped into the realm, not knowing what you would face. Yes, much has changed, but you are so strong, Lyric. That hasn't changed."

I swallowed hard, wondering why what he said hurt, why this conversation felt like something…final.

"Is Brae okay?" he asked. "I didn't see her with you. Did you leave her in the human realm?"

I shook my head. "No, Easton and Rosamond helped with the glamour for her, so she stayed with me in the human realm for a year. No one knew that she wasn't as she seemed, or wondered why I called her Brae. But she's back with Easton's uncles in the Obscurité Kingdom right now. I don't know what to tell Luken. I wasn't sure if it would hurt him that she is so close yet so far away."

Rhodes nodded, looking lost. I didn't know how to help him. "I'll tell him. He'll be sad that she's not here, but I don't know exactly what it would do to him if he saw her not in her original form."

"Doesn't do nice things to me," I muttered.

"I'm sorry. I'm so sorry we couldn't save her. And I'm sorry you're going through all of this." He was silent for a moment, and I tried to figure out what to say. "And I'm sorry, I'm so sorry I left like I did. It was a blow to me to see that everything that I had thought was true wasn't. And I blame myself for it. For how I acted. I shouldn't have left like that. I shouldn't have left you there in Easton's hands without really doing anything over the past year to help you. I was busy here, doing endless things trying to keep my realm together, and training with my father and my uncle. But I walked away from you because I was hurting. And that was cowardly of me."

"You walked away, and yes, it hurt. But I was in no state to try and figure out what I was feeling at that point anyway. I had two new elements within me, and I had just lost my best friend. Not to mention the fact that Emory is still lost to me."

Rhodes cursed under his breath. "She's a siphon, Lyric. I think the Fire Estate is probably the safest place for her until we figure out how to save her. How to help her."

My eyes widened. "What do you mean?"

"Siphons are killed, Lyric. Because they cannot only take the Wielding from others, they can take their life. Just by maliciously using her powers, Emory could kill someone. She's not dead yet, and that's a mercy. But I don't really know what else to do for her right now. I can help bring her here, but I don't think my father would be as merciful as the Lord and Lady of Fire." He muttered that last part, and I swallowed hard.

"I'm going to try and save her," I said. "She might not have treated me the best...actually, she was pretty horrible to me, but no one deserves what she went through. And I hate the fact that I can't help her."

Rhodes leaned closer, and I refused to step away. This was still the boy I knew, and we needed to figure out how to *be* with each other like this. "When the time comes, I'll help you. And I'm sure Easton will, as well. You two seem to be…close."

I closed my eyes, willing back whatever was going through my mind. Because this wasn't about who I could be with Easton…or even Rhodes, but rather what I *needed* to be. And Rhodes…Rhodes looked so lost, so… different. And I didn't know how to help him.

"He helped me. So did a lot of his court. His uncles trained me, and so did Teagan and Arwin and Wyn. Much like you and Luken did before. Eventually, I'll have five elements inside me, Rhodes. I won't just be of one territory, one kingdom. Somehow, I'll need to bring together the elements within me and then do the same for the territories of this realm."

He ran his hand over his hair and then started to pace. I followed his movements, wondering what he could be thinking just then. "I know. And… I'm sorry. I know the Seer magic brought you here, and hopefully, it's to train your new element. But I want you to be safe. Because remember what I told you about how I used to live? It's still the same, Lyric. You need to be safe here, and the politics aren't easy."

I shifted from foot to foot. "I can tell." I didn't mention his father or the weird way everyone was acting, but then again, I didn't have to.

"I'm the way I am for many reasons, Lyric. I don't keep secrets. I know it felt like that before, but… I didn't know what I could tell you. Not because you weren't supposed to know everything, but because I was so afraid if I told you everything, I'd mess up the future. Rosamond is a Seer. She's the powerful one. Not me."

"Rhodes." I reached out, but he shook his head.

"I try to be who I am at all times, but I also have to be the Prince of Water at the same time. For my people. And it doesn't always turn out the way it should. But…there are pressures when it comes to who I have to be, and you above all others know that. I hurt people. I hurt you."

I just raised a brow in answer.

"Yeah. You get it." He looked down at his hands and played with Air between his fingers. Such a small show of power, but the precision was amazing. I was getting better, but I was nothing like him. He sighed before continuing. "But I'm just sorry that I left before. I made you do it on your own."

"Maybe I wasn't completely on my own," I whispered then shook my head. Not wanting to explain that. Not knowing if I could.

He looked at me then, and I knew I could lose myself in those eyes forever.

"We're not soulmates, Rhodes."

It wasn't a question, but he answered anyway. He touched my cheek, and I felt that loss, felt what we couldn't be. "No. We aren't. I think the connection was because of many things, and the way that I feel about you hasn't changed. But, no, we aren't soulmates."

"I don't know what that means in the grand scheme."

"I don't know either. I missed you, Lyric. And I wish there was a way to fix this. I just don't know what that is."

"I need to focus on me," I whispered. "Because life is scary, and I have so much more to deal with than who my connection could be with. I need to know who I am. I need to figure out many things. I don't want to lose you, Rhodes. But maybe just be my friend. Someone I can rely on. Because I don't really know what to think beyond that. And focusing on what *isn't* just hurts. And I have enough hurt right now."

"I can do that," he whispered. "I think...I think that would be best for everyone."

And then he ran his knuckle down my cheek again, the same one he had done before, the opposite side as Easton. And then he left me alone.

I stood in a bedroom that was not mine and wondered what I was going to do next.

It was like a chapter was closing, and yet another was just beginning.

I had been right when I told Rhodes that there was so much more to me and my journey than who my connection could be with.

I just needed to figure out what that was.

CHAPTER 20

Dinner was an interesting affair. The rest of the castle was just as ornate as my room yet on an even grander scale.

The estate itself had water *everywhere*: fish tanks and waterfalls and little pools and ponds. Everything was light and airy with blues and turquoise everywhere. The walls were made of crystal and glass, but unlike in the Obscurité Kingdom, it didn't feel like it was part of the crystal itself, rather the construction was a showcase for what Water could do, as well as the territory's Wielders.

It reminded me of being under the sea, even though we weren't. Everyone seemed to be happy that I was there, but it was all a little awkward as if they weren't quite sure what to do with me. Since I didn't really know what to do with them either, it made sense.

The estate looked like a large mansion. Perhaps some would even call it a castle. But there was an actual *river* running through it. Maybe it was actually one of the small tributaries of a main river, but it was a *river* with rocks and rapids nonetheless. It trickled at some parts but moved quickly and got loud at others. It traversed the building, with open air surrounding the two exits. I wondered how they kept it secure, but I figured that the Water Wielders knew what they were doing. They'd been doing this for centuries, while I had only been thinking about keeping an estate secure from other Wielders for about a year. If that.

We were seated in the dining room, and I kept my shoulders rolled back, trying not to get too overwhelmed.

I had brought clothes with me in my pack, but they had all been fighting leathers, so I had graciously borrowed one of Rosamond's flowy dresses. I didn't think it fit me well, but I didn't really want to sit in fighting leathers at my first formal dinner at the estate.

Rosamond wore a similar dress that cut into her waist perfectly and made her look regal and beautiful. It was a light, airy cream with folds and pockets that made it look like it flowed just like the river that ran through the building. I felt a little dumpy in comparison, but I didn't mind. Rosamond was perhaps the most beautiful woman I'd ever seen in my life.

The frail Lady of Water smiled at me, her dress white with ice-blue trimmings. She was skin and bones with dark circles under her eyes, and when she smiled, the light didn't reach them. I was afraid one touch might break her. I didn't know what was wrong with her, but I didn't miss the looks that both siblings gave their mother. It was as if they were afraid to hurt her. The Lord of Water didn't seem to notice. And that right there was the reason I was inclined not to like him.

Rhodes wore a tunic that mirrored his sister's, and light leather breeches. They weren't really slacks or jeans or anything I was familiar with, so I figured the old-fashioned term would work. He looked just as hot as he had when I first met him, though his eyes held a weariness that I thought might never go away. Not these days.

The rest of my team from the Obscurité Kingdom wore their leathers, although Wyn had added a flowy tunic with hers. It made me wonder why I hadn't thought to do that. Then again, dressing in the Maison realm was still relatively new to me.

I had been placed on one side of the table in front of Rhodes, right next to the lord. The lady sat on the opposite end with Rosamond at her side. Wyn sat to my right, and Easton was seated at the very end of the table, next to the lady.

Arwin and Teagan were scattered in the middle amongst the other members of the lord's inner circle, with Teagan sitting next to the very tall and blond Luken. The two warriors were very similar in stature and attitude, so it was nice seeing them talking to each other.

I didn't know if they had met each other before this meeting, but they seemed to be getting along now.

I, on the other hand, had no idea what to say, so I just sat there, eating quietly as the Lord of Water went on and on about the glory of the territory and how having me there at his side was going to be helpful.

"Now you see, Priestess, with your help, we'll make sure that the Water territory is ready for whatever comes. We will prevail."

"Father," Rhodes said, clearing his throat. "Maybe we should discuss this later. And not at the dinner table?"

I gave Rhodes a thankful smile, and of course, that was when Easton looked over at us. Because why wouldn't he want to make this dinner even more awkward?

"Nonsense, boy. The Priestess needs to know what we can do for her." The unsaid what I could do for *him* was heard loud and clear, even if there were no words.

"So, Priestess, do you know what your next plans are? I know the prophecy has long been ignored, but you're here now. What are your plans?"

For some reason, I didn't trust this man. It didn't matter that he was the father of two of my friends. I didn't want to tell him anything. And I knew I might be making a mistake, considering that I was here to try and unite everyone. Or at least, I thought. For all I knew, the prophecy meant having to destroy everything. And at that weird thought, I held back an involuntary shiver.

"You can call me Lyric," I said quickly. "I prefer to go by that."

"Nonsense," Durin said, waving his hand at me. I really didn't like that word. *Nonsense*.

"You are the Spirit Priestess. You deserve the title. No one should call you just Lyric. Who would just call someone by their name? I am the lord, after all."

"Father," Rhodes began, but the lord cut him off. The fact that I was calling him *the lord* in my head worried me. I didn't understand this man, and I didn't think I ever would.

"Shush, boy. I know what I speak of."

"Father, have you spoken to your brother recently? The king?" Rosamond asked, taking the conversation in a new direction. The Lord of Water grumbled under his breath and then smiled widely. "Of course, dear daughter. Have you Seen something?"

"Oh, one's never sure when it comes to visions. Now, what kind of fish is this? I don't believe I've had this before."

The conversation turned to food, and I met gazes with Rhodes, who just shook his head ever so slightly. Something was going on here that I didn't really understand. Then again, everything seemed fake when it came to the Lord of Water. He kept saying things that didn't really have any substance to them. And while I had been uncomfortable in both the Fire and the Earth

Estates, I hadn't felt like everything was just a complete façade. I only had to guess what I would feel when I hit the Air territory. For all I knew, it would be even weirder.

We finished our meals and then talked about nothing important. Rosamond was very good at keeping the conversation that way.

I was too far away from Easton to figure out what he was thinking, but I couldn't ignore the fact that something was pulling me towards him. That had always been the case, even when I first met him and used my Air Wielding with his Fire. There was just something about him. I looked over at Rhodes as I had that thought and swallowed hard, afraid I was making another mistake. Because I felt as if he knew. He *knew* what I was thinking. And yet it shouldn't matter. I wasn't Rhodes' soulmate, I was the Spirit Priestess. And I had to unravel the prophecy. I had to.

The Lord of Water left the dinner table before we did. Clearly, he had important business to attend to. He took some of his guards with him. They murmured under their breath with each other as they left, and Rhodes gave me a look before going to follow them.

Something was happening, and I didn't know what. But I was going to find out. Not because I felt that it was my business, but because I *knew* it was.

If something was wrong in this territory, I needed to try and fix it.

It hadn't been lost on me that they hadn't let me see the light crystal yet.

Even though it was in the Lumière Court, they hadn't even talked about it. They had been very careful not to mention it.

I knew if I asked Rhodes and Rosamond about it, they would tell me, but the Lord and Lady of Water had been very careful. Something was going on here. And we needed to figure it out.

"Are you ready to go back to our rooms?" Wyn asked. "Maybe fight something. Something feels weird here. I don't like it."

I looked over at her. "I don't like it either."

"It's like something's bubbling just under the surface, and they don't want us to know about it," Arwin put in.

"Yeah, I feel like my skin's just itchy. Like I'm constantly being watched." I looked around, rubbing my arms.

"We probably are," Teagan whispered. "We're the enemies, after all."

"Lyric isn't," Easton said softly. "At least, she's not supposed to be. But you remember what Rhodes said." Easton put his hand on the small of my back, leading me towards the hallway. I let him. Mostly because if I pulled away, it would make a scene. And everyone was already watching us. I didn't want to make it worse.

But I was exhausted. I just wanted to go to bed and then wake up to try and figure out exactly why I was here and what I needed to do next. Why had Rosamond Seen me coming here? Why had the Seer magic pulled me here?

It felt like a game of cat and mouse right now, and I didn't know whether I was the cat or the mouse.

Somehow, I had let Easton lead me to my bedroom, and he closed the door behind me.

"I thought you said we were going to our own rooms," I said, rubbing my arms. I felt a sudden chill, and I didn't know where it'd come from.

"I don't understand you, Lyric," Easton said, shaking his head. "I mean, really?"

I froze and shook my head in return. "What on earth are you talking about? Why would you say something like that?"

"You just threw yourself at him. I saw the way he kissed you. I left you two alone because you couldn't stand to be away from each other. Why didn't you just follow your little dream boy earlier? Why are you even staying with us? You apparently picked your side."

Anger bubbled up in me, and I pushed him. Hitting him hard on the chest. "What the hell is wrong with you?"

"Nothing," Easton grumbled.

"Rhodes is my friend."

"Some friend."

"Easton."

"He's not the one for you," he bit out. "He can't be the one for you."

I swallowed hard, looking at him. "And you are?"

I hadn't meant to say that. Hadn't intended to even broach the subject. But he'd started it, and now I would finish it. At least, I hoped.

Easton froze, his jaw going tight as he looked at me with those dark eyes of his. I wanted to reach out and touch him. Wanted to find out what was wrong. Because I could feel that pull between us, and I knew.

But *something* was wrong.

"No, Lyric. I'm not the one for you."

A sharp pain radiated out from my chest, moving all the way down my arms and sending electric shocks to my fingertips. My Air Wielding slid around the room, blowing my hair just slightly, and Easton's as well, so that same lock fell across his forehead.

I wanted to brush it away from his skin, but I didn't.

The Earth Wielding shuddered within my body, but I held it in, thankful that I didn't rattle the whole castle.

My Water Wielding was the one I had trouble with, though, and it slid from my body, swirling the water in my water pitcher to the right ever so slightly. I knew Easton had seen it, but he didn't say anything.

What he'd said had hurt.

He'd said I wasn't for him.

Maybe he just didn't feel it yet. Yes, that had to be it. Because this couldn't be one-sided. It couldn't be like before. I couldn't take that.

So, I ignored all of it because I had to remember that there were other things to deal with here. I had been pulled into this realm and to the Lumière Kingdom for a reason. I had to stop worrying about my feelings. I had to think about the others.

They were more important. So, I rolled my shoulders back and pulled in my Wielding.

"Then stop pushing at me. Just be my friend." I paused. "I need friends."

Before Easton could say anything in response, there was a sharp rap at the door, and then Wyn poked her head in. "Ah, I thought I felt Wielding. Come on now, Easton, I need some girl-time. Go hang out with the guys. I think Arwin and Teagan are going to train a bit out in the field that Rhodes set aside for us."

Easton gave me a hard look but didn't say anything.

Instead, he turned on his heel and walked out, not saying a word to me. Not telling me why he wasn't mine. Not relaying how he felt about this conversation. He didn't tell me anything.

Like usual.

Wyn took a few steps into my room, closing the door behind her after Easton had left.

"There are things you don't know, Lyric. Things that make Easton the way he is."

She reached out to me and pushed my hair back from my shoulders, just looking at me.

I was done. *So done.* "I know. That's what everyone says. I just don't understand why people keep talking *around* me. Is it because I'm human?"

"You're not human, Lyric."

I swallowed hard, trying to come to terms with that fact. "Fine. I might not be hundreds of years old like all of you, but I deserve answers."

"You might. You might deserve answers. But I can't give you them. And one day, Lyric, you might just reach five hundred years old on your own. If we ever get out of this war, that is."

I blinked, my mind whirling. I'd never really thought about immortality. Other than how I knew it existed within this realm. If I weren't still human, then what did that make me?

My hands shook, and I looked down at my fingers, trying to calm my breathing. This was all too much, and I didn't want to think about any of it.

What was I going to do with so many years ahead of me? And even then, did I really have that?

Because, deep down, I had a feeling that the Spirit Priestess wasn't supposed to rule, wasn't supposed to save everyone by finding a way to come to peace.

I had a feeling that no matter what I did, I wasn't going to be able to control my Wielding, and that meant I wasn't going to reach even a hundred years old, let alone five hundred.

But I wasn't going to think about that.

Instead, I would try to get some answers.

"Why don't you tell me something then?" I said, coming back to our original conversation.

"I can't, Lyric."

"Why? Just tell me one thing. Tell me why it hurts so much. Tell me what you know."

Wyn looked at me, tears filling her eyes. She shook her head before letting out a breath.

"Easton lost his soulmate, Lyric. He's not getting another one."

CHAPTER 21

There was an odd ringing in my ears. Why couldn't I focus? What was that taste in my mouth?

Bile? Was that what it was? Why did I feel so sick?

Soft hands slid down my shoulders and arms and gave my hands a squeeze. I looked up into Wyn's eyes and tried not to see the pity there. Because there was pity. So much of it.

"I don't know if it was my place to tell you, but I needed to. I know I should have waited for him to say something. But I didn't know if he would."

I blinked up at her, trying to clear my thoughts. Because this couldn't be the only important thing. This couldn't be the only thing on my mind.

"He already had his soulmate?" I asked, my voice shaky. I hadn't meant to ask that. I shouldn't need to ask that. I shouldn't be thinking about this at all.

My focus should be on figuring out what the prophecy said and meant. It should be on figuring out exactly what the Lord of Water was up to with his odd speeches and proclamations.

My thoughts should be on how to work on my three elements.

I shouldn't be focused on what Wyn was saying.

But, here I was.

"I'm so sorry, Lyric." Wyn let out a breath. "I don't know much, only that he had his soulmate and lost her. That's why, well…I don't know if that's all of it, but that's one reason he acts the way he does. Because you only get the one. Do you understand what I'm saying? You can't have another one."

I swallowed hard and put a smile on my face. I knew it didn't reach my eyes, and I knew Wyn wasn't falling for it. But that was fine. Because this was not my end.

My life was not going to revolve around this one idea.

I wouldn't let it.

I had grown more and fought so much harder than I had just a year ago when I was trying to figure out how my life could work in the human realm.

I wasn't that girl anymore.

I wouldn't break down.

"Thank you for telling me. That he's not mine. Of course, I think I would have known if he was my soulmate. Right? You know these things."

Wyn didn't say anything, and I didn't need her to.

Because I had been wrong before. And it seemed I was wrong again.

Maybe this overwhelming connection I felt, this powerful feeling I had within myself was just a crush. Just an intense emotion that anyone could have.

After all, I had thought I loved Emory. I had been wrong about her. But when it was all over and done, and I looked back on what we had, I wasn't sure I had actually loved her. So maybe it *was* just attraction. Perhaps it was just me wanting to feel something solid when nothing else was easy.

And that was fine. I would be fine.

I gave Wyn another smile and then backed away, not wanting to be touched, not wanting to be held.

I knew Wyn was just trying to help. I knew she wasn't giving me pitying looks because she felt bad for me. Because that wasn't the case. But I needed to do something.

I had to stop feeling like I needed to be someone else.

I cleared my throat and lifted my chin ever so slightly. "I should focus on training. I think that's important. Because you saw what it was like before." I paused, shaking my head. "I don't want that to happen again."

And I didn't want to rely on Easton to settle me, to help me control what I had within me. Because that wasn't going to happen. After all, he wasn't mine. I needed to do it on my own. It was *my* power. My responsibility. No one else's.

Wyn searched my face for a moment and then gave me a tight nod. "Okay. We can do that. Let's go to that training area that the boys saw before. Do you want to be alone? Or do you want more people with you?"

I thought about being alone, and how maybe that would be better for me, to hide inside myself and just forget everything that was happening around me. But I needed to be stronger than that. And I needed others to help me with my Wielding.

That was what I needed the others for. Nothing more. Nothing less.

"Anyone who wants to join is fine. I could use other's Wieldings to see what I need to do. After all, I don't know anyone else with three elements."

Wyn shook her head. "I don't think they exist. At least not on the surface or out in the open. We're not supposed to have the elements of more than just one kingdom, after all."

At that statement, Wyn walked away. I followed her, wanting to do something.

Because if I did something, I wouldn't focus on what I was feeling. Or the fact that I wasn't feeling much. There was an ache inside me, a hollowness.

Maybe if I could focus on fighting and training, it wouldn't feel like I was breaking inside. Because I didn't like that. I didn't like who I became when I dwelled on the thoughts of who didn't want me, who wasn't my soulmate.

I had spent the first eighteen years of my life not realizing that there were even such things.

Now, I couldn't seem to *stop* thinking about them.

The area where the guys had found a training ring was surrounded by tall trees and waterfall fixtures. It wasn't the same type of greenery that I had seen in the Earth territory. Instead, it was just foliage and greenery that happened when there was a lot of water present.

Plus, every single rock formation or manmade statue had some sort of water feature.

On the ground surrounding the ring were glass rocks that shined in the light with a thousand different blues and greens. Topazes, aquamarines, every single gem that shined azure under the sun. I swore a couple of them were priceless sapphires.

It was all just so striking. So dazzling.

And yet, it surrounded a place where we would be fighting—and possibly breaking the ground with our Earth Wielding.

Since I wasn't sure there had ever been an Earth Wielder to practice here, I was a little afraid what we might do to the terrain.

The others didn't seem to have that concern, though. Arwin and Teagan were already training, with Arwin using his Earth Wielding gently, not wanting to break anything around us. Teagan used his Fire Wielding on top of it. What interested me most, though, was that Luken was there, using his sword and Air Wielding like before.

It had been so long since I last saw him use his Wielding, but it was still amazing to watch.

He had his golden hair tied back in a leather strap, and he grinned and laughed as Teagan shot his Fire Wielding towards him.

Luken rolled across the ground, using his shoulder to take the brunt of the impact before coming back and using his sword to direct his Air Wielding towards Teagan.

The two of them trained as if they had worked together before, but I didn't think they had. They were both just really good at what they were—first lieutenants to their powerful kings and leaders.

When I stepped closer to Luken, however, I noticed that there wasn't as much light in his eyes as there used to be.

There was a sadness there instead, and I knew who it had to be about.

"She's okay then?" he asked in lieu of a greeting.

"She's herself...but with some differences."

He gave me a tight nod. "I've never heard of that happening, but Rosamond says that's the way it's supposed to be. I just hate when prophecies and shit is like that. You know what I mean?"

"I know exactly what you mean." I gave him a look, and he laughed, this time with a little more mirth.

"I wish you could've come, but then again, it might have been a little weird."

"I've been watching her for a year, it is a little weird. But it's like she's still with me. I just hate it sometimes, too. Not that she's actually by my side at the moment since she's safe where she is right now, but she's also not the *same*."

Luken opened his arms, and I stepped into him for a hug, inhaling his light scent. I couldn't remember if I had ever hugged him before or if we had even touched for anything but sparring. But it just reminded me of what had happened last year. It made me recall the fact that he was my friend, even if we didn't know each other all that well.

Others had started to come into the training area, but I didn't care.

Everything was falling apart around me, and I was struggling to keep up, but I had to remember that I wasn't alone in this. I wasn't alone in trying to get everything in order.

Luken had lost Brae as well, and I had a feeling they had been soulmates. I wouldn't ask, that'd likely be too hard for both of us.

But Luken had lost her, and he hadn't seen her since she turned to ash.

So now, we would hold each other, if only just for the moment.

I knew the guys had walked into the circle as soon as they took their first step into it.

I knew it was Rhodes behind me, standing with Easton.

It seemed I would always know.

And maybe that should bother me, but it seemed to be my lot in life.

I would get over it. I'd gotten over a lot of things already.

I had to finish saving the world or whatever was needed of me. After, maybe I could save myself.

I pulled away from Luken, gave him a small nod, and then rolled my shoulders back.

"I suppose I need to start training again."

"We've got this, Lyric," Wyn said, brushing past Rhodes.

For some reason, she kept glaring at him, and I had no idea why.

Maybe it was because he had hurt me before, or perhaps it was for a whole different reason. Everybody was just on edge, and nobody was really getting along outside of their small little cliques.

It felt so weird to have Rhodes and Luken and Rosamond on one side of the training ring, and Easton, Arwin, Teagan, and Wyn on the other.

It was as if both of my worlds had come together, and I had no idea what to do with it. I stood in the middle of them, a product of both kingdoms, even though I hadn't known that until recently.

Maybe this was the first step. Perhaps this was what I needed to do to unite the realm.

If I could bring together two factions of it, two sets of my friends, maybe that would be the first step.

Or maybe we would all just yell at each other, and I would end up breaking apart from not being able to control my Wielding.

Either way, I would have to figure it out.

"I'm going to start with Air since that was the first element I unlocked," I said. "And then Earth. And then Water."

"I'll help," Rhodes said, taking a step forward. Wyn stepped in front of him, shaking her head. "Let's see what she can do on her own while we work in pairs, shall we?" she snapped and then turned her back to Rhodes.

"Don't fight. I'm not in the mood."

I hadn't even realized I'd said the words until Easton took a step forward, his hand outstretched.

I looked up at him and frowned. What was going on in that mind of his?

What was going on in mine?

"Ready?" he asked. I nodded, turning away from him and just focusing on *me*.

We all started training. I started first with Luken and Rhodes as I tried to direct my Air Wielding.

"You're much better than you were a year ago," Luken murmured.

"I've been training."

"With the Obscurité?" Rhodes asked. There wasn't venom in his voice, but Easton still glared.

"Some. But also in the human realm. I haven't just been sitting on my thumbs for the past year."

"I never thought you were." He said the words softly and then slid out his hands, the air around us twirling in soft caresses against our skin.

I smiled at that, remembering the first time he'd learned that move. And then I joined him, allowing my Air Wielding to breathe.

It was like coming home, the power within me settling.

I could feel the other two elements fighting to come out, and they would, but I had to learn to control it.

I had to.

Arwin and Wyn came up then, both of them holding their hands out to their sides. They slid their palms to the front and grinned, and the earth below us began to shake. Just small tremors, not enough to break anything, but enough. It was amazing.

I put my hands out in front of me, as well, both of them outstretched and parallel to the ground, and then I turned my palms up to face the sky.

Both of them smiled widely at me as a sheer mist of soil slowly rose from the ground. I let my Air Wielding slide under it, letting it shake just enough to make waves in the air.

Earth Wielding could be brutal, powerful, and heavy. But it could also be delicate.

Easton took a couple of steps forward, looked at me, and then snapped his fingers. With one snap, the funnel that I had begun to make broke apart into a hundred smaller funnels. I let out a shocking breath.

I shook my head and then slammed my hands together in front of me, bringing the power back. The hundreds of vortexes moved back into one before settling on the ground again.

The others watched, every single person in the group a friend of mine on some level. I had never practiced that move before with Easton, but I had been learning. And he had wanted to show the others what I could do.

And then Rhodes was at his side, one hand out, cupped in the air.

"Are you ready?" he asked. I wasn't sure I could answer.

Slowly, the water from the fountains around us started to come closer, a small wave like a tiny little air dragon filled with water coming towards us. I held out my hand, cupped it towards the sky, and hoped it would be enough.

"We don't know what type of Water Wielding you have, but these are the basics. Just feel it like you do with Air. It's fluid, part of you. Don't fight it."

I nodded, but then the Water Wielding within me slammed against my skin, and I could feel it slowly drowning me. My lungs filled, and I coughed up a whatever could spill out of my throat. Rhodes' eyes widened, and he took a step forward.

But it was too late. The water that I had been helping him hold hit the ground suddenly, and the Earth Wielding that was beneath that fractured, creating a huge crevice down the center of the training circle. Arwin and Wyn both fell to their knees, having been caught in the mayhem. I let out a shocked breath, slamming my palms down to my sides. It sucked all of the Wielding that I had let out right back into me. I choked again.

"Stop it," Easton snapped, putting his hands on either side of my face. "Don't do this to yourself. Let it out, just…slowly. Don't pull it back in. You aren't hurting anyone but yourself."

"What's happening?" Rhodes asked. "What's going on with her?"

"I can't," I whispered, water coming out of my ears and my nose and even out of my eyes. I knew they weren't tears, but it felt like them.

"You can do this. Just imagine it settling peacefully within you. You're scared, and it's coming out in your Wielding."

"Lyric—" Rhodes said and then cut himself off. He seemed to know what was happening and came to stand beside Easton, putting his hands on my back so the three of us were touching, close. Finally, I could breathe. And I hated the fact that I had to rely on them to figure this out. I needed to figure this out on my own.

And as I fell to the ground, my knees aching from the impact, Rhodes and Easton let me go but went to their knees at my sides.

The others were watching, and I was so scared.

Because I was supposed to be the Spirit Priestess.

I was supposed to be the one to unite the kingdoms into one realm that was no longer fractured. But I couldn't even bring together the Wielding within myself.

What was I supposed to do when I gained the other two elements?

When I hurt everyone that I cared about because I couldn't control it? Or would I just die myself?

I didn't have a chance to worry about that though, because as soon as I looked up, Rosamond was running towards us, her eyes wide.

"It's Mother, Rhodes. She passed out. Dad needs us." Her skin was pale, her hair in disarray around her face.

I swallowed hard and let Easton help me to my feet before pushing him away. I ran after Rhodes just as the others did. I couldn't focus on anything else, because I could see the pain in my friends' faces.

Something was wrong with the lady, and I didn't have time to focus on my own failings right now.

"You need to go," the Lord of Water barked at his son as soon as we entered the throne room. "Your mother...this is it. This is the time. We tried to help her. But this is it. You need to get her parents. We've sent word, but you need to be the one to get them."

I took a step back, and Wyn put her arm around my waist as we stood there, watching Rhodes go stiff as he looked at his father.

"What's wrong with my mother?"

"You know she's weak. She passed out. She's not going to last much longer. She needs her mother and father. You need to go."

"Send someone else. Don't make me leave her."

"Your sister will be here. And if you're fast, you'll make it, too. You know your role. Make it happen." Durin looked over Rhodes' shoulder and narrowed his eyes at us. He looked so different than he had at dinner, but then again, I didn't really know him. "Go with him, all of you. You can see the Air territory while you're there. Our family needs time. And you should find your final elements, shouldn't you, Priestess?"

"We will make sure Rhodes gets to where he needs to go," Easton said, and then I remembered that no one knew that he was the King of Obscurité and not just an Obscurité Wielder. He was a king who had just lost his mother and was now watching Rhodes about to lose his.

I didn't know how to help. I didn't know how to do anything. But if Rhodes needed me at his side, I would be there.

I didn't know what else to do.

"Good day," Durin whispered and then ran off down the hallway where I assumed he was going to his wife's side.

Rosamond stood there, her face pale, her eyes wide. "I can't See."

"What do you mean, Rosamond?" Rhodes asked.

"I know it's hard to See my own fate, and that of yours and our parents. But I didn't See this. Something's wrong. You need to get our grandparents. They'll know what to do. You know Grandma has more power than I do. Get her. Maybe she can help." Tears slid down Rose's face, and Rhodes took the two steps between them to hug her close. "I'll get them. Just make sure she stays strong. Okay?"

I turned away, not wanting to intrude on the private sibling moment, but I was so afraid of what was going to happen next. Because all of this seemed off.

We were going to leave the Water territory and head into the Air territory. All to get the Lord and Lady of Air, Rhodes' grandparents.

Even as I knew that this was important, I couldn't help but wonder why we were being pushed away.

And what would happen when we came back.

CHAPTER 22

It wasn't long until we found ourselves once again on the ship traversing the Water territory. I didn't know if any of those at the Water Estate had access to the kinds of magic and portals that Easton had in the Obscurité Court, but I hadn't asked. I was more afraid that if we even dared to try it, we would break the crystal more than it already was. No one had mentioned the Lumière crystal, nor had they really talked about the court.

It was all about Water and Air, not so much about the court that ruled them both.

It had been different in the Obscurité Kingdom, but maybe that was because we were traveling towards it the entire time when I was there. Now, I currently sat next to the King of Obscurité on the ship heading towards the Air territory.

It was all a little bit different, but I was trying to soak in all the information I could. I always felt like I was a couple of steps behind, even though I shouldn't feel that way.

I had learned so much in the past year, but I needed to learn more. It didn't help that everyone kept secrets as if they were afraid to talk about what had been harming their realm for centuries.

No matter how many books I read, it wouldn't be enough. I knew that I needed to see each territory. That once I did, somehow, it would all come together.

It had to.

Because there was no way I could keep going like this, trying to figure out the prophecy when I was so in the dark.

The Spirit Priestess will come of five, yet of none at all.

She will be strength of light, of darkness, and choice.

You will lose what you had.

You will lose what you want.

You will lose what you will.

You will lose what you sow.

Then you will find the will.

Find the fortune.

And then you will make a choice.

A choice above all.

A sacrifice above will.

A fate left denied.

And a loss meant to soothe.

I'd rolled the prophecy through my mind over and over, trying to come to terms with it.

Because I knew it was only the first part. It felt like a beginning, even with the word *sacrifice* in it. The Spirit Priestess will come of five. Of five elements? Five territories? And yet none at all? Was it because I had originally come with no magic at all? Or because I hadn't come from this realm at all?

Strength of light, of darkness, and choice. That made sense to me. Of both realms, both light, and dark.

But light wasn't just good, and dark wasn't all bad. It was only their names, simply what they had chosen to call themselves. It had nothing to do with morality. And that was something I wasn't even sure the Maisons themselves understood.

I would lose what I had? Was that my friends? Or my past?

I would lose what I wanted?

I thought of Easton. Rhodes. Maybe it wasn't as simple as just a crush. As basic as feelings.

I would lose what I will and what I sow? I didn't understand those. Maybe it wasn't my time to understand them yet.

And I would find the will. Did I need to find the will to keep going?

I needed to find the fortune?

And there was a choice. What kind of choice? I was choosing to unlock my elements. Or maybe I wasn't.

I didn't like the word *sacrifice*. It scared me. But then again, everyone around me continually sacrificed what they loved to protect their realm.

Why should I be any different?

I had almost died to discover answers before, would I have to again?

A loss to soothe. A fate left denied.

I needed to go over it all again, there just wasn't time. We were constantly moving, and I barely had time to breathe.

It didn't matter that we were on a ship now, that we were traveling through the rivers of the long land mass that bisected the Water territory. Soon, we would enter the lower seas before we came up to the Air territory's border.

Yes, there was time to go over it, but I couldn't speak openly. Not really.

Because while there was no crew on this ship, I didn't feel like it was the right time to talk about myself when we were here to help Rhodes find his grandparents and bring them back to his dying mother.

That put things into perspective for me.

"Do you want to learn how to do this?" Rhodes asked, his eyebrows lowered as he concentrated on what he was doing.

I stood up quickly and walked towards him, nodding.

"Of course. I want to help."

"Okay. You're going to have to use your Water Wielding to do this, but if it's too much for you, you can also work on the Air Wielding."

"Okay," I said, not really understanding what he was saying.

"Usually, I have Luken work with me on ships like this, but since he's back at the house taking care of Rosamond and making sure she's protected, it's just me and the rest of the Obscurité team. Having another with both of the Lumière elements will be helpful."

I nodded, holding out my hands. "Just tell me what to do."

"Okay, usually we work with a crew about this size, maybe a little bit smaller. Wyn, Teagan, Easton, and Arwin are working with their actual hands rather than their elements. So they're dealing with the sails and directing them and making sure we can get through. I've been working with Water and Air to push us through the Water territory towards the Air border. We will go faster with your help. So, what I need you to do is focus on both of your Wieldings. But just the Lumière ones."

Easton grumbled under his breath, and I looked over my shoulder at him. He turned away quickly, working with something on the mast.

"All I'm saying is that Earth and Fire won't help us at the moment because we are too far above the actual bottom of the sea for Earth Wielding to help. And Fire won't help the ship move forward."

"It would help if there was an engine of some sort, wouldn't it?" I asked and then winced. "Not that engines actually work in the Maison realm."

"They don't, but there are ways to use hot air to get across areas," Easton said cryptically.

"Like a hot air balloon?"

"Somewhat."

"Anyway, let's work on what we have in front of us rather than what we don't actually have."

I looked at Rhodes and nodded again. "Okay, let's do this. What do I need to do with my Wielding?"

"Focus on the water itself and move it in small waves around the ship's hull. Don't press in, we don't want to buckle the wood, but you can move forward with each push."

"You know, if you used some metal in your ships, the Air and Fire Wielders together could probably move you just as fast," Easton said casually.

"I know," Rhodes said softly. "But you try explaining to my father or even my uncle about the need for Earth Wielders who can use metal, and Fire Wielders who can help with Air to push us across."

"Maybe one day we will," Easton said softly, looking at me before turning his head away.

I listened to Rhodes as we slowly moved our hands together in unison, pushing the Water and Air as one towards the south so we could cut the boat through the waves of the sea. There was actual air moving into the sails as well, and every once in a while, Rhodes would throw one hand up into the air to push it towards the front of the ship, moving us a bit faster.

It was easier to work with my Water Wielding right then, not because I was working with Rhodes, but because I was focused on one small task. I wasn't thinking about everything all at once, just like Easton had told me to try and avoid. So, I was using both of their help to try and figure out what I needed to do to control my Wielding.

We were so busy making sure that we were going in the right direction, only taking turns to stop and either rest or eat something, that I didn't have time to feel awkward about anything.

I didn't have time to think about my emotions and my feelings when it came to the people on the ship. For that, I was grateful.

Because this wasn't about me. It was about Rhodes and trying to figure out how to break down the prophecy so it actually made sense. So it could be useful. Right now, the words the old man had told me just confused me. It made me think that nobody knew exactly what Spirit Priestesses were supposed to do.

Maybe I was just an anomaly. Perhaps I wasn't supposed to help people.

Maybe I was just a symbol.

But someone who could get things done. I had to remind myself of that. Symbols were important.

I just didn't want to be useless.

"We should be there in the next day or so," Rhodes said softly. "It really just depends on the headwinds. Even if we're using our Wielding, it takes a long time to cross the distance."

"Still faster than going across the Earth territory," Teagan said, shrugging as the others looked at him. "What? He's been there. We're not giving away state secrets or anything."

"That is true," Arwin said softly. "But there seems to be more people within our territories than this one," Arwin said cautiously.

"Actually, I think the population's around the same," Rhodes added. "I'm just going around any of the water cities. You've probably heard of the floating cities, but we're not going near them. Much like when we went through the Earth territory, there were large swathes of land without anyone living there.

Same with the Fire territory. Everyone really just congregates in cities and towns rather than out in the open."

"It's sometimes like that in the human realm though, too," I added. Everyone looked at me, and I just sighed. "There needs to be places for farming and nature. And the animals need to have places to live, as well. We're constantly pushing them out of their territories, and each city deals with that in their own way. Different wildlife can come into people's homes and towns and are either killed or end up hurting others because they don't know any better. Because it was their territory first."

"It was like that here a long time ago, too. Longer than any of us have been alive," Easton said, looking directly at me. "A lot of the wildlife you see here used to be the way we are, all spread out. Mostly because we don't have as many children as the human realm does. Our lifelines are a little bit longer, so it takes us longer to make decisions, or to do anything for the future like have children and honestly, grow up. But there are many creatures that most have forgotten, those that live directly under the surface or are hidden away."

"And they're coming out," Rhodes added. I looked between the two men. They looked at each other as well, giving one another a look that I didn't quite understand.

"What do you mean?" I asked.

"Easton's right," Rhodes said. Everyone looked a little surprised that he'd said those words, but he continued. "Some creatures have been dormant for a long time. Ones full of magic that needed to be where they were. They used to rule these lands, long before the Wielders came."

"Once, they were all just mysteries or legends, but now they're back. We saw one in the Spirit territory."

At Easton's words, Rhodes' eyes widened. "What did you see?"

"A Domovoi," Easton answered.

"Holy hell." Rhodes shook his head. "If we don't reclaim the magic for those crystals so it can go back into the Wielders, there will be more. Far more than just Domovoi or whatever else we might see in these lands."

"And how do we do that?" I asked, shaking my head. "Because I'm part of the steps. I know that much. I can't be all of them, but I need to figure it out."

"We will," Easton and Rhodes said at the same time and then glared at each other.

Before I could say anything else, Rhodes stood up quickly, his hands outstretched.

"Dear God," he whispered. We were all standing by him in an instant, wondering what he was talking about. And then I saw it.

I remembered when Easton had told me about the sea creatures. About what we could see in the distance and the far more dangerous things that you couldn't see at all. Because the things that lurked in the deep didn't warn you when they came for you. They just came. Attacked.

"Hold on to something and use your Wielding. We're going down," Rhodes shouted. There wasn't a single sound. It was as if we were in a vacuum, just a pin-prick of sensation, and silence.

And then it was upon us.

Large tentacles wrapped around the ship, and a loud crack sounded as the bow of the vessel broke, splitting the thing in two. The sound was deafening. And it echoed in the silence. I knew that if I survived this, I would likely remember it until the end of my days.

Everybody moved quickly, using their Wielding to try and combat the tentacles. Easton had his Fire and Earth rumbling the ship even as he tried to burn the tentacles. Arwin, Wyn, and Teagan worked as one, trying to get one side of the creature, but it wasn't going to be enough.

Rhodes tried to move us past it, using the water to pull the Kraken down while using Air to push us out. I tried to help, using my own Wielding. But it wasn't enough.

And then Easton grabbed me, pulling me close as he shouted, "Let the ship fall but come close. We'll try to get ourselves out." Rhodes was on my other side then, and then the others joined us. Each of us touched each other as if we knew we could find our way out if we just stayed together.

I hoped we would be able to find our way out.

Water started to pool around our feet, slowly coming up to our knees. Then my hips. I looked into the dark eyes of the boy holding me and tried to use my Wielding to press out. Maybe I could use my Air Wielding to create a bubble. To make something so we didn't drown.

Rhodes seemed to know what I was thinking and tried to do the same. He used his Water Wielding to press around us, as well.

And then we went under. All of us holding on to each other but not screaming. There wasn't enough oxygen to yell.

The Kraken was like a thing of nightmares, its large tentacles wrapping around the ship, pulling it down, tugging us down with it.

Light glinted off sharp teeth, and I didn't know where exactly its head was or how it worked. I had only seen drawings of what humans thought it might look like.

Each of us held onto each other and screamed, all of us using our Wieldings except for Fire. Fire wouldn't help here. Even Easton was using his Earth Wielding to shake the seabed far below us to try and push us up, but I didn't think it was doing any good. I didn't think anything would work.

I looked into Easton's eyes, trying to use my Wielding to protect us, trying to get us back up to the surface as the Kraken pulled us down. And then I heard it.

A soft echo. A scream made out of silence and death.

It pulsated around the bubble of Air we had made around ourselves to try and protect us.

It felt like a thrumming in the ears—heavy and sedated.

It burned the edges of the bubble around us, and the hair on my arms stood up.

It was like a soft echo of a waltz, only of death and magic.

And then I was burning, screaming, and all of us shouted. Before I could blink, there was no water, no Kraken, there was nothing.

Just death and absence before, once again, there was light. My knees slammed into the ground, and I found myself on top of Easton, all of us coughing up the water that had filled our lungs when the last of the Air Wielding bubble popped.

I scrambled off him, finding myself on a beach.

An actual sandy and rocky beach.

Everybody was there. And nobody looked hurt. Somehow, we had been transported from one end of the Water territory beneath the surface, to where we were now.

And I had no idea how it had happened.

"Bone magic," Rhodes whispered. His whole body started shaking, and I looked up into those silver eyes, wondering what he was talking about.

"How can there be bone magic?" Easton asked. "There hasn't been that in centuries. I didn't even think you could *make* that anymore."

"What is bone magic?"

"It was the thing that saved us," Rhodes answered.

"And it's going to be the magic that kills us all," Easton added.

And then I looked around at where we were and wondered what exactly had just happened. And why the two words *bone magic* sent shivers deep down into my soul.

CHAPTER 23

"What is bone magic?" I asked, my voice a little shaky. I cleared my throat and rolled my shoulders back. Tried to act stronger than I was. Because those words that they had said? They scared me deep down to my soul. And I didn't even know what their true meaning was yet.

"It's...it's something that's not supposed to exist," Easton mumbled under his breath, not looking at me.

I searched the strong lines of his profile, trying to figure out exactly what he was thinking. But that was the problem with Easton, I never knew what he was thinking.

Rhodes was the one who moved up to me to answer as the others began drying off their clothes, looking around for what might come at us next.

"Bone magic takes sacrifice, the worst kind you can imagine. It's what happens when you strip someone of their Wielding after torture or anything that has them near death. It can take thousands upon thousands of sacrifices, stripping Maisons of their Wielding, taking lives. The bones left behind carry magic. Power that is dark. Not because of the bones that remain but because of who put them there." Rhodes looked at me then, and I stared into those silver eyes, swallowing hard. "It was a type of magic used before the Fall, and why the Spirit Wielders left like they did. Because bone magic is the strongest when the bones of Spirit Wielders are used. Although, all Wielders, no matter their element, can produce bone magic. It just takes the cruelty of another to force it out of them."

I hadn't even realized I was crying until Rhodes reached up and wiped a tear from my cheek.

"So, is this bone magic old or new?"

"We don't know. We can't know. But if it's powerful enough to be beneath the sea floor and push us through a portal of some kind like it did? It has to be newer than anything that could have lain there dormant all this time."

Easton looked at me then, and the anger I saw in his eyes made me take a step back. "It's not like what Lore did with the crystal and the Obscurité Kingdom. He stripped the power from others through the crystal and funneled it into himself to enhance his own Wielding. This is nothing like that. It's worse."

I believed him, but I didn't know what we could do about it. Somehow, the magic within the sea saved us from the Kraken and put us on the shore of the Air and Water border. I just didn't know what it all meant. Or why it had happened at all.

All I knew for sure was that if someone were creating bone magic, there was obviously something far darker in the Lumière Kingdom than had ever been in the Obscurité Kingdom.

I was afraid if I kept digging, I would find darkness so wretched, it would be hard for me to figure out exactly why I was here. And what I could do as the Spirit Priestess in the face of all the brutality.

"So what can we do?" I asked, wringing out my hair. The breeze was starting to come in, chilling me to the bone, and I shivered.

Easton sighed and then reached out and slid his hand over my hair, under the watchful eye of every single person around.

I could feel the heat of his palm, and knew he was using his Fire Wielding somehow. And then suddenly I was dry, as if I had never been dunked beneath the sea as a Kraken tried to drown us.

"That's an interesting way to use your Wielding," I said, keeping my voice light. It was hard to do when all I wanted to do was curl myself into a ball and try not to think about everything that had happened over the past few days.

"It wouldn't do well if the Spirit Priestess caught pneumonia since we're heading into the Air territory."

"I'm fine. Thank you. But what about the bone magic?" I repeated.

"I don't know what we can do. The fact that we know it still exists? That's something we should worry about. But first, we need to get to Rhodes' grandmother. And then we'll figure out the rest." Easton shrugged like it was no big deal. Even though I knew he held the weight of his kingdom on his shoulders.

It didn't help that I held the weight of *both* on mine.

"Let's be off then," Wyn said, stepping between the three of us. She put her hands on her hips and looked around.

"Teagan already dried me and Arwin. So, Easton, if you could get Rhodes over there, we'll all be dry and can head into the very cold Air territory. Lyric, I don't know why, but it's like the breezes come from the tundra over here, it's not a warm breeze. It's going to be interesting. So, let's just get there. And, no, I don't know why the bone magic sent us here specifically. All I know is that we need to get through. Because I'm sure you know just like I do, something's off."

I looked at the others as Easton and Rhodes glared at one another before Easton and Teagan simultaneously dried Rhodes.

I turned away and sucked in a breath as I finally looked at where we were. It was magnificent.

I felt like I thought that every time I hit a new territory, but it was the truth. Because though the people within the realms were dying, fading because of the lack of power, and even though the power in those who still had it was sometimes more corrupt than not, the land was beautiful.

Yes, the monsters were coming back, and the magic was changing, and the realm was literally fracturing, but the setting was still gorgeous.

And maybe that was a metaphor for something, but I couldn't think more about it right now. All I could do was look at how beautiful the area was. Like when we moved into the Water territory, this border was set at a different height than what was in front of us. So, we were higher than the Air territory and the border itself. We were on a cliff of some sort, but everything was green with blue and purple flowers. There were vivid, royal colors everywhere, so bright that it almost didn't seem real. And water burbled, but not in rushes like the Water territory. More like leftovers from whatever the Water territory gave.

The stones here were a mix of pale gray and dark brown and looked as if they were those art installations that I had seen in photos where people balanced rocks on top of one another to create sculptures.

Yes, there were cliffs, but there were also stones that were flat and jagged, all stacked up on one another to make their own pieces with vines and other greenery flowing.

Animals chirped, though I couldn't see them, and birds flew. Avians with two sets of wings in colors I had never seen before in real life. It was like watching one of those documentaries where that man with the British accent talked about the different birds of prey and their mating dances.

Everything was so bold, it almost hurt the eyes to look at it.

But I knew we were still at the border because though everything seemed a little higher than in the other territories mostly because I assumed people with Air Wielding were able to actually get to those places, there was still water everywhere. Rivers and what seemed to be a lake off in the distance. Fish with wings were jumping out of the water in front of us. I just blinked, wondering how all of this could be real.

It was beautiful.

"We should be going," Easton growled, and I looked up at him. When his eyes widened, I sucked in a breath, and then looked back to where I had been gazing.

And that's when I screamed.

Because it wasn't beautiful anymore.

"Are you kidding me?" Wyn snapped. "A freaking gollum? A gollum?"

"You mean the flying fish that's coming at us with very large fangs?" I said quickly, backing away. "That's what a gollum is?"

"Yes. And it seems they are no longer dormant. No longer extinct."

"Well, take care of it, Wyn," Rhodes snapped, sounding angry for the first time in a while. He was always so controlled, so it was odd to see him lose his temper. "We know how to take care of them, but there're only two people here who can actually do it quickly."

Then he glared at Teagan and Easton, and I knew exactly why Rhodes was angry.

"Fire Wielding? You can burn them?" I asked, and Easton tugged me away from the edge of the border.

"Right in one." Before I could actually focus on what to say next, seven more gollums came out of the water in front of us.

We were standing on a cliff that wasn't too high, and there was a beach right in front of us. One that went to the sea before it became the rest of the Air and Water border. And while everything was lush and colorful, the gollums were anything but.

They were gray and a muted green with scales. It reminded me a little of that ghost dragon, and how death-like the Domovoi looked.

The gollums came at us quickly, and I had a feeling it was going to be a bit too much for Easton and Teagan. So I went to Rhodes' side, knowing I could at least use my three elements to do something. At least, I hoped I could.

I had my hands out, my Air Wielding sliding between my fingers as the earth shuddered beneath me, and water lapped at my feet.

Rhodes gave me a look and then nodded before holding out his hands, as well.

It was odd to think that I had two of his elements within me, but I had one more than he did now. Such a difference from when I was just the human girl, looking at the boy with silver eyes and so much power within him.

I had the power now. And I didn't know how to contain it.

A gollum came at Easton, and he held out his hand, Fire Wielding erupting from his palm. He stood there, his legs braced shoulder-width apart as he smirked at it, and the gollum screamed, a terrible sound that echoed in my ears.

The creature burned to ash, but that seemed to ignite the tempers of the other gollums, and they came at us.

I held out my hands and pushed my palms out so my Air Wielding shoved one of the gollums into another. It rolled in the air, its mouth wide, its fangs dripping—dripping with what, I did not know, or *want* to know.

"Don't let those fangs or its venom touch you," Rhodes said. "Its poison will kill you faster than anything else. Just stay out of its way."

"Oh, I have no intention of touching those."

But I wasn't the best fighter, even with all my training, and while I didn't want everyone else to do the work for me, I wasn't going to put myself in a dangerous situation. At least I would try not to.

The other gollums came at us, and while Teagan and Easton used their flames to try and get at them, it only scorched their sides as they barrel-rolled out of the way, screaming at us. It made my head hurt, so much that I had to close my eyes as I tried to block it out.

It was like they were using their screams to stop us from fighting, employing them as another weapon.

But we had to fight back. I just didn't know how.

I used my Water Wielding to create a wave to slam on top of the gollum, but I overshot it, and it only skimmed over the creature before landing back in the sea. I cursed under my breath, and then Rhodes gripped my hand and looked at me.

"Follow my moves."

I looked down to where he touched me. I didn't feel a single thing like I had before, but I knew it had to be the adrenaline. And the fact that this was totally not the time for any of that. I shouldn't even be having those thoughts.

So I nodded and moved my hands up in a cupping motion before pulling them down in front of me and then pushing them out again. It was an odd little wave-dance move that somehow worked, and I didn't know if it was just Rhodes or my help or both that pushed the water into the gollums. It pulled three of them back into the water, giving Easton enough time to get his footing again before he slammed his Fire into the next gollum that came up.

Wyn and Arwin were standing on either side of Teagan, using their Earth Wielding to create waves of dirt, helping Teagan's Fire.

We all worked as one, using whatever we had to slow down the gollums enough so the Fire Wielders could work their magic.

The only problem was that it wasn't like Easton and Teagan created a huge wall of fire to just burn them all at once. For some reason, once they burned one, the flames died out, and they couldn't use the fire for the next. Meaning, they had to start all over with their moves.

It was magic I didn't understand, nothing that had been written in any book for me to read.

But I was learning. And I would remember this.

And so we fought, side by side until the gollums stopped screaming, and the ash in the air rained down on us.

I sucked in a breath, my body hurting, my Wielding feeling as if it had been sucked out of me.

I had used so much power in the past few days without replenishing it. I knew that my well was running dry.

I just didn't know how to find the time and energy to make it come back.

Easton's uncle had taught me to meditate, to focus on my inner power to replenish myself, I just didn't know if I had the time to sit down and cross my legs and focus on it.

I needed to figure out how to do that while moving, while traveling, while finding my own peace.

I didn't know how the others did it, but they had a century or two more experience than I did. And it was starting to show.

While they all appeared a little tired, I felt ragged. I looked the most ragged, too.

My whole body ached, and I didn't feel like I could actually pull up any Wielding on my own without forcing it.

And that didn't bode well for anything else that might be coming at us.

"Well, that was pretty amazing," Teagan said, not looking exhausted in the least. In fact, he looked revved up from the fight. So much so that he grabbed Wyn and smacked a hard kiss on her lips. "Good job, old friend," he said, grinning.

Wyn just rolled her eyes and then kissed him hard on the mouth back. "Sure, honey. It was totally all me."

"Shut up."

Easton gave me a look and raised a brow. I just shook my head.

I did not understand those two.

Teagan grinned and then put both hands on Easton's cheeks and kissed him hard on the mouth, too. "There. Are you happy now? Did you feel left out?" Easton just blinked and then wiped his mouth, shaking his head. "Oh my, oh my. I've never known such glory. Seize the day. Oh my, you strong warrior you."

He said it so deadpan that everyone started laughing. Even Rhodes. I laughed a little, too, but it was hard. I was just so exhausted. And it hurt to want him.

To find more aspects of him that made me want to reach out to him. To be with him.

But it didn't matter. Because that wasn't important.

I knew that Teagan and Wyn were just trying to make people laugh, attempting to bring more warmth into what had just happened. What *kept* happening to us. Everything was being thrown at us, and we didn't have time to settle down and regroup. So the pair was just trying to help.

Even with the forced levity, I still felt two steps behind.

My bones ached, and that just reminded me of the bone magic that had brought us here. We still didn't know why it had.

But I knew something was coming. Something was *always* coming. And

I had to be ready for it.

And that meant I needed to stop worrying about what I felt for Easton.

Because it didn't matter.

We had more important things to worry about.

CHAPTER 24

Apparently, there was still a half-day's journey down whatever trail Rhodes knew through the Air and Water border. If we'd had the ship, it would have been easier, but there was no way to let anyone know that we needed another one. So, we would be walking until we reached the Air territory itself. However, tonight, we'd be resting. Because, apparently, I wasn't the only one who was exhausted after using so much Wielding.

We had lost most of our supplies, everything that wasn't strapped to us when the ship went down thanks to the Kraken, so we had nothing but our Wielding, and even that wasn't as plentiful as it needed to be. After all, we had used so much of it recently. It was just a little too much.

I was exhausted, and sometimes I really just wanted to go back to the way my life had been. When it had been just me, Brae, and Emory, and my

Now that I really thought about it, it hadn't really been that easy then either. Because nothing ever was.

Wyn and I were gathering up firewood, and starting a fire would be easy for Teagan and Easton. We didn't actually have to worry about making it, just setting it up.

Easton and Arwin were out searching for food, while Rhodes had done some fishing and was now getting those ready to go over the fire.

Teagan was on patrol, watching all of us work, but I knew he wasn't just lazing about. He was making sure that no monsters or others could come at us.

And considering that's all that seemed to be happening to us recently, I was grateful for that.

"I think every bone and muscle in my body hurts," Wyn said, rolling her shoulders back.

I looked over at her and nodded. "It's a little ridiculous. Like, you guys are all so much more in shape than I am, yet if you're hurting, you have to realize how bad *I'm* hurting."

"You do look a little ragged."

"I realize how whiny I just sounded, but God, I don't think I could look as ragged as I feel." I let my head fall back as Wyn put another stack of wood into my arms. I almost buckled under the weight of it but ignored it because, even though I was hurting, we had things to do.

There was no rest for the weary, especially Wielders.

I snorted at my little joke that wasn't really all that funny, and Wyn just gave me a look.

"Care to tell the class?"

"I'm just being stupid. And how do you know so many sayings from the human realm?"

"I spent a fair share of my life in the human realm," she said, shrugging as she picked up another stack of wood. "Before I had to go on patrols on the Spirit border, and before I went to try and help the Wielders who were losing so much of themselves thanks to Lore, I was out in the human realm, searching for you. I never found you, but I guess it just wasn't my time. It wasn't Easton's either. Rhodes was the one who was supposed to find you."

She gave me a look, and I just shook my head.

"He's not mine," I said, my voice a little firmer than usual.

"No, but I see the way he looks at you."

"He can look at me all he wants. Anyone can. But no one here is my soulmate, and that's really the only way I would care who looks at me at this point."

I winced as I set the wood down in the center of our camp area. "Well, that just makes me sound like I'm whining more. Like a little baby."

"No, it makes you sound like you're exhausted. You've had a lot thrown at you in a little bit of time. I've never found my soulmate, Lyric. And I've been around a lot longer than you. Teagan and I thought we might have been that for each other once. But that's a story for another time. I've never gone out searching for my soulmate, and I know you haven't either. You searched for other things, and all these maybes and perhaps have been thrown at you. It's kind of hard not to think about that stuff when you know you need to be worrying about other things. So, I won't bother you about it. Because I know it hurts. But just know that I'm here if you need me. Always."

"Thanks, Wyn. It's kind of hard sometimes, trying to figure out exactly what I'm supposed to be doing when there's no set path before me."

"And having a prophecy that doesn't say much and just seems to be a bunch of riddles isn't helping anyone."

"Oh, totally. And I feel like we're always on the move, going from one thing to another, trying to take in as much as we possibly can. Yet it's not enough. You know what I mean?"

"Yes, I do. We came to you in the lower Spirit territory to take you back, to train you. And ever since, we haven't really been resting. There were a few times where we could breathe, so we could get to know each other, but it wasn't enough. And the rest of us, save Rhodes and this group, has had centuries to get to know one another, to make our own stories. To figure out exactly who we are. You haven't had that time. And I know that you have Brae. And I miss her for you. I kind of miss that sweet little cat myself. Even though I know she wasn't a cat before. And I know that you'll eventually want to find Emory, though I've never met her. All of that combined with the fact that you don't really have a girl to talk to... Just know I'm here if you need me. I mean, you have Rosamond, and that's a girlfriend, but you can't only stick with one. So, you're welcome to have me, too."

I reached out and gave Wyn a hard hug.

"Thank you," I said, my voice soft. Sincere. "From the bottom of my heart. Thank you. Because everything seems so vast, so magical, and so out of my hands. Just having someone to talk to may seem silly, but it means everything."

"Well, I'm here. But it's kind of hard to have girl-time when we're surrounded by boys that always sweat and grunt."

She looked over at Teagan then, who flexed his muscles and waggled his brows.

I didn't think he could actually hear us, but he liked making Wyn laugh. Sometimes, I even laughed, as well.

I knew they had a friendship that went beyond what I could see. They were a unit, always there for one another.

I wanted that. Because while I had given in to my fate, I hadn't given in to my destiny. And I didn't want to be alone while I did it.

We finished setting up the fire and then watched as Easton and Teagan made dinner, using whatever berries, fish, and small game they had found.

I had learned how to field dress. I had learned how to take care of the meat and other things that we hunted down while we were in the Earth territory—even though it wasn't my favorite thing. But I couldn't be squeamish when it came to getting protein into my body. It wasn't like the meat that had been pre-packaged in the stores that I used to go to.

We ate in silence, Easton finishing quickly before going to relieve Teagan, Arwin following him.

By the time we cleaned up, and people started to settle down to at least get a power nap in before we started on our next part of the journey, I was exhausted, even more so than before. I wasn't very good at sleeping these days, mostly because I was afraid of the dreams. But I would get used to it.

As I looked over at Rhodes across the fire, I couldn't help but remember the time that I had fallen asleep next to him and woke up—thanks to Lore—with both of us on fire.

Rhodes had been hurt because of the dream, because of what Lore had done.

I didn't know if I'd ever forgive myself for that.

He had forgiven me, but it still didn't feel right.

I needed to take a walk or something before I went to sleep, mostly because my nerves were a little jittery. Even though I didn't have much energy, I just needed to move. So I patted Wyn's shoulder and gestured towards the other side of the fire. She gave me a nod.

I wouldn't truly be alone, and for that I was grateful. Because someone was always watching. With so much coming at us, I knew that was important. Even if privacy would sometimes be nice.

I knew Rhodes was right behind me as soon as I took my first step into the treed area.

"I'm fine, just taking a walk. Everyone can see me." I waved at Teagan, who gave me a chin lift before turning back to what he'd been doing.

"I know. I just wanted to talk to you. Is that okay?"

I swallowed hard and then looked up at him. He was pale and looked just as tired as I felt. I knew he was probably hurting.

"I'm so sorry, Rhodes. I wish we could get there sooner. To your grandparents. That way, we could get back to your mom. I'm just so sorry for everything."

He ran his hands through his hair and nodded. "I'm sorry, too. I don't know what I'm going to do without her. She has to be okay. You know?"

Rhodes was my friend, and even though things were complicated, I had to remember that. So I took a few steps forward, closing the gap between us, and put my hand on his chest. "I hope she's okay, too. We'll get to the Air Estate as soon as we can. And, hopefully, they'll find a way to help her."

"I don't think help is what my dad had in mind," Rhodes said wryly. "I think it has more to do with the whole saying goodbye thing. I just hate the fact that he's forcing me to go and get them on my own. I mean, without the rest of the family."

"Well, we're here for you. Though I wish there was something else I could do."

"I know." He was silent for a moment, his gaze resting on everything but me before he finally looked into my eyes. "I owe you an apology, as well."

I shook my head. "Why? I'm here because you need a friend."

"No, I'm grateful that all of you are here. And I know it's a little weird to be traveling with a bunch of Obscurité." He grinned for a moment, but then delight faded from his eyes.

"I'm sorry for kissing you the way I did in front of everyone. I was just confused. I just…I loved seeing you again. Knowing you were with me. And feeling our connection. I know it isn't the type of connection we thought it was. I would have been able to heal you if that had been the case. When you were bleeding on the floor, I should have been able to heal you. But I couldn't. No one could. And it was a blow that everything I had thought was true, wasn't. And I took it badly. And then I saw you again, and I kissed you because I missed you. And then it just crossed all the wires again and made things weird. So, I'm sorry. I'm sorry that I was so confused that I kissed you without asking. That I made things harder for everyone."

"I..." I trailed off, not knowing what to say. I hadn't expected his apology. After all, it had felt like a lifetime ago that he had kissed me when I first entered the Water territory. Had it only been a few days ago? Had I only been in the realm for a few months?

It felt as if I'd been here forever, yet at the same time, I could still remember everything about where I had been before as if it had been yesterday.

"You don't have to apologize. It was good to see you. Although, I must admit, it was a little shocking to have you kiss me like that."

"Well, I probably should have been a little suaver about it. Or at least not such a dick about it."

"You're apologizing now. But I don't really need that. Because I was confused, too. I guess I still am."

There was silence between us for a minute, and then he looked directly into my eyes again. "Is it Easton?"

I froze, swallowing hard. What was there to say?

"I see the way he looks at you. I see the way that you try *not* to look at him. He comes with a lot of baggage, but then again, so do I. I can't really fight with fate and all that. You know?"

There was something in his voice that I couldn't understand. It was hard for me to understand anything with the ringing in my ears. It was like I was standing on a precipice, far away from civilization, trying to figure out exactly what to say and what to think.

But there really wasn't anything *to* think.

There never was. That was why I was always trying to catch up and push thoughts from my mind, so I could focus on what was important and right in front of me.

I cleared my throat. "He's not mine either. We're not soulmates. He's just a friend. Like you. And, in the end, I guess that's how it should be."

See? I was being so strong. So…adult.

I was being the Spirit Priestess.

Not a teenage girl. Even though I was.

"Oh." Rhodes ran his hands through his hair again and then frowned. "I guess I thought…well, I don't know what I thought. But whoever's out there for you, Lyric, we need them to come for you. Because you can't do this alone."

"Excuse me?" I didn't mean for the bite to come out in my voice just then, but it did, and it surprised both of us.

"That's not what I'm saying." He held up his hands in surrender. "You are so strong, Lyric. And I know you're still learning everything, and I know that whatever comes, you're gonna be able to handle it. But I hope you have someone to lean on when you do. I hope there's someone that you can rely on. Because you can count on all of us. Rosamond, too. And Luken. We'll be your friends. Be your court or whatever word we'll use. Because we're here to stand behind you. But I feel like someone needs to stand *beside* you. Or at least closer to you than the rest of us."

I shifted my head and then pulled out my braid, pacing in front of him. There was so much inside of me, and I really just couldn't handle it right now.

I was tired of thinking about petty things like soulmates and futures. There was a reason I was in this territory, and it wasn't to find my soulmate.

It was to find Rhodes' mother's parents. It was to try and help the lady if we could. And it was to figure out exactly what this territory meant to me.

Because I had to find all the elements. And I needed to figure out the prophecy. Discover the end of it. Decipher it all.

And I couldn't do that with all this other insanity in my head.

"You know, that's nice and all, but I need to unlock Fire and Spirit first. Because the people around us are dying." I felt out of breath. "Literally dying. Their powers are still being stripped from them. The Wielding is being leached from this realm day by day, minute by minute. And I need to help figure it out. There's something wrong in the air. Can't you feel it? There's just something…wrong. I can't think about all of this." I gestured between the two of us. "Because, while you're my friend, what happened between us can't be important. There's something bigger than us at play. Doesn't it feel that way? Like something or someone's orchestrating all of this?"

"I've always felt that way. That we're just stones in a quarry. Drops in a sea. There's something bigger. But, sometimes, you have to remember the smaller things, too, and just focus on what is so you can move forward."

"I guess. But having my mind pulled in so many different directions isn't helping. I'm exhausted as it is."

Before I could say anything else, before I could put my words or thoughts into some kind of action, there was a rush of wind so forceful that it blew back my hair, and I had to reach out and grab onto Rhodes so I didn't fall.

"What is that?" I asked. Rhodes' eyes narrowed, and he growled.

"It's the Creed. They've found us."

CHAPTER 25

"The Creed?" I asked.

"They aren't the League. They aren't spies. They are the Creed of Wings. Assassins. And they don't take no for an answer. If they find you, you're dead—no matter who you call your king."

Rhodes pulled me closer, but I didn't move behind him like he probably wanted.

I wasn't as weak and untrained as I had been before, and from the look in his eyes when he glanced down at me, he was starting to see that.

At least, I hoped he was.

The others moved towards us, Easton and Teagan bringing up the rear as Wyn and Arwin ran forward.

"The Creed of Wings?" Easton snapped as he stormed in our direction,

Rhodes growled. "It's not me. I told you, things are unstable here. It's why I've been here for the past year."

"Things are unstable in my land, too, yet you said I gave up on destiny and all of that. Said I gave up on Lyric because I stayed behind to protect my people."

I stood in between them, anger radiating off me. "We do not have time for this. At all. What do we do, Rhodes? You called them the Creed of Wings. And you said they're assassins. What does that mean?"

"It means they're going to try and kill you, Lyric. For the love of God, get that through whatever fog you're in right now."

I glared at him, ignoring the hurt I felt at his words. "I know what an assassin does, Easton. And don't you dare talk to me like that again. I just want to know what we need to do."

"Fight. We fight. I don't know why they're here. But, like I told you, if they come at you, it'll be the last thing you see."

"Not today," Easton snapped. He rolled his shoulders back and took a few steps away from me.

"He's just a little worried, ignore him," Arwin said softly.

I looked over at the boy and shook my head.

"We're all a little worried. Whatever." I let out a breath. "Have you ever heard of the Creed of Wings before?"

"No, not really. Just as a myth, like the nightmares we've already seen. It seems like everything they wrote about in our children's storybooks is real."

"That's reassuring," I said under my breath.

And then there was no more time to try and figure out what we were going to do.

The Creed was upon us.

There were at least twenty men, and they all flew at us.

Literally flew.

I knew in theory and from Rhodes that Air Wielders could fly, at least the powerful ones. They could use their Wielding to lift them up from the ground and move them in any direction they needed.

But I hadn't seen it in action until now.

I mean, I knew my own Wielding was getting stronger the more I kept up with it, but I didn't think I'd ever be able to do this.

The grace and beauty of their technique was stunning. Even as I knew they were coming to kill us.

All of the Creed of Wings members came at us, their arms outstretched. And then, as one, they moved their hands straight out in front of them, slamming their palms together.

The force of the gust that hit us was so hard, we all staggered back.

I ended up falling, my palms scraping on the soil beneath me as I hit the ground. But then I was up on my feet again, ignoring Easton's and Rhodes' outstretched hands.

I didn't know what was going on, but I didn't have time to be the one falling.

"Kill them, before they kill you," Easton barked out.

When nobody took offense to that or contradicted him, I knew we were truly fighting for our lives.

The Creed came at us again, one moving for Teagan directly, using his Air Wielding like a blade.

Teagan held up a wall of Fire, pushing the Air Wielder back a few feet.

Two more came at Wyn, and she spun in a circle, her arms coming around her head to clasp above her body. She created a vortex of soil that protected her from whatever came at her from the Air Wielder.

Arwin went to one knee, swiping his arm down and bringing up a wall of Earth to take out two more Air Wielders.

Easton used his Fire and Earth as one, taking one step forward and then another, creating a wall of Fire and then a wall of Earth then slamming them into the Air Wielders as he moved his arms forward, protecting us as best he could.

Rhodes and I moved forward together, using whatever water was around us to create an actual wave to slam into the Creed members. And then we used our Air Wielding to create a buffer against the gusts of wind coming at us from our enemies.

I didn't know how to use all three elements at once. When I tried to add one, the others seemed to either fail or get out of control.

I tried to lift up more water and add soil to it so it would create mud and collapse on top of the Air Wielder. But instead, it fell back on itself. I cursed under my breath.

I wasn't trained in this, and I hadn't had enough time to deal with all of these new powers within me. It didn't help that we were already depleted. I could feel myself shaking, could feel myself breaking.

And then the hairs on the back of my neck stood on end, and I let out a gasp.

I turned around, and I knew it was over.

We were surrounded.

"There are more," Easton called out. "Protect your flank."

"No need to do that, son," one of the Air Wielders said, his voice low and deep.

"Not everybody wants your Spirit Priestess in this realm. The realm is exactly how it needs to be. We don't need her, we don't need a prophecy. And you will all listen to what your elders tell you." And then he slammed his hands down to the ground, and darkness came, pulling us all in with it.

I sucked in a breath as my eyes opened, and I found myself chained to the bridge of a ship.

Somehow, they had knocked me out, and now I was on a vessel surrounded by clouds.

I could hear the rush of wind around us, but I couldn't hear water.

I had a feeling we were far up in the sky, like on a plane. But we were on a wooden ship, and none of it made any sense.

This was so far out of my realm of experience.

"Just hold on," Easton whispered from my side, and I blinked, looking over at him.

That's when I realized that all of us were chained to the same deck, only on different parts of it.

Somehow, they had overpowered us, but that really hadn't been a question, had it?

They had outnumbered us three to one. And all of them had been trained to kill, torture, and do so much more.

I only knew that because I could hear the screams.

I could hear the depth of their depravity in the magic around me.

At least, I thought I could…I could see it in their eyes, hear it in the true silence surrounding us.

"Just hold on," Easton whispered again, his voice low.

But I couldn't talk because there was a rope in my mouth, keeping me from saying anything.

I was so scared, I didn't know what to do.

I didn't know who these people were. Not really. Nor did I understand why they wanted us.

They wanted me gone? Then why hadn't they just killed me?

No, instead, they had taken me, taken my friends and brought us here.

And that scared me most of all.

I tore my gaze away from Easton and looked over to the other side of the ship where Wyn was strapped to a piece of wood near the bow.

Her long, dark hair flew around her head, her eyes were wide, and her mouth was open as if she were trying to scream, but there was no air to do so.

"Do you know what we're doing now?" one of the Air Wielders asked as he stepped towards me.

You couldn't hear his feet moving along the wood, and as I forced my head to look down, I realized that he wasn't actually touching the deck at all. He was using Air Wielding to literally walk on air, likely just because he could.

The power within him was clearly immense, and he was wasting it like this? Using it for tricks?

"You're not going to be able to answer me, are you? I forgot we sort of gagged you." He let out a dramatic sigh, and it reminded me for a moment of the pirate king, only this man was nothing like Slavik. Slavik had had a sense of good in him, even if it hadn't made much sense to anyone but him. There was clearly nothing good about this man.

"Your friend...Wyn is it? She's a decently strong Earth Wielder. Yet nothing. All of the Obscurité are nothing. Their king is nothing. He'll be dead soon, and then the Lumière will take their rightful place at the helm. And we can stop talking about this fracturing." He rolled his eyes, and I did my best not to look at Easton. Somehow, the glamour still held over him. No one knew that they were talking near the King of Obscurité himself.

"But, as for your friend, Wyn," the man continued, "Air Wielders can do so much. It's not just creating little puffs of air and moving things around. Yes, we can walk on air. We can use it to do many things. But as you know, your body needs oxygen to survive. But did you know that with a snap of a finger, we can pull it from someone's body? Molecule by molecule, gasp by gasp."

He snapped his fingers, and Wyn let out a large gasp as her body folded in on itself, and she struggled to keep breathing.

Tears fell down my cheeks, and I wrenched against my restraints.

I could feel Easton doing the same by my side, but I could only focus on Wyn.

I couldn't reach her.

She was being tortured. The air literally being sucked from her body, and there was nothing I could do.

The man let out a sigh and snapped his fingers again. Wyn stopped panting, stopped struggling. Instead, her chest puffed out, and her eyes widened, and I knew he was hurting her again only in a different way.

And there was nothing I could do.

I thrashed against my restraints, and then two more Air Wielders came up from behind the other man, glowering at me.

"I don't like her in restraints. Make sure she's standing so she can see everything. But don't let her go. Keep the gag in. It'll help."

I kicked out and tried to use my Air Wielding or any of my Wielding to get free, but they had somehow put a block around me, using just Air to press on me so tightly that I couldn't even reach my own Wielding.

I was supposed to have all this power, yet I didn't know how to use it.

I felt useless. Depleted. And I was going to die after I watched my friends die.

I couldn't let this happen.

"Yes, I like this much better." The Air Wielder's gaze raked over me, and I felt like I needed a shower. "Turn her to the other man. Let her watch this."

They turned me to Arwin, and tears once again fell down my face.

The boy was upside down, hanging from what looked like nothing, except it had to be Air Wielding holding him aloft.

He was unconscious and looked as if he had been thrown against the bow of the ship, but now, he was hovering over the side of the vessel as if he might be dropped to his death at any moment.

I could see his chest moving, and I knew he was breathing. At least he wasn't in pain at the moment. I hoped to God we would find a way to wake him up and get us all out of this. Because I didn't want him to get hurt.

I didn't want any of us to get hurt.

All because some of those in power liked what they held and didn't want the crystals to find their way back to wholeness. They didn't want the prophecy, whatever it truly was, to come to pass.

They liked their individual power, but they were scared of change.

So, they were lashing out.

"This one sort of bored me. Someone hit him in the head a little too early, and he passed out far too quickly for me. But when he wakes up, we'll figure out what else to do with him. Because you see, dear Spirit Priestess, Air Wielders are much more than just the pretty ones with the puffs of air. Turn her to the next one," he barked out.

And then they turned me, and I swallowed a scream.

"Do you see this one? He's strong. So this is worth it. You see, those same air molecules that are in your body are right beneath the skin. With just a small bit of energy and precision, Air Wielding's so technical, you can actually peel the flesh from someone's bones."

Teagan looked at me then, and small strips of flesh and skin peeled from his arms and his chest, but he didn't scream.

Instead, his jaw clenched, and he narrowed his eyes at me.

He didn't say anything, but I knew he was telling me the same thing Easton was. To stay strong. Because we were going to get out of this.

Because there was a prophecy for a reason.

I just needed to unlock the rest of my elements. But how could I unlock them when I didn't even know how. How could I do anything when I couldn't get through this Air shield that they had put around me?

They turned me again, and I let out a choked sob around the rope in my mouth.

Rhodes was bloodied, bruised, and also gagged.

I wanted to reach out and make sure he was alive, but I could barely see his chest moving.

"You see, we can also use the air within you to blow you up from the inside out. But that ends things far too quickly. For this one, and the weak one next to you, what we did was throw them up as high as we could into the air just to see what our Wielding could do. And as they landed, we tried to test the precision of our Air Wielding to ensure that we could catch them."

He shook his head as he came into my line of sight. "Sometimes, we threw a little too hard or missed when they came down. That's why this one's so bruised."

He snapped his fingers, and Easton was moved towards me, two more Air Wielders pulling him. "Now, let's see what happens with this one."

The Air Wielder bowed to me, and I wanted to kill him. I wanted to use every single Wielding technique I knew, and everything that I had learned in the human realm to kill him.

He was torturing my friends just because he could. Because he wanted to show what an Air Wielder could do.

But the thing was, I knew that every type of Wielding had its darkness. That was why there was light, because there couldn't be darkness without light and vice versa.

There was good and there was bad in everything, and there were people that lived in the gray.

But this man was nothing in between.

This man was darkness. Even if he called himself Lumière.

Easton looked at me, his eyes dark, and I wanted to reach out, wanted to tell him that I'd find a way to help him. To save us.

But then two Air Wielders flipped up their hands, and Easton flew into the air.

I looked up, holding back a scream as he became just a dark dot so high in the sky that I knew if he fell from that distance, or any height even close to that, he would die. It didn't matter that he was one of the strongest Wielders I had ever met.

He would die, and it would be my fault.

And then the Air Wielders let their hands go, and Easton fell. I didn't hear a scream, but Easton wouldn't yell out. Of course, he wouldn't.

Easton came closer and closer to the ship, the black dot creating a form. Soon, I could see him, but I couldn't hear him.

I screamed then, reaching out, and the leader laughed, flicking his hand so Easton stopped about two feet from the top of the bridge of the ship.

"Ah, this one's important to you. As is the other we've bruised. That's good to know."

"You're nothing," Easton growled out. "And you'll learn that you are nothing."

"You're boring me. We are the assassins. Usually, we kill quickly, but when we want information, we do have interesting ways of getting it."

But they weren't asking us anything. They were doing these things just because they liked it. I wanted them dead.

"However, getting rid of the Spirit Priestess now would do us all some good. Did you know that there's a weapon we can make of Air? A blade that can pierce your heart just as precisely as anything metal or any other kind of tool. Only those that are pure with Air can make it so, though. But all of us have trained. You cannot be a Creed of Wings without it."

And then I looked up at him, and I knew this was the end.

They were holding me down, not even letting me fight back.

This was how I was going to die.

Stabbed. Again.

And there weren't going to be any Spirit Wielders to protect me this time.

Then the Air Wielder threw his hand forward, and I swore I could see the glint of light on a blade, even though it was made of air.

I screamed, not because I was going to die, but because I knew what was going to happen next.

Easton threw out his arms, his Wielding finally overpowering what was holding him back, and then he jumped, though he didn't push me out of the way. No, he would never do anything like that.

Instead, the King of Obscurité jumped in front of the blade of air and shouted. And I knew.

I knew as soon as the blade hit his body, as soon as it sliced through his heart, that it had hit home.

And that was when my own Wielding broke through. Finally.

I threw back my head, and all the Wielding I had been trying to push through moved past me like a wave. Water and Earth and Air slammed into the others around me. It missed my friends, only hitting the Air Wielders. They shouted and screamed, but were tossed over the sides of the ship.

I knew some would come back, but others wouldn't. Because I had heard the bones in their necks snap as the wind hit them hard.

My friends moved around me, each finally free. Teagan grabbed Arwin, but Wyn and Rhodes were fighting, using their powers to get free.

I was on the deck, my hand over Easton's chest as he smiled at me.

Smiled.

"I'll be fine. Missed the heart," he said, coughing up blood.

Still, tears fell down my cheeks.

Because I couldn't heal him. I wasn't a healer.

And I didn't know if he was lying.

The others fought around me, and I let them.

I had led the first strike, but if I let go of Easton just then, if I didn't stop the bleeding, he was going to die, and there was nothing I could do about it. I closed my eyes, not willing to look at him in death, not knowing what to do. My Wielding surged within me, pushing up from under my skin. It seeped out of me, bit by bit, moment by moment.

I didn't know how much time had passed, but soon, Rhodes was at my side, looking between Easton and me.

"Easton will be fine," he muttered under his breath. I looked up at him, my whole body drained.

"You saved him."

I blinked. "What? How?"

Easton was asleep in front of me, his dark lashes looking stark against the pale of his skin. He never looked fair. But right then, he looked pale as death.

"Apparently, a Spirit Priestess can heal."

I sat down, unaware that I'd been kneeling the whole time. My knees ached, but I ignored the pain. "Heal? I can heal?"

"You can. It wasn't a mortal wound, so I think that's how you could heal him so quickly."

If it had been a mortal wound, and I had healed him, that would have meant that I was his soulmate. But I knew that wasn't the case. Though I didn't say that.

And Rhodes didn't either.

I finally looked around at the ship and noticed that all of my friends were standing around me. Somehow, we were still in the air, but there were no Air Wielders around us anymore. I didn't know if the Creed would be back, or if they were all dead.

All I knew was that I was exhausted, and this was only one step.

Another battle, and we weren't even where we needed to be. I wasn't where *I* needed to be.

"The Air sentries are coming," Rhodes whispered. I looked up at him, frowning.

"What?"

He looked off into the distance, pale, bloody, and broken like the rest of us. "I can sense them. My grandparents must have sent them. The Creed is gone, but they're not dead. Not all of them anyway. They vacated the ship because I think they were a little scared. Good on you. Let's get Easton ready to go. Because I have a feeling it's only going to get worse from here."

And with that prophetic announcement, I looked down at Easton, and at the blood on my hands, and wondered what the hell had just happened.

And why I felt like everything had changed.

CHAPTER 26

Everything moved quickly from that point on, and I wasn't sure if I'd ever be able to remember exactly what had happened. Mostly because I didn't know if what I saw had happened at all. I had been so focused on Easton and keeping him alive, I'd missed it.

The Air sentries had indeed come aboard the ship. Their Wielding felt different. It was as if it weren't tainted with evil or greed.

Considering that it had been a while since I had felt anything as fresh as that from people that weren't lying destitute, or in a small town that had nothing to do with power, it was almost refreshing.

The sentries had shown up in light gray, almost cream robes and smiled at us, telling us that they'd been looking for us. Then said we should go. So, here we were, entering the Air territory, finally traveling to where Rhodes needed to go…and to where, hopefully, we could heal.

The Air territory was like something out of a dream. As someone who tried to run from her dreams, it sounded like a most apt description.

Everything was tall and high up in the air. There were large canopies everywhere, and the homes were built into the cliff faces as if anybody who needed to get anywhere could just fly, as if they had wings to go from one area to another.

I knew that the ground and water and all of the other elements were below, but everything in the inner sanctum was just higher, it's elevation grander.

There were flags and billowy canopies everywhere, the wind harsh in some respects. But this high up, you would have thought it would have been even worse.

I knew it had something to do with the Air Wielders themselves because they controlled the element.

And they wouldn't let it hurt their people.

Rhodes had explained as we came in that some of the Wielders could actually fly from area to area, though I had only been half listening because my attention had been on Easton. Others used rope bridges or different ways of getting around. Not everybody had the strength to use their Air Wielding in such a manner, of course, and he'd said that it was becoming even rarer as time passed because of the crystals failing.

I knew I needed to get to the court of the Lumière at some point, to see the crystal for myself.

I was drawn to it, much like I had been drawn to the Obscurité crystal.

I knew that once I figured out my five elements, I was going to have to figure out what to do with those crystals, too.

Or at least help someone else figure it out.

Because even though I had met some strong Wielders, the fact that so many were losing their Wielding and becoming weak as time passed, meant that the realm was indeed fractured. That people were dying.

But I was so exhausted right then, I couldn't care. I couldn't help.

I just had to focus on what was happening in front of me and take it one step at a time.

We had taken another airship, this one not as pirate-like as the Creed of Wings had. It had gone over the Air territory itself to get to the estate.

We had moved quickly, all of the Air Wielders using their Wielding in such a dramatic fashion that it didn't feel as if we had been on the ship that long at all.

Though I knew the land mass must've been the same distance away as any of the other territories.

Everyone was in a hurry, and I had a feeling that things were going to get worse.

"We're here," Rhodes whispered. I looked up at the estate in front of us and sucked in a breath.

It was all white with large turrets and billowing flags and silks everywhere.

It was gorgeous and looked like a princess castle out of a fairy tale.

"It's beautiful," I replied.

"My grandfather may be the Lord of Air, but my grandmother is the Lady of Air and helped design it. She wanted something welcoming, something pure so others knew that they could come for safety even as they came for hope. But it was so long ago, that I don't know if anyone actually remembers that message anymore."

I gave him a strange look, but I couldn't really ask him more because we were landing at the edge of the estate, and everyone was moving around quickly.

We were all bruised, and even I had some cuts and scrapes and blood on me.

Although Teagan, Arwin, and Wyn were bleeding, as well, they wouldn't let anyone else take Easton from them. Instead, they used the gurney that the others had provided and carried their king out towards where the infirmary must be.

I wanted to go after them, but Rhodes held my arm. I blinked.

He was hurt as well, one eye sealed shut, and blood all over him, but he just shook his head.

"We'll go to them soon. But first, you need to meet my grandparents. And I need to go, too." He swallowed hard, and I watched the long, lean line of his throat work.

Yes, it was probably protocol for the Lord and Lady of Air to meet the Spirit Priestess, but I knew that was only part of it.

Rhodes didn't want to be alone.

He was going to his grandparents to tell them that his mother, their child, was dying.

And he didn't want to be alone.

I would be here for him for that. After all, that was why I was here. At least part of it.

Rhodes took my hand and kissed it, and I looked at him, frowning. My hands were covered in blood, except for the very tops, where he had placed his lips.

It didn't feel romantic. If anything, it felt like a thank you. My head hurt, and I didn't want to think about anything so difficult—more than I already was anyway—so I rolled my shoulders back and gave him a nod.

"Let's go."

"Thank you," he whispered but didn't let go of my hand as we walked down the plank towards where the estate was located.

People milled around, some shouting at one another and talking about different things that I couldn't really hear. I heard the word Creed, and the words Spirit Priestess, but I ignored it all. Instead, I paid attention to the two people running towards us, the two who looked to be only a little older than me. But I knew they were Rhodes' grandparents.

It was a little shocking, and I had to remind myself that someone who was five hundred years old could look the same age as someone who was twenty here. Age was a different construct in the Maison realm, and I had to remember that.

"Rhodes." Rhodes' grandmother ran towards us. "My darling. What's wrong?" She cupped his face, and I looked over at her. I couldn't help but stare. She had long, dark hair that had a similar wave to Rosamond's. She was paler than both Rhodes and Rosamond but had the same sharp cheekbones and features.

Rhodes' grandfather had dark skin that glistened under the light, with short-cropped hair cut almost in a military style. They both wore long robes, but I could see the battle leathers under Rhodes' grandfather's. It looked as if they'd both been waiting for us, and since that was what the sentries had said, it made sense. But it was also confusing. Because how could they have known?

How.

"It's Mom," Rhodes whispered and then cleared his throat. "Grandpa, Grandma, I want you to meet Lyric."

Both of Rhodes' grandparents looked at me, and they smiled, though it didn't reach their eyes.

"We know who you are, dear Priestess," the Lord of Air said, smiling, even though it didn't really reach his eyes.

"I'm Lanya," the Lady of Air said softly. "This is my husband, Holdar. Let's get inside. We can check on your friends, and we can get you both bandaged up. And you can tell us what has happened to Áine."

"I would say it's good to meet you, but I know this isn't under the greatest of circumstances," I said softly.

Lanya moved forward and hugged me close. "Think nothing of it. Now, tell us what has happened to Áine, and we will discuss it more. I assume we will be headed towards the Lord of Water's territory," she said under her breath. I could tell there was tension there.

It just reminded me that there was so much more for me to learn.

"Rhodes, tell us what you know as we head inside," Holdar ordered, though his voice was soft. "What's wrong with our daughter?"

"She's sick," Rhodes answered, his voice breaking. "Dad sent me here to get you."

"Why did he not send a note?" Lanya asked then shook her head. "No, don't answer that. We know the answer. Because he likes ordering others around."

Holdar and Rhodes shared a look, and I wondered what was going on. However, I didn't think it was time for me to really know. After all, these were also the Lord of Water's in-laws, so in a strange way, it made sense that they might not like their son-in-law. It just seemed out of place since we were also talking about territories and power. Then again, Maison and human nature seemed to parallel in some respects.

Eventually, Lanya led me to a room where someone helped me get bandaged up after washing my wounds, and then I showered, trying to wash away the grime and sweat while keeping my bandages dry at the same time—Water Wielding at its oddest.

I sighed, trying to figure out what I was going to do next. I knew I needed to see Rhodes, knew he might need me, but first, I needed to check on another. Easton had been so close to dying, and all because he had sacrificed himself for me. It hurt just to think about. So, I needed to make sure he was okay.

I stood in the shower for a while, ignoring my aches and pains, just letting everything wash away from me. I hurt, my head hurt, my body hurt, and my soul hurt. I hadn't had time to just breathe, to figure out what was going on, but I knew this wasn't over yet. It couldn't be.

If I sat in the shower any longer, I knew that things weren't going to get better, they would only get worse.

I dressed in soft, clean leathers that those of the Air Estate had left for me, and I was grateful. From what I'd seen, everyone either wore leathers like these or long, billowing dresses and robes that always seemed to be blowing in the wind. I liked the fact that they'd given me something to fight in instead of a dress because no matter how hard I tried to avoid it, it seemed I was always fighting.

I was exhausted and just wanted to go to bed, but I couldn't. Not anytime soon. I didn't trust myself. Not when I couldn't control the power within me.

I looked down at my hands and tried to do what I normally did when I started my day, just stretch. I attempted to let my Air Wielding out, flicking my fingers ever so slightly, like I was rotating a shiny coin. Only it didn't come. It was just a puff. I frowned.

I focused on what was inside of me, on the Wielding that I could feel pulsating within me, but it wouldn't come out. I looked over at the pitcher of water and pointed my finger at it, just to see if I could float any water. Nothing came.

I couldn't reach for the earth, not when I was in a building that I could bring crashing down by accident, so I just looked down at my hands again and tried to Wield.

Nothing came.

"You need to rest," a deep voice said from the doorway. I turned quickly, and the water pitcher suddenly shattered, all three of my Wieldings hitting it at the same time.

I looked up at Easton and blinked.

"What are you doing out of bed?" I ran to him and put my hands on his face, then moved them down to his chest where he had been bleeding. Though he was wearing a shirt, it wasn't laced in the front, so I could see where he had been stabbed. Everything looked healed, and there wasn't a single scar on him.

"I'm fine, Lyric. They have good healers here. Everyone is getting patched up. Even you." He reached out and pushed my hair from my face, and I tried not to lean into that movement. "It seems you healed me, as well."

I looked up at him again, and then down at my hands where they still touched his chest. I quickly removed my hands and took a few steps back. I could feel myself blush, but I ignored it.

"I don't know how I did it."

"I don't know either, but you can do surprising things, Lyric. Once you have the energy and the training." He paused. "And once you believe in yourself again."

I didn't realize I was laughing until I was shaking with it. "Believe in myself?"

"Believe in yourself," he snapped, but it wasn't harsh. "You've had some knocks. Remember what Uncle Ridley said? Wielding comes from within. You need to focus on who you *are* so you can delve deeper into what you can *do* with your Wielding."

I shook my head, studying his face. "I don't understand what's happening."

"You used too much of your Wielding. It'll come back. Plus, you're shaking on what little ground you have. I get that."

"I don't know, Easton. I just don't know anything anymore."

"You're awake," Rhodes said as he pushed past Easton, careful not to actually jostle him.

"I am," Easton said, his voice low.

I looked between them, and all of a sudden, they appeared exhausted, weary, and battle-worn. It didn't matter that they were in different clothes and were both clean.

We all just seemed worn out.

It felt like this was the beginning again.

"You will need more training, and understand what the legend says, and then you'll be able to work out all of your Wielding. No one has three elements like you do. So, of course, it's going to take you time."

"Well, I guess we're eventually going to need to make it to the southern Spirit territory to figure out exactly what the rest of the prophecy is."

"You know part of the prophecy?" Rhodes asked, his voice high.

"Part. But we don't know exactly what it means. There's only one place we haven't really been to yet, and that's the ruins of the southern Spirit territory. There's got to be something for her there."

"Well," Rhodes began before I stepped in between the two of them.

"I love the fact that you two are talking about me like I'm not here. But we will deal with the next part of the plan after we deal with this. Because I don't know what's wrong with me. I think I'm just tired. That has to be it."

Easton met my gaze, and the look he gave me said he knew I was lying. He likely knew I was afraid. I was scared because every time I attempted to use all three of my Wieldings at the same time, something bad happened. And Easton had been the one to save me each time. I hated that.

I refused to rely on him.

No matter what.

"If that's what you want," Rhodes said softly.

Before anyone could say anything else, there was a scream, and we all started running towards the throne room.

Air billowed about, and Wyn, Arwin, and Teagan were right on our heels as we made our way in.

The Lady of Air was standing on the dais, her face in her hands as she sobbed. The Lord of Air stood and watched over her, his eyes also filled with tears, his body shaking with rage.

I noticed a piece of crumpled parchment in his hand, and I knew.

I knew that someone had sent a note, even though they had sent Rhodes and the rest of us here.

Someone had sent a missive, just like they could have before. Rhodes should still have been in the Water territory.

Because as soon as the Lord of Air started speaking the words, I knew what they would be.

"The Lady of Water is dead. Áine is dead. My daughter is dead."

As Rhodes fell to his knees beside me, I didn't move, I couldn't do anything.

Because I could feel the grief and didn't know how to help. We had been sent away for a reason, I just didn't know what it was.

We weren't there, at Rhodes' home.

And now the Lady of Water was dead.

Rhodes had lost his mother.

Still, somehow, we needed to figure out what was going to happen next.

CHAPTER 27

I stood there, watching as Rhodes calmly walked to his grandmother and pulled her into his arms. She sank into him for a moment before pulling back to look stoically like the queen she wasn't but the lady she was.

I might have said *calmly*, but there really wasn't anything calm about Rhodes. I could see the strain in his shoulders, the way his hands were still fisted as he held his grandmother close.

There was tension in him, grief, and all the pain that I could feel, though I couldn't reach out and help.

I stood back, feeling lost and as though everything had once again changed. But could things actually change when I didn't even know what my base was anymore? What if this was just life, the next breath, the next moment. Because everything altered with each breath these days, with each

The Lady of Water was dead.

The daughter of the Lord and Lady of Air was dead.

Rhodes' mother was dead.

The Lord of Air looked at us, fire in his eyes, and just glared.

The heavy brocade drapes in the tall windows that were at least three stories high blew, and it felt as if we were suddenly in a tunnel, the Air moving quickly.

The Air didn't touch us, it was only around us, threatening but not hurting.

"Holdar," Lanya said under her breath. "Don't."

"I'm not touching a soul," he growled, glaring at the world. It was like he wasn't looking at any of us but rather seeing something far off in the distance that he couldn't touch, that he couldn't save.

"Did you know that I am almost two thousand years old? Two thousand years have passed, and I have watched this world crumble and rise and then crumble again. Two thousand years, and my daughter should still be alive. She should still be here at our side, married, happy, and not a casualty of this war. But now she's gone. I want answers. Somebody'd better give me answers."

Then the winds died down, and he swallowed hard.

Rhodes was standing in front of him then, one hand on his grandfather's shoulder as we looked on.

Easton was by my side, and I hadn't even realized he had moved so close. It was as if he wanted to protect me, but there was nothing here to protect me from.

Even in the height of the lord's anger, Holdar hadn't attacked us, hadn't used his powers in a way that would have hurt anyone. He had lashed out and released all his anger, *so* much energy, yet he had been in control enough not to harm any of us.

That kind of power was breathtaking.

Teagan, Wyn, and Arwin were behind me, and I knew that they were ready to use their Wielding at a moment's notice, but I didn't think we would need to.

At least, not yet.

"Grandfather," Rhodes whispered. "She's been weak for some time. You know that."

"She was never weak when she lived here. She was strong. Happy." He beat his chest with his fist just once, but I saw the anger there, the strength of the warrior.

"Things change over time, my husband," the Lady of Air said softly. I could hear the steel beneath her words though. There wasn't anything calm about her.

No, she was ready to take a blade to the throat of anyone who dared to come at her family. Yet there was no one to attack here. We were hundreds of miles away from the Water Estate. Hundreds of miles away from their daughter. We had only just come here to tell them about their sick offspring. I didn't know if we were supposed to bring them back to try and heal the Lady of Water, or maybe to say goodbye.

I hadn't known the answer when we set out, and honestly, I didn't think anyone did.

Now, it was too late.

And because they had just gotten a message about Áine's death, that meant someone could have told the Lord and Lady of Air without Rhodes having to be away from his mother as she took her final breath.

I didn't think I could ever forgive the Lord of Water for that.

I didn't know if he was my enemy, wasn't sure if he'd had anything to do with what had been attacking us over and over again since we neared the

Lumière Kingdom.

But I knew that no matter what happened in the end, even if he became my most loyal ally in this new war, I would never forgive him for pulling Rhodes away from his mother in her final days.

Never.

"Help him," Wyn whispered, tears streaming down her face. And then I remembered that she could feel emotion, at least sometimes, and she didn't know how to help. But then again, neither did I.

"We'll be right outside that door," Teagan said, pulling Arwin and Wyn back. I nodded at them, grateful that they understood that the family needed privacy. I wasn't part of this family either, and I knew I should probably leave. But one look from those silver eyes made me stop. Rhodes needed me here.

I looked over at Easton, who gave me a tight nod, his jaw clenched as he turned on his heel and walked out with the others, leaving me behind with Rhodes and his grandparents.

I stood apart from them, feeling alone in the grand throne room, a place that had once been filled with love. I could tell that just from the aching memories.

It wasn't power, it was just a feeling.

And now, it was fading.

There was no daughter left.

Just a grandson in pain.

And more family members far away, like Rosamond.

The King of Lumiere's family was tied to Rhodes on his father's side, so none of those in the court would be grieving like this family.

Instead, it was just us, and I didn't know what to say.

"I'm so sorry for your loss," I said, trying to keep my voice steady.

"Thank you, Spirit Priestess," Lanya said, not looking at me.

"Call me Lyric." I swallowed hard. "I don't have any words. I wish there were some, but there aren't any."

I moved towards them, unsure whether I'd be welcome, but they didn't tell me to go away, didn't stiffen or even look elsewhere. Instead, the family stood on the dais, the actual thrones empty, no one looking at each other, but grief so immense in the room I could taste it on my tongue.

"I should ready the airships," Rhodes' grandfather said, his voice hoarse. "Come with me, Rhodes. You can tell me about my daughter. Tell me about the years that I missed because her husband wanted his estate *perfect*. Tell me about your mother. And then we'll go. We will say goodbye. And then I want answers."

Rhodes gave me one last look and then followed his grandfather as the Lord of Air stomped towards the doors.

I reached out, brushing my fingers along Rhodes' arm, and he gave me a grateful smile that didn't quite reach his eyes. Then I was alone with the Lady of Air.

I hadn't meant to be. I didn't know her, but I had a feeling she didn't want to be alone. Neither did I, honestly. I had lost people, but never like this.

I could still remember the pain, the agony I had felt when I watched Brae turn to ash, when she died in front of all of us.

But now she was back in another form, and although it wasn't really the same, and sometimes watching her reminded me that she would never be the smiling and laughing sweet girl I had known, she was alive. Though she'd never truly be my best friend again.

Maybe it would have been easier if she were gone forever, but even that thought was selfish of me.

I didn't know what Brae thought, no one did. She was back in some form, and I had to be grateful for that.

Emory was gone too, but she was still alive, in captivity as far as I knew.

Rhodes had said that he would help me save her, that he'd help me figure out how to fix her.

I just didn't know if she *wanted* to be fixed. I didn't know anything about her anymore.

It had been so long since I had seen her, that I didn't think about her every day.

Maybe that made me a bad person, but with so much going on, it was hard to remember every single aching pain in my life.

"Did my Rhodes ever tell you how his parents met?" Lanya asked as she looked off into the distance at one of the windows.

I followed her gaze and watched as birds with double wings and long, flowing tails flew into the air, cascading down into a beautiful array of lights and sparkles.

There was a song in the distance, and it pierced my heart.

I knew that song. It was one of sorrow and pain, though I didn't know exactly how I knew that.

"That is a sorrow dove," the lady said under her breath. "The territory is learning of my daughter's death, and the birds and those of the air are mourning with us."

I cleared my throat. "It's a beautiful song."

"She was a beautiful girl. Stunning, and so sweet. She was never frail, not like she became later on in life. She wanted to be a warrior, and I was always scared that she would succeed. I was afraid that she would die in battle because of what the old king fought. And then the Fall came, and she stayed in her castle, safe. Or so I thought."

I just stood there listening as the Lady of Air spoke, trying to imagine what it would be like to know thousands of years and have so many memories in your head that you had to shuffle through them to try and remember each and every detail. I didn't think I would ever be able to do that, but then I remembered that I might reach that age. Though I didn't think so.

I didn't think the prophecy of the Spirit Priestess would end well. But that wasn't something I was going to think about right then.

If ever.

"My daughter wanted to be a warrior like that Aerwyna of yours. She wanted to be everything. But then she met Rhodes' father. I hadn't wanted her to marry a lord. There's so few of us, only the four of the territories. The offspring get the titles as well, of course, but it depends on the family as to what they are called. The children lose their titles once they grow up or grow out of the territory itself. Or the title moves to the next person. It's been five hundred years under the rule of the current King of Lumière, and changes don't happen often. The fact that there is a new king in the Obscurité Kingdom is something far different. Further change."

She looked at me then.

"Most don't remember that with a new king comes change. Sometimes, for the good. I always liked Queen Cameo, though I probably shouldn't have. She was kind to me, though she didn't need to be. We were near the same age, and we grew up together—although far apart. She wanted change, and those around her didn't. She was not like the Lumière king, my king, the twin to my son-in-law."

She shook her head. "But all of those stories are for another day. As I was saying, your Wyn, the daughter of the Lord of Earth, is a warrior. She fights with that Frederic of yours," the lady said with a wink.

I stiffened.

No one was supposed to know that Easton was under glamour, but then again, others with magic were always around us, and I remembered that Rhodes' grandmother was a Truth Seeker, something that was passed down in Rhodes' blood, just not fully. Lanya could sense the truth of others. Perhaps she could see through glamour, as well. And Rosamond was a Seer. I wondered what Áine's power had been. Though I wasn't sure she could have used whatever it was. It looked as if the life had been pulled from her. And in the end, it had.

The Lady of Air reached out and patted my cheek. "Don't look so worried, my husband and I know who lies under that glamour. He didn't see, of course, but I told him. I don't keep secrets from my husband."

Her gaze went far away for a moment.

"We were good people, and we tried to keep our territory whole and safe. But sometimes it's not easy. Sometimes, we have to make decisions that hurt others, and it takes part of our souls in the process. But we always try to be on the side of good, on the side of right. Though sometimes those two don't end up on the same side."

She shook her head as if clearing her thoughts.

"I'm sorry, but my mind is running in a thousand different directions today, and I'm not making much sense."

"I'm following you. Say whatever you need to say."

"Your Wyn is a brilliant warrior. That is who my Áine wanted to be. And so, we let her train, we let her learn. Because I refused to clip my daughter's wings. My husband eventually learned to be understanding."

She smiled then, but it didn't reach her eyes. This poor woman. All I could do was listen, learn, and try to help.

"And then we went to the court under the old king's guard because there was a ball that we had been forced to attend. We were the Lord and Lady of Air then, as well. Therefore, we were required to attend. The current King of Lumière was the Lord of Water then, his father being the King of Lumière at the time. It's all very incestuous when you think about it, but titles go to eldest sons or daughters if there are no boys. And so, we went to the court with the others and brought Áine with us. She couldn't wear her battle gear because the old king hated the idea of women in power." She snorted. "It would have been a surprise to him that the King of Obscurité's daughter, Cameo, would one day become queen. He would have hated it."

Lanya smiled then, and I smiled with her.

"My daughter Áine was forced to wear clothing that spoke of a daughter of the Lord and Lady of Air. She was a lady in her own right, a lady of the Lumière. A simple title that is often called a princess—or prince for the males—although only in hushed whispers if they aren't actually within the court. All the words mean is that you're somehow connected to power. It doesn't really mean anything in the end."

Lanya shook her head and then continued. "Áine was forced to dance with all of the noble brothers then. Brokk, the former Lord of Water, now king of the Lumière Kingdom, was already courting Delphine, Rhodes' aunt. But Áine didn't have eyes for him. Instead, she had eyes for Durin. The other twin. The younger brother."

"It's odd to think about them as young...as people finding their loves," I said softly.

"They were your age at the time, it was that long ago. Áine had eyes for Durin, and there was nothing I could do. He was sparkly and a warrior and he made her feel like no one else ever had—or so she said. And so, she fell for him. And we could do nothing but stand back and let the marriage happen. Brokk and Delphine married around the same time as Áine and Durin. It was the idea that their children would grow up at the same time and be like siblings. Although they didn't have Eitri, Rhodes' and Rosamond's cousin, for many years. My daughter had Rosamond first, over four hundred years ago. And then she had Rhodes two full centuries later. But Rhodes and

Rosamond are as close as twins, no matter their age difference. My daughter was a good mother. And she tried to be a good wife. But I know that every time we tried to visit, seeing her became harder as the centuries passed."

It wasn't lost on me that the Lady of Air spoke of her daughter in the past tense. It was as if she'd lost her Áine long ago and time had finally caught up.

"Áine was no longer the daughter of Air, no more a future warrior. Instead, she was a centerpiece, a piece of lace to be strewn upon Durin's arm as he showed her off to his brother. She didn't fight in the Fall, none of us did. Not really. My husband and I tried to fight you see, but the king wouldn't let us. He banned us from unlocking our powers, so we couldn't actually fight and save our people. You see, he wanted to keep the blood pure. And that was why we fell. Why our power broke. Why the kings died, and there was nothing left but ash as we tried to rebuild."

She shook her head, and I reached out and ran my hand down her arm. She took my hand tightly in hers, and then loosened her grip, though she didn't let go.

The lords and ladies hadn't fought in the Fall? The great war that had split the realm as it was so the crystals had to work harder? No wonder the realm was failing. Their leaders had been held back, bound by their kings to surrender to the nothingness.

"My Áine became a shadow of herself. I knew she was becoming frail, so unlike the girl that I had raised, the daughter I loved. But there was nothing I could do about it because she still loved Durin. And she loved her children more than anything. She told me once that she felt more for them than anything she could have felt as a warrior, and I believed her because I loved my daughter more than any power I could have as a lady of the Lumière."

Lanya turned to me then, tears falling down her cheeks, but her chin raised. "I never wanted my daughter to marry a lord. I wanted her to have peace. But maybe she found peace." She shook her head and looked at me. "Peace. Such a small word for a rather momentous thing. You are the Priestess, Lyric. You can be so much. You could be the one who takes out the rot that has overtaken our kingdoms, our entire realm. You could be so much and save us from ourselves. The Spirit Priestess is more than a title, it's a calling. You are not meant to be a queen. Not a king. You are not a leader. You're a savior. But in order to know what you need to save, you must know your people."

I swallowed hard, transfixed. This was the most anyone had ever said to me about what I needed to do. I couldn't look away. "I've seen the territories, the people, and I know they need hope." I hadn't meant to say the words, but they seemed right.

"You *are* that hope. And when you find the right time, the key, you will be able to unlock the final two elements and save us all. Because, yes, the realm is dying. The people are doing much the same. My daughter is dead. We need you. You need to ensure that Rhodes and Easton find a way to repair the rift. Because they need to be the future."

I blinked, wondering what on earth that could mean. *They* were the future? Then what was I?

She must have seen the confusion on my face because she continued. "You are our future, but so are they. Easton is the King of Obscurité, he is one of our paths. And Rhodes will be the other."

I shook my head, trying to keep up. "But isn't Eitri the heir to the Lumière Kingdom?"

Lanya nodded. "But Rhodes is the future."

And then she squeezed my hand and left me alone to my thoughts on everything that she had just given me. She wasn't a Seer, and yet she spoke of truths and futures that didn't make any sense to me. Had Rosamond told her something? Or had she seen the *truth* somehow?

There was so much history, so much depth within this realm, but it was fracturing, turning to ash as she had said.

Rhodes and Easton were the future of the realm, but I was the savior.

If only I knew what that meant.

CHAPTER 28

The trip to the Water territory was uneventful compared to our journey to the Air territory. On our trip to Rhodes' grandparents' estate, it had felt like everything was stacked against us. From mythical creatures to the League and the Creed of Wings, so much had come at us, trying to kill us in unimaginable ways.

In comparison, this trip was almost serene. As much as it could get considering that we were headed to the Water Estate for the funeral of the Lady of Water.

So, no…not serene at all.

But a deep sense of mourning and confusion cloaked us like a sickly second skin. One that tightened with each passing mile as the airships moved over the land and sea of the Lumière Kingdom.

I didn't know how to help, so I sat there, listening as the Lady of Air

Unlike the previous trip, we weren't alone. Instead, the Lord of Air had brought a lot of his men with him, and some of the court who had wanted to go and mourn their former princess.

It was odd, though. Because while I knew we were headed to a funeral, to a place where Rhodes would say goodbye to his mother, it also felt as if we were going into battle.

I knew that shouldn't be the case since this was Rhodes' father, his other family. And yet something felt off.

It could be that I was just picking up on the very obvious undercurrents of how the Lord and Lady of Air felt about their son-in-law.

There was clearly no love lost there. I didn't know if it was because of how they'd felt about him before, or now.

After all, all they could see was what their daughter had turned into, year by year as her life slowly faded in the presence of her husband.

And from what I had seen of Lanya and her husband, I didn't think they would have just stood by and let it happen.

They must have tried to stop it. Must have tried to do something.

But the politics when it came to royals was so far out of my purview, it wasn't funny.

But I was learning. For now, though, I just had to sit back and watch.

"We're almost there," Easton said, standing up to start pacing again.

He had been doing that often lately, as if lost in his own thoughts. I didn't know what to say to him. Something had changed between us since I found out that he had lost his soulmate and learned that whatever I was feeling for him wasn't what I thought it was. That he wasn't mine. It was almost as if he knew that I knew and was now keeping his distance. Only, he wasn't really. He was just keeping emotional distance, and I had no idea what that meant exactly.

But he and Teagan kept taking their turns pacing along the extended deck of the airship we were on. Wyn and Arwin spent most of their time with Rhodes up front, either talking to him or just standing near him. I didn't know exactly what that was about, but I had a feeling that Wyn's emotional Seeing or whatever she called it, was drawing her to those who needed her.

I just sat there, sometimes talking to Rhodes, sometimes talking to the Lady of Air.

I took it all in, wondering how I could help.

Easton sat next to me then, and I looked over at him. "I know we're almost there," I said, not knowing if he needed a reply. "You can tell by the landscapes. We're starting to actually have land rather than just the sea."

"We're moving far faster on the way back than it took us to get there."

"Well, we haven't had a Kraken come at us yet," I said drily.

"Let's not risk bringing that one on, shall we?"

"Yeah, I'd rather not see another Kraken 'til the end of my days."

"If you see another Kraken, it'll *be* the end of your days." He leaned back on the bench where I sat and rubbed his temple.

"What's wrong?"

"Other than the fact that the Lady of Water is dead, and I have a feeling that it's only the beginning?"

I winced, looking around just to make sure no one was listening. Thankfully, everybody was busy getting ready to reach our destination and weren't paying attention to us.

"Yeah, other than that."

"I just have a headache. It's fine."

"Do you need to rest or something?"

"No, using so much glamour after all this time isn't the best for me. I didn't realize we'd be gone so long."

I sat up, alarmed. "Is there something we can do? Do you need to go somewhere and hide so you can drop the glamour? Or maybe you could, I don't know, use some of my powers or something. Is that a thing?"

He gave me a small smile, and my heart leapt. I stomped that down quickly though. It meant nothing.

"No, I don't think that's a thing. But, thank you for offering." He winked, looking like the old Easton. It was almost as if we were back training and everything was okay. But it wasn't. It never would be again. I had known that before, so it shouldn't be a shock now. And, sadly, it wasn't.

"Oh," I said lamely.

"And I can't drop the glamour because I'm also holding back some of my power beneath it."

I leaned closer so I could hear him. "I didn't notice."

"Because you can see through the glamour. And, well, other things." He shook his head as if not wanting to finish that line of conversation. I wanted to know what he'd meant, but I knew if I asked, he wouldn't answer. "Anyway, as soon as I let go of the glamour, I'll be at my full strength again, and everyone will be able to tell who I am. There's no hiding the king," he whispered.

"Wait, you haven't been at your full strength this whole time?" I asked, leaning forward, stiffening.

"No. I had to hold back some of my powers to keep the glamour on. That's why we keep getting so close to death."

"Because you weren't able to use everything that you had."

"Yeah, but it was either that or not come at all. And I don't want to think about what might have happened if I hadn't been here." He looked at me then, and I swallowed hard.

What was he searching for? What was going through that mind of his?

I knew there was more that he wanted to say, more I wanted to know, but he didn't say any more. Instead, he looked at me for a few moments longer and then stood up and started pacing again.

Teagan took his place near us, and I frowned. "What's wrong?" I asked, echoing my statements from earlier.

"Easton's stressing out, and if he's stressing out, then I'm stressing out."

"Well now that all of you are stressing out, I guess my stress levels are increasing, too."

He snorted and looked over at me. "Easton doesn't stress. He's calm, methodical. For a Fire Wielder, that's practically unheard of. His mother was the same way, though." An echo of pain washed over Teagan's face, but he quickly dampened it. "Easton sees a problem, looks for a way around it, and then blasts his way through it. Usually, anyway. But none of us can actually see what's in front of us now. It's like there's a block. And it's annoying him because he's worried that something's happening that he can't stop or even figure out what it is to begin with. And if he's worried, I'm worried. Because I'm his backup. I need to make sure he's safe so he can protect our kingdom." He shrugged as if the weight of the world weren't on his shoulders, as well.

I reached out and gripped his hand, giving it a squeeze. He looked startled by the contact for a moment, and I realized that I didn't really know Teagan that well, other than what we had learned about each other during our travels. I was closer to Wyn and even Arwin, but Teagan was a little more remote. He laughed, but he was still a warrior that took everything seriously in order to make sure that his king was safe.

"We'll figure it out." I laughed then, and he gave me a weird look.

"What's so funny?" he asked.

"Only that I keep saying that. I've been saying it for over a year now. Almost two, now that I think about it." I sat back, thinking about how much time had passed since I first saw the Neg when I was out for a burrito after a run of all things.

I wasn't that girl anymore, and honestly, I wasn't the same one from a year ago when I lost everything.

I didn't know what to make of any of that.

"I keep saying that I'll figure it out. But at some point, we just have to. I've been to all of the territories now. I don't have all of my elements yet, but I will. I don't think there's any getting away from that. And when I figure that all out, when I have all of my elements, I have a feeling there will be no going back at all. Everything will be going forward a hundred miles an hour, and we'll just have to hang on for dear life."

"It must be so weird to come at this so new. I've had my entire life put in front of me, and I knew what I would be. I knew I would be a Fire Wielder, and I knew that I'd protect Easton. Even when he was just a prince and the son of the queen. I knew I would be his friend, and I knew where I would be in the end. Wyn came later, but I knew we would be connected somehow." He gave me a wry look. I was not going there. That was their business, not mine. "And I knew we would be warriors. Arwin came next, and I instantly knew we would be a team. The three of us have been fighting for quite a while now, but not as long as others because Arwin is still so new. But we have always been the king's guard, Easton's guard. It was just never foretold that we would also be yours."

I blinked and looked at him. "You're not my guard. You're Easton's."

"You're the Spirit Priestess. We're your guards, too. Even that warrior, Luken, the Air Wielder. Rhodes, as well. Don't you see that everywhere we go, someone fights us? Someone doesn't want to lose their powers, doesn't want to lose their place in this fractured realm. And because of that, they want to take you out. Because they're afraid of peace and what change it will bring. The quieter ones, they are the ones who see you as their savior. So, when you reach the next step in your priestesshood, your guard will be there for you. Though Luken is Rhodes' guard, and I am Easton's, and we're on two sides of an immortal war, we will both still be on your side. Remember that when the time comes."

And with that, he walked away, leaving me confused.

I didn't know what to think about any of that, or how I should feel. And before I could figure out exactly what he'd meant by any of the things he'd said or how I felt about them, we started to descend. I stood up, going towards the front of the ship where Easton and Rhodes stood side by side. They parted slightly, and I stood between them.

Each of them looked down at me, but I couldn't read their faces. I didn't know what to do, so I reached out and ran my hand over Easton's arm and then Rhodes', just to tell them that I was here. Because I knew Easton was weakening from his power being bound and used, and Rhodes was in pain.

They weren't my soulmates, they weren't my future. But the Lady of Air had said that they were the futures of these kingdoms, and they were my friends.

So, there was no choice, there was only my place. By myself as the Spirit Priestess, following my own path.

By the time we settled on the Water Estate's grounds, everyone seemed a bit nervous, even though I didn't know why we should be. At least, not on the surface. After all, we were here for the funeral of the Lady of Water.

Not for war.

And yet, it felt just like before when we had been ready to fight Lore, the Creed, and the League. There was a sense of anticipation that worried me.

I just didn't know what it meant or what was to come.

The Lord of Water came towards us, Durin's face a mask.

It slipped for just a moment, though, and I didn't see the grief that I thought should be there. I didn't see the agony of a man who had just lost his soulmate, his one true love.

Instead, I saw rage mixed with surprise.

Why would he be surprised to see us?

I couldn't help but wonder why he had pushed us away to begin with.

Something was going on here, and whatever it was, it wasn't pretty.

We would figure it out, though.

Because even though I didn't know the rest of my prophecy, I wasn't going to allow people to get hurt because of those in power. That was one thing I could do. Or, at least begin to do.

"I'm surprised to see you," Durin said, his voice low.

I froze beside Rhodes, who stiffened.

"What do you mean, Father? Surprised to see me here for my own mother's funeral? Why did you send me away? What were you thinking?"

Rhodes' voice grew louder with each question, and I reached out and tugged on his arm.

People were staring, and I could feel the power of Wielding around me.

Durin looked as if he wanted to strangle his son, but still, there was no hint of grief there. Just anger. And all of it directed at Rhodes. With no outlet.

"Let's go for a walk," I whispered to Rhodes. "Just a walk."

He looked down at me and glowered for a moment before rolling his shoulders back and masking his emotions. His face went carefully blank, and then he looked at his father and bowed.

"If you'll forgive me, I'm just shocked. I'm going to walk off my emotions. I will be back later to talk about Mother."

There were so many pieces in play, so many others watching, that as much as I wanted Rhodes to lash out at his father and figure out what had happened, this wasn't the time or place. Not when so many people could be hurt, and not when we didn't know exactly what was going on.

And so, without a word, Rhodes stalked off, and I followed him, looking over my shoulder at Easton, who gave me a tight nod. I could see the relief on his face. He was glad that we weren't going to be around. Because if Durin lashed out, using the full force of his Wielding, innocents could be hurt. And we needed to find out why we'd been sent away first.

I walked with Rhodes in silence. We didn't say anything. There wasn't anything *to* say.

We just walked, and I tried to take in the sights, to look at the waterfalls and the bubbling brooks, but it all seemed so muted now. As if it were mourning its lady, as well.

How would the rest of the realm react to the loss of the Lady of Water?

"I'm sorry," Rhodes growled under his breath. "Something's going on here, and I want to know what it is and why. But I shouldn't have said that. I should have waited until we were in a place where Father might actually answer me, instead of doing it when he felt so superior."

"I'm sorry about your mother, Rhodes."

He looked at me then, his silver eyes watery. "Me, too. I loved her. The mother you met? That wasn't the one who raised me. She wasn't always so frail. I don't know what happened, but now she's gone, and there's nothing I can do."

"I wish there was something I could do to help you."

"I know." He sucked in a breath and then shook his head. "Let me get you back to your room so you can get some rest. We have a long day ahead of us with the funeral coming up and all of the politics that come with that. And I need to see Rosamond. She and Luken weren't out there to greet us, and I just need to see my sister."

I opened my arms, and he stepped into them. I gave him a hug, holding him tightly and him grasping me tight in return. I inhaled his scent, the one that had always made me dizzy before, but it wasn't the same now.

This was my friend, the person who'd helped me see the realm which I had been born to live in yet hadn't known. And he was grieving. And there was nothing I could do.

He hugged me tightly for one more moment, and then let me go without saying a word. He led me to my room, the place I had stayed before, and then nodded and walked away.

I found myself alone in my suite, missing Brae, missing my old home. Missing everything that had once been.

Because I didn't know what was going to happen next. It seemed I never did.

I showered and got ready for bed, the lateness of the hour surprising me. We had traveled for so long, and I never seemed to just be able to rest.

With so many things going on inside my head, I didn't know if I would be able to rest at all, even though I knew I needed to.

There was a light tap at the window. I narrowed my eyes at Easton, who stood on the ledge, looking in.

I opened it for him and snorted. "What are you doing?"

"It's bedtime." That was all he said as he jumped into my room, walking around.

"That doesn't answer my question. What are you doing here?"

"Something's up. And none of us are alone. Arwin, Wyn, and Teagan are in one room, each taking shifts. I don't know what's going on, but we're going to stay on guard."

I put my hands on my hips and just glared. "So that means you think you're going to be in my room tonight?"

He gave me that grin that always did something to my insides, but I just glared at him. "I promise you, nothing's going to happen, little girl. Just go to sleep. I'll watch over you."

I did not like the fact that that made me feel better. It shouldn't make me feel better. It should make me feel creeped out.

Instead of thinking too hard about it, though, I just pushed past him and got into bed, careful not to look at him. Because I wanted to sleep, my whole body was tired. And I knew Easton was likely exhausted, as well.

"Wake me up halfway through so that I can take the next shift."

He just raised his brows.

"Don't give me that look. You said the others were taking shifts. I'll take the next one for us. You need sleep too, Easton. Especially since you had that headache earlier."

Something came over his face, but I didn't know what it meant. Instead, he just took a couple of steps forward and then tucked me into bed. It was such an intimate gesture, so out of character for the two of us. But then he leaned down and kissed the top of my head as if he were tucking in a family member and not the girl who wasn't his soulmate.

"Sleep well. I'll watch over you."

"And then I'll do the same for you."

He smiled but didn't answer.

I didn't think he would.

After all, nobody was allowed to take care of Easton. Let alone me.

CHAPTER 29

I vaguely remembered the first funeral I had ever attended. It was that of a coworker of my father's, one who had died too young. I'd been too young to understand what was going on, had been shushed more than once by my mother for asking questions.

I remembered the casket, the way everybody sniffled and cried but didn't speak. Or, if they did, it was in hushed whispers that seemed to echo within the chamber.

I couldn't remember much of it, not that there *was* much to remember.

I'd been to a few other funerals in my lifetime, one for a grandmother, and another coworker of my father's, but never for anyone that I had truly known or had a connection to in my adult life.

So, as I sat on a bench next to Easton and behind Rhodes, I wondered what we were going to say, and what would happen.

Only a day had passed since we arrived from the Air territory and we were already laying to rest a woman I hadn't really known. I couldn't remember if I'd even heard her voice.

Isn't that odd? Shouldn't I remember if I had heard her speak? She was the mother to Rhodes and Rosamond. The daughter of the Lady and Lord of Air, people I already respected after knowing them for only a short time.

And she was gone.

Others were silent around me, but there wasn't a single tear in the place.

Nobody was crying or talking or using hushed whispers to let their voices be heard.

We all just sat there in silence as the water of the stream that went through the estate itself trickled along.

Burble. Drip. Drip. Drip. Burble.

It was just a trickle, but it was the only thing that echoed in this tomb.

I sat on the left side of the pulpit along with Easton and the other Obscurité. We were the only ones that got looks since everyone else in the room was Lumière.

No, not the Lumière as a whole, just the Water territory.

The only other people there, were those on the left from the Air territory, the ones who had come with Rhodes' grandparents.

Everyone else was from the Water territory only.

I found that odd and wondered about it.

The King and Queen of Lumière weren't here. No one from the court either, from what I could tell.

It was just those in the Water territory. It was as if we were in our own little world with this funeral happening so fast that either no one else had had time to come, or they hadn't been invited at all.

The whole thing seemed almost a farce.

But I would never say that.

Because the people in front of me truly were grieving, as were those that had known the Lady of Water as a child.

They were mourning, and I didn't know how to help them.

The Lord of Water wore dark gray. The others wore black, but he didn't. He stood out like royalty amongst the rabble.

He didn't smile, he didn't frown. He had the perfect look of a royal who knew his due and wanted the praise and consolation of someone who had lost his wife.

I didn't see grief there, didn't see a single inkling of sadness at all.

And I couldn't help but wonder *why* we had lost that frail woman so quickly.

And why we couldn't be there for her.

"My wife is gone," the lord began.

"She is gone, my Áine. My sweet Lady of Water. Though she was never truly Water. Her Wielding was that of Air."

I stiffened and looked over at Easton, who gave a slight shake of his head. This was not the time for questions, but I didn't know what this was. At all.

"My wife is gone, but we must remember who she was and what she stood for. We must remember that the time of change is upon us, and we have the Spirit Priestess on our side." He gestured towards me, and I refused to look away, refused to look at anyone who was now murmuring under their breath. There were whispers, words that I couldn't hear, not with the ringing in my ears.

How dare he bring me up during his wife's funeral? This was not *my* time, nor the time to talk about change.

This was a time to remember a woman who was no longer with us. A woman who had been a warrior but had been stripped of that when she fell in love. A woman who had been a mother but hadn't been able to say goodbye to her only son.

I didn't like Durin. I hadn't liked him before, but now I loathed him.

"The Spirit Priestess is among us, and that means we are truly fruitful indeed. Let us not weep for Áine. For she has gone to a better place. A place where the old kings and queens and those who have fallen before us reside. Let us remember that she was weak, not strong enough to lead us into the new era. But that is fine, for the weak have their place, as well."

I'd noticed that those in front of me were holding Rhodes down, and Rosamond's body was shaking next to him. The Lord and Lady of Air didn't say anything, they just sat there staring at their son-in-law as if they were waiting for the right moment to end his life.

And though I wasn't truly bloodthirsty, I would hold their robes for them as they pummeled him with their Air.

"My wife is gone. But the future remains. Let us rejoice in what she has left us and what we have. For the Lord and Lady of Water will always be with you. I am the Lord of Water, who rules this territory. The lady is gone, long live the lord."

And then he turned on his heel and left, his guards hurrying after him.

I narrowed my eyes at a few of them as they passed, wondering why they looked so familiar even though I hadn't seen them the last time I was at the estate.

People started getting up then, whispering fiercely to one another. I just sat there and then looked over at Easton.

"What on earth?" I asked in a shaky voice.

"Not here. Go back to your room. We're leaving."

He stood up then, and I followed him. I did not want to stay in this estate any longer. And while I wanted to make sure that Rhodes and Rosamond and their grandparents were okay, a weird, sinking feeling had crept over my skin, and I knew that I couldn't stay for long.

Something was coming, and something was wrong with the Lord of Water. We couldn't stay here any longer. The fact that they had let the Obscurité stay for as long as they had didn't seem like a boon any longer. It seemed like a threat.

I had to remember that while I might be of neither kingdom, not truly, the Obscurité and the Lumière were at war.

All of this talk of change and weakness…that meant something.

We needed to go.

I was just at my door, Easton practically pulling me by the arm, when Rosamond came running up from behind us.

"You must go, quickly," she said, her eyes glossy. "I don't know what's coming. They've blocked my Sight somehow. But you must go. Protect the Priestess, King," she said, her voice low as if not hers. "Protect her and protect the prophecy. I can't See what's coming. Why can't I See what's coming?" She put her hands over her face, and I reached out to help, but then Wyn was there, holding Rosamond close. "Go, grab your things. Easton, grab mine. If we can, let's take Rosamond and Rhodes with us. I have a feeling it's going to get dicey soon."

"Bet they're not going to like that," Easton said dryly. "But you're right, there're more important things than old rivalries to worry about," he said and then looked at me. "Go. Grab your stuff. Something's wrong."

"What about the Lord and Lady of Air?"

"They have their staff, and either we'll bring Rhodes and Rosamond with us, or they'll go home with them. I don't know which yet, but we need to get out of here. Be quick."

And then he kissed me quickly, surprising us both it seemed. Then I was in my room, trying to grab the last of my things. I wanted to get out of here quickly. I hadn't truly unpacked, as if I knew that this was just a way station.

Everything just seemed wrong right now, and I was scared. So scared.

Because while I had been at every estate now, this one seemed the most tainted, even more so than the Earth Estate.

This man was the twin of the King of Lumière, and I had never met the king. Only his twin. Just the man who seemed to want to use me for something.

Though I honestly didn't want to know what that was.

The door opened behind me, and I turned. "I'm ready."

And then I froze.

It wasn't Easton or the others who stood there. No, it was one of the guards. I looked at him, trying to remember exactly where I had seen him before. It hadn't been at the estate. It had been somewhere else.

Who was this?

"The lord requires your presence," the man said, his voice deep.

"Oh, well, I-I need to do a few things. I'll meet him there soon?"

"No, you won't. You will come with me now. This is the Lord of Water's territory, and you will listen to what he says."

And then he reached out to me, and it wasn't Water Wielding that came for me but Air.

My eyes widened, and I let out a shocked breath.

"You're an Air Wielder," I whispered.

"Clever girl," he said and then winked.

Suddenly, I knew where I'd seen him before. He was one of the Creed of Wings. One of the assassins.

And he was working with the Lord of Water.

What on earth was going on?

I looked down at his other hand and froze. There was something that looked like a stone in his palm, but it wasn't a stone. It was a bone.

Bone magic.

How did this man have bone magic? And why was he working for the Lord of Water?

But before I could reach any of my Wielding, he slapped his hand out, and I flew off my feet, my back hitting the wall behind me.

I coughed, scrambling to stand as I tried to shake the ringing from my ears.

"The Lord of Water requires your presence," he growled out, and I tried to use my Wielding again but froze mid-air.

The Lord of Water was behind him, his eyes narrowed as he stared at me. I looked down, and he too had a piece of bone in his hand, a snarl on his face.

"Tut-tut, Spirit Priestess. He told you that I required your presence."

"Where are the others?" I snapped, once again trying to use my Wielding. But something was blocking it. It had to be the bone magic. I didn't understand it. How was this happening?

"You'll see them soon," the Lord of Water said. "But first, you're a very important part of my plans."

"I'm not going to help you. Ever."

"I was afraid you would say that."

He snapped his fingers, and another Creed of Wings member dragged along a very familiar person.

My eyes widened, and I blinked, my mouth going dry.

"If you want this boy to live, you'll come with us. The others are already taken care of. You don't want any more deaths on your hands, do you, Spirit Priestess?" Durin asked, his voice sickly sweet.

I looked down at Arwin's face, at the blood covering his mouth and one eye.

I didn't know what to do. But I wasn't going to watch my friend die. I wasn't going to watch the boy that always seemed so young die because of me.

"I'll go with you. Just leave him alone."

"You've made the right choice, Lyric." And then he took the bone, slid it into his other palm, and slowly dragged it across Arwin's neck.

I watched, my body and my soul frozen in place as Arwin's eyes widened ever so slightly, before a thin trickle of blood slid down his neck. It was just a tiny amount, as if it were nothing.

But I knew it was too much.

It was as if everything in front of me had stopped, as if I could hear every single intake of breath and watch the seconds tick by.

It had been the same when Brae died.

That echoing, hollow sadness gripping me.

Arwin fell to his knees, his hands outstretched, his body pale as blood slowly slid down his neck and onto his shirt, darkening the material to a red that could only mean death.

He didn't blink, didn't scream, he just fell to his knees and then to his side as the blood pooled around him. I wondered why everything was so silent.

Why wasn't there a scream of death as Arwin died in front of me?

But there was nothing.

Durin had said that he had taken care of the others, and then he had killed Arwin right in front of me after saying he would keep him alive.

As the Creed of Wings surrounded me, and the Lord of Water brought the bone to my chest, I wondered if this was going to be the end or only a new beginning.

He smiled.

And then there was nothing.

CHAPTER 30

Drip.

Drip.

Drip.

I opened my eyes and then shut them again. A vibrant light was above me, blinding me. It hurt.

Where was I? What had happened?

I wasn't in my room, wasn't in any of the rooms that I had called my own for the past few years. No, this was somewhere different. I couldn't remember what had happened, how I had gotten here, or where I needed to be.

There was something wrong, though. That much I knew. What was that sound? What was with all the dripping? The slow water coming from all around me.

I opened my eyes again and gasped.

There was light, something artificial as if it were bouncing off whatever bubble was above me.

Bubble, as in an air pocket within water.

My breaths came in quick pants as I panicked.

I fisted my hands, trying to move and figure out exactly what was happening, but I felt chained. Chained down so I couldn't get up.

"Breathe," Easton said next to me. I froze before slowly turning my head as far as I could to see him.

He wasn't wearing his glamour anymore. No, he was back to looking like Easton without the blur, but someone had beaten him badly. His whole body was covered in bruises and cuts, and he had a wicked gash on his forehead that looked like it hurt a lot.

He looked worse than he had when we were on the ship, and the Creed of Wings had taken us.

The Creed of Wings. They were working with the Lord of Water.

My eyes widened, and Easton tried to reach out, but he was secured to something, as well. The same something I was chained to most likely.

But my mind wasn't working all that quickly just then, and I couldn't really focus on what we were secured to. Whatever it was, I knew the whole situation was bad. I knew that whatever we were chained to wasn't something I wanted to think about. So my mind just didn't let it happen.

It was all a blur. There was just water, Easton, and from the moan to my left, there was someone else. Rhodes? I looked. Yes, it was Rhodes.

The three of us were chained to something, and I didn't think we were going to get out of this.

I licked my dry lips and tried to focus again. I was so tired. As if something had hit me hard in the head and took everything out of me. I just didn't know exactly what it was or what any of this meant.

"What happened?" I asked, my voice shaky.

"It's my father," Rhodes said, his voice emotionless and dull. There wasn't even the anger that I had heard before there anymore. And that scared me. Because Rhodes needed that anger. Despite how calm and collected he usually was, he needed his emotions. And if he was so calm now? So emotionless? Something bad was definitely happening. Or it had already happened.

And then I remembered Arwin and the blood on the floor, and the way that Durin had come to me, the bone in his hand as he slammed it into my chest, making me pass out.

I didn't know what type of magic he had used, other than bone magic since he had been holding a bone. And I didn't know what that bone magic could do, other than somehow open portals like the one that had saved us from the Kraken.

"Yes, the Lord of Water put us here. In case you couldn't tell, we're under the actual sea," Easton snapped. "The damn sea."

He pulled against his chains and growled.

"They've infused bone magic into the chains. We can't even use our Wielding, it's completely blocked."

I thrashed against the bonds myself, the clanking sound of chain against whatever we were attached to echoing in my mind.

"I thought the bone magic saved us from the Kraken?"

"Bone magic isn't inherently horrendous," Easton said slowly.

"It's made by using the bones of the murdered, how can it not be horrendous?" Rhodes asked, growling. At least there was emotion there, even though it happened to be directed at Easton. Regardless, I would take it.

"Yes, in order to make bone magic, you have to sacrifice other Wielders and then strip their magic from them, directing it into yourself somehow. And in doing so, the bones left behind sometimes create echoes. If someone uses the bones for evil, then the bone magic is for evil. Just like any Wielding.

But, somehow, I believe the bones we're currently lying on protected us. As if the souls that were forced to stay beneath the sea didn't want us to drown or be destroyed by the power of the Kraken."

I listened to Easton even as dread filled my belly. And then I looked under him and to the left beneath Rhodes.

We had been chained to bones.

Not just rocks or the bottom of the sea.

As far as I could tell, it was an actual layer of bones. Likely the Wielders who had been murdered.

There were leg bones and arm bones, and I could even see finger bones and a couple of skulls. Some were shattered fragments of whatever had been crushed, but others were still whole and new.

I turned my head up just slightly and noticed the empty, hollow eyes of the skull placed right by my head.

I couldn't scream. I couldn't feel anything.

Because this wasn't just morbid curiosity, a macabre display, this was death.

And they had chained us to it.

They had used these people for something, and even though somehow, as Easton had said, the souls had saved us once, I didn't think it was going to happen again.

Not when we were chained to them, not when we were under a bubble of Air beneath the crushing weight and pressure of the sea.

I didn't understand the physics of it, considering that if we had been in any other vessel beneath so much ocean or sea, the pressure would have been an issue. But maybe with Wielding, it negated science and physics. I had always been afraid of going in submarines or going too far under the water where your ears popped. Where you could lose oxygen and die because you couldn't rise to the surface fast enough. Where your lungs couldn't regulate to the new pressure.

It was one reason I had never been scuba diving, even when my parents went on vacation and wanted me to take classes so I could dive with them.

Instead, I had stayed behind on the beach and played in the waves, enjoying the sand beneath my feet, the heat of the sun on my face, the water lapping at my toes, and the wind in my hair.

I'd enjoyed those elements, but I hadn't wanted to be beneath the sea.

Now, here I was, under so many feet of water I couldn't even comprehend it.

"Lyric? Breathe."

I looked over at Easton and let out the breath I hadn't even realized I'd been holding.

"How do we get out of here?"

"I don't know, but we will. This isn't how it ends for us, do you get that? This is not how it ends." I looked into Easton's dark eyes and tried to feel like he was right. That there was a way out of this.

Everything just felt so far out of my hands. Especially when the bone magic had taken away my Wielding. I might still be new to it, but in cases like this, it was the only thing I could rely on. I was becoming a fighter, but only through my Wielding.

Using my fists or even the ability to run as far as I could wouldn't help me while trapped at the bottom of the ocean.

"How did you get down here? How did *I* get down here?"

Easton let out a curse and then looked up and around as if he were trying to find a way out just like I was.

"They bombarded us, one at a time. Waited until we were all separated and gathering our things." He paused, and I could feel the pain in that beat. "I saw the blood, I didn't know who it belonged to. It was in your room. I didn't see a body."

I tried to say something, but Arwin's death and everything that came with it caught in my throat.

"You're not covered in that blood, so unless they washed you, it wasn't yours."

"It was Arwin's." I whispered the words and then swallowed hard. Because Arwin deserved more than my crying, more than my pain. He deserved everything. He deserved to be alive. "Durin used an actual bone to slice Arwin's throat. He died. Right in front of me."

A tear slid down my cheek, and Rhodes muttered to my left. I could hear him moving, trying to get out of the chains. Easton just looked forward, not glancing at me, but I could see his throat working, I could see the pain cross his features.

Arwin had been one of his. Had been part of his inner circle, a unit so small that Easton felt alone a lot of the time. He never told me that, but I knew.

I knew so much about him, even though it had only been a year since I met him, and even less time that we'd actually spent together.

"I didn't know about Arwin. I didn't know where any of you were, nobody was near me when the eight guys came at me, using bone magic to take away my Wielding. I just saw the blood as they dragged me past your room. I thought it was you." Easton paused, breathing hard. "I thought they had killed you. But instead, I woke up here with you right by my side, passed out just like me. And the son of the traitor the same way."

I winced at those words and then turned slightly so I could see Rhodes. "You can call me much worse. I knew there was something wrong, I thought I could fix it, but I couldn't. I think he killed my mother. And not just by taking away her will. There's no way she could have died the way she did, we don't die from illness."

"You're right about that, son," Durin said as he came out from the shadows. I hadn't even realized he was there, but maybe he hadn't been before. Because as seven Creed members and some League members appeared with him, I realized that the group had somehow made a hole in the bubble so they could walk along the seabed.

The Lord of Water was working with the League *and* the Creed. These weren't the same League members I had seen at the border of the Spirit and Water territories, so that meant that maybe the League members who had come at us before truly were from the King of Lumière, and these were just other League members. The only way I knew it was them was because of their robes.

Everybody seemed to be out to deceive one another. So, for all I knew, the League was playing both sides.

But the Creed of Wings did not work for the Lord of Air. No, they definitely worked for Durin. "Your mother was useless. I thought she would help me gain power, but all she did was give me a weak son and an even weaker daughter. She thought she could be a warrior?" Durin scoffed. "She couldn't even fight for herself. So, I slid bone magic into her food every day for years. She died just the way she lived. With nothing. But now, my territory mourns for me. They see me as the man who could do so much for them because I am grieving my wife. They will give me everything, they will give me gifts, they will give me their power. They will know that I am righteous because they will see the man who was left behind."

Durin, the Lord of Water, was clearly insane.

And he was going to kill us.

I really wanted to kill him first.

"I hate you," Rhodes growled. "And I'm going to get out of this. I'm going to escape, and I'm going to kill you myself."

"Strong words for a boy who can't even find a mate with the Spirit Priestess. You found her, and it did nothing for us. You couldn't take her power, you couldn't make sure that the King of Obscurité died along with his mother. What are you even worth? I thought maybe we'd get something out of having Lyric by your side, but she doesn't want you. She wants the Obscurité boy."

Durin shook his head and then glared over at Easton.

"And you. The so-called King of Obscurité. It took a while to get through that glamour of yours, but I knew you couldn't be who you seemed. I knew it."

From the way he sneered it, I didn't think he had known at all. I had a feeling that whatever bone magic he used had stripped the glamour from Easton. It was the only thing that I really thought could break through that.

"And I see you're just as much of a pompous ass as ever," Easton snapped.

"Watch your language, son. One day, I'm going to be the King of Lumière, and then I'm going to war with your sad little kingdom to take all of their power. Because you don't deserve it. Fire and Earth have been the dirty, inbred Wielders for centuries. My father should've eradicated all of you. Instead, we had the Fall, he died, and we were split into two kingdoms that can't fix anything on our own. Because your blood isn't pure."

He was raving and literally made no sense. But I knew if I worked hard enough, maybe I could get out of these chains. I might not be able to use my Wielding, but I had been human long enough that I had learned how to rely on just being myself. Maybe I could wiggle my way out. I wouldn't die like this. Not without a way to fight back. And not between Easton and Rhodes, who couldn't fight back either.

"It's taken me a long time to figure out exactly what I needed to do to find my place in this world," Durin began, pacing between the Creed and League members.

"Still a monster," Easton drawled.

"Am I?" He lifted his hand, a bone in his palm. The chains around Easton tightened.

I heard Easton's inhalation of breath, but he didn't make another sound, just stared as the chains dug into his skin, bruising, pulling so tight that I was afraid they would cut into him. But I didn't make a sound either, because if I did, it would likely make things worse for everybody.

But all the while, I tried to work my way out of my chains. I was the Spirit Priestess.

I needed to find my way out of this.

Because if I didn't, what was the damn point of any of what we'd gone through?

"As I was saying, I needed to make alliances." He pointed towards one of the Creed members. "The Creed has always been in its own little world, don't you think?"

The man who had to be the Creed of Wings leader gave Durin a look and then nodded. "We do not work for the Lord of Air. We are…allies. But an alliance with the Lord of Water and his plans seemed just."

"You see? They didn't want my father-in-law. They wanted me. All the connections to my wife? Useless."

Rhodes made a pained noise, and I wanted to reach out and help. But instead, I just kept working on my chains.

"The League works for my brother. They are spies and very good at what they do. But, sometimes, they work for me."

Two of the League members gave each other looks behind Durin's back, and I wondered what that was about.

Maybe the League had been there that day along the waterfalls to push me away and kill me as well as the rest of my friends on behalf of the king.

I would have to remember this for later, but first, I needed to make it out of this alive.

"So, I've made my plans, but I had to gain power. Because my brother has the crystal. The crystal of the Lumière, which some say is fading, but it's only because of my brother. If I were the king, born just two minutes earlier, then it wouldn't be a problem. I would have found a way to save my kingdom and get rid of the low-born Obscurité. But there was nothing I could do. At least, until now. Because he may have the crystal, but I have the bones." He held his hands out, and the seabed beneath us shook, but it wasn't just the ocean floor, it was the bones of the souls he had trapped and killed.

"Did the boys tell you exactly how you make bone magic?" Durin shrugged and walked towards me, looking down at me with eyes so like Rhodes' but without their luster.

"You see, each Wielder has magic within them. I have been taking some of the Wielding from Air and Water Wielders who don't understand their role in my territory. Because while I can't siphon their Wielding like the knight of the Obscurité did through their kingdom's crystal, I can create my own type of siphon with these bones. So, I took the sea, for I am that powerful. I could use the entire sea with my Wielding of Water and crush my Wielders. With just a precise number of artifacts. Artifacts I have been searching for longer than the Fall itself, I can create the bone magic."

He smiled then, and my whole body chilled.

"People thought that bone magic had been eradicated, that it was a mere whisper or myth. But I am the one who brought it back. I am the one with the power. Whenever someone goes against me, I emerge victorious. My enemies will quake in front of me because I'm the one who can take care of those who aren't my allies. So, Air and Water Wielders that come too close, who don't understand their purpose, those are the ones I've used. Other Obscurité who dare to enter my territory? They learned a lesson and paid the price. Only they couldn't tell others because they never made it out."

I looked over at Easton then. He just glared as if he were planning to rip the flesh from the Lord of Water's bones.

Not that I actually blamed him just then. The atrocities that this man had committed were horrendous.

And if we didn't get out of here, no one would know. And he would find a way to get rid of all evidence of his lies and horrors.

"So, I used these bones to protect my territory so I can one day take over Brokk's rule and become the high king."

That wouldn't be the high king. The high king ruled over *both* kingdoms like before the Fall, that much I remembered. So, Durin was going to take out Easton now, and then take out Brokk so he could rule both kingdoms somehow.

I needed to find a way to stop that. Durin looked at me and smiled. But it didn't reach his eyes. I didn't think anything could.

"But, Lyric, in order for me to have all the power, I know there's one piece I'm missing." I stiffened, my whole body frozen.

"And while I would've preferred you to have all five elements, four will have to do. I had heard that it takes great distress for you to unlock an element. So, sending the Kraken like I did should have worked. But, somehow, you escaped. As did the others. We sent the Creed to you, and yet you survived that, too. And none of that brought out your new elements. But there is no more time. I need what you have, so I will use you, Spirit Priestess. You will be what brings me the power to take over the lands and be who I was born to be."

Rhodes and Easton pushed against their bonds then, and so did I, all of us trying not to feel as if our efforts were futile.

"The Spirit Priestess is among us, long live the Spirit Priestess."

And then the water came.

CHAPTER 31

At first, it was just a drip, as if the top of the dome were leaking. But then it was more. The Lord of Water moved back, his Creed and League surrounding him as they disappeared into the shadows.

I assumed they made their way to the surface using their combined Water and Air Wielding, their ticket to safety. But as they did, they didn't close or seal the bubble. The water came in a wave then, crashing into the side of the dome as if it were a snow globe and the water was just being poured in. The water smashed into one side and then curled into a wave before folding in on itself to hit the seabed. The action splintered the bones, moving them in all directions. A few came at me, slicing my skin, scraping my face, my hands, my arm, my leg. Any part of me that wasn't held down by chains or completely covered.

"Try to get out!" Easton yelled.

"Just try," Rhodes whispered.

"I can't!" I screamed.

I looked at Rhodes as we each tried our best to overcome the bonds. "I'm so sorry," he shouted. "So sorry."

I swallowed hard and rocked, trying to break free.

"Just hold your breath, Lyric," Easton called out. "I'll come for you. No matter what, I'll find you."

I wanted to believe that. Wanted to trust that the three of us would find each other. That we would win. Would live.

But it was hard when the world seemed to burn around us. Burn…and drown.

The bubble quickly filled with water, and we were the pieces inside our makeshift snow globe of death.

The pressure was too much, and our Wielding wasn't protecting us anymore. There was nothing.

This was what I had always feared, too much water pressing down on me. My lungs burned.

My eyes were open, but it was so dark I couldn't see anything. I couldn't hear Easton over there. I couldn't even hear my own breathing because I couldn't breathe. I couldn't do anything.

I could just hope, pray, and thrash against my bonds. But I knew it wouldn't be enough.

I would never be enough.

Not like this.

It was all too much, the pressure, the water, the fact that I couldn't reach out and help the others.

We were going to die like this. And the Lord of Water was going to use whatever artifact he could to suck out our Wielding and make himself more powerful. And then he would use our bones for more magic, to take more souls, and enslave an entire kingdom. An entire realm.

I couldn't let that happen.

I pushed against the bonds, even as my head went light, the lack of oxygen too much. But it was no use, there was no coming back from this.

And then I blinked, and I was suddenly standing at the center of a clock, twelve shadowed figures staring at me as the four elements slammed into my body. I dripped on the ground beneath me, creating a mud pile in the soil.

I had been here before. Many times, in fact. When I first learned of the Maison realm and these magics, I had been called to these dreams. I had seen the clock with the twelve Spirit Wielders, though I hadn't known who they were at the time.

I had seen courts and ladies and lords. I had heard the whispers and saw the balls and gowns of a time when there hadn't been war.

And then I'd seen the elements of five. Each one calling to me as if a siren song. I had seen them all. But it hadn't made sense. Hadn't been anything at all to me. Not really.

It had only been a dream. Just an idea of where I would be one day, though I had never truly made it there.

I looked up, drenched, covered in cuts and bruises, gasping for breath.

A blink.

A blink, and I was here.

But this was still a dream, I wasn't *really* here.

Was I dead?

Was this my eternity?

"You must unlock," the one at twelve whispered. "The Gray is coming."

The Gray?

"Say what you really mean," I shouted. I was so done with all of this. I had been thrust into this world with nothing but a promise of answers, and yet no one had given any to me. I had lost my friends, my future, and my family. And yet they expected me to just *know* what to do.

What the hell was this prophecy anyway?

It didn't make any sense. And it never would unless someone told me why I was here and how I could help. No one seemed to care about that. They just wanted to wait for me to have all the answers and save them.

I was done.

Spent.

Because I didn't *have* the answers.

And I was scared that nobody else did either.

"Where am I? Am I really here, or is my body dying down there below the sea? What about Easton? And Rhodes? Why can't you just do something?" I threw up my hands, and Water, Earth, and Air raged all around me, creating a spiral of causation and causality.

"You will not know the answers until you know them all. The Gray knows. The Gray sees."

I glared at Four, the one to my right and slightly behind me.

"Now you're speaking in riddles that don't even make sense. I know part of the prophecy. But it's not enough. I'm dying down there, and you bring me back inside my head? I'm not breathing. I'm dying. I'm probably already dead. Is this my hell?"

"You're not dead, Lyric. But you must unlock the final element. You must break it. This one will be the worst. The one you can't completely control. But you will find a way."

I turned on my heel and looked at Six.

"Why can't you help me? Why does it all have to be shrouded in mystery?"

"Nothing worth fighting for is easy," Seven said, and I swear it took everything within me not to throw something at her. Old sayings and platitudes that meant nothing weren't helping. Nothing was helping.

"You won't tell me what I need to do. You won't get me out of this. You won't do anything. For all I know, this *is* my actual hell and I did die down there. Why can't you let me out? Why can't I break the bonds? Why won't you at least let me help Rhodes and Easton? They didn't ask for this. They were just trying to help me."

"You would sacrifice yourself for the two boys who you thought might be soulmates? Who you must find a connection to?" Two asked, and I turned to the Spirit Wielder.

"Isn't that my role? To sacrifice everything?" Two sighed and looked at me, the Wielder's eyes vacant and shadowed. I didn't know what else Two meant by his or her statement, but I didn't have time to ask. It wasn't like I'd get an answer anyway.

"Your role is to save the kingdoms, to fuse together the realm. But in order to do that, you must use your elements. So, you must unlock the fourth one. You will know what to do when the time comes. As will we."

"Are you saying that you don't know now?" I asked, exasperated and growing colder. I might be in my mind right now, but my body was dying. I had a feeling that when I was in this type of thing, time moved far faster than in real life, and that was the only reason I was still alive to do this.

But I was running out of time.

I was going to suffocate, die from the pressure, and then I wouldn't be here to yell at the Spirit Wielders who couldn't help me.

"Much is unknown. We don't live where you do. We can't know. We are not all Seers and foreseers. We are the ones who are here to try and help. But we were banished long ago. We are not what we once were. And although we try, it's not enough. We can only do so much. You must do the rest."

I looked at One, and my shoulders fell. They were right. No one knew anything, just a prophecy laden with mystery and what seemed to be untruths.

"You must unlock the final element, not for yourself, but for those you love." I looked at Three and shook my head.

"How do I do that?" I asked, tears falling down my face. "How can I help them? They're dying, and there's nothing I can do."

"Look inside yourself, Fire is there. Fire can take Water, and such the element that you are. You will use the four, and you will find a way to protect those you love. Because it is not you for who the elements Wield, it is for those you love."

"But…"

"You can love both. And in the end, you will choose. But that is not for now. First, you must save yourself and then the world."

"I have to unlock Fire," I whispered, looking down at my palms.

"The others just happened. I was angry, or we were dying…just like I am now. So, why isn't Fire coming?"

"Because you're afraid." I looked at One as the Wielder spoke. "You cannot control the other three, and you are afraid you are not going to be able to control the fourth. But it won't matter whether you can control them if you can't unlock them. So, first, you must find a way to get through the fear and find the Fire. Not for yourself, but for the boy who lost his mother, for the boy who is losing his father. Do it for the boy who looked at you with wide eyes as they slit his throat. Do it for the others. Your Easton and your Rhodes will die right now in the next few moments if you do not unlock Fire. You will die too, but you already knew that."

"Unlock the Fire," they whispered as one.

"Become the Fire."

"Find the Fire."

"Unlock. The. Fire."

"Do not let the souls of those you love die," One shouted.

"I can't," I gasped. "I'm trying. I promise I am." I looked down at myself and tried to imagine a lock surrounded by flame and then tried to pull at it. I attempted to picture a key unlocking it. Nothing was working. Why wasn't it working?

It had happened on its own before. But I couldn't make it happen.

"Your soulmate is dying, save him."

I looked up, my eyes wide. "What?"

"Save him."

And then I looked down at myself and imagined the Fire, imagined the answers, imagined so much.

They were wrong, I didn't know anything about who could be my soulmate, but I needed to save my friends. I needed to save those who had protected me for so long.

I needed to save myself.

So, I thought of Arwin. Of Easton. Of Rhodes. I brought to mind the old woman who had died giving me the last bit of prophecy in that cave with the Earth pirates. I could see Rosamond's face when she tried to get us out of the estate. I imagined the weak-looking little boy who had cried in the Fire territory because there wasn't enough food.

I imagined all of it, and I watched it burn.

Because if I weren't careful, the world would burn, it would drown, it would suffocate. There would be no more saving it from itself without a savior.

I had to fulfill the prophecy.

And that meant I needed to unlock Fire.

I imagined Rhodes, and then I pictured Easton, and I thought of what they were feeling right now, the crushing weight of their suffocation, each oxygen molecule escaping them one by one. They were dying.

I couldn't be too late.

And then it snapped into place, making a slightly audible sound that didn't even echo.

It just slithered out of its shell as if it were afraid. No, as if *I* were afraid.

I focused on the flame, what I had always admired. I had always wanted to hold the Fire in my hand and watch it dance upon my palms. Even when I was younger, I had looked at fire and was transfixed.

Now, it was within me.

So, I held up my hand, my eyes closed, and the Fire came.

But with Fire, came danger and power.

And then I was no more.

I was just the flame.

The roar was immense, shuddering through my body as the bonds broke around me, as did Easton's and Rhodes'.

I wasn't controlling it, it was controlling me. Somehow, the water sloshed away from us as if the sea were parting, and we staggered to our feet. Standing on the bones of those who had been sacrificed before us and surrounded by towering plumes of the sea as fire fizzled all around us, a swirling vortex that flew into my hair and into the others as if the air were mixing with it, the Wielding having a mind of its own.

Easton and Rhodes gasped, their bodies shaking as they looked at me, each reaching out to me. But I wasn't Lyric.

I was Fire.

The ground beneath us cracked, and all four elements moved around me, trying to compete for which could win, but I was the Fire.

Rhodes and Easton yelled at each other, commenting and then using their own Wielding, and then we were airborne. Somehow, Rhodes pulled us to the cliff's edge. We were no longer in the water, but I was not the same.

I was not Lyric.

I was the Fire.

And as I stepped one foot and then the other onto the land belonging to the man who had tried to kill us, who had attempted to take us all, I knew that I needed to protect those who couldn't save themselves.

I needed to fight.

And when we fought, my foes would die.

They would burn.

Because I was the Fire.

CHAPTER 32

"Lyric."

The voice drew me back. I knew that voice. I loved that voice. I blinked again, and suddenly, I could see, I wasn't surrounded by fire, or even by the terror of what had just happened. Instead, I stood on a cliff face, the wind blowing in my hair so violently that the small strands seemed to cut into my face. I looked over at Easton and then down at my hands.

"I…I…oh, God."

I leaned down, put my hands on my knees, and tried to suck in a breath.

"It's good that you unlocked your fourth element," Easton said carefully, then came to me. He helped me stand, putting his hands on my shoulders. "But we're not done yet. Can you do this?"

I looked at him and tried to nod, only I felt like I was a few steps behind. I wasn't going to let the Fire control me. I couldn't.

But I still felt like I wasn't all there.

I hadn't felt like myself when all of that had happened. I'd felt like I was only watching, that I had actually been the Fire, and that was scary.

Considering what had happened when I unlocked Water, I was terrified of what would happen if I let Fire go again.

"What are we going to do?" I asked, trying to keep my voice steady. I wasn't steady.

"We're not going to have enough time to plan it," Rhodes said. "They're coming."

I turned to him and then looked forward. That's when I saw them.

The Lord of Water had used the time we'd been under to start assembling his army. The League, the Creed, and some of his own men were standing, all in battle leathers, shouting at each other and at the Lord of Water as they tried to amplify their messages.

I didn't think it was a fight. No, they were just revving each other up so they could fight whoever came at them.

I didn't know if anyone could actually see us because we were slightly downhill, but we could see the line of soldiers. There were so many, and I didn't know what to do.

But I couldn't let the Lord of Water go. Not with everything he had done.

"Rhodes, your father can't create this army. He has to atone for his actions."

"I know." Rhodes looked at me then, his silver eyes filled with pain. "And I know you don't want to be the one who has to deal with it. I don't want you to either. I'll take care of him." He raised his chin, and I reached out and put my hand on his upper arm.

"We can do it together. I think that's why I have the four elements now. Why I'm here. You can't bring together a realm if its core is rotten."

"I'll be by your side, too," Easton said, coming up right behind me.

"Unless it wouldn't do to have the King of Obscurité helping you."

I looked over my shoulder and tried to give Easton a grateful look.

It was going to be complicated, but we couldn't let this go on. Not when the bones of those who had died in silence screamed at us from beneath the sea.

"I don't think it's Lumière versus Obscurité at this very moment. We'll deal with the consequences later. But I could use your help. I don't know who on my father's side truly knows who he is. Or if they do, they might not care. Because he's been the pretty face, the one who has lied about his power for so long. And people have been afraid of what they're losing, afraid of the world failing around them. So, they've clung to my father, even through his lies."

"You won't fight alone. We're stronger than he is. Together."

"What about the power he's stolen from the other Wielders?" I asked. "Because I felt those bones, and the Spirit Wielders told me it would be hard."

"The Spirit Wielders?" Easton asked.

"I'll tell you later, but I don't think we have a lot of time."

"You don't," Rosamond said, coming towards us.

I looked at her and almost wept in relief.

I hadn't known where she, Wyn, Teagan, Luken, or Rhodes' grandparents had gone, but now they were all here, coming from the other side of the hill where Durin and the others couldn't see them. There were others with them, those who had come with us from the Air territory.

"Rose," Rhodes said, his breath coming out in a quick, choppy pant before he crushed his sister to him. "I thought he'd taken you. Or worse." He kissed the top of her head, and Rosamond patted his back.

"He's been using the bone magic to stop me from Seeing," she said as she pulled away. "That's why I couldn't See what he had been doing to Mother all this time. Why I couldn't See why he wanted you to go to the Air territory. I saw none of it. Because he was blocking me. But he will not be able to do that any longer. The disasters I See? The end of our eras? That will happen if he becomes king or finds a way to start this war within the Lumière Kingdom. He can't see us now because he's so blinded by his own ambitions that he won't even bother to look for magic beneath the hill. But he will know us soon." She raised her chin, looking more like a queen than I'd ever seen her.

She was the Lady of Water, in truth.

A Seer, and a brilliant tactician.

I wouldn't want to face her as my enemy.

"We will help, as well," Lanya said, hugging Rhodes to her. "We might be the Lord and Lady of Air, but we come with powers of our own. He killed our daughter."

"And he will pay," Holdar growled.

"I've been able to See it all now," Rosamond explained as we all looked at her. The others hadn't been down below the surface of the sea with Easton, Rhodes, and me when Durin had revealed his plans. "It was like as soon as I was able to figure out where to look after his speech at the funeral, I could See what I had been missing. But by then, it was too late."

"It was too late to save Arwin," Wyn said softly. She looked at Easton and me and blinked away tears. "We put his body in one of the caves nearby so we can take him home." I reached out and gripped her hand before letting go.

"We evacuated as many as we could from the estate," Teagan explained. "Rosamond said she Saw that we needed to, so here we are. But it's us against an army. It's not going to be easy."

Teagan and Easton shared a look, one that spoke of warriors or long-ago battles, but I knew we would fight. Because we couldn't allow Durin to win.

"I think if we make sure the others know exactly what he has done, some of his army won't fight with him. I think they'd fight against him."

They all looked at me, and I held up my arms. "If we could use the Water and Air Wielders, and perhaps even the other Wielders, we can pull some of the bones up from the sea floor, and they will speak their truths."

"Lyric," Lanya said, putting her hand over her mouth. "Are you sure?"

"I'm sure. I think that's the last part of the puzzle for me. Once I unlock my Spirit Wielding, maybe I'll be able to figure out what to do with them."

"I know, dear," Lanya said. "My husband and I, along with Rosamond, will know what to do with the bones. Once we are done here, they will find their place. First, you are right, this territory needs to know what rot lies beneath the surface. Are we ready?"

The Lord of Air smiled, just for a moment, and it reached his eyes. "My daughter was not the only warrior," he said to me and then kissed his wife hard on the mouth. "We will avenge our Áine. And then we will help rebuild this kingdom. We will not let our daughter's death be in vain."

"My mother will have a name and memory that was of truth and strength," Rhodes said. "Trust in that."

I let the family have a moment to themselves, and then we planned.

We didn't have long because the army couldn't ignore us for too long, but as we rose and walked to the top of the hill, I knew this might be our last moment to speak, to form a plan, to do *anything*, but we would not let Durin die today without the world knowing what he had done. And we would not let him rule.

"Look at your Lord of Water and know what he has become," I called out, my voice low, sounding much more like the Spirit Wielders' than my own. The others gave me a startled look, but not Easton. He just smiled and then winked at the guards and others in front of him. He wasn't in his glamour. No, he was out in his pure King of Obscurité glory.

Now they knew. But they would know the rest, too.

Luken came up from behind Rhodes then and nodded. "We're ready," he whispered.

"What is the meaning of this?" Durin shouted. "Seize them. The King of Obscurité is here, and he's come to take my children."

"No, first, you will listen to the truths." I held up my arms, my palms out as I lifted them. The other Air Wielders around me did the same, and the Water Wielders put their hands out to their sides as if parting a sea.

The Earth Wielders put their hands down, palms facing the ground. It shook beneath us.

Teagan didn't use his Fire Wielding, but that was fine, that would come later.

It wasn't lost on me that Arwin's Earth Wielding would have helped, but we would avenge him. We would avenge them all.

"You think to stop me on my own lands?"

"Your Lord of Water has committed a grave sin. He has killed thousands for power. Listen to the bones."

"You have no proof."

"We have *all* the proof," the Lord of Air snapped back. "You killed our daughter. You killed so many."

But before the Lord of Water could defend himself with lies, the sea shook, and the bones of those who had been lost slid up into the air, shining beacons of magic and depravity.

"Look at what your Lord of Water has done."

And then Rosamond took a step forward, one step and then another, her hair blowing in a breeze that wasn't there.

"My father is a bad man. You know I am the Seer. You know I can See what is coming and what is lost. But he used bone magic to cripple me. He used bone magic to kill my mother. Watch and listen to the bones of those who have died before us." And then she held out her hands, and every single person in front of us opened their eyes wide, their eyes going glassy.

I hadn't known that she could do this, that she could send her visions to others.

From the way she swayed on her feet before Luken and Teagan reached out to steady her, I knew she didn't do it often for a reason. It took too much out of her, but this time, it was worth it.

Some of the army looked surprised, some looked aghast, some even threw up where they stood, dry heaving as they watched what the Lord of Water, their so-called future king had done to the innocent.

What he had done to their lady.

What he had done to me, Rhodes, and Easton.

Some started to scurry away, and some even came to our side.

Nobody else moved, nobody tried to fight. Not yet.

But I knew this peace wouldn't last for more than a moment.

"She lies. The King of Obscurité and his men have jaded my daughter and son. They've put lies in their heads and made them commit treason. They have corrupted and befouled the Spirit Priestess. We must protect our realm. And to do that, we must end them. For the change that is coming cannot be on the shoulders of those in front of us. We have the strength. Not them." He held out his hands, looking fearful for just a moment, but then the power within him ignited around the bone necklace he wore, and in the bones in his crown.

"Save our kingdom, save our territory, and take out what is putrid, what is wrong."

And then he shouted, and the battle was truly upon us.

The League and the Creed stayed on the side of the lord, as did some of his men, but some of them had moved to ours. Some were just Water

Wielders, others with dual powers, and some were even Air Wielders who maybe lived closer to the border.

I didn't care what they could Wield, as long as we all worked together.

Wyn and Teagan worked side by side as usual, while Rhodes and Luken worked together with their Air Wielding. It was a familiar sight to see Luken use his sword to direct his Air Wielding before he smashed his body into the others, a warrior of old and one that protected his prince.

Rosamond looked weak but stood between her grandparents, doing her best to use her Wielding to protect everyone.

I stood with Easton and tried not to be overwhelmed.

Because I'd never fought with four powers before, and I'd never really used Fire before at all. So I didn't this time either.

It wouldn't be safe. So, I used what I knew. What I had been trained for.

A man came at us, his Air Wielding weak but not weak enough. I threw out my hands and slammed them to my sides, creating a gust that rammed into the man. He fell back, rolled around, and then came back at me, shooting a blade of Air towards me.

I put my hand in front of my face and then shoved it towards him, fingers splayed. Rocks formed between us, and the man slammed into them, knocking himself out.

"That's a good one," Easton said, grinning, using his Fire Wielding to burn anyone that came close to us.

People shouted. I had never seen a battle like this. All four elements were in play, Fire, Earth, Water, and Air. The only thing missing was Spirit, though I didn't think that would help any of us.

The bones that had been in the air before now lay in a long line at the edge of the cliff, safe and protected from those who might hurt them or use them.

We couldn't let the Wielders' deaths be in vain, so we protected their remains while we defended ourselves and the territory.

The Lord of Water stood in the middle of the fray, fighting with all of his power, everything shaking around him.

I knew what he was feeling. Far too much power all at once.

I couldn't control mine, so I wasn't using it. I was trying to be safe.

But Durin wanted all the power, and he was going to explode from the inside out if he wasn't careful.

He came towards me, one step after the other, but stopped when he saw the Lord of Air in front of him.

"You will fight me, Durin," the Lord of Air growled, his hands outstretched, two cyclones on each palm ready to go. "I shouldn't have let her marry you."

"You were always a weak prick." Durin scowled. "I should've gotten rid of you long ago. She cried when she said she wanted to go back to you. But it was never enough. She acted as if I wasn't enough. Well, she's not here to complain anymore." Holdar threw one of his cyclones at Durin, and Durin used his Water Wielding to create a shield in front of him, water pouring out of the pouch at his side. The magic was shaky at best, but far stronger than it should've been.

He was adding bone magic to his Wielding.

Even as I fought some of the Creed and League with Easton, I watched what was happening. I was afraid.

There was no one else around Durin and Holdar, only small skirmishes.

It was just the Lord of Water and the Lord of Air, two leaders of the Lumière, fighting. Not for territory or for power.

No, this fight was for Áine.

"You were nothing," Durin snapped.

"You took my daughter. You won't take anything else."

Slam, smash, crinkle.

Holdar sent out another cyclone, and Durin blocked it. The Lord of Water sent out a wave, and Holdar made it mist before it even slammed into him. Things shook around the lords, and mud flew as they fought. Sweat beaded on both of their brows, but then Durin tapped the bone right at the side of his temple, and I shouted, knowing I was going to be too late.

Durin held out both arms, his fingers splayed as blades of Air shot through the distance between them.

It was silent. There were no screams, no shouts, nothing.

One second, Holdar was fighting. The next, his eyes were wide, and then he was down on the ground.

The scream from Lanya was deafening, and the ground beneath us shook, not from Earth, but from the Air coming from all around us, shaking the molecules themselves.

Rhodes came running, doing his best to fight through the pack, but then Durin turned, facing his son, and smiled.

That expression scared me more than anything I had seen or experienced. More than the chains, more than the dragon that spat venom.

That smile spoke of death and everything that was wrong with this realm.

The Lord of Air was dead, lying on the ground as Lanya ran towards his body, but I was watching Rhodes. Wyn moved to my side then since Teagan was near Luken and I was on my own. She fought off another attacker, and I tried to help, but I still only had eyes for Rhodes, afraid of what he'd do in the heat of the moment.

And because of that, I didn't see when Durin turned to me and threw out his hand, a bone in his other palm, blocking me from my own Wielding. A shockwave of Air slammed into me, and I fell back, Wyn toppling along with me, but we were on the cliff's edge, scattered among the bones of the lost, too close to the side where we could fall to our death. I looked down at my hands and noticed a crack along the edge. I scrambled, taking one step after another, but Durin threw another wave of Air at me. This time, the bones in his crown lit up as he pulled on their magic.

I knew if I didn't get out of the way, I would fall, and there would be no coming back from that. There'd be no using my Wielding to try and get out of it. I dug my hands into the soil, trying to claw myself back up, but then Rhodes was there, and I watched as he took the full brunt of the Air assault into his body, blocking Wyn and me from what Durin had sent with the bone magic of death on the air.

Durin grinned while I shouted, trying to get up, trying to do *anything*. Rhodes' body shook, lighting up as if he'd been hit with lightning instead of wind.

I staggered to my feet while Wyn dragged me away from the edge and tried to reach for him, screaming his name. But I was too late.

The rock face gave way, and Rhodes fell.

He looked at me, his silver eyes wide but not scared. There was no fear there, only purpose. The wind ruffled his hair, and while he had his hands out, trying to reach for his Wielding, it wouldn't come. It couldn't. Not with what Durin had used on him. Not with the bone magic that must be blocking Rhodes from his Wielding.

The bones were surrounding him, those waiting at the edge of the cliff.

But nothing could help him.

He fell, a scream on his lips that echoed in my head. The rocks took him, and then I couldn't see him anymore.

I couldn't see anyone.

CHAPTER 33

This can't be happening.

Not again.

Rhodes...

He'd fallen.

Off a cliff.

He...he couldn't be dead. He had to come back. He had to be able to use his Wielding. Right?

He couldn't be dead.

There was no body. I didn't see him die. He wasn't dead. I refused to believe it.

"Lyric," Wyn shouted, shaking me. "Lyric! Are you all right? Did the magic touch you? It takes away your Wielding and who knows what else. Lyric!"

I blinked, trying to focus on my friend as the battle raged around us.

Rhodes had pushed Wyn and me out of the way, had taken the assault of the bone magic mixed with the Lord of Water's own Air Wielding straight to his body. He hadn't been able to protect himself, hadn't been able to use his own Wielding to stop his fall.

Instead, he had fallen off the cliff, with the rocks and the bones and everything else falling on top of him. An actual rockslide, where the magic of the Lord of Water had slammed into him, and there was nothing he could do to save himself.

And Rhodes hadn't uttered a sound.

"Lyric. Snap out of it. We have to keep fighting. The Lord of Air is down, the Lady of Air is losing her shit," Wyn snapped.

I looked up and shook my head, trying to pull myself out of wherever I had just gone.

"Okay, we can do this."

"Oh, we're *going* to do this." Wyn held out her hands, and the earth shook beneath us powerfully. I hadn't even realized Wyn possessed that much Earth Wielding within her. "That Lumière prince does not *get* to die for me," she growled.

"No, he doesn't." I slammed my hand into hers, and we clasped fists. The earth around us rumbled in waves. While the water in the sea below the cliffs started to rise up, and the air whipped my face, and flames danced along my fingers.

I was the Wielder of four elements. The only one in existence as far as we knew.

I would not let the Lord of Water take control. I would not let Rhodes' sacrifice be in vain.

And so, I grinned at Wyn, who smiled wickedly back at me, the look in her eyes manic. Because we weren't happy, we weren't gleeful.

We wanted revenge.

So we let go and stalked towards the Lord of Water.

Rosamond had her arms outstretched, the air around her whipping as she brought some of the soldiers and the League and Creed to their knees. They clawed at their eyes, bleeding and screaming.

I knew that Rosamond was using whatever Seer magic she had to force visions into the others. I didn't know how long she could do that, but I was going to help however I could. Because as soon as she faltered, she would pass out, spent from using so much of her power.

The Lady of Air stood above her husband's body, her own hair blowing in the wind as she stood there, a serene look on her face even as war battled around her. She had her fingers spread, and I could tell by the way she just stood there that she was gathering up her power. An assault was coming.

Easton and Teagan and Luken were running towards Wyn and me, their faces pale and bloody.

"He's gone?" Easton asked, his voice a growl.

Why did those two words break me?

Why?

"He's gone," I answered, my voice not sounding like my own. Easton must have understood though because he gave me a tight nod before reaching out to cup my face. "Use the power within. I'll be right beside you."

And I believed him. I had faith that he would be right beside me no matter what power I gave into, no matter what ran through me.

I just refused to lean on him. I would not let another person die for me.

So, I backed away and then moved towards the Lord of Water. The others flanked me, the Lady of Air coming out of her trance as she and Rosamond moved to the west side. Whatever Air Wielders were left that had been on our side, as well as the Water Wielders that had moved away and joined our army moved with us so we walked in a line, all towards the enemy above.

"You think to destroy me?" Durin asked, his voice sounding amplified. "I hold the power of the bone magic. I hold the power of so many lost before. I will be the true king. I will be the one who towers above them all. You are nothing. You can't even use your own Wielding to protect those you thought you cared about. Everyone keeps dying for you, and you can do nothing. You stand by and watch the world pass you by. You were never meant to be here. You are but a babe in the eyes of the world. You weren't born to be here. You were born to be nothing. You are just a human, weak and defenseless. And now you hold what you think is power, but it is nothing. You will die with the rest of them because you have forsaken all that is the Maison realm. You are nothing, Lyric."

The others started shouting, but I wasn't listening. I just tilted my head and looked at the man who called himself the Lord of Water, the man who wanted to be the high king.

"I am the Spirit Priestess. The one who was prophesied to unite us. But in order to do so, the rot must be gutted."

"You call me rot while you lay like a snake in the grass waiting to take what is not yours?"

"Stand down, Durin. Before you die at the hands of those who will protect this realm. Before you sacrifice any more lives for your greed. For your dishonesty."

"I'll never stand down. This role is mine. And you are in my way."

And then he held out his hands, the bones on his crown and necklace glowing once more as they had when he killed his own son.

His army stood behind him, their arms outstretched as they each held their Wieldings, ready to attack at a moment's notice.

I wouldn't let this happen. I was the Wielder of four elements. The Spirit Priestess. I had fought countless dreams and other monsters. I might not know the histories of them all, might not know exactly how to control any of what I held yet. But I was here for a reason.

And I would not let Rhodes, Brae, Arwin, Holdar, or anyone else die in vain for me.

I would not let anyone else die for me period.

And so, I held out my hands and let the power flow.

Air began first, a slow swirl of sensation through my body as it flowed out of my fingertips and into the open space in front of me. I could see it like a wave creating a wall in front of my friends and me.

And then Earth came, strong and unyielding. It leapt from the soles and arches of my feet into the ground and then rumbled up to combine with the wall of Air. It wasn't as thin as the microscopic wall that the knight of the Obscurité Kingdom had made when he tried and succeeded in killing me. But it was power.

The others gasped, and I could feel their eyes on me even as they held back their own Wielding, ready to fight.

But I wasn't done yet.

I pulled my arms back a little farther and crooked my fingers ever so slightly. In doing so, I could feel the water in the air around me, as well as the sea behind me start to collect. Drop by drop, drip by drip, my Water came slowly, reaching up the cliff's edge as if it were crawling back from the abyss. It slid along the ground beneath us as if it were an overflowing river before it crept up the wall of Air and Earth that I had created, mixing with the wind and dirt.

And then there was Fire.

My new friend, my new element.

My head fell back, and the heat and the anger and the burning within me crashed out of my face, through my eyes, my nose, out my mouth and ears, all of it erupting from a place deep within.

I knew I could not create Fire like Easton, not yet. I could not Wield it with any accuracy unless only to do harm to myself and the world crumbling around him.

But I could become it, if only for a moment.

And so I screamed, the Fire erupting from me before it slammed into the wall of my other elements, mixing with them and strengthening their hold.

If I had had the fifth element, I knew it would have been the next step, but it was not time for that yet.

My body shook as the Wielding reached out to me, wanting to hold me in its embrace. But I wasn't ready to let go.

It was only for a moment, all of the elements coming together as I focused on what was in front of me, using instinct and not skill, no knowledge.

I knew if I thought about it, I would fail, and that it would be my undoing. Because I didn't have the training or the strength to handle all of these yet, but I could at least use what was within me to protect the others.

And maybe if I survived this, I would actually learn to call upon the elements without fear, without loss of control.

But that wasn't now.

Durin looked worried for only a moment and then he smiled, a grin that I knew I would see until the end of my days even if those days happened to be numbered.

All of the power that he had held for so long, that slowly ripped from every single person he had killed over the centuries, slammed into him, and his entire body glowed. Even his own men, the Creed, and the League, took steps away from him as if haunted and scared by the man that wasn't a man anymore.

No, he was power. But it was stolen power.

And that had to make a difference.

"Kill the Spirit Priestess!" the Lord of Water screamed. And then it began.

The onslaught of power hit my wall with such ferocity that I took a staggering step back. Wyn put her hand on my right shoulder, Easton's on my left hip, both of them holding me in place.

It was because of them and their strengths that I could push more of myself into the wall.

The lord slammed his Water Wielding mixed with bone magic into the wall, and I could sense the tiny fractures. But that was fine. I had more Wielding, and I would use it. But first, I had to tire him.

If I could take away some of the power that he had stolen, even putting it into the wall itself, then it could give us a fighting chance. It might not necessarily be even ground, but it would be better.

It had to be enough.

"Take her down!" one of the League members said, and then the other Wielders ran towards the wall that I had created.

Every single person on our side of the battlefield was protected by the wall, but as soon as it fell, as soon as those fractures split open completely, they would all have to use their own Wieldings to protect themselves.

But it would be enough. It had to be enough.

"Don't burn yourself out," Easton said, his voice a shout over the raging wind and inferno. "Let us help you."

I turned to him. He didn't move back, didn't look scared at what he saw on my face. I knew I didn't look like myself. I didn't feel like myself. He wasn't afraid of me. Instead, he leaned forward and rested his forehead against mine. "Don't kill yourself trying to protect us. Let him burn out his bone magic, and then let the wall fall. We'll take the rest."

"Don't die for me," I whispered as a tear slid down my cheek.

"Never. But you can't die for us either," Easton said, sounding softer than he ever had before. And then he wiped the tear from my face and turned away, but he kept touching me.

Wyn had her hand on me, and then Teagan and Luken and Lanya and Rosamond and the others.

So many touched me, infusing me with their strength, even though I wasn't taking their Wielding. Just knowing that they were there, knowing that we were a unit was enough.

And then the Lord of Water took a step to the right, leaning heavily, and I knew he was almost spent. He might still have his Water and Air Wielding, but he was losing the bone magic.

Because the light of his crown and the other bones he had put on himself as if in fashion were starting to dim.

But he came at us with another onslaught, and I shook, the wall ready to fall.

I didn't know how to end it, I didn't know how I'd even made it this far.

But I knew it was almost over.

And as the last light of the crown faded into nothingness, the wall fractured, leaving us bare and out in the open, but not useless. Not inhibited.

Because we were Wielders, and I was the Spirit Priestess. And I had more.

The others let go of me, and my whole body shook, but it wasn't enough. I had used all four elements in a way I hadn't known I could, in a way I hadn't before.

And now it was too much.

Fire erupted from me, and I held out my hands, standing with my legs braced apart as the others fought the onslaught of League and Creed members and the other Wielders who fought for the Lord of Water. I only had eyes for Durin, and he was weak.

He had used too much, and now, this would be his end.

I had killed before, and I would again.

But I would look into his eyes as I did so, and I would carry it on my soul for the rest of my days.

And so I moved my left arm forward and pointed towards the Lord of Water.

He screamed as the Fire touched him, engulfed him in a wall of flame and ash.

The others looked at me askance, but not my own people. My friends understood what I had done and why. I knew they would have done the same.

He had killed so many, and he would do it again and again unless he were stopped.

As Durin screamed his last breath and fell into a pile of ash, I couldn't help but think of Brae.

My best friend had become ash but had come back as my Familiar.

The Lord of Water wouldn't be coming back.

But the Fire whispered to me. It was too much, but it wasn't done yet.

I wasn't done yet.

The Lord of Water and everything he had done couldn't remain.

And so, I lifted my palms to the sun and let the Fire burn.

It scorched a trail through the enemy, burning those in its wake, and slammed into the castle itself. The estate had been made of ostentatious water and stone to showcase the power that Durin had stolen.

It was empty now, evacuated because Rosamond had Seen this.

And now it would be no more.

As the power erupted from me, and my other elements fought for control, the world burned, and the castle turned to ash and ruin. The others ran from me, not from the Spirit Priestess but from what I had become.

Because I couldn't control it.

And the Fire kept coming as if there were no bottom to the well.

And then the other Wielding came at me, and I couldn't control any of it.

I couldn't control myself.

CHAPTER 34

The Fire slid from my fingertips as the Earth caused the stones to rumble beneath my feet. The Air whirled around me, and the Water slammed into the side of the cliff as if reaching out to me.

All four elements warred for control, and it was all I could do to keep my breath.

The Fire was still raging, and I turned slightly to the left. Others screamed, running in fear of my power.

I didn't want this. I didn't want people to fear me, I didn't want any of this.

But I couldn't control it.

I hadn't been able to control it when Water had taken me over, and now Fire would be worse.

I remembered when someone had once told me that Fire was the hardest element to Wield. Because no matter what happened, it was always within you, forever trying to burst free. Fire Wielders needed to have more control than others, so much that they turned to stone when they had to hold everything in.

And while Teagan might laugh and joke with Wyn, he was incredibly controlled in his fighting, and trained harder than anyone else I knew.

And Easton was the same way. He used so much of his power just to control it, along with his Earth.

I remembered meeting that little baby Firedrake, watching it dance along the desert that was the Fire territory.

There had been such innocence in that flame, but there was nothing innocent about the flames I now possessed.

I remembered using the fiery blooms of the cactus in the Fire territory with Easton's Wielding to take out the Negs that had tried to kill us.

The first time I had met Easton, I had been standing with Rhodes, trying to fight for my life using only one element. Air. The only one I had at the time.

I had used my Air to help Easton's Fire, and we had worked together without even knowing who we were to each other. Not knowing who each other was at all.

I remembered all of that, but it wasn't enough.

Because I wasn't that innocent flame. I wasn't the cool and collected Wielder.

I was out of control, and I couldn't hold back.

A river of Fire surrounded me, slowly crawling to make a full circle and blocking off my friends and the others who might come at me.

I couldn't think, could barely breathe, and while the other three elements were slamming into me, trying to either stop me or protect me, or just take over Fire so they could be the one that took me, it wasn't enough.

The Fire was too strong. I had never Wielded it with any accuracy.

I had burned a castle to ash, had turned Rhodes' and Rosamond's childhood memories to dust.

I was of flame and ash and nothingness.

And I couldn't stop.

The battle had ended, those who had survived on the other side had run, and I could see some of the Air and Water Wielders who had been on our side chasing them. But I couldn't focus.

I didn't know if the Creed or the League had survived, or what would happen to them. I didn't know anything right then.

I couldn't tell if my friends were near or even if they had survived, I could just feel the flame on my face and know that this was how *I* would end.

Maybe this was what I needed to do all along, collect the four elements and stop an uprising. The others would survive without me.

At least those who had survived to this point.

Because Rhodes had died for me, and so had Brae, and Arwin, and Holdar, and so many others.

They had died, and I had survived.

But now, the Fire would take me because I couldn't stop it.

It sang to me, that siren song of death and destiny.

I didn't want to die, but I believed this was the end.

Nobody could get through the flames. I could hear shouting, but I didn't know if they wanted to kill me or stop me.

Maybe they knew I would burn up from the inside and that nothing would douse the flames, not even the other elements I Wielded.

People should be scared of me. I was afraid of myself.

But then someone shouted my name, and it was as if I heard it as an echo. I wondered who it could be. Questioned why.

And then I felt hands on my face, and Easton was there, his face singed but Fire running along his body, his own Wielding protecting him from mine even as he held me close.

"Control the Fire. You can do this, my Lyric. I believe in you."

"No," I said, my voice a song. "I can't. I've done so much, and yet it's not enough. No one told me it would be like this. I wanted Fire, but I never wanted this. But now it's here, and I can't control it."

"I told you I would be by your side. And I'm here. So, if you burn yourself up, I'll burn right along with you."

I pushed at him, but he didn't let me go.

"You promised you wouldn't die for me," I snapped.

"I did, and I won't die for you, I'll die with you. Because you have to be the one that ends it. You have the control. It's in you. You just need to find it."

"I'm trying!"

"Try harder. You can do this. I believe in you."

And then his lips were on mine, and the flame danced between our mouths and along our bodies as it engulfed us.

I clung to him, needing his kiss, his taste, just one last moment of peace before the end came and there was nothing but ash.

He kissed me harder. I arched my back as I tried to hold in everything that I had, everything that I had done.

I had never thought I would end a life, but I had ended so many. They didn't have a chance. They had screamed, and then they had died, and their bodies and bones were now ashes. And it was all my fault.

But I couldn't let my friends die. Because if *I* died, what would happen to my Fire?

Would it hurt the others? I couldn't let Rosamond or Wyn or anyone else die for me.

I couldn't let Easton die for me or *with* me, whatever word he chose to use.

And so I kissed him back, and the tears fell down my cheeks. The flames slowly receded.

It lifted from our skin, and then it was Air. I fell to my knees, but Easton caught me, holding me close as he kissed my forehead and I crumbled, tears streaming down my face, my body racked with sobs.

My body shook, and I just wanted it all to end.

It was as if something had been pulled from me. My soul, my heart... something.

I saw the ash around me, the dirt and soot on the others' faces as they stared at me.

Did they fear me? They should. Because who was I? *What* was I? Why couldn't I save the realm?

How *could* I if I couldn't save those I loved.

Couldn't save myself.

Because, once again, Easton had been the one to bring me back.

I might have saved us all from the lord, but I couldn't stop the power within me.

I never knew I could resent a part of myself.

Sure, I was the Spirit Priestess, but I obviously couldn't do it alone.

CHAPTER 35

I wasn't dead.

But it felt as if I were one of the few that wasn't.

Cleaning up after a battle wasn't really something I'd ever thought about. Mostly because the movies ended before the cleanup, and I had never been to war nor truly seen it.

The first time, I had been passed out, bloody and broken and back from the dead after I'd woken up in a room, the same one I had later stayed in when I trained with the Obscurité. Everyone else had done the cleanup. And then the time I had been in the human realm, Easton and the others had rebuilt the castle. They had made the crystal room better and protected it from themselves and others.

So, I had never seen the cleanup.

And I never wanted to see it again.

When I finally wiped my tears and stopped feeling sorry for myself, I stood up and pulled away from Easton's arms, not wanting to lean on him anymore. The fact that I knew I might have to in the future because I couldn't control all my powers shamed me.

And though some part of myself reminded me that others had had centuries to learn their powers and not mere minutes like I did, it still didn't make the pill easier to swallow.

"We're clearing the dead, but it's not going to be easy," Wyn said softly as she came to me. We were all covered in soot and blood and God knew what else.

But we were alive. At least most of us were.

I nodded, swallowing hard. "Okay. What do we do next?" I asked, knowing the question was one that needed to be answered even though I didn't think there were actually any answers.

"I know we need to bring Arwin's body back," Wyn said, her voice shaky. She swallowed hard, rolled her shoulders back, and looked more like the warrior she had been before. Teagan put his arm around her shoulders, gave her a squeeze, and then let her go, moving closer to Luken so the two of them could discuss something I couldn't hear.

"I think that's a good idea. I can't even really think about it all, you know?" I asked, worried.

"I know. It doesn't seem real. None of this does. But his parents were farmers, you know? They're Wielders that slowly lost some of their magic in the siege when the crystal was being misused. But they raised him well. They'd want to bury him there among the trees and the ground that he grew up around. So, we'll bring him back."

"We'll help you get a boat and then a wagon and other things to get through the territories," Lanya said softly as she came up to us. Her eyes were haunted, but the rest of her looked strong. I knew she was grieving, having lost her soulmate, but there was nothing I could say or do.

She had lost her husband, her lord, so soon after losing her daughter. And now she'd lost her grandson, too.

I didn't know how she was even standing. I could barely stay upright myself.

"We'll get you to the Obscurité Kingdom."

"Is that what we're doing then?" I asked, looking down at my ash-covered hands.

"I think we need to," Easton said, looking off into the distance. "We'll figure out what to do. All of us." He looked over at the Lumière who were part of our group. "Any of you who want to come to my kingdom are welcome. We are not the Lumière versus Obscurité at this point. We are those who want to save our realm, and those who don't want change."

"I'll go," Luken said, his voice wooden.

"My prince is gone, and though there is no body, he's gone. And he would want me to fight on the side of good. So, I will go with you."

Luken had lost so much, the bastard of the Lumière as some called him, he had no family. He had lost Rhodes, and he had lost Brae. But I remembered that Brae was at the castle of the Obscurité Court, so maybe that was something.

Not that I knew *what* it was.

"We'll go, of course," Teagan said. "We need all the warriors we can get, I think," he added, looking at Luken.

"I will go, as well," Rosamond said, surprising us all. "I haven't Seen much of what is ahead, and I need to focus. But I can't be here. I must be with the Spirit Priestess. And that will be first in the Obscurité Kingdom before we move."

I reached out and grabbed her hand, holding it tight.

"I will go back to the Air territory with my men and women who are still here," Lanya announced. We all looked at her. She looked like a queen, so regal yet broken.

"We will rebuild and help protect. We must fight from within the Lumiere Kingdom itself. And you will need allies, Lyric. The Water territory will need allies, as well," she said, looking at Rosamond.

The Seer let out a breath. "I am the Lady of Water now, I suppose," she said shakily. "Unless we find Rhodes." Her eyes went a little glassy, and I moved forward, a lump of hope in my throat. "I could never See him, you understand. He is my blood. My brother. My best friend. But I don't know if he's gone for sure. There would be a body. I would be able to See. I would know. But I can't stay here. Not with my uncle. I don't know what the king's plans are, and though I may be the Lady of Water in title, he has to be the one to sanction it in the end. So when it is time, we will come back to rebuild the Water territory. When it is time. But not before."

There was so much in her statement. I tried to focus, tried to understand what we were doing.

"So we're going to the Obscurité Kingdom to recuperate and figure out the next steps. And determine what to do with all of my elements." *And for me to control them.* But I didn't say that. "And unravel the prophecy and unlock the fifth element and all of that. We're going to do it together."

They all looked at me and nodded, and I knew these were my people, my court. Those who I would protect and who would protect me as we tried to piece this realm back together and figure out if the King of Lumière was really with us or against us.

"We must leave quickly," Wyn said.

"Yes, I believe my uncle will want revenge," Rosamond said. "Even if he doesn't know all of the details, he will see this as an act of treason and an act of war."

"Before we go, we have to release the magic from the bones," Lanya said, reaching out to grip her granddaughter's hand. "Some of the bones went back to the sea with Rhodes, and we will find those."

And maybe we would find Rhodes.

I didn't think so, but I needed some hope. I needed something to hold onto.

There had to be something.

I had four of my elements, and I knew I needed to find Spirit. I just didn't know where or when I would and what I would have to sacrifice to make it happen.

The Lord of Water had been right when he'd said that others died or were hurt around me in order for me to unlock my powers. And I was afraid of what would happen for me to find that fifth one. And I worried if I would be able to control it.

So we began the cleanup, buried the dead, and gathered what we could.

I saw the fear on some of the Wielders' faces. Not those who knew me, but those who had only seen the Spirit Priestess engulfed in flame. I didn't know what to think about that.

I honestly didn't know what to do about any of it.

When it was all over, and we were ready to go, I stood at the edge of the cliff where Rhodes had fallen and just stared out at the sea, wishing he would come back. Wishing I knew where he had gone.

The wind whipped my hair, and I tried to find some victory in what had happened.

I had four of my elements, and the Lord of Water could no longer hurt anyone else.

And we were making a plan, we were unraveling my prophecy. So, maybe that was a win. Perhaps it was something we could take in stride.

It was just hard to do when so many had been hurt and lost for that to happen.

Easton came up behind me, putting his hand on my shoulder as I stood staring out into the distance.

"I will fight with you no matter what. I hope you know that, Lyric. It's not me as king, just me as a man."

I turned to him then, looking into those dark eyes of his, wondering what it all meant. Because one of the Spirit Wielders had said that I needed to save my soulmate, and I knew it wasn't Rhodes. And Easton had lost his before. But maybe they were wrong. Perhaps it was all wrong.

"I know you'll fight with me. You haven't let me down yet." I tried to smile, and he did the same, but it didn't reach either of our eyes.

I relied on him, maybe too much, and I didn't know what would happen if he wasn't there. That meant I needed to be stronger. I didn't want to rely on anyone. Not if it meant their possible death. Rhodes' face filled my brain again, and I tried to push those thoughts away.

I couldn't break down. Not now. Not in front of everyone.

"There's something you need to know." I looked up at Easton, wondering why he looked so confused, so lost. "It's not what you think," he said, speaking quickly. It was if he were running out of time for something. I stood up straighter, wondering what it could mean. "What Wyn said before? About my past? About everything? It's true, but it's not at the same time."

He swallowed hard as if fighting for each word. I reached out, putting my hand on his chest.

"What is it?" I asked, scared.

"Lyric…" His voice trailed off, and something dark came over his eyes. Suddenly, he wasn't Easton anymore. He was other.

"Easton? What is it? What Wyn said?"

And then it hit me.

Soulmates. This was it. This was what Easton needed to say. He just needed to get it out, and then it would be okay. We would figure out the next step.

"I need you," I said, not meaning to say the words aloud but knowing they needed to be said. I was baring my soul, and I knew if he walked away, it would break me. But maybe it would be for the best. Because I shouldn't rely on anyone. Still, I needed him.

"Can't you feel it?" I asked, my voice hoarse.

He just looked at me, not blinking, his eyes cold.

"I can never love you."

Five words, and I couldn't breathe.

Five words, and I was broken.

And then he took a step back and looked at me. For an instant, he was Easton again, the boy I had fallen for, the man I wanted to be with. He looked…*scared*. And then something dark and shadowy wrapped around his waist as if a rope emerged from the air and *tugged*.

He reached out once more…and then he was gone.

Gone.

It was if someone had flipped a switch and opened a vacuum. The sound was deafening, echoing in my ears and amongst the rest of the world.

Easton was gone, sucked into whatever had opened in front of me, pulled into the abyss.

I was alone.

Alone on a path I didn't know the ending to.

Someone or something had taken Easton. I had seen the surprise on his face as it happened. And now he was gone.

Just like Rhodes.

Like so many others.

Easton was gone.

And I was alone.

Just like I had known I would be.

Because the Spirit Priestess didn't get to find their future. They *were* the future.

All of the loss and pain and uncertainty hit me.

And I screamed.

Lyric's journey and the *Elements of Five*
series continues in...

FROM
SPIRIT
AND
BINDING

A NOTE FROM
CARRIE ANN

Thank you so much for reading FROM FLAME AND ASH! I do hope if you liked this story, that you would please leave a review! Reviews help authors and readers.

This series means so much to me and I'm truly honored you're taking this journey with me. Lyric is still on her path, as well as Easton and the others. The series has more to come and I cannot wait to show you where we're going.

If you want to make sure you know what's coming next from me, you can sign up for my newsletter at www.CarrieAnnRyan.com; follow me on twitter at @CarrieAnnRyan, or like my Facebook page. I also have a Facebook Fan Club where we have trivia, chats, and other goodies. You guys are the reason I get to do what I do and I thank you.

Make sure you're signed up for my MAILING LIST so you can know when the next releases are available as well as find giveaways and FREE READS.

Happy Reading!

THE ELEMENTS OF FIVE SERIES
Book 1: *From Breath and Ruin*
Book 2: *From Flame and Ash*
Book 3: *From Spirit and Binding*
Book 4: *Title to Come*

MORE TO COME!

ABOUT
CARRIE ANN

Carrie Ann Ryan is the *New York Times* and *USA Today* bestselling author of contemporary and paranormal romance. Her works include the Montgomery Ink, Redwood Pack, Talon Pack, and Gallagher Brothers series, which have sold over 2.0 million books worldwide. She started writing while in graduate school for her advanced degree in chemistry and hasn't stopped since. Carrie Ann has written over fifty novels and novellas with more in the works. When she's not writing about bearded tattooed men or alpha wolves that need to find their mates, she's reading as much as she can and exploring the world of baking and gourmet cooking.

FOR MORE INFORMATION, VISIT:
WWW.CARRIEANNRYAN.COM

MORE BOOKS FROM
CARRIE ANN

THE MONTGOMERY INK: BOULDER SERIES:
Book 1: Wrapped in Ink
Book 2: Sated in Ink
Book 3: Embraced in Ink

THE LESS THAN SERIES:
A Montgomery Ink Spin Off Series
Book 1: Breathless With Her
Book 2: Reckless With You
Book 3: Shameless With Him

THE ELEMENTS OF FIVE SERIES:
A YA Fantasty Series
Book 1: From Breath and Ruin
Book 2: From Flame and Ash
Book 3: From Spirit and Binding
Book 4: Title to Come

Book 6: <u>Destiny Disgraced</u>

Book 7: <u>Eternal Mourning</u>

Book 8: <u>Strength Enduring</u>

Book 9: <u>Forever Broken</u>

REDWOOD PACK SERIES:

Book 1: <u>An Alpha's Path</u>

Book 2: <u>A Taste for a Mate</u>

Book 3: <u>Trinity Bound</u>

<u>Redwood Pack Box Set</u> (Contains Books 1-3)

Book 3.5: <u>A Night Away</u>

Book 4: <u>Enforcer's Redemption</u>

Book 4.5: <u>Blurred Expectations</u>

Book 4.7: <u>Forgiveness</u>

Book 5: <u>Shattered Emotions</u>

Book 6: <u>Hidden Destiny</u>

Book 6.5: <u>A Beta's Haven</u>

Book 7: <u>Fighting Fate</u>

Book 7.5: <u>Loving the Omega</u>

Book 7.7: <u>The Hunted Heart</u>

Book 8: <u>Wicked Wolf</u>

<u>The Complete Redwood Pack Box Set</u> (Contains Books 1-7.7)

THE BRANDED PACK SERIES:

(Written with Alexandra Ivy)

Book 1: <u>Stolen and Forgiven</u>

Book 2: <u>Abandoned and Unseen</u>

Book 3: <u>Buried and Shadowed</u>

CPSIA information can be obtained
at www.ICGtesting.com
Printed in the USA
LVHW081502081119
636785LV00012B/279/P